CHASING STARDUST

CHASING STARDUST

A Novel

Erica Lucke Dean

LAKE UNION
PUBLISHING

This is a work of fiction. Names, characters, organizations, places, events, and incidents are either products of the author's imagination or are used fictitiously. Otherwise, any resemblance to actual persons, living or dead, is purely coincidental.

Published by Lake Union Publishing, Seattle
www.apub.com

EU product safety contact:
Amazon Media EU S. à r.l.
38, avenue John F. Kennedy, L-1855 Luxembourg
amazonpublishing-gpsr@amazon.com

ISBN-13: 9781662531859 (paperback)
ISBN-13: 9781662531866 (digital)

Cover design and illustration by Jarrod Taylor
Cover image: © Misha Kaminsky / Getty

Printed in the United States of America

To the Starman
for eternal inspiration

Music is the universal language of mankind.
—Henry Wadsworth Longfellow

1

Ashes to Ashes

There should be a law against having a funeral on a beautiful summer day. How can the world keep spinning as if Mom didn't die? Roses bloom. Bees pollinate. Mrs. McHugh's scruffy schnauzer pees on every stationary object in the park across the street. And none of it matters because Mom's still gone.

Life isn't fair.

Hugging her silver urn to my chest, I plop down on the old church's crumbling front steps and blink into the bright midday sun. Somehow, I made it through the entire service without shedding a tear. I simply couldn't bear having the whole town watch me fall apart like a carnival attraction. It took every ounce of self-control, but not one tissue was sacrificed on my behalf today.

My older sister, Jeanie, walks up beside me, her blue eyes puffy and rimmed in red. At least one of us isn't afraid to cry. A twinge of guilt threatens to slip through my carefully constructed defenses, but then I catch a whiff of stale weed under her flowery perfume. Not crying. High.

Part of me wishes I had a little of her reckless spirit.

Then she opens her mouth, and I change my mind. We're nothing alike and never will be. "Douchebag still a no-show?"

"He'll be here." No sooner are the words out of my mouth than my confidence wavers. It wouldn't be the first time he's broken a promise, and it probably won't be the last.

"Yeah, whatever. I'll believe it when I see it." Jeanie cranes her neck, searching the distance for something . . . or *someone.* "Why are you still seeing him anyway? You can't possibly have anything in common with that Neanderthal. And please don't tell me you think he's been pining for you every night while he's off at college. Trust me, that asshole is getting—"

I cut her off with a searing glare, but it doesn't slow her down in the least.

She sighs. "Dating the star quarterback might've made sense when you were in high school. That's what cheerleaders do. That's what *Mom* did." Her eyes soften. "But you're not in high school anymore."

"Harsh," I mutter. "Even for you." I refuse to admit that her thinly veiled accusation hit its mark. Jeanie has no clue what my life's been like for the past two years. She wasn't here.

When Mom got sick, Damian became the bridge between my old life and my new reality. When I was with Damian, I didn't worry about Mom's next chemo appointment or which prescriptions needed to be filled. For those few stolen hours each day, I got to be the old carefree Zoey. God knows he isn't perfect, but he brought me some measure of comfort when I needed it most, chasing away the bone-deep loneliness and paralyzing fear—at least for a little while—and I'm not sure I'm ready to give that up just yet.

"Come on, Zo. You know Mom only went down that path because it was the opposite of—"

"Don't. Mom's not here to defend her choices anymore." The last thing I want today, of all days, is to have a conversation about what Mom did or didn't do before we came along. Or why I've always been so damn determined to follow her example.

She raises one shoulder in surrender—likely the only apology I'll get from her.

"Why do you even care?"

She shrugs for real this time. "I guess I don't."

"Then, for Christ's sake, drop it. It's not as if Damian's the only no-show." The implication hangs in the air like a feather caught in an updraft, picking up subtext as it floats around, unanswered.

Her spine stiffens, her eyes narrowing. "You can't compare G-Lo to your *boyfriend*."

"You're absolutely right. So where *is* Grandma Lola?" I refuse to call Mom's eccentric mother *G-Lo*. She isn't a rapper. She's a crazy old hippie, still living in the carefree sex, drugs, and rock and roll lifestyle of her past.

Jeanie slips out of her black pumps and hangs them from two fingers. "You're the only one who expected her to show up."

Stunned, I stare into my sister's glassy eyes. "Let me get this straight. Damian, who you despise, by the way, has somehow offended you by not being here, but you're fine with our *grandmother* skipping her own daughter's funeral?"

She brushes her hair out of her face and shifts her gaze to the street. "Even Mom knew G-Lo would blow off her funeral."

Jeanie doesn't get it. My virtually nonexistent friends, my inconsiderate boyfriend, the whole damn town for that matter . . . none of them make the slightest difference to me, but our grandmother should be here. "That doesn't explain where the hell she's been for the past two years."

"Give it a rest, Zoey. She's a free spirit." She shrugs, her porcelain skin glistening with a light sheen of sweat. "That's just G-Lo."

Easy for her to say. Jeanie wasn't the one sacrificing her freedom to take care of a sick mother for two years. She didn't have to smile and pretend Mom didn't look more horrifying every day.

"And you're right," she says. "I don't like your boyfriend. I especially hate how he'll make the two-hour drive from campus every weekend for a booty call but can't—or won't—carve out a few hours to show up for you today. That's seriously messed up. Even that pencil dick, Rick Hansen, showed up for me. We went out three times last summer. I barely recognized him with his clothes on. But he showed up." She flicks her gaze toward me. "I thought maybe a few of your high school friends would come, but I guess two years is a long time."

The two years since graduation feel like an eternity. Before Mom got sick, there was no question I would head off to college like my sister before me. But with Jeanie already gone, I couldn't exactly leave Mom to fight cancer alone. And I couldn't blame my friends for scattering to the wind, leaving me behind to forge their own futures while I watched mine wither and die. And I wasn't exactly blameless. They weren't the ones who changed, I was. They tried to include me in their lives . . . for a while. But I didn't give a damn about current fashion trends or the latest world events when my entire life was crumbling around me. Maintaining friendships with people I no longer had a single thing in common with anymore was exhausting. So I stopped trying.

Oblivious to the tempest swirling inside me, Jeanie rattles on. "But *Damian* is your *boyfriend.* Two-hour drive or not, he has no excuse for ditching you today."

I bite my tongue to keep from telling her that he's home for the summer and only five minutes away. That the "booty calls" are as much for me as him. Where the hell did she think I'd find someone else my age when I spent all my time in hospice with Mom? How else was I supposed to distract myself from the soul-crushing sadness? And God knows I needed that distraction. Under the circumstances, putting up with his control issues and toxic masculinity for a few hours every weekend seemed like a small price to pay.

Jeanie drops onto the step beside me, scooting me over with her narrow hips. "Wanna know what I think?"

I count my heartbeats to keep from fleeing our excruciating conversation. "Not particularly."

"I think you only started dating him because you thought he was the kind of boy Mom would've picked."

My jaw drops, my head whipping in her direction. The words *you're wrong* stick in my throat. I close my mouth, going back to counting heartbeats, half convinced she's working through a playbook filled with every one of my insecurities.

"He'll be here," I whisper, no longer believing my own lie.

"Not that it matters anymore. The funeral's over. Everyone's already gone. Wait all day for all I care, but I'm going home. Reverend Tom and the ladies' church league are probably sitting in the driveway with another month's worth of crappy casseroles as we speak. Better be nice to me if you want me to save you any." Jeanie snickers.

When I don't respond, she hops up with a huff as if I've insulted her. And maybe I have. Somewhere during the past couple of years, I outgrew her. Jeanie may be two years older, but she acts as if she's twenty-two going on eighteen, and after all the time I spent caring for our sick mother, I feel as if I'm twenty going on forty.

"You don't laugh, you don't cry . . . you really need to drop the robot act, Zo. Mom died. It's okay to show some freaking emotion." Her hands tremble as she reaches for Mom's ashes, and my fragile hold on those emotions slips for half a second.

"What are you doing?" I tighten my grasp on the urn, fighting the urge to set my tears free. I can't cry now. If I do, I may never stop.

She arches an eyebrow, slowly enunciating each word as if I don't speak her language. "Taking Mom's ashes?"

"No. You're not." I squint up at her, burning my retinas in the process. Sunlight streams through her icy-blond hair, making it glow like a halo behind her. An involuntary snort slips out of me. Horns would be more like it. "Not unless you've changed your mind about her last wishes . . ."

"No." Losing her own battle with tears, Jeanie blows out a breath, deflating along with it. "We're doing it, so get used to the idea."

Head pounding, I curl my fingers into a fist, sinking my freshly manicured nails into my palm, welcoming the sting. We've already had this argument more times than I can count, but if she wants to go at it again, I'm in.

"Do you even know why she wanted us to spread her ashes along some fifty-year-old concert path?" I demand.

"Does it matter?" Jeanie locks her shimmering blue eyes on mine. "That's what she wanted."

"It's just so . . . *wrong*." I pick at a loose thread on the black dress Mom bought me the day she found out her cancer had spread to her lymph nodes and then check my phone again. Three spam texts asking me about my car's extended warranty and a calendar reminder to refill my birth control, but nothing from Damian. "She was half out of her mind on opioids at the end."

"Right or wrong, we need to do it soon. This is my last free summer. I start my new job in less than a month."

When I ignore her, she flicks a loose pebble into the grass with her big toe. Neither of us wants to tackle the elephant in the room—how she's a college graduate with a bright future, and I'm a twenty-year-old high school graduate who's never even had a real job.

"Is Mr. All-American picking you up, or are you walking home?"

"I don't know yet." I shift my weight again, squirming on the uncomfortable stone steps.

"I really have no idea what you see in that guy." She snorts. "I've never liked him. Neither did Mom."

Red-hot rage sears my veins. If we weren't on the steps of a church, I'd slap the smirk from her lips. "What would *you* know about what Mom did or didn't like? You've been gone for almost four years!"

"I wasn't gone. I was in college." She lowers her gaze as if my accusation wounded her. "And I talked to Mom every day."

"That's nice for you. But I'm the one who gave up my entire life to take care of her. Watched her slip further and further away every single day. And do you know what she never said? 'Break up with the quarterback, Zoey. Don't follow in my footsteps, Zoey.' Because she *wanted* me to have the kind of life she had."

Jeanie's head snaps up. "Damn it, Zo, maybe you don't remember how bad things were before Dad left, but I do. Mom divorced him for a reason. Marrying the quarterback isn't all it's cracked up to be."

"I never said I was gonna marry him." The words tumble out on a breath. The mere thought of seeing Damian every day for the rest of my life makes my soul itch. But I'll be damned if I tell Jeanie that.

"Good, because we both know that didn't work out so well for her. And despite what you think, that's not what she wanted for you."

"Like that matters now." My shoulders sag, the fight draining out of me. *Mom's dead.* Every single sacrifice I made over the past two years pales in comparison.

She chokes out a bitter laugh. "Whatever. I'm outta here."

For someone so eager to ditch me, she waits almost a full minute before stomping down the steps toward her electric-orange Nissan—an early graduation gift from Mom. I would've gotten one, too, someday . . . if life had unfolded differently.

"I'm not coming to get you if you change your mind." Jeanie climbs behind the wheel and slams her door.

"I won't!" I yell as she pulls away from the curb, determined to walk all the way home if I have to just to spite her.

The rumble of a broken muffler draws my attention from Jeanie's retreating taillights. My chest tightens as a familiar banana-yellow coupe turns the corner onto Church Street and backfires twice. I instantly recognize my grandmother's signature bottle-dyed, flame-red hair flying around her face as she speeds toward me, a cloud of smoke billowing out of her open window. A sudden burst of emotion punches me right in the feels, and I squeeze my eyes shut to keep from giving in to it. Seeing her again—*today of all days*—has my ten-year-old self longing to play dress-up with her hideous costume jewelry, her brightly colored scarves, and every shade of red lipstick ever made.

Her 1973 Oldsmobile Cutlass pulls up to the curb and she climbs out, hacking up a lung as she slides her giant bug-eye sunglasses into her fiery-red curls.

"Zoey Marie, is that you?" She rolls her eyes at my halfhearted wave and barks out a throaty laugh. "Get your pretty little ass over here and give your G-Lo a hug."

Swallowing a mouthful of resentment, I kick off my heels and hook them with my fingers, letting my bare toes sink into the cool grass as I traipse across the thick lawn. With one arm still around Mom's urn, I wrap the other around my grandmother's narrow waist and suck in a lungful of stale Camels, cheap perfume, and the skunky stench of fresh weed.

"Good to see you, Grandma Lola."

"Language," she croaks, a thousand packs of cigarettes coloring her voice. "What did I tell you about using the *G-word*?"

"Oops." I grin. "Guess I forgot."

It's been forever since I've seen her, but other than a few extra lines around her eyes when she smiles, she's barely changed. Wearing weathered jeans with frayed knees and a vintage Sex Pistols tee that's probably older than I am, she looks more like a college student than someone's grandmother.

"Now, let me get a good look at you." She cups my face in her warm hands, and the tears I've battled all day threaten to break free. "You've grown into a beautiful young woman, and I'm sick to death that I've missed it."

I hold my breath as she studies every inch of me, combing her black fingernails through my dark-blond waves. My eyes flutter shut, and my imagination replaces her touch with Mom's.

"You look so much like her . . . when she was your age. Same wispy frame, same dishwater-blond hair."

The fragile illusion pops like a soap bubble, and I release the breath with a groan, my hand drifting to my clean hair. "Can we *not* compare my hair to dirty dishwater? Please?"

Grandma Lola erupts in loud laughter. "Your mother said the same thing when she was eighteen."

"I'm almost twenty-one. Damn near old enough to drink, for god's sake," I snap with a little more bite than necessary.

She waves her hand through the air, making her stack of gold and silver bracelets clink like wind chimes. "When you get to be my age, everything under thirty-five runs together."

I have a thousand questions, starting with a big fat *Where the hell have you been?* But she beats me to the punch.

"You're probably wondering why I'm late."

Understatement of the century.

I nod as a million other questions swirl around my brain, each one more painful than the next. With my unresolved feelings stacked in a reckless game of emotional Jenga, one wrong word could send it all crashing down around me.

"Oh, sweetie, I know what you're thinking, but I couldn't bear to see her like that." She dabs at her dark-rimmed eyes with the hem of her black tee, flashing lacy side-boob to the world.

"She missed you." *I* missed you. The thought takes me by surprise, and my next breath catches in my throat as I blink back more tears.

Grandma Lola pulls the latest iPhone from her back pocket and holds it up. "I texted. I called."

"Not the same." Eyes burning, I tighten my grip on Mom's urn and focus on the tall blades of grass jutting between my toes.

"You *sound* a little too much like her, too." Grandma Lola's smile falters. "Cut me a little slack, kiddo. Funerals are for the living, not the dead, and I'd much rather remember your mother the way she was. Full of vibrancy and life."

"*I'm* one of the living." I level a scorching glare at her. "So is Jeanie. Did it ever occur to you that *we* might've needed you today?"

"I'm here now." Throwing an arm over my shoulders, Grandma exhales a breath heavy with unspoken apologies. "Come on, let's get some lunch. You look like you could use a sandwich . . . *or two*, and I've got a serious case of the munchies."

I shift the urn to my other hip, the weight of Mom's judgment pressing down on me. "What about Reverend Tom and the church ladies?"

She raises an eyebrow. "Unless you're talking about a new punk band, they can get their own damn lunch."

"No, I mean, they're at my house. With food. Probably tons of it. Jeanie went home to let them in."

"Good. Let Jeanie eat Crock-Pot delight and lime ambrosia with the denture squad. You and I have a date for triple-decker sandwiches from Mimsy's."

A fleeting memory of shiny chrome stools and vanilla Cokes with paper straws brings me to the edge of losing it again. "Mimsy's closed. Last year."

"Closed?" Her mouth hangs open, exposing several silver fillings. "As in closed *down*?"

"As in, there's a nail salon there now."

"Damn. Guess it's church lady surprise for us, too." The Cutlass creaks and moans as Grandma yanks her door open. "Come on, hop in."

Empty fast-food wrappers and Styrofoam cups litter the passenger seat, and I shove everything to the floor before climbing in. A grainy photo of my grandmother smiles up at me from the trash pile—a laminated ID card, attached to a purple lanyard—and I fish it out.

Bold black letters spell out P-R-E-S-S above her photo, her name scrawled in red ink at the bottom. "What's this?"

"Isn't that obvious?" She chuckles as she pulls away from the curb.

I flip the ID over, looking for proof that it's authentic. "Where'd you get it?"

"I didn't *steal* it, if that's what you're wondering. Did you think I wandered the country going to rock concerts for fun?"

"Maybe." I shrug. I'd never questioned my grandma's motivations for what she did. Mom called her an old hippie, so that's how I always thought of her.

This time, she throws her head back and laughs. "Even an old girl like me has to make a living somehow. Classic cars like this don't pay for themselves."

Lost for words, I give the press pass another quick once-over.

She nods toward the glove box. "Put that where I won't lose it, would you, sweetie?"

The latch sticks, so I give it a yank. The little door flies open, launching the contents toward me like projectile vomit. Without missing a beat, Grandma slams the door shut, but not before a few crumpled packs of Camels, a baggie with three joints, and several mini liquor bottles land at my feet with a clink.

"Just toss it in the back seat."

From the time we leave the church until we pull into the driveway alongside Mom's ancient, faded-green Explorer, Grandma Lola waxes poetic about coleslaw and turkey sandwiches, making whatever casseroles the church ladies left us seem all the more unappetizing.

"I still can't believe Mimsy's went out of business. I've been craving one of their turkey Rachels since hitting the state line." When I don't respond, she follows the path of my eyes to the shiny black four-door parked along the curb. "The church ladies, I presume?"

"No." I sigh. "Just Reverend Tom."

"What the hell's he still doing here?"

"Probably waiting for me." I don't tell her I slipped out after the funeral without saying goodbye. Or how he spent a lot of time at our house when Mom was sick. If she had gotten better, I have no doubt he would've come around even more. I didn't mind so much then. It gave me a chance to breathe once in a while. Doesn't mean I'm ready to discuss my feelings now.

"Oh, hell. If I'd known I was about to face the wrath of God, I would've fired up another doobie." Grandma cuts the engine and turns to me. "Guess we'd better get this over with."

We don't get far before Jeanie bounds down the front steps as if the devil himself is on her heels. She plants her bare feet in the grass and presses her fingers to her pink lips, staring at our grandmother as if seeing a ghost. She looks so small standing there, so much younger than her twenty-two years, and for the first time, I recognize the weight of grief in her eyes.

"I knew you'd come," she whispers. "I just knew it."

Grandma Lola opens her arms. "My goodness, Jean-Jeanie, you've grown up!"

"One of us had to." Jeanie's eyes glisten with unshed tears as she falls into Grandma's arms.

"Well then." Grandma pats Jeanie's back. "I'm glad it was you."

Reverend Tom wanders out of the house dressed in casual Dockers and a Mister Rogers sweater. Without his church uniform, he looks more like a substitute math teacher than a preacher.

His gaze skips over me, drifting from Jeanie to G-Lo, and he offers a consoling smile. "I'm guessing you're Vida's mother. I was quite fond of your daughter. I'm so sorry for your loss."

Grandma releases Jeanie and stalks forward, grinning like the Cheshire Cat as she holds out her hand. "Lola Stone." She studies the man as if planning to cook him and eat him. "And you must be Reverend Tom."

"Uh, yes. Tom Randall. I've, uh, heard a lot about you. Wish we could've met under different circumstances."

"Guess we'll have to make up for lost time then, won't we?" she purrs.

Reverend Tom backs away slowly, turning as red as Grandma's lips. "I really should be going. I'm sure you'd like some time to catch up with the girls."

"See you around, Reverend." She wiggles her fingers in a flirty wave as he stumbles the last few feet to his car and slips behind the wheel. As he pulls away from the curb, she turns to us and releases a whoosh of air. "I thought he'd never leave."

"He's gonna be absolving himself all night long after that little exchange." Jeanie's eyes sparkle with amusement.

I'd sooner gouge out my eyes than imagine anything Reverend Tom does under cover of night. "We probably should've been nicer to him. He was really good to Mom."

"Your mother was always drawn to complicated relationships." Grandma wraps her arm around Jeanie's shoulders. "But let's not talk about men. I've driven halfway across the country to see you girls." She pins me under her knowing gaze. "I understand we have things to discuss, so we should probably get right to it."

Jeanie eyes the urn in my arms.

I shift my weight, balancing Mom's ashes on my hip. "You can stop pretending you haven't been talking behind my back. It won't change how I feel about Mom's crazy request."

"It's not so crazy when you understand her reasons. May I?" Grandma nods toward the urn and holds out her hands. "Let's take her inside so we can talk."

I reluctantly surrender Mom's ashes and follow my sister and grandmother into the house.

2

Ziggy Stardust

Our kitchen looks like Paula Deen exploded. From the doorway, I count at least three homemade pies resting on the glass cooktop. Assorted casserole dishes litter every available flat surface, and the light reflecting off the aluminum foil is blinding. Stacked around the Pyrex graveyard are plastic containers in nearly every color of the rainbow, as if our house is where Tupperware came to die. The church ladies thought of everything—right down to the tub of whipped I Can't Believe It's Not Butter! nestled in a basket of freshly baked brown 'n serve rolls.

"Hungry?" Jeanie holds out an oval dish filled with what looks like regurgitated dog food.

The stench of boiled cabbage and scalloped potatoes slaps me in the face like a wet sneaker, making my stomach roll over and play dead. "I'd rather starve."

"Suit yourself." Jeanie shoves the dish into the overcrowded refrigerator before taking a seat next to Grandma. She taps a shimmery pink fingernail on the table in a quick staccato, mimicking my erratic heartbeat, and the hairs on the back of my neck stand on end.

I alternate my gaze between Jeanie and Grandma Lola. "Is this an intervention?"

Instead of answering, Grandma gives me a syrupy smile that all but confirms my suspicions.

I pivot on my heel, ready to march back the way I came. "If you need me, I'll be in my room yanking out my fingernails, one at a time."

"Sit!" Jeanie points at the open seat across from her.

"Fine." I scrape my chair across the floor before falling into it with a grunt.

The two of them share covert glances, speaking in code with their eyes.

"Sooo . . ." I drag out the word, filling the uncomfortable silence. "What's the mysterious reason Mom wants us to spread her ashes between Cleveland and Santa Monica?"

Grandma finally releases her stranglehold on the urn and sets it in the center of the table. "It's a long story."

"It's not like I have anything better to do." I cross my arms and straighten my spine. If I miss the rapidly closing window to register for classes, I'll have nothing *but* time.

"As you both know, I haven't exactly lived a conventional life," Grandma starts.

I snort. "Understatement."

Jeanie pins me with a glare. "Let her talk."

"As I was saying . . ." Grandma folds her hands on the table. "I've always been somewhat of a nomad, floating from one place to another like a leaf in the wind."

I open my mouth to mention the press pass, but she holds up a finger, preempting my question.

"I may have parlayed my love of music into an actual job, but long before I snagged my first paycheck, my cousin Penny convinced me to sneak off to Cleveland to see Led Zeppelin with her." She gazes straight through us, as if she's found a window into the past. "Penny was a little older than me, but far more worldly than her years. She was 'nineteen going on thirty,' as Momma used to say. She smoked pot, drank cheap whiskey, and ran around with the best-looking boys in town. So, naturally, I wanted to be just like her."

Almost against my will, her story draws me in. "How old were you?"

A gravelly chuckle rolls up her throat. "Barely seventeen—and if my mother had known how long it would be before she saw me again, she would've nailed my windows shut."

"You ran away?" Jeanie's jaw drops. "Just like that?"

Grinning ear to ear, Grandma nods. "With nothing but a change of clothes, the last seven dollars from my piggy bank, and my brand-new driver's license."

Even in the 1970s, I doubt she would've gotten far on seven dollars. "How did you pay for the tickets?"

"Oh, we didn't have tickets." She snickers. "Penny knew the guy at the gate. When we got to Cleveland, she not only got us into the concert without a single ticket between us, but she sweet-talked the security guards into letting us backstage to meet the band. I spent the weekend sleeping in the back seat of Penny's powder-blue Pinto, and I never went back. That beat-up old hatchback was practically my home for the next two years while we hit every concert in Ohio. The rest, as they say, is history."

"So you were a rebel. What does that have to do with Mom?" I sneak a peek at my phone. *Nothing.*

"I'm getting to that." Grandma takes a deep breath. "In September 1972, a young Englishman with flaming hair and four-inch platform boots walked onto the stage at the Cleveland Music Hall and changed everything I knew about the world. I'm not exaggerating when I say he blew my mind. None of us had ever seen anything like it before—the hair, the makeup, the elaborate costumes. He was this glittering alien, oozing sex appeal."

I shudder.

Grandma waggles her eyebrows and lets out a barking laugh. "Oh, Zoey, honey, you have no idea."

"This is so wrong." Groaning, I cover my face with both hands. "You're my *grandmother*. I don't want to think about you cavorting with oozing rock stars."

"I wasn't always your grandmother. And trust me, Bowie oozed. The man was out of this world. I was . . . more than a little obsessed to be honest. I practically got down on my knees and begged Penny to follow Ziggy Stardust and the Spiders from Mars to Memphis for the next stop. She was up for almost anything in those days, so we hopped in the Pinto and followed the tour bus the whole way there. The first several stops on the tour were hardly sellouts, but it gave us a chance to get to know the band. To talk with them. Party with them. I may have only been nineteen, but I was mature beyond my years."

"That's a fascinating story," I deadpan, stealthily checking my messages again.

Finally, a text from Damian: Hey babe, whatcha doing?

As if he doesn't know.

But since I can only fight one battle at a time, I simply text him a quick call ya later before pocketing my phone and going back to the conversation at hand. "I still don't see what any of that has to do with Mom."

"Your mother was conceived somewhere between Memphis and Malibu." Grandma's smile turns wistful, as if reliving the moment.

Jeanie leans in, hanging on every juicy word.

"So you . . . hooked up with one of the roadies or something?" No wonder Mom never wanted to talk about her dad.

"No." Grandma laughs. "Not one of the roadies."

"Another groupie?"

Jeanie cackles as if she already knows the answer.

"No, Zoey. I didn't sleep with some random groupie."

Frustration finally gets to me. "Then who?"

Grandma's green eyes sparkle with untold secrets. "Ziggy Stardust himself."

◆ ◆ ◆

"Wait . . . you're going where?" Damian's voice roars down the line, and I pull the phone away from my ear. All things considered, he's taking the news about as well as expected.

Swallowing a groan, I shove my old Pooh Bear to the side and fall into a stack of pillows. "Cleveland, for starters."

He snorts. "Why the hell would you go to the Mistake on the Lake on purpose?"

Ignoring his tired joke, I switch the call to speaker and gaze down at the old photo of him grinning up at me from the phone display. His olive complexion is even darker in person, especially now that it's warm enough to be outside all day. I reach for the discarded bear and hug it to my chest. "I'm going with Jeanie and my grandma to spread my mom's ashes. It's a long story."

"Oh. Right." He clears the attitude from his throat and lowers his voice. "How long will you be gone?"

"Not sure yet." I pick at a loose thread on Pooh's butt. Mom probably sewed the same seam over a hundred times since I was a toddler. "A week . . . maybe longer?"

"For Chrissakes, Zoey! You're supposed to be registering for classes and coming to look at apartments with me this weekend." And just like that, the attitude's back.

"I didn't plan this, you know?" Everything—Mom's death, Grandma's bombshell, the road trip—weighs down on me until I damn near boil over like a pot of potatoes.

Damian lets out a defeated sigh. "I'm sorry about your mom, Zo. I, uh, would've been at the funeral but . . . you know I'm not good with emotional shit."

"Yeah, I know."

His aversion to "emotional shit" is one of the many reasons for rethinking my decision to join him at Penn State. The plan was always to go to college together. I enrolled—went to orientation and everything—but then right after graduation, Mom took a turn for the worse, and I couldn't leave. Now that she's gone, I'm not sure I want the same things I did two years ago.

My eyes and nose prickle as I fight back tears.

"Don't cry, baby," he pleads.

"I'm not a baby . . . and I'm *not* crying!" My voice cracks, taking a bite out of my anger.

Damian releases a ragged breath. "Don't worry about school right now, okay? Do your thing and come back."

"Thanks," I say, the word bitter on my tongue.

How dare he act as if I need his permission to spread my mother's ashes. He doesn't need to know I hate the idea. Or how many times I tried convincing my sister to spread Mom's ashes damn near anywhere else. How I'm only going because she gave me no choice.

"Will I see you before you leave?" he asks.

"Maybe."

Shouldn't he be more concerned about your emotional state than whether or not he gets laid before you go? The voice in my head sounds a whole lot like Jeanie's, and I quickly block it out before it says something I can't ignore.

"I don't know. I'll ask Jeanie and call you in the morning." Or maybe I won't, and there's absolutely nothing he can do about it.

"Whatever. Have a nice trip." Damian hangs up, still fuming over a decision even *I* don't understand, and I'm more than over his childish dramatics.

The streetlights outside my window flicker on. One after the other, they come to life, glowing orbs stretching out in both directions as far as the eye can see, like fireflies lining up for dinner. I shove the window sash as high as it goes and climb onto the porch overhang—the secret spot I go when I need to be alone with my thoughts.

With my back to the weathered blue siding, I sit on the scratchy gray shingles and pull my knees to my chest, trying and failing to picture my grandmother—even a much younger version of the woman I know—kissing an actual rock god. I tug a loose thread on my sleep shorts, unraveling the hem halfway around my leg before realizing what I've done.

Shit. I break off the string, letting it float through the breeze.

Do ashes float when you spread them?

A tear rolls down my cheek, and I wipe it before it hits my chin. This is not how my life was supposed to go. I should be halfway through college by now. Maybe changing majors because I can't decide between math and science. Spending spring and summer breaks barhopping at the beach with friends. Making plans for the future. Not burying my mom. Definitely not spreading her ashes in far-off places.

"What the hell were you thinking, Mom?" I close my eyes, and she's waiting for me behind my lids.

"Promise me, Zoey." Her reedy voice rings through my memory. *"Promise me you'll spread my ashes in each city he played."*

Her pale, cracked lips barely moved as she whispered—the sound little more than vapor to my ears. Her request made no sense. It didn't the first time, and it doesn't now. But her unwavering determination chipped at my defenses . . . wearing me down.

"I don't understand, Mom."

"You will." She smiled and closed her eyes as if she knew she'd won.

At the end, I didn't argue with her. The absolute last thing I wanted was to say anything that was less than perfect when I didn't know how long we had. She was so pale. So thin. With her eyes closed, it was hard to tell if she was still in there anymore. Watching her wither away little by little, connected to machines via tubes and wires, broke my heart. My only comfort came from the rhythmic beep of the machine counting her remaining heartbeats like a ticking time bomb.

"Mind some company?" My sister pokes her head out the window, scattering my memory to the wind. With her ice-blond hair pulled into a loose ponytail, and her face scrubbed clean, she could easily pass for a teenager.

"How'd you find me?"

"You always come out here to brood." Jeanie throws a bare foot over the sill and ducks under the sash to climb out.

So much for my secret spot.

Without another word, I slide over to give her room. Instead of sitting beside me, she brushes a few leaves aside and sits across from me with her back to the street and her eyes on the stars.

"Hell of a day, huh?"

Leave it to Jeanie to understate the obvious.

In her pink yoga pants and matching hoodie, she looks exactly like she did when we were kids. Even now, she's all pretty in pink, and I'm moody blue with the whole world on my shoulders. For some reason, I find it hard to stay mad at her when she strips away the mask and turns into the little girl who taught me how to crack open an Oreo to eat the cream filling first.

"I talked to G-Lo. If we leave first thing tomorrow, we can hit Cleveland before lunch, get shit done, and make it halfway to Memphis before dark," she says without taking a breath.

Tomorrow? My empty stomach clenches into a tight fist. Tell her you don't want to go. "Okay."

Chickenshit.

"We'll be gone two weeks. Three at the most. I absolutely have to be back by the last week of July. I start my job August first."

"I don't have any plans." Damian would disagree, but he'll get over it. There's always spring semester. "But I still don't understand why we're doing this. I call bullshit on G-Lo's story. I get people were all about the free love back then, and maybe she banged every roadie along that tour—"

"She named Mom Davida."

"Which is totally weird but doesn't prove anything. There's no way in hell she got close enough to Bowie to smell his sweat, let alone swap bodily fluids." Visions of the Goblin King humping my grandma pop into my head, and I quickly banish them before they take up residence. "Sorry. Not buying it."

Jeanie wraps her arms around her legs and rests her chin on her knees. "It doesn't matter if it's true or not. Mom believed it."

Mom may have *wanted* to believe it, but I don't believe for one minute she actually did.

"Come on, Jeanie. David Bowie? You're as unhinged as Grandma if you let her suck you into her delusions."

"I read her diary, Zo."

"Grandma Lola's diary?" Graphic visions of drug-fueled orgies dance through my imagination, and I shut them down just as quickly. "I'll bet that was . . . weird."

Her laugh echoes in the night air. "No, dumbass. Mom's."

"Hold on . . ." My mouth goes dry, and my lungs still. "Mom had a diary? Why am I just now hearing about this?"

Jeanie lifts her head, but her arms tighten around her legs. "I guess she didn't think you were ready to read it."

"But you were?" My heart rattles behind my ribs, my stomach twisting painfully as I try to make sense of what I'm hearing.

"You were just a kid."

"I'm only two years younger than you!"

Jeanie exhales a sharp breath. "She gave it to me for safekeeping. She'd just started chemo. You were studying for finals. She didn't want to distract you."

I blink, then blink again. "You've had it for two years and never told me?"

"I didn't read it. Not until after . . ." Jeanie drops her gaze. "She made me promise to wait until she was gone. So I'd understand."

Something inside me snaps. White-hot anger rises up, lashing out like a cracking whip. My whole life I've been stuck with Jeanie's hand-me-downs—her clothes, her toys. Everything was hers before it was mine . . . even Mom. Even now.

"Why you?" My anger unfurls like a giant sail, catching the wind. "I'm the one who took care of her all this time. I'm the one who gave up everything and stayed behind!"

"Maybe she was afraid you couldn't handle it then."

"And now?" Feelings of inadequacy, of desperation, well up in me. Mom hadn't trusted me. Hadn't thought I could handle the truth. But Jeanie could. My hands shake as I roughly grip my thighs, holding myself still before I jump across the roof and tackle her. "Where is it now? Or am I still unworthy?"

Jeanie rolls her eyes as if my request is beneath her. As if she still sees me as that fragile little girl who cried over spilled ice cream. "It's in my carry-on."

"Go get it. Right now."

She shifts her weight but doesn't get up. "Not until you calm down."

"Damn it, Jeanie!" I release my thighs and the blood rushes back in. "You're such a bitch!"

Jeanie's lips take on a cruel slant, and she chuckles under her breath. "*I* may be a bitch, but *you're* acting like a child."

Her words sting more than they should, and I suck in a breath.

"Whoa! What's going on out here?" Grandma Lola leans out the open window. "Keep this up and one of you is going to fall and break your neck."

"She started it." The instant the words tumble past my lips, I know I've lost. *Congratulations, Zoey. You just proved Jeanie's point.*

I half expect Grandma to hug us into submission. Instead, she plops down beside Jeanie and crisscrosses her legs. She pulls a cigarette from behind her ear like a hippie magician and lights it with a rainbow-colored Bic from her pocket. "Now what's all the ruckus about?"

With a sigh, the fight drains out of Jeanie. "Mom gave me her diary, and—"

"And I don't think it's fair for her to know all Mom's secrets while I'm left in the dark," I say.

"I was planning to let you read it," Jeanie mutters.

"When? After I graduate college?"

Grandma leans forward and exhales a smoke ring. "Is it the diary from our trip?"

Jeanie cocks her head. "How'd you—"

"As far as I know, it's the only time your mother kept a diary."

A sad smile crosses Jeanie's lips. "It starts on the day you told her about her dad . . ."

"And ends on the last day of our trip . . . on Santa Monica Pier." Grandma takes another drag on her cigarette and nods as if she's reliving the memory.

Alternating my gaze between them, I heave a heavy sigh. "Will one of you tell me what the hell you're talking about? What trip? How old was I?"

"You weren't even born yet, Zoey," Grandma says. "The summer before your mom started college, I told her the same story I told you girls this afternoon. She wanted to see all the places I'd gone on that tour. Wanted a way to connect with her father . . . and me, I suppose."

Eager to hear more, I crawl across the roof until I practically land in my grandmother's lap. "So you took off on a road trip? Just like that?"

She nods. "We spent the entire summer retracing my steps from '72. She never told you about the time we snuck her into a pub to sing karaoke?"

"No." I laugh at the thought of my straitlaced mom sneaking into a bar.

Grandma's face lights up. "You should have seen her. She wore one of my ripped band tees and a pair of frayed cutoffs. And the things we did in New York City would curl your toes! It was before camera phones, but I think your mom took photos at every stop."

"She did." Jeanie swipes a stray tear from her cheek. "She taped them to pages inside her diary."

Grandma snuffs out her cigarette on a shingle and tosses the butt over the side. "We had the best time that summer."

Dozens of questions pick at loose threads in my soul. Five minutes ago, I wanted nothing to do with Grandma Lola's ridiculous story, and now I can't get enough to quench my curiosity. "Just that summer? You didn't go on any other wild trips together?"

"Sadly, no. She went off to school, met your father, started a career and a family. We were on different paths right from the beginning. The road's no place for a baby. I should know." She blinks several times before changing the subject. "What do you girls say? Should we leave in the morning?"

"Sounds good to me." Jeanie turns to me, eyes probing.

"I don't know." It was easy to get caught up in her story, but I still don't understand how a summer trip Mom took over thirty years ago factors into her final resting place. "Why can't we just spread her ashes under the big tree in the yard? At least then we can go talk to her sometimes."

Jeanie's nostrils flare, her jaw clenching and unclenching. "Because Mom's gone, Zo. She's not coming back. But you know what? I'm here. And you're here. And she wouldn't want us spending every damn minute of every damn day mourning her. Sticking around this shitty little town, or tied to this shitty little house, just to visit her tree every day. She'd want us out there"—Jeanie points into the night—"experiencing life. So pack a damn bag, because we're going!"

A twinge of guilt silences my objection, the words turning to ash in my mouth. I jerk my head in a curt nod.

Jeanie's features relax, as if the weight of the world was lifted from her shoulders. "I think we should re-create the pictures Mom took in each city. Zo and I can even pose the same way she did. In the fountain in Cleveland . . ."

Grandma's eyes light up. "On the pier in Santa Monica?"

"Exactly!" Jeanie beams.

"I love that idea." Grandma pulls out a hand-rolled cigarette from her pocket.

My gaze locks on her fingers as she lights it and takes a long drag, holding her breath for what seems like forever.

The skunky odor hits my nostrils, and I flinch. "Is that pot?"

She finally exhales, coughing as she waves the cloud away from my face. "Don't have an aneurysm, dear. It's perfectly legal. I have a prescription."

She seems to forget that Mom had cancer. I know all about the law. Sure, people did it, but not out in the open. Not on the roof where the neighbors can see.

"This isn't California!" I hiss. "You can't *smoke* it here!"

"What the hell else are you supposed to do with it?" Grandma takes another drag.

Panicking, I turn to my sister. "Tell her!"

Jeanie laughs. "She's freaking out because the guy across the street is a mall security guard."

"Ooh, a mall cop?" Grandma snickers. "That *is* scary."

Rough asphalt scrapes my skin as I scramble to my knees. Just being here makes me an accessory. Guilt by association, like Mom always said. "You two are gonna get me arrested!"

"Honey, it's only a crime if you get caught. And it'll be legal in all fifty states before you know it, mark my words." Grandma passes the joint to Jeanie, who takes it without hesitation.

I stare at Jeanie as a wave of panic threatens to drown me. "You said you were quitting!"

She smirks. "Today wasn't the day to quit."

"What if your new job drug tests you?"

Jeanie rolls her eyes. "They won't."

"You don't know that!" I grab her wrist, but she won't give up the joint without a fight.

The roof is like sandpaper under my bare feet as we dance around, hands locked in the most epic thumb war ever. Jeanie rotates her wrist to the right, and I counter with a twist to the left.

"Let me go, you lunatic." She jerks her hand free and stumbles backward, a scream caught in her throat.

"Be careful!" Grandma Lola squeals. "Don't drop the doobie!"

Jeanie teeters precariously near the edge for half a second before regaining her balance. "That was close." She barely gets the words out before the shingles beneath her break free and she disappears over the side with a bloodcurdling shriek.

"Jeanie!" I scramble to the edge and peer over, unable to catch my breath. My chest goes quiet as I gape down at her still form sprawled across the top of a thick boxwood shrub. She can't be dead. Not her, too.

In the shrub below, Jeanie groans, her arm twitching.

"Call 911!" I throw a leg over the side and shimmy down the vine-covered post before the rational side of my brain takes over. The second my feet touch the ground, I race to her side, high on adrenaline as I kneel on the damp grass and grab her wrist to check for a pulse. She moans at the contact, and I release a breath. "I thought I'd killed you!"

She cracks open one eye. "Not unless hell looks like Western Pennsylvania. But . . ." She opens the other eye and winces. "I'm pretty sure I broke something."

Relief washes over me, allowing anger to sneak in. "I told you drugs were dangerous!"

Jeanie's glare threatens to burn me to a crisp. "You seriously have your priorities messed up, Zo."

3

The Jean Genie

Grandma parks her ancient Cutlass in front of the house just as the first glow of morning crests the horizon. It takes both of us to help Jeanie out of the car without bumping the cast holding her leg together.

"G-Lo, your car is gross. I need to be disinfected." Jeanie glares at her Nissan still parked in the driveway and snatches the crutches out of my hands. Even high on pain meds, irritation oozes from her pores as she hobbles toward the house. "I can't believe neither of you know how to drive a stick shift."

I stab my key into the lock a little harder than necessary. "I would've asked someone to teach me if I'd known you were going to fall off the roof."

"Fall?" Jeanie growls, balancing on one crutch as she teeters on our front stoop. "I didn't *fall* off the roof." She points at me with her bandaged hand. "You *pushed* me!"

My mouth falls open. "Did not!"

"Did, too, and I have the broken bones to prove it."

"Let's not argue over who did"—Grandma Lola wipes the smile from her lips—"or didn't push who off the roof. There's something else I'd like to discuss with you both." Her eyes dart toward Jeanie. "I know we'd planned to go together, but since Jeanie won't be in any condition to travel for the next six weeks, maybe I should—"

"I'm going." The words bubble past my lips before I realize the weight of what I'm saying.

"Honey, your sister needs someone to—"

"You stay with her," I snap, suddenly angry with everyone for taking my choices away. From Mom keeping her diary secret, to Jeanie ordering me to pack a bag without bothering to help me understand her reasoning. She read Mom's damn diary. She *knew* why. Even Damian, for thinking he gets a vote as to where and when I start school. I'll be damned if I let another person tell me what to do. I swing the front door open and step inside. Today is the day I take control of my own destiny. "I want to go."

With the words fresh on my lips, I realize how true they are. And not because I'd do almost anything to avoid playing Jeanie's personal nurse while she recuperates. Or because I haven't had a good night's sleep for close to two years. But because, for the first time since Mom got sick, I have a sense of purpose.

I'd be lying if I said I understand why Mom wanted her ashes spread across the country, but if I have any hope of understanding how she felt at the time, why she asked us to make this trip, I need to read her diary in the places she wrote it. And maybe . . . just maybe . . . I need to start living my life for *me* for a change.

Jeanie snickers. "Good one."

"I'm not kidding." But the terrifying realization slowly sinks in. I may be more than a little unhinged for even considering something so bold.

I'm doing this by myself.

"What? No!" Jeanie's left eye twitches—from pain meds or panic, I'm not sure. "You can't go!"

"Yeah, I really can." Straightening my spine, I gaze at my sister, refusing to back down. "Listen, I know I wasn't on board with the whole ashes thing from the beginning, but you said it yourself. This is what Mom wanted. And by the time you're cleared for travel, it'll be too late."

"But . . ." Jeanie trips over her own tongue as she struggles to spit out the words. "You can't drive stick, remember?"

"I have Mom's car."

Her eyes go wide and she gestures toward the dark shadow parked in the driveway. "You mean the piece-of-shit Explorer that hasn't been serviced since Mom got sick?"

The thought of driving Mom's shitty SUV beyond the town limits sends a bead of sweat racing down my spine, but I won't let Jeanie talk me out of it. "It works fine."

"For grocery runs maybe, but you can't drive it across the country! The whole electrical system shorts out at least once a week, and the damn thing leaks more fluid than a Dollar Store diaper. It's only a matter of time before it heaves its last breath and leaves you stranded by the side of the road."

"You're the one who drilled into me how important this trip was to Mom. It took me long enough, but I finally get it."

She lets out a primal shriek before turning toward Grandma. If not for her broken leg, she'd undoubtedly stomp her foot like a three-year-old in the throes of a temper tantrum. "G-Lo, tell her she can't go!"

Grandma presses her pot leaf key chain into my hand, then folds my fingers around the huge wad of keys and squeezes. "You can take my car."

"W-What?" Jeanie sputters, her mouth hanging open like a giant flytrap. "Compared to your car, the Explorer looks new! How that fossil even starts, let alone drives, boggles my mind."

"Don't hate on the Betty." Grandma pats Jeanie's unbandaged hand, guiding her toward the sofa. "She may be old, but she runs like a dream."

"And smells like a nightmare!" Jeanie's death glare isn't nearly as scary with her eyelids drooping.

"Smelled like fries and ancient tacos to me." I swallow my laugh.

Grandma shakes her bony finger at me, but there's no heat in her expression. "Those tacos were from yesterday."

"Do you even hear yourselves?" Jeanie says, the fight fading from her voice. "Joking about Zoey driving your ancient death trap across the country? That's . . . you've *both* lost your minds!"

"Come on, Jeanie." Grandma grabs her elbow and helps her sit. "The sun's coming up, and your pain meds are probably wearing off. I have a spliff of Sour Diesel with your name on it. A few puffs of that, and you won't even remember you *have* a sister."

For every shirt I stuff into my backpack, Jeanie pulls out two.

"Stop packing." Her voice cracks, warning me how close she is to losing it.

"Why?" I close my eyes, reminding myself I'm doing this for Mom. We wouldn't even be having this argument if Jeanie hadn't told me about the diary. But now that I know, I can't *un*know.

"Because maybe you're right." She fidgets with her crutches. "Maybe we should spread Mom's ashes under the big tree. She loved that tree."

Ignoring her, I go back to packing. "That's the Percocet talking."

"Maybe . . . but damn it, Zo. I can't let you drive across the country by yourself!"

"I don't need your permission. I'm more than capable of making my own decisions."

"Well, this is the dumbest decision you've ever made. Mom would never forgive me if anything happened to you out there."

With a sideways glance at my sister, I go back to shoving clothes into my bag. "Nothing's gonna happen to me."

"You don't know that." She lets out a frustrated growl, then snatches the bag out of my hands and drops it to the floor. Balancing on her good leg with both crutches tucked under one arm, she reminds me of a beat-up old Raggedy Ann doll. "You may be an adult on paper, but you're not exactly street smart."

I scoop my bag from the floor and place it on the bed, out of her reach. "Then I guess it's a good thing I won't be spending a lot of time on the streets."

"As your older sister, I . . . I forbid it!"

"Nice try." I laugh. "I'm still going."

Jeanie juts out her chin. "If Mom was still alive, she'd never let you go."

"*Mom* begged us to do this. Remember?" I say the words through gritted teeth and cram my favorite jeans into my already-stuffed bag, stretching the seams as far as they'll go. "Yesterday, you ordered me to go, now you want me to skip the whole thing? Make up your mind. I'm getting whiplash."

Red blotches stain her cheeks, and she presses her lips together until they pale from the strain. "Because yesterday I was going with you. We're supposed to be doing this together. That's what she wanted."

Memories of Mom planning one last trip to the beach for the three of us before she died hit me like a gut punch. "She wanted a lot of things."

Jeanie's fingers tremble as she picks at the Band-Aid on the back of her hand. "Zoey, please. Be reasonable."

"*You're* the unreasonable one." I glance from the scrapes and bruises on her arms to the cast on her leg. "You can't travel like that."

Her shoulders deflate, and she nods. "So we wait."

"Until when? Next summer when you've accumulated enough vacation time at your new job? Four years from now, if and when I finally graduate college? There's never going to be a perfect time. Maybe . . ." A sliver of guilt works its way under my skin, and my mouth goes dry as I fumble for the right words. "Maybe it's my turn."

Jeanie's attention snaps back to me, and the used Band-Aid flutters to the floor. "Your turn?"

"To be first. You've always been first. Born first. Graduated first." *Read her diary first.* "You didn't have to share her with anyone for the first two years of your life. The only time I got to do that was when she was dying. You read her diary. You already know everything there is to know about her. Give me a chance to have her all to myself for a little while. To say goodbye to her the way she wanted us to." Tears blur my vision as my gaze locks on hers. "Please let me do this."

The silence stretches between us while I wait for her to say something. Anything.

"Jeanie?"

A single tear streaks down her face, and she roughly swipes it away with the back of her unblemished hand. "Fine. You win. Go."

"Really?" I hold her gaze, waiting for her to change her mind, to put up another compelling argument.

She sighs. "I still think you're crazy for doing this alone. But if you're determined to risk your life, I can't stop you."

"No." I give her a watery smile. "You can't."

As if she knows how close I am to bursting into tears, she switches gears. "What about your muscle-head boyfriend? What does Damian think about you going on a road trip by yourself?"

I almost forgot about Damian. If I tell him now, he'll only try to stop me. Maybe I'll text him when I get to Cleveland. Then again, maybe I won't.

I shrug. "It doesn't matter. He can't stop me any more than you can."

"Are you sure you want to do this?" She grips her crutches so hard her knuckles whiten. "How will you eat? Where will you stay? You don't have any money."

"I have money." Several years' worth of birthday and Christmas money in the bank, courtesy of Dad's guilt. "And a credit card."

"And no job to pay it back."

I sear her with a glare. "Stop trying to talk me out of going."

Defeated, Jeanie lets her crutches fall and then flops onto my bed. "I hate this. Really, really hate this."

"Grandma Lola was only seventeen when she ran away to be a freaking groupie. I think I can handle a two-week road trip."

"That was the seventies."

"Exactly." I chuckle. "The most dangerous serial killers of all time wandered the earth back then."

"That doesn't mean it's safe now." The vein in Jeanie's neck pulses. "You could get raped. Or kidnapped by sex traffickers. Or come face-to-face with a serial killer no one's heard of yet."

"Oh my God, stop. Have a little faith in me. I'm not a kid anymore, Jeanie. I'll be careful. I won't talk to strangers. I won't drink anything I don't open myself. I'm not gonna get kidnapped, killed, or raped."

Grandma Lola pokes her head into my room, spinning a pair of shiny, black-and-white-striped Lycra undies from her pointer finger. "Not if you have these."

"Magical underwear?" I snicker, eyeing what looks like a hybrid between shapewear boy shorts and a Victorian swimsuit.

"No." She laughs and tosses them to me.

I catch them in midair, surprised at how heavy they are. "What are they?"

"They're anti-rape pants."

"Oh, great!" Jeanie fights her way out of my mattress like an upended turtle, rocking back and forth for momentum before launching herself to her good foot. "She'll just get murdered. That's so much better."

"Are they clean?" Cringing at the thought of wearing someone else's underwear, I hold the thick fabric away from my body.

Grandma scoffs. "Of course they're clean. They're brand new. A friend of a friend picked up a pair for me in Europe a while back as a gag gift. I never even tried them on."

"So they're . . . a joke?" I study the underwear, trying to figure out the punch line. They're heavy, as if lined with steel cables. "Do they shock you when you put them on?"

Rolling her eyes, Grandma marches toward me and snatches the panties from my hand. "No, they don't shock you. They're a legitimate protection device. Look . . ." She flips them around, and with a few clicks of her fingers, demonstrates how to unlock the waistband. "It has a secret code built in so only the wearer can remove them. They're knife proof, scissors proof . . . hell, they're practically indestructible. You'd need wire cutters to get them off without the code. It's printed on the tag, so don't lose that. Trust me, your virtue will be safe in these."

Grandma winks as if she knows my *virtue* was lost in the back of Damian's mother's Suburban after the homecoming game senior year.

With a shrug, I stuff them into my leather tote-slash-purse. "Thanks, Gra—"

"Cut the grandma shit, already, will ya?" She pins me with a glare.

"Yeah, sure." I cringe, surrendering to her preferred moniker. *"G-Lo."*

"Thank you."

I snicker at her victorious smile.

"Laugh it up, sis." Jeanie props herself on her crutches, tears clogging her throat as she hobbles toward the door. "Go ahead and wear your fancy superhero panties if that makes you feel safer, but when shit goes south, don't come crying to me! It's a big world out there, Zo. I hope you know what you're doing."

At the crack of dawn, with Jeanie and G-Lo trailing me like a pair of lost kittens, I load my overstuffed backpack, a lightweight blanket, and my favorite pillow into the back seat of G-Lo's car and then toss my tote into the front with Mom's ashes, her diary, and—thanks to Jeanie—enough food to feed an army.

Jeanie's blue eyes lock on mine. "Are you sure?"

Am I? I don't know anymore. The farthest I've driven alone was just across the state line, trailing a school bus filled with football players, in what may as well be a past life at this point.

"I'm positive." I offer her a confident grin.

"If you insist on doing this, can we at least rent you a car from this century?"

"That's not really in the budget." I tug at the bottom of my frayed shorts, unraveling them a little more.

"Oh, please." G-Lo rolls her eyes. "My car has been carting me around for damn near forty years. I think she can survive the next two weeks."

Jeanie heaves out a heavy sigh. "Then drive carefully, for Christ's sake. Stick to the highways—no back-road shortcuts. Don't talk to strangers. And whatever you do, don't eat gas station hot dogs or sketchy vending machine sandwiches."

"Why the hell would I eat vending machine sandwiches?" My stomach gurgles at the thought.

"Just trust me. Don't do it. Here . . ." She hands me her AAA card and a handwritten list. "I added you to my membership, just in case. And I jotted down all the best places to stay in each city. They're in the nicer parts of town but they won't break your budget—and since you're not twenty-one yet, I weeded out the ones that have age restrictions."

I open my mouth to ask how long that took her, but she shoves a wad of cash into my hand.

"And take this. It's not much, but it should cover your gas for a while, even in that rolling fossil. Don't spend it all on snacks, okay?"

"I won't." I stuff the cash into the front pocket of my shorts. The emotion in her eyes brings tears to mine, and I blink fast to keep them from falling. I almost tell her I changed my mind. That I don't really want to do this all by myself. That we can wait until her leg heals, until she has vacation time, until the pain of losing Mom doesn't fill my every thought and threaten to crack my chest in two. Instead, I whisper a quiet, "Thank you."

She swipes a hand under her nose, covering a sniffle. "You'd better text me pics of everything you do."

"I'm not—"

"I'm serious, Zo. I want pictures of every meal you eat, every bed you sleep in, every damn place you go. If I can't be there, I want to feel like I am. Promise me."

It finally hits me what she's giving up by letting me go, and I swallow the lump in my throat. "I promise."

"I'm glad I'm not going. Really. It's too damn hot for a road trip. It's supposed to be in the nineties all week. That's some crazy global warming shit, right there. Better you than me." She tears her gaze away, focusing on anything but my face. "Now, go, before I change my mind."

"She's right, you should probably get going." G-Lo checks the time on her phone. "You've got a long drive ahead of you."

Before I can wrap my fingers around the door handle, Jeanie pulls me in for a quick hug.

"Please don't get killed." Her hot breath fans across my neck as she sobs out the words.

"I won't." I squeeze her a little too hard, then let go and climb behind the wheel of the Betty. Sucking in a deep breath laced with the stench of stale tacos, rotten milk, and Sour Diesel, I slide the key into the ignition. After a few tries, it finally cranks, and the growl of the engine rattles my bones.

G-Lo dips her head through the open window and flicks her eyes to the dash. "Don't trust the gas gauge. Once it dips below half a tank, start looking for a gas station. If you let it get down to a quarter, it's probably too late."

"Got it." I cringe, hoping I don't forget that tidbit along a dark, deserted highway.

"Oh, and . . ." She lets out a nervous laugh. "The blower doesn't work unless you run the wipers. And they're temperamental. You might need to give the dash a good *whack* if they don't come on right away."

Great.

I force a smile. "Anything else?"

"Uh . . ." She leans in and taps the instrument panel. "Ignore the check engine light if it comes on. It's glitchy."

A dull throb pulses behind my eyes, and for a split second, I rethink the entire trip. "Maybe we should have someone look at it before I go?"

"You worry too much." G-Lo pats my cheek, then presses her glossy red lips to the spot. "This old girl will take good care of you. I've been driving her without a problem since before you were born."

"Oh-kay." I laugh, but it comes out a little hysterical. "Take care of Jeanie. Make sure she doesn't have an aneurysm worrying about me out on my own in the big bad world."

"Leave your sister to me. I've got plenty of weed to keep her happy." G-Lo winks, then backs away from the window.

"Don't tell me that." I chuckle, buckling myself in.

"And, Zoey, I know you said you have money, but if you run out of cash out there, let me know. I can always wire you some the old-fashioned way."

I roll my eyes. "It isn't 1972. Nobody wires money anymore."

"I'm well aware of what year it is, but a lot can happen on the road. It doesn't hurt to be prepared."

"Now who's worrying too much? I have Venmo and Apple Pay, and if I need cash, I have my debit card. I'll be fine. Really."

"If you say so." G-Lo thumps the hood and barks out a raspy laugh. "Go on, now. Get out of here."

With a quick wave and a silent prayer, I pull away from the curb. Visions of Mom keep me moving forward, but by the time I reach the turnpike, I'm running on pure adrenaline. I have no idea what I'm doing, but I have no doubt it'll be an adventure.

4

Wild Is the Wind

The Betty has at least ninety-nine problems, but the prehistoric 8-track player isn't one. The clear blue sky and miles of black pavement inspire me to roll down the windows and blast vintage Bowie from the speakers. Somehow it seems appropriate. Pushing the speedometer needle toward seventy-five, I belt out "Rebel Rebel"—the only song I know all the words to.

More than once, Damian's face flashes across my iPhone display, and each time, I hit the big red eff-you button. I'm nowhere near ready to deal with him. I have no desire to hear him complain about how my life choices affect him. That doesn't stop his cheesy grin and dark eyes from getting under my skin. But with every mile I put between us, the easier it gets to breathe. Maybe Jeanie's right. Maybe it's time to give Damian his walking papers.

"What now, Mom? Am I doing the right thing here?"

I can't help wondering what she'd make of my solo trek across the country. Or my joke of a love life. God, it isn't even the whole joke, just the punch line. What I wouldn't give to hear her voice again. She always said exactly what I needed at any given moment.

"Are you sure you wouldn't rather join the theater club?" Worry stained her voice, and her mouth twisted into a lopsided bow as she gnawed

on her bottom lip the way she always did when I was about to take the field.

We were standing at the bottom of the stands, just before the homecoming game junior year. My first year as the top of the pyramid, and the first time Damian paid me any attention. I was a tangled knot of anxiety, but Mom should've been thrilled. It was everything she'd ever wanted for me. So why did it seem like she wanted me to quit?

"Like Jeanie? No thanks." I pulled my laces tight and stood, tugging my pleated skirt over my spankies. "You did cheer. You said it was the most fun you ever had."

"No. I said it helped shape who I am." She handed me my blue-and-gold poms, then gave me a crushing one-armed hug.

"Same thing."

With a dry laugh, she tucked a lock of my dark-blond hair behind my ear. "Not really."

"Don't worry about me. I'm gonna be just like you, remember?"

"As long as you don't end up like your grandmother," Mom muttered, her smile faltering.

"Never gonna happen." With a laugh and a wave, I turned and bolted toward the rest of the squad as the marching band played the school fight song and the crowd roared.

A horn blares behind me, startling me back to the present. I dry the tears collecting at the corner of my mouth with my shoulder. Mom may not be here, but something tells me she'd say it was time to suck it up and get this over with.

I hit the automatic redial and put the call on speaker.

"Hey, babe," Damian purrs into the phone, using his smooth John Legend voice. "You just now rolling outta bed?"

A twinge of guilt pierces my chest. "Actually . . ."

Before I can get the rest of the sentence out, a minivan full of kids cuts me off, and I swear under my breath.

"What's wrong?" Damian asks. "You sound stressed."

Understatement. "I'm, uh, on the interstate heading toward Ohio."

"Ohio?"

A loud noise clatters through the line, making me jump.

"Hold up, I thought you said you couldn't go because your sister fell off the roof?"

"No." I choose my words carefully, making sure he comprehends what I'm saying this time. "What I *said* was my sister fell off the roof so *she* couldn't go."

"Ah, okay." He snickers under his breath. "Stuck with your crazy grandma all week?"

"Uh . . . not exactly." *Come on, Zoey, grow a pair and spit it out.* "My grandma stayed home to help Jeanie, and—"

"Who's driving you to Cleveland?" Damian's voice turns icy.

My stomach clenches, and I clear my throat. "Me?"

"Nice one." He laughs. "For real, who's driving?"

"I'm not kidding." It takes every drop of willpower to tamp down the moral outrage. "I decided to go on my own."

"What the hell, Zoey?" Damian shouts. "You can barely drive!"

"That's not true!" As if making his point for him, I slide in front of a Prius, barely missing their bumper. "I can drive."

Damian snorts. "My eighty-three-year-old great-grandpa can drive. He also drove his car straight into the Tastee Freez last August. Thought he was pulling into the drive-through window. Unfortunately for him, they don't *have* a drive-through window."

"I'm not your grandpa, and I'm not gonna drive into a Dairy Queen."

"Tastee Freez."

I roll my eyes. "Whatever."

"Listen, Zo." He switches to his I-have-two-years-of-college-under-my-belt-so-I-know-best voice. "It's early. You couldn't have made it to the state line yet, so it's not too late to turn around."

"No. *You* listen." Tears of frustration burn my eyes, but I refuse to let them fall. He's made me doubt myself for the last time. "I'm not turning back. If that's not okay with you, then break up with me. Otherwise, get over it."

"I don't wanna break up, I just want—"

The asshole in the car behind me lays on his horn.

"I gotta go." I swipe at the traitorous tear rolling down my cheek. "I'll call you when I get to Memphis."

"Zo, wait!"

I hang up and toss my phone into my tote where I won't hear it if he calls back, then crank up "Rebel Rebel" again.

A few hours, one pit stop, and several 8-track changes later, I reach the Cleveland city limits. With my legs sticking to the cracked vinyl seat and my pulse jumping, I exit the interstate at East Ninth. My sweaty palms make gripping the steering wheel almost impossible as I navigate the dense traffic. Even the voice on my GPS sounds nervous as she guides me past the baseball stadium and through the city toward the Music Hall at the Public Auditorium.

I loop the square several times before finally landing a parking spot a few blocks away. Then, using the faded Polaroid I lifted from Mom's diary as a guide, I set off on foot.

Jeanie wasn't kidding about the heat. At barely ten thirty, it's already close to eighty degrees. An unappetizing combination of sizzling hot dogs and sulfur from the nearby steelyard wafts through the air. And for a Wednesday morning, the park is packed with an odd assortment of people. Between the babies, the old people, and the underlying stench, it's as if I've wandered into a diaper ad.

A pair of businessmen in starched suits eye the silver urn poking out of my tote but don't say anything. Then a group of shirtless guys pauses their game of Frisbee to stare at me as I wander toward the fountain in the picture, but I don't let their unspoken questions distract me from my mission. I keep moving, eyes locked on the statue in the distance. Perched on top of his orb in the center of the fountain, the tarnished bronze man appears to be climbing out of a sea of fire, reaching toward the sky like a shimmering green merman.

By the time I reach the Fountain of Eternal Life, my nerves are live wires, sparking and snapping with electricity. Everything looks exactly as it does in the photo, giving me the weirdest sense of déjà vu. I can almost see Mom sitting on the polished granite rim of the shallow pool with the imposing statue looming behind her, her blond hair whipping in the breeze.

With Mom's smile sparkling in my mind's eye, I pull out her diary and flip to the page titled "Cleveland."

> *June 1992*
> *It rained all week, the heavy kind that drenches you to the bone the second you step outside. Grammy Jane said the powers that be knew something was up. Three days later, the sun came out. Not even an hour after that, Mom pulled into the driveway in her god-awful yellow Cutlass after almost six months of zero contact, saying it was time I knew the truth. Maybe I should've told her to turn back around. But for some reason, the mischief in her eyes sucked me in. Now here I am, in Cleveland, right outside the first place Bowie played in the US, and I swear I have more in common with the damned marble guy in the fountain.*

This is it. The thought hits me like a lightning bolt. This is where I need to spread Mom's ashes.

After setting my bag in front of the fountain, I pull out my phone to take the pictures I promised Jeanie. But before I can snap even one, a guy whistles at me.

"Hey, girlie! You can't get a good shot that close up." The guy jogs toward me. He doesn't look much older than me, but he's dressed like someone's grandpa, wearing faded navy Dockers with splotchy bleach stains from the pockets to the knees, and a blue-checked, short-sleeved button-down shirt. Sweat beads on his forehead as he reaches a hand toward my phone. "Here, let me."

Instinct tells me I should back away, but his wide smile and perfect white teeth draw me in.

I hand him my phone. "You press the circle—"

He laughs and backs up a few feet. "I know how to operate an iPhone. Smile pretty, now."

With a cautious glance over my shoulder, I climb onto the rim of the fountain and position myself exactly where my mom stood thirty years ago. A slight gust blows my hair from my face, and my stomach flutters as if sensing her with me.

Are you here, Mom?

The man snaps a few shots, then hands me my phone.

"Thank you," I tell him.

"You are most welcome. It was my pleasure." He overexaggerates his diction, speaking with an accent I can't place—a weird cross between British and French—but his English is perfect.

I expect him to jog back in the direction he came, but he sticks around and watches the clouds slide by as I shove my phone into my back pocket.

"What brings you to the city today?" He tears his face from the sky and eyes the silver urn jutting out of my bag.

"Uh . . ." For reasons I can't quite comprehend, I tell the truth. "I'm here to spread my mom's ashes."

"Ah." He nods, dropping his dark eyes to his beat-up leather shoes. "Sad day, then."

"Yes. Very."

He peers around me, as if expecting an army to descend at any moment. "Where is your family?"

I twist a strand of hair around my finger, then let it drop. "They, uh, couldn't be here."

"Then I'll stay with you. So you won't be alone." He sits on the edge of the fountain beside me, folding his hands in his lap.

"You don't have to do that." Damian's disappointed face flickers in the back of my mind. I can imagine what he'd say about me hanging out in the park with a total stranger.

The man flashes a friendly smile. "I know."

Shoving Damian out of my thoughts, I smile back and pull Mom's urn from my bag. After twisting off the lid, I sink my fingers into the coarse sand. With a shudder, I quickly pull them back out again. "I've never done this before."

He winks. "Neither have I."

"I'm Zoey, by the way." I shift the urn to my other arm and hold out my clean hand.

"Nice to meet you, Zoey." He shakes my hand. "My friends call me Junior."

"Nice to meet you, Junior." Something about Junior's open smile puts me at ease. I plunge a hand into the urn again and tighten my grip on a fistful of sand, slowly drawing it from the jar. "Should I say something? A prayer maybe?"

Junior gently squeezes my shoulder. "God knows your heart."

I nod and face the fountain, closing my eyes as I raise my hand, ready to release Mom into the air. "I love you, Mom."

One at a time, I open my fingers . . . just as the wind shifts. The light gust blows the ash back into my face, and I gasp, inhaling the tiny particulates.

Air whistles in and out of my lungs as I struggle to breathe. "Are you kidding me right now? What in the actual hell, Mom?"

My nose and throat burn, and every time I think I have a handle on the coughing fit, I inhale and it starts all over again. *Oh my God!* I totally snorted my mom, and she smells kinda like Sour Diesel.

I wipe my tongue on the bottom of my shirt, but even that's covered in a layer of ash. *Why is it so . . . salty?* The briny taste sets off my gag reflex, and my breakfast climbs up my throat. "Holy shit, I think I swallowed . . . oh God. I need water."

Panicking, I scramble over the edge of the fountain like a rabid squirrel and stick my face in the pool. After thoroughly rinsing my mouth without swallowing, I plop down on the rim to catch my breath.

"I really hope I don't die from E. coli. I blame my mother for this. She's the one who wanted her ashes spread."

Beside me, Junior's laughter slowly dies down as he wipes a layer of gray dust from his face. "Your mother, she has a good sense of humor, no?"

"No." I toss an icy glare skyward. Water drips down my nose and chin, soaking the front of my thin white T-shirt until it's practically see-through. "She has a shitty sense of humor."

A stern woman marches toward us, wagging her finger at me. "Can't you read? No swimming in the fountain!"

"I wasn't swimming, I was spreading my mom's ashes and the wind—"

The woman's eyes go straight to Mom's urn.

"*Human* ashes? In the park? You can't do that!" Her voice inches its way up the scale until dogs from miles around can hear her. "I'm calling security."

"Uh." A fleeting desire to pitch a fistful of ashes into the lady's face grips me, but I shake it off. "That's my cue. I need to go." Without another word, I screw the top onto the urn and shove it into my bag. Slinging my tote over my shoulder, I make a break for it. "Thanks for your help, Junior."

With one last wave, I leave my new friend to face the music and sprint all the way back to the car. With Cleveland safely in my rearview, I set off for Memphis, hoping I don't end up eating Mom's ashes at the next stop.

5

Rock 'n' Roll Suicide

Just over nine hours and three and a half stops for gas later—depleting nearly all the cash Jeanie slipped me in the driveway—major regret seeps in. Abandoning Mom's piece-of-shit Explorer for G-Lo's ancient Cutlass sounded like a solid plan at the time, but it probably wasn't one of my best decisions. Being trapped in a rolling steel box without working AC on one of the hottest days of the year was not on my road trip bingo card.

After driving close to twenty miles under a clear blue sky, with a minivan of kids making faces at me while I slapped the hell out of the dash to keep the wipers going so the blower would work, I discovered that the air conditioner is actually broken. When G-Lo said the wipers had to be on for the blower to work, she failed to mention that the blower only serves up hot air. A layer of sweat formed over every inch of me, making my damp clothes cling to my skin and plastering my hair to my neck.

The temperature finally dipped below ninety after the sun went down, but somewhere west of Nashville, the sky opened up and pummeled the Betty with fat raindrops, forcing me to play Whac-A-Mole on the dashboard again to keep the wipers on.

The farther west I drive, the harder it rains until it's hammering the car like tiny projectiles. Massive trucks whip past me doing more than eighty, and unless I keep hitting the dash every few minutes, I can't see a damn thing. To make matters worse, the GPS on my phone lost signal before I remembered to plug in my next destination, so in the pitch-black of night, I have no idea where I am.

To top it all off, I officially hate the 8-track player. It's been stuck on the same song for over four hours—no skipping the track, no ejecting the tape, and no lowering the volume. I swear on every one of Harry Styles's tattoos, I'm going to lose my damn mind if I have to listen to "China Girl" one more time. If I didn't need the crappy wipers to battle the downpour, I'd snap one off and use it to pry that sucker out.

At least the headlights on this hunk of junk still work. They're the only things keeping me alive out here.

A massive eighteen-wheeler rolls up behind me, its high beams shining in the rearview completely blinding me. As it speeds past, a wall of water washes over the side of the Betty like a tsunami, and the road becomes a giant Slip 'N Slide. I should pull over, but the last sign I passed was for Bucksnort and Barren Hollow, so I'm pretty sure I'm literally in the middle of freaking nowhere. Jeanie's threat of serial killers and rapists around every corner suddenly doesn't seem so ridiculous. Even with David Bowie belting through the speakers, I can almost hear the rhythmic twang of dueling banjos playing in the distance.

I hit the autodial on Jeanie's contact, hoping she'll talk me off the ledge, but I don't have service. "Damn it, Jeanie, why'd you let me do this?"

The first notes of "China Girl" play again, drawing my attention from the road for a split second as I vow revenge on that tape if I ever manage to evict it from the player.

I look up just in time to see a dark shape in the road ahead.

"What the hell is that!" My heart stops cold before racing to life again.

Staring straight at me from dead center in the lane ahead is what looks like a weaponized opossum, its armor glistening in the glow of the headlights.

"Holy shit!" A scream rips from my throat as the freaking battle ninja leaps into the air, connecting with the front of G-Lo's car like a bag of wet cement.

Oh my God, I killed it! With no time to think, I slam both feet on the brakes. The Betty skids sideways, rising off the ground for the span of several heartbeats before slamming against the pavement with a horrible crunch. The tires squeal and my ears ring as the Cutlass does a full circle across both westbound lanes, finally coming to rest in the center divider, half in and half out of the ditch and facing oncoming traffic.

With my brain scrambled and my fingers locked in a death grip on the wheel, I peek over the dash and inspect the front of the car. The headlights look cross-eyed, casting shadows in the wrong direction, and an angry hiss of steam pours from under the hood. Never a good sign.

Now I've gone and done it. I killed the Betty, too!

After spending almost an hour in the ditch, polishing off the last of my Doritos and burning through my iPhone's battery searching for a signal, I finally flag down a dairy truck. Or as Jeanie would likely insist, a refrigerated serial-killer-mobile. For all I know, the tank is filled with bodies, and I'm destined to be his next victim.

A bone-rattling shudder runs through me as I force the gruesome image from my brain and focus on the Betty's mangled grill.

"I'll be damned." Ernie—according to the swirly script embroidered across the flap of his blue coveralls—scratches his gray-stubbled chin. "Ain't never seen nothin' like this a'fore."

"What?" I peer around him into the wash of his flashlight, shivering in my ripped cutoffs and thoroughly drenched T-shirt.

Ernie taps a stiff back claw with a stubby finger. "Looks like it used to be an armor-diller, but it don't belong in your radiator."

Thanks, Ernie, now tell me something I don't know.

"Can you, maybe . . ." I wince. "Pull it out?"

Ernie snickers like a twelve-year-old before wiping the grin from his chapped lips. I can almost hear him thinking, *That's what she said.*

"I s'pose I could, but that won't fix the radiator none."

"Yeah, I was afraid you'd say that." My spirit deflates. "I guess that means I'm stuck here for a while."

"Looks like it." He bobs his head, scratching under his hat. "I can radio for a tow, but at this hour, in this storm, I don't s'pect it'll get here none too soon."

Just my luck.

"Or . . ." Ernie gives me a once-over before glancing toward his eighteen-wheeler. "I s'pose I could give ya a ride to town."

"I don't . . ." My gut clenches so hard my belly button hits my spine. The words *oh, hell no* clog my throat as a blinding flash of lightning zigzags above us, followed closely by a clap of thunder that practically cracks the sky in two. It would seem the cosmos—*or maybe Mom*—has other ideas. The storm that had all but passed us by rages back with a vengeance. "H-How far is town?"

"Fifteen . . . maybe twenty miles."

"Okay." Bottom lip clamped firmly between my teeth, I nod. "I guess I'll be safer with you than out here alone. I, uh, need to grab my stuff."

Ernie pulls off his hat and palms his bald head. "Ain't got a lotta room in the cab."

"Oh, I don't have much." I reach into the back seat for my overstuffed backpack before grabbing my tote and Mom's ashes from the front. I lock the car and yank my yellow Penn State hoodie over my head before beaming at Ernie, hoping he won't notice I'm scared shitless. "See? Hardly anything, really."

We both jump at another boom of thunder.

Ernie side-eyes my stuff. "Guess we'd better be on our way."

I follow him from the muddy ditch to the truck, where he takes my backpack and tosses it inside. Then he sweeps a pile of debris from the passenger seat and helps me climb in.

Balancing Mom's ashes in my lap, I tug the seatbelt around me and settle in.

The inside of the truck looks like an episode of *Hoarders*. Stacks of empty gas station coffee cups and chip bags litter the floor. A half-empty jar of generic peanut butter, a dirty plastic spoon, and a sleeve of Ritz crackers take up the cup holders. Multiple cords snake from the outlets to various electronic devices. A collection of Christmas tree air fresheners in assorted colors dangles from the radio knobs, and a faded-purple rabbit's foot swings from the rearview mirror.

Ernie hops into the driver's seat and turns the key, making the truck roar to life. "She ain't clean, but she's my home away from home."

Though I'm all too aware I'm living the opening scene to almost every horror movie I've ever seen, once Ernie cranks the heat and I start to warm up, keeping my eyes open becomes a struggle. He doesn't look like he wants to kill me and make a suit from my skin, but what do I know? I've been awake for close to twenty-four hours, and I didn't exactly get a great night's sleep before beginning this fool's mission, so I drift in and out of consciousness while Ernie rattles off his riveting life story.

"We're here." Ernie pokes my damp shoulder. "Sorry, but this here's the only place in town open all night."

I startle awake, blinking up at the sign for BB's All-Night Diner. A ginormous neon guitar juts from the roof, flickering off and on like the fluorescent bulb above our kitchen sink, almost as if sending out a secret code: *That wasn't chicken.*

I swallow a laugh and clear the cobwebs from my throat. "What time is it?"

"Almost three."

"In the morning?"

"Yup."

Wiping the drool from my chin, I dig for my iPhone. The battery is deep in the red zone, but at least I have a signal. "I guess I should call someone to get my grandma's car."

"I radioed the wrecker on the way here. They'll pick her up at first light and bring her to Mack's garage on Sixth."

Relief rushes through me. "Thank you."

"Need to be on my way now. Gotta make Memphis a'fore morning, but if you're hungry, BB's makes the best damn chili this side of the Mississippi and all the coffee you can drink. Steer clear of the tuna . . . unless ya got a death wish." He looks down his nose at me as if questioning my sanity.

Mister, I'm way ahead of you!

"Good to know." I shove Mom's ashes into my tote and sling the strap over one shoulder before sliding down from the passenger seat, hanging on to the door handle until my soggy Skechers hit the cracked pavement.

The truck growls as Ernie throws it into gear. "Mack's opens at nine. Good luck to ya, miss."

"Thank you." I slam the door and back away as memories from the last few days flicker before my eyes. This trip was supposed to take two weeks—three at most. Now, who knows if I'll even be able to finish what I started.

As Ernie's taillights disappear into the distance, I glance down at the mud caked on nearly every visible inch of me. What I wouldn't give for a shower and a clean pair of—

"My backpack!" I scream into the darkness.

My thoughts scramble, trying to decide who to call first. I don't know Ernie's last name, or even if his name is really Ernie. For all I know, he bought the overalls with the name already on them. And even if the dairy company could locate him based on his description, I doubt they'd pick up the phone at three a.m.

The only thing saving me from total meltdown is Mom's ashes, still safely tucked in my tote with her diary and my wallet.

BB's giant neon guitar flashes another secret message: *Time to admit defeat.*

I'm all for that idea. I gave it my best. I don't control the weather . . . or suicidal armadillos. And I sure as hell can't be held responsible for the Betty and *her* death wish.

As I fish my phone out of my pocket, the battery gasps its last breath and dies in my hand.

6

All the Young Dudes

The sky belches out a loud boom of thunder as the storm rolls in for another round. I have two choices: Stay outside in the rain and hope Ernie realizes my bag's still in his truck before he reaches Memphis, or go inside where it's warm and dry and get something to eat. My stomach growls, making the decision for me. After all, woman cannot live on Doritos alone.

The scent of burned chili and greasy french fries greets me the moment I walk through the door. A smaller version of the guitar from outside hangs above the long counter, where the after-bar crowd sits shoulder to shoulder on a row of red-vinyl-and-chrome stools, conjuring the sour smell of liquor and cigarettes from my imagination. The whole place—from the matching red-vinyl booths lining either side of the room and the framed rock and roll prints covering almost every square inch of the neon-pink walls, to the old-fashioned black-and-white linoleum tile floor—is coated in a thick layer of grease.

A middle-aged waitress delivers a juicy burger and a chocolate shake to the nearest table, and my mouth waters. But after the night I've had, I have other matters requiring my attention.

"Great Balls of Fire" blasts from the jukebox as I follow the sign to the restroom, praying it isn't occupied.

A lady changing her baby in the booth adjacent to the ladies' room smiles at me. "If you can hold it, I would."

"That bad?"

"Worse." She folds the discarded diaper into a stinky burrito and shoves it into an outer pocket of her bag, then scoops up her baby and holds him to her chest.

"I think I can hold it." Mom once said I was part camel . . . time to prove her right.

"Good idea." She lowers her voice and tosses a quick glance over her shoulder. "The night manager, Rob, doesn't give a damn if the ladies' has TP, or if the toilets are clogged. And he doesn't give a shit if some drunk takes a dump on the floor or pukes in the sink."

My mouth drops open, and I quickly snap it shut.

"Now, the morning shift manager, Becky . . . she'll be here in like"—she checks the neon clock on the wall—"an hour . . . two tops. She won't put up with that shit. She cracks the whip, and those boys jump. Rob included."

"I think I'll wait for Becky."

"You'll be glad you did. Oh, and here." She smiles and pulls a wad of wipes from her bag. "You might wanna clean up before sitting down."

"Thank you." While I scrub my face and neck, my stomach releases a loud rumble.

"Somebody's hungry." She pins me with a serious look. "Don't eat the tuna. Stick to the burgers . . . or the chili. It's pretty damn good."

"So I've heard."

"Go get you a seat over there." She nods toward the opposite side of the diner. "The smell can get pretty ripe over here by the restrooms, and you don't wanna ruin your appetite. And do yourself a favor and steer clear of Travis," she says as I walk away. "That boy is nothin' but trouble."

I slide into the only clean booth, which also happens to be the one directly next to the jukebox, and place my tote with Mom's ashes under the table. Other than me, and the couple making out in the back, the only other person not sitting at the counter is a guy with dark floppy hair two booths away. Nose buried in a tattered copy of *On the Road*, he seems completely oblivious to the world around him.

Travis.

As if plucking his name straight from my thoughts, his head snaps up.

Picking at the loose thread on my shorts, I bury my face in the dirty menu in front of me, avoiding the dark eyes glaring at me from behind a pair of black-framed glasses.

I jump as a throat clears loudly at my side. Roughly the same age as me, the waiter—T. J., according to his name badge—isn't tall or particularly good looking. His sandy-brown hair is too short, his nose bends too far to the right, and his muddy-brown eyes are too close together. But he has a nice smile.

"Hey, beautiful." He grins down at me. "Ready to order?"

"No," I blurt without thinking, too focused on Travis still watching me over his book. "I mean, yes. I'd like a cheeseburger—medium well, no pickles, extra onions—with a side of fries and a Diet Coke."

"Sure you want those onions?" T. J. winks.

Two tables away, Travis's eyes dart to T. J., and he snorts.

With no witty comeback at the ready, I mutter, "Yes, please."

The guy behind the counter beckons T. J. to pick up his next order, mercifully putting an end to the awkward moment.

"Comin'!" T. J. yells, then leans in and dials up the charm again. "Be right back with that Coke."

Distracted by Travis's impressive scowl, I mutter a quick, "Thanks."

Once T. J. disappears into the kitchen, I slide out of the booth and switch sides, putting my back to Mr. Tall, Dark, and Broody.

Within a few minutes, T. J. drops off my drink and then sticks around to ask me where I'm from before he's dragged away again. A little later, he brings my food, hovering as I take my first bite.

"Everything okay?" He flashes a wide smile.

I chew and swallow as quickly as I can without choking. "It's good, thanks."

"Let me know if there's anything else you need. Anything at all." With another wink, he slowly backs toward the kitchen. His smile slips as his gaze lands on something over my shoulder, and he stalks off.

Behind me, Travis's scoff morphs into an impressive imitation of a cat hacking up a fur ball. *Asshole.*

Ignoring the beautiful troublemaker, I devour my burger and down two sodas while I wait for the morning manager to arrive. Almost an hour later, my bladder reaches the tipping point. Every pair of headlights draws my attention to the door, every passing minute urging me to take my chances with whatever horrors await in the neglected ladies' room.

While I weigh my options, T. J. slides onto the bench across from me and snatches a cold fry from my plate. He props himself on his elbows and leans forward until he's practically on my side of the booth. "I get off in fifteen minutes if you need a ride somewhere."

"Really? You'd do that?" I rest my elbows on the table, meeting him in the middle. The possibility of a clean bathroom, and maybe even a shower, silences the voice of reason in my head. And with a lethal combination of sleep deprivation and desperation, the words come out in a stream of verbal diarrhea. "That would be awesome. I'm basically stuck here until Mack's opens—that's where they're supposedly towing my car. Hopefully, they can get the armadillo out of the radiator. And I should probably track down Ernie's dairy truck to get my backpack and phone charger. If they can't fix my car by tonight, I guess I'll need to find a motel, and I don't have a clue where to look."

"Whoa!" T. J. laughs. "Slow down, I didn't catch half of that. Lemme go finish up and clock out, then we can figure out what to do next."

"Thank you so much!" I beam at him. "You have no idea how grateful I am. Really and truly."

"Hey, no problem. I'm here to serve." He winks, then dips his head, going in for a . . . a kiss?

The hell? I jerk back before his lips land.

He straightens in the seat, shock registering in his muddy eyes, but he keeps his thoughts to himself. "Sit tight. Be back in a few."

T. J. saunters to the kitchen while I reassess our tentative agreement.

What have I done? Accepting offers from two strangers in the same night? Jeanie will have my head . . . if I don't lose it first.

"You shouldn't trust that guy."

The seductive murmur startles me, and I whip my head around to find Clark Freaking Kent casually leaning against my bench with his tattered book tucked under his arm. Travis may be trouble, but up close, the guy is seriously hot—all tall and sinewy in a wrinkled short-sleeved button-down and dark jeans. He could use a haircut, and probably an attitude adjustment, but if I didn't know he was bad news, he would be exactly my type.

"He's only trying to get laid." He stares down at me from behind those black frames.

I raise a single eyebrow, trying and failing to avert my attention from his sinful body. He could easily be a model for designer eyewear. Or a superhero disguised as . . . *a complete douche canoe?*

"Believe me, don't believe me. Either way, I've done my good deed for the day. The rest is on you." He glides onto the bench across from me uninvited and flips to a page in the middle of his book.

The balls on this guy!

Stunned by his arrogance, I openly gape at him. "Who do you think you are?"

Clark-slash-Travis stares at the open book in front of him. "The guy who's watched redneck-Romeo make a play for every woman under the age of forty who's walked through that door since he started his shift almost five hours ago. He's remarkably persistent considering how many times he's been shot down."

An undignified snort sneaks out of me as I peek toward the kitchen.

"You're the best looking of the bunch, if it makes you feel any better. But definitely not the first."

"You've been sitting here since before midnight?"

Travis lifts his gaze to mine. Behind the black-rimmed glasses, he has one blue eye and one that's more brown than blue. As if someone got bored while coloring his iris and quit in the middle.

For the second time in the span of an hour, words tumble past my lips without permission. "Your eyes."

"Yes." He sighs and goes back to his book. "I've seen them."

Tired or not, I'm fully aware I'm staring. "They're just like David Bowie's."

"No. They're not." He flips to the next page, obviously not reading. "I was born with heterochromia. David Bowie got punched in the eye when he was a kid and it blew out his pupil."

I cock my head to the side, studying him. "How do you know that?"

He shrugs. "Everyone knows that."

"I didn't."

A devilish smile curves his perfect lips. "Everyone but you, then."

The dig doesn't bother me as much as it should. "My grandma would probably know that."

No response.

"My mom loved Bowie." I barely get the words out, the simple sentence nearly gutting me in the process. I turn to the window and take several short, steady breaths to keep from crumbling.

Across from me, the beautiful troublemaker lifts his head and studies me, a furrow forming between his dark brows. "Mine, too. She cried the day he died."

Tears clog my throat, and I manage a weak nod, barely holding myself together.

Unaware of my fragile emotional state, T. J. bounds to the table and flicks his gaze toward Travis before dialing up his smile. "You ready?"

"Almost. I need to pay my check." I pull three crumpled dollar bills from my pocket.

T. J. raises his hand, his grin wolfish. "I got you covered."

"No, really. I have money." Against my will, my eyes are drawn to Travis as I reach under the table for my tote. I place Mom's ashes on the seat next to me while I dig for my wallet.

"Oh, hey. Nice, uh . . . martini shaker?" With a nervous laugh, T. J. juts his chin toward the urn.

Travis shakes his head. "It's an urn, dumbass."

My blind search comes up empty, so I lay Mom's diary beside her ashes and tip the bag upside down, spilling the contents onto the table. "It has to be here."

Fear blooms in the pit of my stomach as I dig through the assorted candy wrappers and juice boxes, tubes of cherry lip gloss and blackest black mascara, several stray M & M'S, a travel-size deodorant, toothbrush and toothpaste, a bunch of loose change, the keys to the Betty, Jeanie's AAA card and her handwritten list of safe places to stay, a hairbrush, three tampons, and G-Lo's striped anti-rape panties.

But no wallet.

My cheeks burn as I shove the underwear and tampons back into the tote and pick through the rest as if my wallet will suddenly appear out of nowhere. "I know I grabbed it before I left." Did I leave it in the car? God, maybe something living in the Betty's back seat ate it.

"T. J.! You forgot to clock out, again," the guy from the kitchen shouts.

"Hold on to your hat, Rob!"

Rob pokes his head out of the back. "Becky's here."

T. J. groans. "Aw, shit."

An older woman with faded red-orange hair strolls out of the kitchen wearing a crisp white apron over her pink uniform and a pair of green rubber gloves up to her elbows. "Travis James Masterson, I don't pay you to flirt. Get in here and clock out before I call your mama and tell her I fired you again!"

The breath in my lungs freezes, and I lift my head in slow motion. Missing wallet momentarily forgotten, I gape from one Travis to the other and clear my throat. Instead of words, incoherent nonsense sputters past my lips. I try again, this time focusing my attention on my waiter. "*You're* Travis? I-I thought you were . . . and he . . ." I dart my eyes toward the man I *thought* was Travis.

"My friends call me T. J." He shrugs, oblivious to the gears frantically turning in my head as he backs toward the kitchen. "Be right back. And don't worry about your food. I got it covered."

While the real Travis disappears behind the counter, the fake one throws back his head and explodes with laughter.

"You thought *I* was . . ." *Not*-Travis cackles so hard, air wheezes in and out of his lungs.

Horrified by the dawning realization, I nod.

"And Mandy warned you to steer clear of Travis, right?"

My head buzzes as I search the room in a daze. "Mandy?"

"The lady with the baby?"

I nod again. "I saw her by the bathroom earlier."

Another bark of laughter. "I knew it! They're related—*somhow*. I haven't figured that out yet, but she was bitching up a storm when I got here. Spilled *all* the dirty deets about Travis James Masterson." He pulls a napkin from the holder and a pen from his back pocket and then furiously scribbles words I don't bother to decipher.

As if invoking his name conjures him from the back, Travis—a.k.a. T. J.—strolls to the booth with a big smile. "Okay. All set. Ready to roll?"

"No." I blurt the word.

"Awesome!" T. J. does a slow double take. "Wait. What?"

"I think . . ." I shoot daggers at the-stranger-formerly-known-as-Travis, also known as Clark Kent.

Clark shoves his ink-covered napkin into his pocket, trying and failing to hold himself together.

I blow out a breath. "I should stay here."

T. J.'s eyebrows form a deep V as he studies Clark, still snickering in the seat across from me. "Did I miss something?"

My attention drifts to the contents of my tote scattered across the table, and suddenly T. J. is the least of my worries. "I can't do this. I don't know what I was . . . I guess I wasn't thinking at all, was I?"

"I see." Arms folded across his chest, T. J.'s gaze drifts from Clark to my stuff before settling on my face. He nods, eyes tight, smile stiff. "Well played. I'm, uh, gonna take off. You're welcome for dinner."

"It wasn't like that," I call after him as he storms out of the diner.

With T. J. gone, the fog slowly lifts, leaving anger in its wake. Whether he deserves it or not, I direct the venom toward Clark. "Why didn't you tell me you weren't *him*?"

"What?" He chokes on a chuckle. "How was I supposed to know you thought I was? You never said anything."

"Why would I?" I snap.

Despite my glorious display of fury, he laughs again. "Is that why you've been mean mugging me since you sat down?"

"I thought you were someone else! But that doesn't explain why *you* were giving *me* nasty looks. *I* didn't do anything."

His laughter dies down, every trace of humor fading from his expression. "I figured you were another empty-headed idiot willing to ignore Mandy's warning."

"Well, I'm not."

His lips twitch. "Good to know."

The T. J. situation behind me, I shove my stuff back into my tote, trying to remember the last time I saw my wallet. A sudden memory of white teeth and green marble turns my stomach as the puzzle pieces fall into place. I *am* an idiot. But not for the reason Clark thinks.

"That slick sonofabitch took my wallet!"

Clark's head snaps up from his book. "Travis? I would've seen—"

"Not him." I wave my hand. "Junior."

Clark scans the room. "Who's Junior?"

"A guy I met in Cleveland. He must've lifted my wallet while I was spreading my mom's ashes. Damn it!" Exhaling a loud breath, I slump against the bench. Jeanie was right. I have no business making this trip alone. "I'm so stupid."

"I'm sure you're not—"

"I am. My sister tried to tell me." Determined not to cry in front of a stranger, I fold my arms across the table and press my face into the center. I should've known I couldn't manage a cross-country trip by myself. Everyone else did. I may as well be a kid playing dress-up.

G-Lo has faith in you.

G-Lo was wrong.

7

Heroes

"Honey, you wanna use the phone to call someone?" Becky hands me a new roll of toilet paper as I cry in the freshly scrubbed bathroom stall.

"No." I may be a total failure, but there's no reason for G-Lo and Jeanie to know until I salvage the tatters of my self-esteem. "I don't want to call my family until I talk to the mechanic."

"I suppose that's reasonable." Becky shoots me a side-eye. "But you should probably call and tell someone you lost your wallet. The bank maybe?"

The paper seat cover crinkles beneath my shorts as I blow my nose, and the sound echoes in the tight space. "Why would the bank care if I lost my wallet?"

"They might if you lost a checkbook or debit—"

"My debit card!" I leap to my feet and bolt out the door as if my life depends on it. The contents of my bank account just might.

"Honey, wait!" Becky swipes at my backside. "You've got something stuck to your britches."

The stupid paper seat liner flaps behind me like a cape as I scurry through the diner, too focused on Clark, scribbling on another napkin across the room, to care.

My feet hit a patch of grease, and I nearly collide with the table, lips moving before my brain catches up. I realize a moment too late that I still don't know his real name. "C-Can you help me?"

He lifts his gaze, nothing but detached curiosity reflecting in his weird eyes. "What do you need?"

"To call my bank. I-I don't know the number, so I'll need to search it up online and, um . . ."

Eyes still locked on mine, Clark reaches around me, snatches the paper cape from my butt, and crumples it into a ball before chucking it into the corner of his seat. Under any other circumstances, I'd be mortified. But today, I'm on a mission.

"My phone died, and no one in this godforsaken diner has an iPhone charger, so I hoped maybe . . ." I dial my smile to eleven.

He lifts his brows. *"Maybe . . . ?"*

"You'd let me use yours?"

"Yeah. Sure." He pulls a sleek silver rectangle from his back pocket and hands it to me.

"Thanks." I flip the device over. Other than the tiny camera lens, it's the same on both sides. "What am I supposed to do with this?"

"You—" He blows out a breath and holds out his hand, palm up. "Give it to me." He snatches the thing from my fingers and opens it like a clam. After clicking a few keys, he presents what looks like a miniature web browser. "I assume you can handle things from here?"

"Uh . . ." I stare at the tiny screen. Mom had something like this when I was about six. When she got her first iPhone, she gave the old device to Jeanie to play with. I may have snapped it in two trying to wrestle it out of her hands. "Can't you just ask Siri to call my bank?"

"No." He laughs. "I can't ask Siri to do anything." The laugh dissolves into a groan. "What bank do you use?"

◆ ◆ ◆

Several phone calls later, after divulging everything but my height, weight, and blood type to my bank, the Cleveland police department, and practically everyone within earshot in the diner, including the hot guy sitting across from me, I settle into my booth with Mom's diary to watch the sun come up. Until I know how much damage the armadillo caused the Betty, there's nothing else I can do.

"I don't mean to pry, and I promise I wasn't eavesdropping, but I heard you talking to the police . . ."

Clark's statement catches me off guard—as does the sympathy radiating from his eyes.

"Oh." So he knows the full extent of my idiocy. Great.

He glances at the silver urn sticking out of my tote and exhales a breath that smells like syrup. "When did she die?"

"It's been . . ." I glance at the clock above the door and do a quick calculation in my head. "One week, four days, and almost eleven hours."

He opens his mouth but closes it just as quickly.

"Cancer." I answer his unspoken question as a lump grows in my throat. "She, uh, fought for as long as she could—chemo, radiation, even tried some experimental thing in New Mexico that sucked nearly her entire life savings dry because her insurance wouldn't cover it—but it caught up to her in the end. Almost two weeks ago, she closed her eyes and never opened them again." A tear slips down my cheek, settling into the seam of my lips, and I lick it away with my tongue.

Clark clears his throat. "I'm sorry. That's rough. What about your—"

"My turn," I interrupt. "What brings you to this greasy diner in the middle of the night? Waiting for someone? Hiding from the law? Or . . ." I narrow my eyes, studying him in the harsh fluorescent lights. "Scoping out your next victim?"

He leans in, his expression devoid of emotion. "I wouldn't be a very good serial killer if I divulged all my secrets, now would I?"

I flinch, and he lets out a whoop of laughter.

"None of the above." He drops his gaze to his book again, a secret smile on his lips.

"Oh, no . . ." I reach across the table and snatch the tattered thing out from under his nose, slamming it onto the stained Formica with a huff. "You do *not* get to do that. You know all about my failed road trip, from my mom's ashes and my stolen wallet to my armadillo grill ornament, and I don't even know your name!"

Lips twitching, he slides the book back to his side of the table, tucks his latest napkin doodles between the pages to mark his spot, then closes it again. "Dash Hammond. Dashiell, actually, but no one calls me that unless I'm in deep shit. I'm sort of on a road trip of my own, trying to decide between two very different versions of my future, and BB's seemed like as good a place as any to kill time while my car charges. Trust me, you don't want your battery to run out in the middle of nowhere."

With a fleeting glance toward my deceased iPhone, I nod. "Are there even car charging stations in Hicksville?"

"Not for a quick charge. But if you're patient and"—he peers over his shoulders, then lowers his voice—"*resourceful*, you can charge anywhere with an outlet."

"So here you are, patiently people-watching for the next however many hours?"

He checks his watch. "It probably has enough juice to get me the rest of the way to Memphis. I can get a rapid charge there, but . . ." He shrugs. "I'm not in a hurry."

"And you're not tired?" The instant I get the words out, I realize how exhausted I am. A yawn catches me off guard, and I laugh.

He holds up his coffee cup as if staying out all night is normal. And maybe it is . . . for nerdy superheroes on cross-country road trips.

"I'd give just about anything for a warm bed and a hot shower." I catch myself gawking at his eyes again and quickly look away.

Dash throws another glance over his shoulder, this time toward the parking lot, where the first streaks of morning light color the sky. "What are you going to do if they can't fix your car?"

"I don't know what I'll do if they *can.* As soon as I charge my phone, I guess I can use Apple Pay in place of a credit card, but . . ."

"But you canceled all your cards, didn't you?" Dash rests his elbows on the table as if he didn't just light my last shred of hope on fire.

"Damn it." I let out a breath, strangling the napkin in my hands. "I'll tell you what I'm *not* going to do. I'm not going to call my boyfriend to rescue me. He'd get far too much satisfaction from that. I'd sooner become vulture bait than ask him for help. My sister can't drive with a broken leg, and my grandma can't drive Jeanie's car because it's a stick shift. Maybe I should count my losses. Go home. Nobody expected me to get this far, so they won't be shocked to see me crawling back with my tail between my legs."

Dash slides his glasses down his nose and stares at me over the top. "Cop out much?"

"Are you kidding me? I snorted ashes in Cleveland. Had my wallet stolen. Got lost. Twice!" With each item I list, I stick up a finger. "Damn near died in a rainstorm, thanks to my grandma's beat-up Cutlass, and crashed into a freaking ninja armadillo! I don't normally believe in signs, but trust me, I got the message."

"Hold up." Dash laughs. "You snorted ashes? Like on a dare?"

"Not on purpose. It's a long story." Defeated, I sink into the booth.

Shaking his head, he settles back against his bench. "Long or short, quitting still sounds like a cop-out to me."

"Listen, Mr."—I glance at his well-worn copy of *On the Road*—"I-read-Jack-Kerouac-for-fun, you and your hipster friends might not think twice about wandering the country like nomads, but going on a cross-country quest to spread Mom's ashes wasn't my idea."

"Did you just call me a hipster?"

I cross my arms and cock an eyebrow. "If the glasses fit."

"I prefer beatnik."

"Whatever, same difference."

"No." He chuckles. "Not even a little."

Groaning, I drag my gaze away from his spectacular face and eye the busboy as he clears tables. "If you say so."

"Come on, I'm curious." He leans forward again, folding his arms on the table. "I get that your trip is about spreading your mom's ashes, but what I don't get is why Cleveland? And why Memphis? I'm guessing that's your next stop."

I nod.

"And what's after Memphis?"

"New York. I think." I grab the diary from my tote and flip to the next entry after Memphis. "Yep, New York. And after that, Boston. Then . . . I guess it doesn't matter anymore."

"That's an impressive trip. Kinda random, though."

"Not random at all. I'm basically taking the exact trip my mom took in '92. She and my grandma spent two weeks retracing the steps of the '72 Ziggy tour. She wrote everything down in her diary, and I'm supposed to be re-creating the pictures—"

"Wait. Go back." His eyes light up. "Are you talking about David Bowie's 1972 Ziggy Stardust tour?"

I realize too late that I offered more information than I intended. The last thing I want is to air my family's dirty laundry to a stranger.

He locks his gaze on me, giving me his full attention. "Why did your mom and grandma go back and visit all the old Bowie tour stops?"

I shrug and flip through the pages of Mom's diary, avoiding eye contact. "Just because."

"No way." He shakes his head. "No one embarks on a cross-country road trip, visiting the stops of a twenty-year-old concert tour, 'just because.'"

"Fine." I lower my voice. "Grandma Lola was a rock groupie in the seventies."

"Now we're getting somewhere. Are we talking Penny Lane from *Almost Famous*?"

I snort. "I don't know about *then*, but *now* she's more like one of *The Banger Sisters*."

He waves his hand like he's tugging the truth out of me at the end of a rope. "Keep going."

I give the diner a quick scan, then lean in and whisper, "According to her, my mom was conceived during that particular tour."

"Was your grandfather someone famous?" Dash brings his head closer, lowering his voice so we're both speaking in hushed tones.

My cheeks burn. I know a lot of girls who would jump at the chance to tell the world they had even the shakiest connection to a rock legend, but I have zero interest in that kind of attention. I haven't even told Damian about the whole Bowie thing. I'm not about to tell Dash.

"Well?"

"You'll laugh." With a nervous chuckle, I move to lean back but he grabs my wrist, holding me hostage in the center of the table. My first instinct is to snatch back my hand, but his palm is so warm, I don't.

"Come on, Zoey," he whispers. "You can't leave me hanging here. I'm invested in the story now."

The soft rumble of his voice turns my guts to mush, and my throat threatens to close. I swallow hard. "It's not like I believe her, anyway. She smokes a lot of pot."

Dash laughs, then releases my hand and settles against the bench again. "I don't know what your secret is, but if it has you this twisted up, it must be good."

"It's really not." I collect the shredded remains of my napkin, twisting the pieces into corkscrews. "My mom was pretty high on pain meds when she asked us to spread her ashes across the country, but a promise is a promise." And the truth definitely won't set me free.

8

Let's Dance

"Wake up, sleepyhead. I made pancakes."

I jerk awake as the ghost of my dream fades into the ether. The sudden loss leaves me cold and empty. Instead of Mom gently nudging me, I'm greeted by the aromas of fresh coffee, bacon, and maple syrup, and the boisterous laughter from at least a dozen voices all speaking at the same time. The quiet, predawn diner I fell asleep in is now packed with the breakfast rush. The clatter of forks on plates and ice clinking in glasses drags me further out of my sleep hangover. I lift my head, breaking the long string of drool tethering my chin to the table, and use my shoulder as a rag.

The empty seat across from me makes me weirdly uneasy, and I search the crowd for a familiar face. Becky gives me a three-finger wave from the counter. I wave back, wondering where Dash disappeared to. Did he leave?

"You're awake." He drops into the booth with a bounce.

A startled squeal catches in my throat. The words *Where were you?* pop into my head, but I shove them back. "What time is it?"

"Almost eight thirty. I would've woken you sooner, but, uh . . ." He snickers, giving me a quick once-over. "You looked like you could use the rest."

My hands go to my face, then slide into my matted hair. An inhuman sound rolls out of me. I can only imagine how horrible I must look.

Dash grins. "You mumble in your sleep."

A quick intake of breath sends saliva down the wrong pipe. "What did I say?" I choke out the words.

"Something about church ladies and green Jell-O." He laughs, and his whole face lights up.

"Excuse me." I scoop up my tote and the tattered remains of my self-esteem and stumble out of the booth. "I'll be right back."

My dirty Skechers slap the greasy linoleum as I scurry to the restroom. Safely inside the subway-tiled walls, I lift my chin and approach the mirror. *How bad can it be?*

My reflection stares back at me in horror. Faded-black streaks of mascara trail from my eyes to my chin like creepy shadows against the sickly glow of death, courtesy of the yellow hoodie. Hardened mud and ash have turned my ponytail into a tangled nest, minus the sticks and leaves. Every exposed inch of me from my Skechers to my dishwater-blond hair is coated in a thin layer of filth. I look like I clawed my way out of the grave.

Worse than I thought.

Balancing my tote between my feet, and armed with nothing more than cheap diner supplies, I yank off my hoodie and tie it around my waist, ready to get down to business. The hot water tank groans as I crank on the taps and dump a handful of powdered soap from the rusty wall dispenser into the chipped sink. The basin quickly fills with bubbles, and the sickening scent of old lady perfume wafts through the air as I unfurl half a roll of paper towels and get to work.

After scrubbing my skin raw and yanking a brush through my tangled locks, I feel almost human again. Not exactly my best, but a giant step up from what had to have been my worst. I brush my teeth and add a bit of cherry gloss to my lips before tossing everything I own into my bag, a little too eager to get back to the booth. And Dash.

When I reach the table, he does a double take and then hands me his no-frills phone and a steaming cup of coffee. "I hope you don't mind. I dialed the number for Mack's. It's ringing."

"Great. Thanks!" I press his phone to my ear and wait.

"Mack's Garage," a deep voice answers. The rest of his garbled greeting is lost between a thick Southern accent and what sounds like a mouth full of pennies.

"Hi! Um . . . I'm calling about the yellow Cutlass that came in last night?" I dump two sugars into my coffee, fidgeting with the empty packets while I wait for his reply.

"We got a yellow '73 Cutlass in this morning."

"With the armadillo in the radiator?" I ask.

He chuckles. "Yup, that'd be the one."

"Can you tell me if she can be saved?" I dart a nervous glance at Dash.

"Nah, that armadillo most likely died on impact."

I clear my throat to cover a laugh. "No, I mean the car. Can the *car* be saved?"

"Oh, sure. Nothing we can't fix with the right parts."

Relief courses through me, sending a warm tingle from my fingers to my toes. "Great. When can—"

"Gonna need to order those from Atlanta."

"Seriously? *Atlanta?*" Dread sets in. "How long will that take?"

"Oh . . . not long. We can probably have them in by noon tomorrow."

"I-I guess I can hang out here for another day." I look at Dash, and he nods along with me. I hope the Betty has armadillo coverage. "I'll have my grandma call her insurance—"

"But . . ." The voice cuts me off again. "With the holiday comin' up, it'll likely be Tuesday before we can crack 'er open."

"Tuesday?" My insides plummet and the blood drains from my face, leaving me cold. "What am I supposed to do in Hicksville for a whole week with no money?"

"Well . . . the town puts on a pretty good fireworks show for the Fourth. And Memphis ain't that far away, if you can get a ride."

"Of course." If I had a ride, I wouldn't need the stupid car to begin with. I sink deeper into the booth and let my head fall against the seat back with a groan. "I guess I don't have a choice, do I?"

He doesn't say anything, and I can almost see him shrugging into the phone.

"Can I at least come get my charger and my pillow while I wait?" If I'm going to be stuck in this diner for a week, I'd at least like my favorite pillow with me. And that's if they don't kick me into the street for loitering.

"Sure thing. Come on over and get it."

"Thanks." I end the call with no clue how I'll get to Mack's, or what I'll do in this one-horse town for the next week. I still haven't called G-Lo to tell her about her car.

Dash gives me a sympathetic smile.

"So . . ." I tap my toe to the rhythm of my pulse as I contemplate the inevitable. "I guess your car is all charged up by now?"

He nods, still wearing the unreadable expression from earlier.

"Thanks again for letting me use your phone." Sighing, I pass it back to him. "And for warning me about Travis. And for not letting anyone steal my stuff while I slept." I let out a hollow laugh. "Too bad you weren't in Cleveland."

"Right?" He shreds the napkin in his hands, then grabs another one and starts over. "I've been thinking . . ."

"At least one of us has." I lay my cheek on the cool table and stare into the crowded dining room. Mom would've had a backup plan.

"No, really, listen." He wads the napkin confetti and chucks it at my head. "Memphis is just over an hour from here. If that."

"Great." I snort. "Close enough to Uber. If I had my wallet. Or my charger—"

"No." He exhales. "You're not getting what I'm saying."

His frustration piques my interest, and I lift my head. "I guess not. What *are* you saying?"

"I'm saying . . ." He rakes long fingers through his dark waves. "I could take you there. If you like."

"Why?" Somewhere in the dark recesses of my brain, a warning light flickers and then goes out. *What are you cooking up in that gorgeous head of yours?*

He pins me with a solemn look. "You promised your mom you'd spread her ashes."

"So?" With my brain finally firing on all cylinders, I pick apart his body language.

"So it's on my way. And . . ." He shrugs. "It might be nice to have some company, even for a little while."

The adventurous part of my brain that somehow convinced me to climb behind the wheel of G-Lo's car not twenty-four hours ago perks up. But the rational voice in my head tells me not to get my hopes up.

"Let me get this straight. You're saying you want to drive me to Memphis—which is on your way. Then bring me back here—which is definitely *out* of your way if you're heading west. Just so I can spread my mom's ashes?"

He bobs his head a few times, lips twitching with the threat of a smile. "Sounds about right."

The idea should thrill me, and yesterday it definitely would have, but after the events of the past twenty-four hours, I can't help but wonder about his motives.

I narrow my eyes at him. "What's in it for you?"

"What do you mean?" He turns his book over in his hands a few times before laying it face down on the table. "Can't a guy simply want to do the right thing? Is it wrong of me to want to help you?"

"Not at all." With my voice of reason battling the newly awakened adventurous spirit for control, a dark laugh bubbles out of me. "But I don't exactly have a great track record when it comes to trusting men."

He arches a brow. "I'm not Travis. Or the guy in Cleveland, for that matter."

Or Damian, but Dash doesn't know me well enough to realize he's being compared to him, too.

"I know that." Jeanie's warnings flash in my peripheral vision, and I stare him down like the criminal he *could* be. "But how do I know you're not trying to lure me into the desert so you can kill me?"

He laughs. "Memphis isn't in the desert. Come on, Zoey, road trips get boring. There are only so many diners you can eat at before you start getting lonely."

"Get a puppy. Dogs love car rides." I grab my tote and scoot toward the end of the bench.

"Wait!" He tugs on his hair. "You're so stubborn. Why won't you let me help you?"

With my tote in my lap, I lean forward until my chest rests on Mom's urn and lock my eyes on his—first the brown, then the blue one. "Because I don't buy it. No one sacrifices their summer vacation for someone else without some level of self-interest."

A sliver of guilt works its way under my skin as I realize the ugly truth in my statement. Didn't I tell Jeanie I wanted Mom all to myself, if only for a little while? Maybe I was even a little relieved she couldn't make the trip. Doesn't that make me selfish?

"Damn. You're relentless." Dash goes back to shredding napkins, adding them to his growing pile of casualties.

"Me?" I snatch the napkin holder, dragging it to my side before he kills again. "You're the one dipping out on his own road trip to tag along on mine. Do you *always* pick up randos in the middle of nowhere? Because a habit like that could be bad for your health."

"No." He chuckles and relaxes into the booth again. "I've never picked up a stranger in a diner before."

"Then why me?" I glance down at my dirty hoodie and catch a whiff of my stale-flower odor. "Must be my dazzling personality."

"Okay, fine." He shakes his head, accepting defeat with a laugh. "I set out on this trip because I have three weeks to make the most important decision I've ever had to make—a choice that will decide the path I take for the rest of my life—and I have absolutely no idea what to do. Helping you gives me a much-needed distraction. And yeah, maybe I'm a little curious about your secret connection with Ziggy Stardust. I wasn't kidding when I said my mom loved Bowie. She's practically a Bowie encyclopedia, and thanks to her, so am I. Your adventure sounds way better than mine, and maybe . . ." He leans closer, lowering his voice to a low purr. "Part of me wants to come along for the ride."

9

Suffragette City

Becky throws me a smile, and I mouth "thank you" for letting me use the diner's phone. Like everything else in BB's, it's retro—a bubble-gum-pink, wall-mounted model with a long spiral cord tethering the handset to the base and rotary dial that takes me several tries to figure out. I send up a silent thanks that G-Lo's is one of the three phone numbers I have memorized.

"What should I do?" I pivot toward the dining room, wrapping the curly cord around myself in the process.

G-Lo took the news of the Betty's fate a lot better than my estranged boyfriend. After making the walls in BB's shake with his furious tantrum, Damian demanded I give him my exact location so he could come save me—an idea I shot down immediately. I can only imagine how he'd react if he knew about Dash. That I'd rather hitch a ride with a total stranger than allow my boyfriend to swoop in and rescue me should tell me all I need to know about our doomed relationship. For the first time in maybe forever, I'm glad my phone died.

"I can't stay here, camped out in a diner for a week like some weirdo, but what's the alternative? Hop in the car with a guy I met *five hours ago* and hope he doesn't throw me in a wood chipper somewhere? Would you take that chance?"

"Is he cute?" G-Lo whispers through the phone as if she knows people are listening. Knowing Jeanie, she is.

With a nervous tingle blooming in my stomach, I glance at Dash, squirming in our booth across the room while waiting for me to decide his fate. Behind the glasses, his eyes draw me in, making me forget to breathe. Cute doesn't come close to describing him. "He's not bad."

"I could never turn down a cute boy." G-Lo sighs like a teenage girl.

"What if he's a serial killer? Ask her *that*!" Jeanie screams in the background. "They said Ted Bundy was cute, too, you know!"

"Hold on, Zoey." G-Lo whispers something, but I can't make out what. After a few seconds of hissing back and forth, G-Lo comes back on the line. "What does your gut tell you?"

"Her guts will be telling the police what she had for breakfast if she's not careful!" Jeanie shrieks.

"No they won't," G-Lo snaps at Jeanie. "Now, that's enough. Go smoke a bowl while I finish talking to your sister."

I can't tell if she's trying to scold Jeanie or soothe her, but Jeanie's voice gets fainter as she takes her tirade into another room.

"Don't listen to Jeanie, she's had way too much oxy and not nearly enough reefer. Take it from an old hippie who hitchhiked all the way across the country and back without so much as a scratch. Trust your instincts. Your gut won't steer you wrong." G-Lo rambles on as if dictating a self-help book.

"I don't know." Keeping Dash in my peripheral vision, I lean against the wall and gnaw on my thumbnail.

As if he senses me watching him, he glances my way and smiles.

Cringing on the inside, I smile back and wave like an awkward teenager. "I don't think he's a psycho, but I haven't exactly had time to psychoanalyze him, so how can I be sure?"

I was wrong about Junior—and T. J.—but I don't mention either of them to G-Lo. She already has more than enough evidence to doubt my survival skills in the wild.

"Ask him what color crayon he'd be," she says.

I snort. "What does that have to do with anything?"

"I have no idea, but they always ask that in interviews. I'm definitely blue . . . with a swirl of chartreuse."

I choke back a laugh. "I'm not trying to hire him. I'm trying to make sure he won't kill me and wear my skin as a suit."

"Then you should steer clear if he says he's scarlet or crimson . . . too close to blood."

"Gee, thanks."

"Life is an adventure, Zoey, but it isn't without risk." G-Lo rattles off her fortune cookie wisdom without a drop of sarcasm. "What if you took a picture of him beside his car? You could get his license plate in the photo and send it to me."

"My phone died. Remember?"

"Oh, right. Does what's-his-name have a phone?"

"Dash?" I roll my eyes. "Barely . . . but yes, I guess that's pretty much all it does—call and text." I remember the lens on the back. "Oh! It has a camera."

"Good! Grab it and call me so I can trace his number."

"You can do that?" I spin around again, tangling myself in the pink phone cord until the spiral is pulled taut.

"No, but I used to sleep with a private investigator in Cincinnati. The sonofabitch owes me one."

"I'm afraid to ask."

"Last time I stayed over, I found an empty tube of wild cherry lube, a purple dildo, and a picture of his mother beside his bed."

"G-Lo!" I'm half a second from shoving my fingers into my ears and singing *lalala, I can't hear you.*

"Tell me about it! It was my lube!" She bursts out laughing, and it takes her several moments to collect herself again. "Send me a text from Dash's phone—don't forget to get his license plate number in the photo—and I'll get Cecil to run it."

I nod, sneaking another peek at Dash. "What do I do until then?"

"Did you pack the anti-rape undies?"

Her question catches me off guard, and I hesitate for an instant. "I did."

"Good. Put those on. They'll give you peace of mind, if nothing else."

They're more likely to give me a wicked case of diaper rash . . . or a yeast infection.

"If you say so." I pull the heavy underwear from my tote and stuff them into the front pocket of my hoodie before anyone sees them.

"This could be the biggest adventure of your life, Zoey. Don't fight it. Enjoy the ride!"

"All I want to do is spread Mom's ashes and come home." The lie stings on the way out. Despite everything that's happened, I want the adventure.

"You'll see."

Her voice surrounds me like a hug, and I close my eyes, imagining her bony arms wrapping around me. "What about Jeanie?"

"Don't worry about Jeanie. She's so high, come tomorrow she'll think she dreamed the whole thing." She barks out a laugh. "And don't worry about the car, either. The Betty will be fine. Trust me, I've run over worse things than a damn armadillo."

I don't even want to know.

After promising to call her as soon as I charge my phone, and to text her from Dash's phone before setting one foot inside his car, we say our goodbyes. The instant I hang up, Dash is out of his seat and heading my way.

"What did she say?" He adjusts his glasses and gazes down at me.

"If I take a picture of you beside your car with the plate visible and text it to her from *your* phone, you probably won't kill me."

He nods, a mask of cool indifference on his flawless face. "That's a fair assessment. It would completely ruin my alibi. I'd be an idiot to kill you after that."

"Right." I listen for my gut to send me some sort of sign. Other than a sharp twinge in my bladder, the only message I'm getting is that Dash is really hot up close.

"So we're doing this?" he asks.

I nod, and his whole face lights up.

Unbelievably hot up close.

Still grinning ear to ear, he walks backward toward the counter. "I'll order us burgers for the road—extra onion, right?"

"Yeah, but I don't have—"

"You can Venmo me after you charge your phone."

"Oh, um, Dash?" I wrap a finger around a loose string dangling from the bottom of my shorts, gripping it for dear life.

"Yeah?"

"If you were a crayon, what color would you be?"

His brow furrows and he cocks his head, but his smile stays in place. "What a strange thing to ask."

I hold my breath, eagerly awaiting his reply.

"I don't know." He shrugs. "Way too many colors to choose from."

"Right." I exhale, twisting the string into a knot before releasing it. "So many colors."

While Dash orders food I can't afford, I duck into the deserted ladies' room to put on G-Lo's anti-rape underwear.

What the hell have I gotten myself into?

After relieving my bladder for what could be the last time in who knows how long, I fish the striped undies from my hoodie pocket and give them a few vigorous shakes in the tiny stall, cracking them like a whip the way Mom always did before pulling on new pantyhose. Then, with my bare feet resting on top of my shoes to avoid the puddle of what I *hope* isn't pee surrounding the base of the toilet like a moat, I begin the weirdest game of solo Twister ever played. I step into the first snug leg hole, then shift my weight and shove my other foot through the second hole before tugging the garment from my shins to my knees.

"Damn, these are tight," I mutter. At least one size too small. Maybe two.

Gripping the waistband until my knuckles whiten, I drag the European knickers over my knees, huffing and grunting while wriggling them up my thighs. Almost there. Just a few more inches. *Damn it.*

Shimmying down a freaking drainpipe naked would've been a hell of a lot easier.

A loud flush from the next stall echoes through the small restroom.

Then someone clears their throat. "Excuse me?"

With the unforgiving boy shorts wedged just below my crotch, I freeze in place and choke back a laugh. "Yes?"

"Could you pass me some paper?" the timid voice whispers. "This stall is completely out."

Instead of earning my sympathy, her panicked voice sends me over the edge. With the fingers of both hands wedged into my waistband, I laugh. "I'm sorry. I . . . my hands are occupied at the moment."

After a few seconds of silence, she clears her throat again. "I-I'll wait."

Once I've vacuum sealed myself into what basically amounts to Spanx-on-steroids, I pass what's left of the TP roll to the lady in the next stall and finish dressing.

Dash is wearing a fresh shirt and a big smile when I step out of the restroom a few minutes later. "Ready to roll?"

"What's all that?" I ask, catching a whiff of french fries.

In his left hand, he balances a drink carrier with four large cups, while his right hand clutches the extra-large white paper bag resting on his right hip. He rolls his eyes. "Lunch."

"For what army?"

He laughs. "Just us."

"How much do you think I can eat?"

He shoves away from the wall with his cool facade of feigned disinterest firmly in place. "Oh, this? This is all for me. I got you a Snickers. It's melting in my back pocket."

"Ha ha. Very funny." A nervous chuckle catches in my throat.

His mask slips, replaced by a genuine smile. "I got you a cheeseburger, no pickles, extra onions, and a side of fries."

Almost exactly what I'd ordered last night.

"Thank you."

"Don't mention it." Hands full, he prods me with his elbow. "You ready? We're wasting daylight."

"Lead the way." I reach for the drink carrier, and to my surprise, he lets me take it. Damian would've flexed his bulging muscles and flat-out refused my help.

Dash just smiles and leads me through the door.

Once we're outside, curiosity gets the best of me. "Why four drinks?"

He eyes me as if the answer is obvious. "Two coffees and two Cokes."

"Do we really need coffees *and* Cokes?"

"Absolutely."

"Why?"

"Because, duh. Coffee is a necessity of life."

"And the Cokes?"

"Trust me." He points his chin toward the sun. "In less than an hour, you'll be thanking me for that icy-cold beverage."

I laugh. "If I drink all that, we're gonna need to make a pit stop."

"Would it be a road trip if we didn't?"

My laugh turns into a groan as I consider the real possibility that I'll have to pee before we get back.

"Still afraid I'm a serial killer?" he asks.

"Maybe?" The memory of wriggling into the sadistic panties is still fresh in my mind, and the inevitability of having to do it all over again strikes fear in me. Get in and get out. That's the goal for Memphis. I can hold it until we get back.

Dash leads me around the side of the building.

I glance over my shoulder, wondering if I'd spoken too soon. "Where are you taking me?"

"I told you I had to be patient *and* resourceful." He stops in front of a cherry-red Tesla.

And not just any old Tesla, either. I recognize the expensive vehicle from the cover of one of Damian's many luxury cars magazines.

"Hang on . . ." My eyes follow the long extension cord running from the car to the building. "You drive a *Model X* and you can't afford a decent phone?"

"I never said I couldn't afford a smartphone. You assumed. I *choose* to use a basic phone. There's a big difference."

"It's barely a phone at all."

"Actually, it's *primarily* a phone. And without all the other useless nonsense, it holds a charge for a lot longer with way less distractions. Plus, I'll bet I get a better signal in rural areas than you do." He scratches the back of his neck and clears his throat. "Best of all, my family can't use an app to track me everywhere I go."

Hmm, interesting. "Speaking of your phone . . ." I hold out my hand.

He stops and gapes at me. "I thought you were kidding."

"Nope." I wiggle my fingers until he slaps the phone into my palm. I crack open the clamshell and stare at the display. "How do you—" I click the menu button and find the option for the camera. "Ah, got it. Smile pretty for the camera."

Dash poses at the back of his car with a stony expression that, somehow, makes him hotter. After taking a few snaps, I send the best ones to G-Lo and return his phone.

"I don't know how you can use that thing. It doesn't have iTunes, or Spotify, or anything."

"There's more to life than iTunes, you know." Dash rests the burger bag on his hip while fishing the key fob from his pocket. He clicks a button and the front passenger door swings open on its own. He clicks another button and the rear doors open upward, like wings, folding up and tucking in above the sleek body.

"How do you listen to music?" I mutter, mesmerized by his futuristic vehicle.

Dash sets the white bag in the back seat. "Ever heard of this thing called a *radio*?"

"There's never anything good on the radio."

With one more press of a button, the trunk opens with a quiet snick. "There is when you have satellite."

"How does a college student afford a hundred-and-twenty-thousand-dollar car, anyway? You didn't steal it, did you?"

"College *graduate*." He grins. "And no, I didn't steal it. It was a graduation gift. If I was going to steal a car, I would've picked something a little less flashy."

My fingers itch to glide across the glossy finish, and I tuck my hand under my arm to stop myself. "Must be nice."

"If you say so." He snorts. "Gifts from my father always come with strings."

"Still . . . could be worse. You could've gotten stuck with a '73 Cutlass with an armadillo in the radiator."

"True . . ." He grimaces. "One of the few perks of being Daniel Hammond's only son."

He spits out his father's name like a curse, and I wonder if I should know who he is—a famous Hollywood director or music producer, maybe—but I don't ask.

After loading the car, Dash runs around and disconnects the power cord from the diner outlet and then stows it in the back.

"How'd you get them to let you charge this thing all night long?"

"Resourceful, remember?" He taps his forehead. "Now, get in."

I scoop a magazine from the front passenger seat and climb in, unloading the drinks into the car's cup holders before setting the empty carrier in the back seat. Taking extra care not to scuff the white leather upholstery, I slide my tote between my feet. While Dash buckles himself in, I flip through the magazine's wrinkled pages. From what I can tell, *Tattle Tale* is a little bit *Rolling Stone* and a whole lot *National Enquirer*, leaning heavily on salacious rock and roll news. Basically, the same tabloid garbage found in grocery checkout lines.

I recite the first heading that draws my attention. "Which heavy metal guitarist has the biggest—"

Face flaming the same bright red as the car, Dash snatches the magazine from my fingers and flings it into the back.

I bite back a grin. "A little trashy for a guy who reads *On the Road* for fun, don't you think?"

"It's not . . . I wasn't—"

"It's not . . . you weren't . . . what?"

He shifts his gaze skyward and blows out a breath. "Would you believe me if I said it's my mother's?"

I snicker. "Definitely not."

"Yeah, I figured." Dash rolls his eyes and punches the ignition button. The car whirs to life, sounding more like a spaceship than a car, and we ease out of the lot.

After a quick pit stop at Mack's for my charger, we hop on the highway and head toward Memphis with the most glorious, ice-cold AC pouring from the vents.

10

Starman

With my iPhone finally up and running, I set out to retake control of my destiny. After gaining access to my bank account—though, sadly neither my debit nor credit card—I manage to track down Ernie and my backpack, thanks to a nice lady at the dairy company. But with my clothes officially en route to Mack's Garage, fate swoops in like an evil harpy and rips the rug right out from under me again.

"Damn it." A wave of sadness rolls over me as I scroll the Wiki page for Memphis.

"What's wrong?" Dash snickers. "Battery die already, or did you lose signal again?"

"No, smart-ass." I release a defeated sigh. "They demolished Ellis Auditorium in 1999. Where am I supposed to take the picture now?"

Dash leans in and reads over my shoulder, surrounding me with his rosemary-and-clean-laundry scent. "That sucks. It was practically a historical landmark."

Hot breath fans across my neck, sending a delicious tingle down my spine. "Eyes on the road, Dash."

"We're good. The Tesla has autonomous driving." He says *autonomous* as if it's synonymous with *magic*.

With visions of ninja armadillos dancing through my head, I shoot him an icy glare. "I don't know what that means."

"It's basically autopilot." He turns his attention back to the road, dramatically gripping the wheel at ten and two. "Happy?"

"Yes. Thank you." Flashing him an obnoxious smile, I continue my frustrating search.

He shakes his head and circles back to the original topic. "Did they replace it or just tear down the old one?"

"There's a shiny new auditorium in its place, but that's not where Mom had her picture taken."

Just like with Cleveland, Mom documented all the places she went and things she did while in Memphis. All but one of those is still there—the place from her photo. And as far as I can tell, nothing of the old auditorium remains. "How am I supposed to re-create a photo in a place that doesn't exist anymore?"

"We'll figure it out." Dash hovers, studying the picture of Mom. "She was beautiful."

"She was." I trace the lines of her neck and shoulder with my finger. My head used to fit in that spot. From as far back as I can remember, after every bad dream or any time I was sick, I'd snuggle into the crook of Mom's neck to fall asleep. Even after she got sick, she did her best to be a shoulder for me whenever I needed one. Near the end, she was simply too frail. "My sister looks just like her."

Dash clears his throat, and I catch him staring at me.

"I think you look like her," he says.

A shiver runs through me, and I tug my hair forward like a shield. "We have—*had*—the same hair." I coil a thick lock around my finger. "But Jeanie's her clone in every other way."

Dash sweeps my hair over my shoulder, and my stomach somersaults. "I don't know your sister, but I think *you* look a lot like your mom."

"You . . ." I lift my gaze and find myself trapped in his mesmerizing eyes.

Inconvenient or not, you still have a boyfriend, remember? I may *finally* be ready to put Damian out to pasture, but even *he* deserves more than an impersonal text message breakup before I start shopping for his replacement.

Swallowing the lump in my throat, I look away while I still can. "You're not watching the road."

"Sorry." He shifts his attention to the traffic ahead.

As if he has a sixth sense, or some sort of Zoey radar, my phone rings and Damian's face lights up the display. Speak of the devil. With a panicked glance at Dash, I accept the call.

"Finally!" Damian's voice booms through the line, and I can almost see the vein in his neck pulsing with every breath.

Twisting in my seat, I face the window and lower the volume on my phone. "Hi."

"Are you ignoring my calls?"

"No, Damian." I grit my teeth as I grind out the words. With my insides coiled like a snake about to strike, it's a wonder I haven't reached through the phone and strangled him with my bare hands. "I told you my phone died."

"For Christ's sake, Zoey! Why didn't you charge it?"

"Because—" My breath hisses out like an Instant Pot releasing steam. Nothing I say will make a difference anyway. "Never mind, it doesn't matter."

"Call it a sign and scrap the whole trip. You can come with me to my brother's place on Rehoboth for the Fourth."

"I can't just scrap my trip," I whisper, hoping Dash isn't paying attention.

"Why not? You'd have way more fun at the beach with me. And as an added bonus, I can help you register for classes."

A dull ache builds behind my eyes, and I contemplate ending things right here and now. With a glance at Dash, I change my mind. This isn't the time or the place to make those kinds of decisions. "I told you I wrecked my grandma's car."

"Exactly my point. Nothing you can do about that now, right? I'll get you a bus ticket and you can—"

"I got a ride to Memphis." I hold my breath and peek over my shoulder at Dash, watching the road with his jaw clenched tight enough to shatter bone. "To spread Mom's ashes."

The line goes quiet, and for half a second I think the call dropped, but then Damian chuckles. "Where'd you find someone to give you a ride in the middle of East Jesus?"

"Uh . . ." I fiddle with the frayed hem of my shorts, tugging another loose thread free. "West Tennessee, actually."

"What the hell ever." Damian snorts, and I can hear the eye roll from here. "Who gave you a ride, Zo?"

Dash shifts in his seat, opening and closing his mouth as if itching to say something.

My skin prickles, sensing his eyes on me. "Sorry, Damian, I'm losing the signal. Can I call you later?"

"Zoey, wait."

"Sorry, I'm losing you." I rub my finger over the speaker, hoping to make the line crackle.

"Don't hang up."

"Gotta go!" I mash the button, disconnecting the call, and put my phone on Do Not Disturb.

Eyes locked on the road ahead, Dash exhales through his nose. "So that's him, huh?"

"Yeah."

"Well, he sounds . . ." He laughs, abandoning whatever polite flattery he was about to spout. "He's not happy you're still here, is he?"

"Nope." I draw out the word, emphasizing the *p*. "He didn't want me coming at all. Had *other* plans in mind."

He tears his eyes from the road and gapes at me. "Don't tell me he expected you to go party in Daytona."

"Rehoboth, actually. But it's a little more complicated than that."

He shakes his head and turns back to the road. "What a dick."

Desperate to put Damian out of my mind, I change the subject. "What about you? Girlfriend? *Boyfriend?*"

Dash snickers. "I don't have a boyfriend."

"Girlfriend, then?" We're barely friends, let alone anything more, yet I get an unpleasant twinge in my chest at the thought.

"No." A dark cloud crosses his features. "No girlfriend."

Curiosity gets the best of me. "Never?"

"No, not never." He rolls his eyes. "You wanna listen to some music?"

"Wait! You can't leave me hanging like that. What happened?" I lower my voice dramatically. "You didn't kill her, did you?"

He bursts out laughing. "No. I didn't kill her. Although . . ."

"Dash!"

"I'm kidding. She's alive. If you can call a soulless creature *alive*."

"Sounds like she and Damian would get along," I mutter under my breath. Then, louder for his ears, I say, "How about that music you promised me?"

"Sure." Dash cranks up the eighties station on Sirius just in time to catch the chorus of Talking Heads' "Psycho Killer."

"The plan is to spread Mom's ashes at Mud Island Park." Until reading her diary, I hadn't realized how absent G-Lo had been when Mom was growing up. They'd been at odds for nearly all of Mom's young life, but during a picnic at Mud Island, some of that icy indifference thawed. "I think she'd like that."

"Don't inhale this time." Dash keeps his eyes on the road, but his lips curl up at the corners. "I don't care what your grandma says, you can't get high from ashes."

"Smart-ass."

He pins me with a smoldering look that sends ribbons of warmth through my limbs.

"You know"—he cocks an eyebrow—"it's not too late to bury your body in the woods."

I tear my gaze from his and flash a saucy smile. "Don't forget, my grandma knows what you look like."

"How could I forget? It's not every day someone's hippie grandma threatens to dig into my sordid past." His easy grin tells me he isn't the least bit worried.

If he only knew . . .

"So . . ." He changes the subject. "Should we start at the new auditorium? I know it's not the same building, but it's *technically* the same place. I could even take some pictures, if you like."

"I'd like that." With our itinerary set, I finish my Coke with a loud slurp.

"Want some of mine?" He holds out his cup, beads of condensation spilling over his fingers.

"No thanks." My stomach sloshes, warning me to pace myself. "I'm trying to avoid unscheduled pit stops."

"I don't mind stopping. Besides, I suspect we'll find at least one public restroom every few blocks."

"Great." I force a smile. If Dash knew what it took to squeeze into this shiny Lycra chastity belt, I doubt he'd be so eager for me to wiggle out of it so soon. My insides clench at the thought of getting the clingy pants down and not being able to get them back up again.

No. Not happening. I glance out the passenger window and unravel the hem of my shorts a little farther. My bladder will have to wait until we get back to Hicksville.

Dash pries my fingers from my shorts. "How long were those when you left home?"

"Ha ha. Very funny."

We exit the highway, and Dash parks in the Mud Island garage, just a short walk in either direction from our planned destinations. We step out of the car and straight into the drum of a clothes dryer. But instead of smelling of damp laundry, the sticky wall of heat envelops us in the loamy stench of mud and fish from the nearby river.

I gather my long hair into a loose ponytail to get it off my neck. "Why is it so humid here?"

"Welcome to Memphis." Dash chuckles, sweat already running from his temple to his jaw. "Come on." He clasps my hand. "Adventure awaits."

The city is a flurry of activity. The aroma of sizzling meat and spices emanating from the small army of food trucks parked on every corner fills the air. The rattle of vintage streetcars rises over the din of voices as assorted tourists and businesspeople pack the sidewalks, every one of them on a mission of their own.

We make our way through the throng to the Cannon Center for Performing Arts, but it's the giant metallic *spaceship* parked out front that captures my attention. Resembling a swirling tornado of liquid mercury, the columns and funnels of the mirrored sculpture draw my eyes and reflect my conflicting emotions.

"Incredible." Dash gazes up at the shimmering work of art.

Despite the impressive sight in front of me, I direct my attention to the ground at my feet. Did my mother stand in this same spot three decades ago? My eyes sting as I crouch and place my hand on a four-by-four concrete square as if the sidewalk holds the secret of my entire existence. This isn't even the same auditorium and yet . . . I didn't expect to feel her presence here, but I do.

Dash squats beside me. "You want me to take your picture?"

I wordlessly hand him my iPhone, and he snaps several photos before joining me on the sidewalk. Ignoring the noise and the crush of people fanning out around us, we sit shoulder to shoulder on the pavement and stare up at the giant silver structure.

"Seems fitting," he says after a few minutes.

"Fitting?"

"Definitely." He nods. "Since, in some weird twist of fate, you were sent here by a Starman."

11

Under Pressure

A hot gust ruffles my hair as the last particles of ash drift through the sky and float down the Mississippi River. Two down, only seven more to go. I peek at Dash over my shoulder. Unfortunately, I'll be on my own for those.

Unlike Damian's constant nagging from almost a thousand miles away, Dash relaxes on a bench, never once complaining while I choke back tears and say goodbye to Mom. All things considered, I couldn't have asked for a better travel companion. But I know I can't keep him forever. And maybe that's for the best. It would be too easy to get attached . . . too hard to say goodbye.

I wipe my dusty fingers through the tall grass, then make my way to the bench.

Dash smiles as I sit beside him. "All done?"

I nod, focusing my attention on my gritty fingers. "I have sand under my fingernails." As the words tumble out, I realize it isn't sand at all. It's Mom.

Dash bumps me with his shoulder. "At least you didn't snort any this time."

With his sweat-soaked hair pushed away from his face and his glasses tucked into his front pocket, he looks like Superman. All he's missing is the suit.

I glance at his glasses. "Don't you need those to see?"

He pulls them from his pocket and slides them on. They instantly fog.

"Can't see much with them on." He slips them into his pocket again. "But without them, everything kinda looks like an impressionist painting. I'm pretending I'm at the museum." His lips twitch as he turns toward me. "You ready?"

"Yup." My good humor vaporizes like water in a hot pan. "I guess you can take me back to Hicksville."

"That's it?" He wipes a drop of sweat from his cheek with the back of his hand. "No sightseeing? You came all this way to spread some ashes and leave?"

Unable to meet his gaze, I shrug. If I look at him, I'll cry. I'd give anything to spend the day visiting all the places Mom went, but every minute I spend with Dash makes it harder to say goodbye. I don't know what the hell's wrong with me. I've known him for less than a day. Maybe it's the emotional roller coaster I've been riding since discovering the existence of Mom's diary, or maybe it's the stark contrast between Dash and Damian, but if I don't break free of Dash's orbit soon, I won't have to worry about getting attached, because it'll be too damn late.

And I can't forget about the ticking time bomb in my bladder.

"Don't tell me your mom drove all the way to Memphis, took a picture, then left. I call bullshit on that." Dash reaches for Mom's diary. "May I?"

I hand over the journal, knowing exactly what he'll find.

He wipes the fog from his glasses and then slips them on, holding Mom's diary open like story time at the library.

"I knew it! They hit Beale Street . . . Sun Studio. Skipped Graceland because your grandma said it was a giant tourist trap—she wasn't wrong about that. And look . . ." He taps the page. "They ate barbecue and deep-fried Oreos."

"Okay, I get it." My chest tightens as all the reasons for staying add up, making the reasons for leaving seem ridiculous in comparison. "That's not nothing."

"Got drunk at Jerry Lee's," he continues.

"Okay, stop right there." I reach for Mom's diary with a nervous chuckle. "I'm not getting drunk at Jerry Lee's . . ."

Or anywhere else in a strange city with a guy I just met.

"Don't look at me like that," he says with boyish innocence. "I wasn't planning on drinking, let alone getting drunk. I'm driving, remember?"

I raise an eyebrow and fold my arms over my chest. "And if you *weren't* driving?"

"Well, I seriously doubt I'd be drinking if *you* were driving, either, after the whole armadillo incident." His innocent facade slips, the gears in his head turning as he holds my gaze. "You *could*, though, right? Without breaking any laws?"

"Of course." I shift my attention to the swirling script on the page and mutter, "In Europe."

He laughs. "But not here?"

His glasses fog again, saving me from his penetrating gaze.

"If you must know, I'll be twenty-one in three months."

He nods and releases a breath. "Good to know."

With that subject firmly behind us, I stow Mom's ashes and her diary in my tote, still torn about what to do next. Dash is right, I should stay and do all the things Mom did—and not out of some sense of duty, but because I *want* to do all those things . . . with him. But I also don't want to get caught with my pants literally around my ankles when I need to pee and can't get G-Lo's personal protection undies back on in the damn Memphis heat. Thanks to countless hours of binge-watching *Friends* with Mom, visions of Ross and the leather pants plague my thoughts.

Dash bumps my shoulder with his. "Maybe you didn't get to re-create the picture at the old auditorium, but you're here. In Memphis. Breathing the same air your mom breathed, however long ago. You can't really want to leave already. Let's . . . I don't know. Let's go to Sun Studio and Beale Street. We're in the home of the blues. We didn't drive all this way to turn right around and go back, did we?"

"No." My willpower deflates like a sad party balloon. "We didn't."

Excited, he dials up his smile. "Then let's do this . . . Listen to good music. Eat good food. And experience what your mom did when she was here. What else do we have to do? Your car won't be ready until Tuesday."

"You can stop selling me on the idea." Laughing, I nudge him and he slips right off the bench.

He's right, and he knows it as well as I do. I can't dump a handful of ashes and go home. Mom was alive when she came here, and I have a chance to truly follow her footsteps. I can't turn my back on that.

"Hey, that's fine." Grinning, he stands. "If you want to camp out in the diner for the weekend, or waste half your budget on the Hicksville Inn where you can search for patterns in the carpet stains and watch *The Bachelor* reruns all weekend, I won't—"

"Dash!" I drag my bottom lip through my teeth as an army of butterflies takes over my insides.

"What?"

A grin explodes across my face. "Let's do it."

His eyes widen. "Really?"

"Come on, before I change my mind." I hook my arm through his.

He does a quick fist pump before towing me back toward the footbridge and the nearest trolley. "You won't regret this."

Two hours later, I am filled to the absolute brim with regret. Regret for eating my weight in pulled pork and barbecued baked beans. Regret for inhaling half that again in gator gumbo and deep-fried Oreos. And *so much regret* for every single drop of Memphis sweet tea that passed my lips.

The heavy wood and glass door falls shut behind us, barely muffling the live music blaring from inside the historic Beale Street café. My stomach sloshes in time with the sound of blues guitar, and the first real twinge of fear creeps into my consciousness as my bladder finally reaches maximum capacity.

"Don't lie. You loved the gator, right?" Dash loops his arm with mine and tows me toward the river. "And the music. Too bad we can't stay longer. I'll bet it's amazing after dark."

The sound of a trolley bell in the distance steals my attention. If we catch the next one, how long will it take to reach the car? I rack my brain to remember how long it took us to get here from Hicksville. Can I hold it that long?

Dash pokes a finger into my side. "Hey! Earth to Zoey?"

My bladder spasms, and I let out a squeal, clenching my pelvic floor as hard as I can.

Dash roars with laughter. "Wow, ticklish much?"

"No." I inch away from him, making him laugh even harder. "You just scared me."

I'm not even lying. I'm *terrified* if he pokes me one more time, I'll explode. *Oh, God, please don't make me pull these medieval torture panties down in some sketchy restroom on Beale Street!*

Oblivious to my growing panic, Dash drags me toward another sweet shop. "How about some homemade fudge?"

"How are you even hungry? You ate more than I did, and I'm literally a breath away from bursting."

In more ways than one.

"Fast metabolism. Come on, *Zo-ey*." He says my name like a kid whining to stay up late on a school night. "You know you want to. Besides, this is the perfect opportunity to hit the restroom."

"I'll wait. I'm good." I force a smile and block out the smell of sweets in the air.

"How can you possibly hold it that long?" He winces. "That can't be good for you."

It's all I can do not to cackle at his expression. Laughing with a full bladder would be . . . unwise.

"I'm fine." I keep lying, like the great big liar I am, and clench harder. Simply talking about peeing makes the urge more unbearable. And standing still? Nearly impossible. I dance forward, beckoning him to follow. "Come on, Dash. Let's go. I'm exhausted and beyond full. If we hurry, we can make it to Mack's before they close. I miss my backpack, and I'd pretty much *kill* to be able to change, uh"—I swallow another hysterical laugh—"my *clothes* again."

"If you insist." Dash sighs and pivots from the sweet shop, jogging to catch up. "But I'm starting to believe one of us is actually a psycho killer . . . and it isn't me."

A few blocks later, he swings into a bakery for a quick pit stop—his third since we arrived in Memphis. Just imagining the sound of a toilet flushing nearly brings me to my knees.

"How much farther?" I whine, my voice climbing another octave until it's nothing but a breathy squeak.

At this rate, there's no way I'll make it back to Hicksville. If I clench any harder, something down there is bound to break. Medieval device be damned, I need to stop soon. If I'm lucky, I'll find a nice clean Starbucks around the next corner.

"That's it." Dash stops dead in the street and faces me, all stony and hot. "I don't know what kind of weird hang-up you have about public restrooms, but this is getting ridiculous. Just pee already."

A whimper sneaks out of me before I can stop it. I'm so close to the breaking point, I can taste it. "Fine! You're right. I can't do it. I can't hold it anymore."

Dash releases a massive breath. "Jesus, finally." Grabbing my hand as if he's the one with the critical bladder situation, he drags me into a little café and walks me all the way to the ladies' room. "I don't know what you're afraid of, but I promise I'll be right here when you're done. I'm not going anywhere. Okay?"

Blinking back tears, I nod and then scurry into the restroom, barely pausing to close and lock the door behind me.

After launching my tote onto the hook behind the door, I drag my shorts down my thighs, the taste of impending relief on the tip of my tongue. Goose bumps erupt over my skin as I struggle with the waistband on the stupid prison panties for what feels like hours but . . . They. Will. Not. Budge.

Then I remember G-Lo's warning. "The tag!"

Heart stuttering behind my ribs, I snatch my tote from the hook and dig through its contents for the brown paper square with the secret code.

"Come on! Where are you?" Rising panic grips me as I dump my bag onto the filthy floor, dropping to my knees and foraging through the chaos. "No, no, no. Not again."

Teetering on the edge of desperation, I pitch everything back into my bag and search my memory for the damn code. I vaguely remember the pattern, but no matter how hard I try to re-create it, I fail.

A wave of nausea washes over me, and goose bumps form on top of my goose bumps.

In the next stall, a toilet flushes, and the sound of rushing water echoes around me. "Are you kidding me, right now?"

Since I basically locked myself up and threw away the key, I have two choices: Stay in this bathroom forever or ask Dash for help. I yank up my shorts, and with as deep a breath as I dare take, stumble out of the restroom.

Dash is exactly where he said he'd be, oblivious to the tears streaking down my face. "We should stop at the charging station before we—"

"Dash?" I whisper his name on a sob.

"Zoey?" He glances behind me as if the source of my distress is anywhere but directly in front of him. "What happened? Are you okay? You look kinda sick. Was it something you ate?"

More like something I drank. My bladder spasms again, and I whimper.

"Say something." He locks his concerned gaze on me. "You're scaring me."

"I-I have a problem." My voice cracks.

He flinches, but to his credit, he doesn't back away. "Like, a *female* problem?"

I *freaking* wish.

A hysterical laugh breaks free, and I choke it back, on the verge of losing it. "Not exactly. I, uh, my grandma Lola gave me a pair of . . . of *special* panties."

"Special?" Dash cocks his head to the side, brows furrowing as he processes the new information. "Special how?"

Another spasm threatens to drop me to my knees, and I snap my eyes shut. "There's a secret code to get them off, and I—" Tears spill over my eyelashes. "I lost it."

He nods and blows out a breath. "So we get a pair of scissors and you cut them off, right?"

I look up at him through wet lashes and shake my head.

"No?" His eyebrows dart up his forehead.

"G-Lo said they're practically indestructible."

"Indestruct—" Dash chokes out a nervous chuckle and wipes a bead of sweat from his forehead.

"She said I'd need wire cutters to get them off," I whisper.

He shoves his hands into his hair and swears under his breath. "Okay, come on."

He practically lifts me off the ground, dragging me down the street in a half run, half power walk.

We pass the trolley stop, and my body goes into a full-on spasm. "Aren't we taking the streetcar?"

"Too slow." He scoops me up and tosses me over his shoulder. "Just . . . Please don't pee on me."

I swallow a snarky reply. At this point, my sense of humor is full-on drowning.

Like freaking Usain Bolt at the Olympics, Dash sprints the last few blocks, practically hurdling the summer tourists and chanting "please don't pee on me" the whole way back to the parking garage.

When we finally make it to the car, he deposits me at the front bumper and opens his trunk. He pulls out a sleek black bag, and my first instinct is to run. But since I'm incapable of moving without my bladder spontaneously emptying, I stand, frozen in place, while he digs out a giant tool that looks like it would easily cut through bone.

"W-Why do you have *that*?" My shriek echoes through the parking garage.

Dash cringes. "You said we needed wire cutters. These"—he gives the instrument of death a shake—"are the closest thing I have."

"But why do you just *happen* to have a pair of bone cutters in your car?" A jolt of fear spikes through me. "I should've waited for G-Lo's background check. Jeanie was right. You're way cuter than Ted Bundy. I should've known!"

"They're not bone cutters." Dash rolls his eyes. "They're *bolt* cutters."

"But—"

"I'm on a cross-country road trip. I have flares and a flat tire kit, too. Does that make me a serial killer?"

My voice refuses to cooperate so I shake my head.

"Take these." He extends the long handles toward me, and motions toward the back of the car. "I'll be over there . . . if you need me."

I snatch the tool from his fingers. "I won't."

Once Dash turns his back, I tuck the heavy cutters under my arm and fumble with my shorts. My trembling fingers can barely get the button through the hole to unzip. After peeling back the denim like a ripe banana, I grip the tool in both hands and bring the cutting end toward the edge of the death-trap undies. But either the handles are too long or my arms are too short, because I can't quite master the angles.

"How's it going over there?" Dash calls over his shoulder.

"Fine!" Another tingling ripple runs through me.

"Once you cut yourself free, you can use an empty soda cup—"

"Shut up! I'm trying to concentrate." I rise onto my toes, hoping the action will somehow make me taller, or make my arms longer, or anything that will get the freaking mouth of the tool into my waistband. It doesn't. And I can't. Tears spill over my lashes and down my cheeks. "I-I can't do it."

"Need my help?"

I let out a defeated whimper. "Hurry!"

Dash's eyes soften, but he eases toward me as if approaching a live grenade. His hands are no steadier than mine as he takes the tool from my trembling fingers.

Keeping his gaze locked on mine, he brings the bolt cutters closer. "I'm only gonna cut enough so you can get these off, okay?"

I nod, mentally preparing myself to strip out of my shorts the instant he cuts me free.

"Okay, here goes." Dash opens the jaws wide and gently slides them into position.

The instant the cold metal touches my hot skin, I release a hard shudder. Then just as the cutter's teeth bite through my steel-lined waistband, everything inside me lets go. Sweet relief rushes through me like a river breaking through a dam, and no amount of clenching will stop the flow.

The sound of running water echoes through the parking garage, and Dash's eyes widen with horror.

"Shit!" He dances out of the way of the stream, climbing halfway onto the hood. "That's a lot of pee!"

"It's not my fault," I cry. "I tried to hold it. Honest, I did. It was all that Coke!"

Dash bursts out laughing, cackling so hard he can't catch his breath. Every time he gets himself under control, he crumbles into another laughing fit.

"Don't feel bad, Zoey," he wheezes. "I heard Bowie had a pretty bad coke problem once upon a time, too."

12

Where Are We Now?

After what has to be the longest stretch of awkward silence in my entire life, Dash hands me an open packet of wet wipes and a pair of Superman boxer-briefs. "Here. You, uh, might need these."

Darting my eyes from the crisp new royal-blue underwear to Dash's red face, I grin. It's as if someone threw me a life raft in the middle of my ocean of shame. I know I should keep my mouth shut, hope he forgets what he witnessed not minutes ago, but the part of me desperate to wash away the sting of humiliation can't help herself.

"Don't say it." His voice echoes through the parking garage as he pins me with one of his stony stares. "They were a graduation gift from my little sisters. They picked them out themselves, so I wasn't about to refuse them."

"I didn't say anything . . . *Clark.*" I bite the inside of my cheek to keep from laughing. I'm obviously not the only one to make the connection.

A dark chuckle rolls out of him like distant thunder. "After what you just . . . you know what? I'm not going there. My mother raised me to be a gentleman, so I'll let you have this round."

"See, that's exactly what I mean." I look down at the puddle at my feet and shrug. My poor Skechers. "I was just thinking how nice you are to help me like this. It's really . . . *super* of you. You're totally my *hero*."

"Keep it up, and I'll—" His lips quiver as he loses the battle to maintain his stony exterior.

"You'll what?" Somehow, I keep my features neutral. I may be far from innocent, but I'm not above playing dumb.

He balls up the matching Superman T-shirt as if he doesn't want me to see the big red *S* emblazoned across the front and chucks it at me, hitting me square in the chest. "Don't say a word. Go change. And please throw those things out." He nods toward the black-and-white stripes peeking from my open zipper.

I finger the mangled waistband while he grumbles about his leather seats.

"I get it," I say. "Not like I can ever wear them again, anyway." Not when they look like a badger chewed through them.

"I can't believe you wore them in the first place."

"I was being safe." My face heats. "You never told me what color . . . and you could've been a rapist."

He flashes a wide smile. "You think I'm cuter than Ted Bundy."

A wave of fresh heat envelops my face. "I-I can't be held responsible for anything I said while I was freaking out."

"Hmm." The grin fades into a frown. "Speaking of things you said, is your grandma really running a background check on me?"

A ripple of laughter slips out, bouncing off the concrete walls like ping-pong balls. "Maybe."

"Perfect." He rolls his eyes. "Hurry up so we can get out of here."

"Zoey, wake up." Dash nudges my shoulder.

I wipe the drool from my cheek and blink in confusion. The last thing I remember is washing my shorts and my sneakers in a public bathroom and then climbing into the front seat, barefoot and wearing Dash's underwear and T-shirt, looking like a kid in a pair of Superman Underoos. I peer out the window at the Mack's Garage sign hanging above a pair of closed garage bay doors.

I straighten in my seat and search for signs of life in the empty parking lot. My breath hitches as I turn toward Dash. "What time is it?"

He winces. "A little after six."

"We missed them?"

"I'm sorry." He rubs the back of his neck. "The car took longer to charge than I expected."

With a halfhearted laugh, I sink into the warm leather seat. "What's one more day without my clothes, right?"

Dash blows out a breath. "Listen, it's been a long day. We're both exhausted. Let's head over to the Hicksville Inn."

"Together?" Heat prickles over my skin. "I . . . do you think that's a good idea?"

He laughs. "I reserved two rooms."

"Oh! Okay. Good." The air in my lungs whooshes out.

"I'm so far past exhausted." He presses the heels of his hands into his eye sockets and rubs. "I need to sleep for at least twelve hours. But I *promise* I'll bring you back over here to get your stuff in the morning."

"That's fair." I drag my bottom lip through my teeth. "But I can't let you pay for my room."

"Zoey—"

"I've got it. It's fine." I wave my device in front of him like a victory flag. How much could a room in Hicksville possibly cost? "I'll go online, book a room, and pay for it. Venmo to the rescue."

He lifts his brows. "With the cards you closed? And no ID?"

A low groan creaks out of me. "No."

"If you're that worried about it, you can pay me back." His lips curve into a slight smile, not mocking but definitely amused. "You can even transfer it to me with your fancy phone."

Relieved, I relax into the seat. "I can do that."

"Good. Now that that's settled . . ." A jaw-cracking yawn interrupts him. "Let's go check in before I fall asleep at the wheel."

◆ ◆ ◆

My room smells like a basement—decades of wet towels and cigarette smoke hiding under cheap pine cleanser. The ancient air-conditioning unit rattles away as it pumps stale icy-cold air into the room. I drop my tote on the corner chair and lay my wet things over the vent to dry before stripping off Dash's clothes and stepping into a hot shower. Once every square inch of me is thoroughly scrubbed, I dry off and slip on Dash's boxers and T-shirt, wrap a towel around my hair, and crawl across the bed to call G-Lo.

"Well . . . ?" She drags out the word. "How'd the trip go?"

"Really good." I leave out what happened in the parking garage. "We went to almost all the places you and Mom went."

"I'm glad."

"Me too." I crisscross my legs and pat the temporary swell of my stomach. "I ate too much—probably gained five pounds—but it was worth it."

"Did you get your picture?"

"I did. The old auditorium isn't there anymore, but Dash took some pictures of me in front of the new one. And at least twice as many around town." The weight of the day finally catches up to me, and I uncross my legs and lower my voice. "I felt her there with me."

"She was," she agrees. "I'm sure of it."

Letting her words wash over me, I scoot down and settle into the pillows. "I've decided to finish the trip once the car's fixed."

"Good." Her voice softens. "Life moves pretty quickly. You can't let a little thing like a broken radiator slow you down. And don't worry about the car. Everything's taken care of. You're good to go once they install the new parts."

"Dash said something today." I swallow the lump in my throat. "I finally get how important it is to finish what I started." Saying his name sparks a warm tingle that spreads from the center of my chest down my arms to the tips of my fingers.

"You like him."

The smile in her voice makes me wonder if she's been eavesdropping on my thoughts. I sit up and yank the wet towel from my hair, tossing it aside with a groan.

"Come on, now," she prods. "You aren't fooling me with your brooding silence."

"What difference does it make if I do?" I shake out my hair, sending microscopic water droplets everywhere. "He's taking me to get my stuff in the morning, then taking off to wherever. I'm never gonna see him again."

"You don't know that. With all the technology out there these days, there's no reason you can't stay in touch."

"He doesn't have social media. Even *you* have Facebook. He doesn't have *anything* on that stupid phone of his."

"I still have his number. I'll text it to you." She pauses and a moment later, my phone vibrates with an incoming message. "And don't forget, Cecil's busy digging up all his dirty little secrets."

"It doesn't matter. After tomorrow, I won't have any reason to talk to him again. Besides, I have a boyfriend, remember?"

"Right. Fabian."

"Damian." His name leaves a sour taste in my mouth. I flop back again, spreading my wet hair across the pillow. "Which reminds me, I need to call him. He's been blowing up my phone all afternoon."

"Okay, honey. You call Dominic."

"Damian."

"That's what I said." She chuckles. "I'll talk to you tomorrow. I love you, Zoey."

"Love you, too."

After we hang up, I pull up the pictures Dash took in Memphis. I look sad, sitting on the sidewalk with the silver spaceship behind me and total strangers walking by. I scroll through the images until I reach the selfies of us in front of Sun Studio and the Memphis Rock 'n' Soul Museum.

In every shot, Dash gazes down at me as if he wants to kiss me senseless. My stomach flutters. Damian has never once looked at me like that.

As if the thought summons him, Damian's face replaces Dash's on the screen, instantly sticking a pin in my good mood. Steeling myself against a wave of anxiety, I accept the call.

"Who drove you to Memphis?" he demands.

I recoil from his biting tone, unable to remember any of the reasons for staying together. Determined to defend Dash's honor, I stiffen my spine. "A nice guy I met at the diner. He was going that way anyway and asked if I wanted to tag along."

"A *guy*?" As expected, Damian lets out a string of colorful curses that would make even *Jeanie* blush. "You're taking rides from strangers now?"

"Yes." My stomach flutters as I think of said—*really hot*—stranger. "In fact, I'm doing *many* things you'd probably disagree with. I drank a drink I didn't pour. Sat on a dirty sidewalk and didn't wash my hands afterward. Spent the whole damn day hanging out with a guy I barely know."

A guy who actually seems to give a damn about what I'm going through, unlike the selfish prick on the other end of the line.

"And you know what? I had fun. For the first time since Mom got sick, I'm experiencing life for myself. And I like it."

"That's great. I'm happy for you." His lack of enthusiasm tells me otherwise, and I suddenly understand what Jeanie's been saying all along. "You've had your fun, now come home."

"I'm not coming back!" The words erupt in a rush as the pent-up anger I've been keeping in check for months—longer than that if I'm being honest—bubbles to the surface.

How freaking dare he order me around? And why the hell did I let him get away with treating me this way for so long? I sure as hell don't want to spend the next decade asking myself the same questions.

"We can still—" He chokes off his sentence. "What did you say?"

My breath hitches. "I said I'm not coming home. I'm finishing my trip."

"After everything that's happened, you're still finishing your damn trip? What happens if next time, instead of a possum in the road, the goddamn engine falls out? Or the tires blow?"

"For the last time, it was an armadillo, not a possum. And if the engine falls out, I'll get another one." Shrugging off his excuses like a wet blanket, I finally breathe for the first time in months.

"Zoey, you can't just 'get another one.' Engines are—"

"I don't care, Damian. Nothing you say will scare me into running home." My chest tightens as I realize I mean every word. "I won't be back until I've spread Mom's ashes in every one of the stops on that tour. I don't care how many auditoriums were torn down, or wallets I lose, or accidents I have, I'm finishing what I started."

"W-What about school?" he stammers. "Your mom's cancer was the reason you couldn't start two years ago, but now that she's gone . . ."

"She *just* died, you heartless asshole."

He lowers his voice. "And I'm sure you're really sad right now, but you're finally free to start living your own life. No more playing caregiver. Hell, if you're determined to spread her ashes first, come with me to the beach. There's a whole ocean at your disposal. She liked Rehoboth, didn't she?"

Damian's words rattle around my head like pennies in a can. "What is wrong with you? My mother *died*, and all you care about is what *you* think should happen next. You never asked what *I* want to do with my life! Maybe I don't want to go to Penn State. Maybe I don't want to go to college at all!" My voice creeps up another octave, and I draw in a deep breath before I inadvertently summon security to my room.

For two damn years, I've gone through the motions, desperate to keep my head above water while the tsunami washed over me. Staying with Damian was the easiest decision in a sea of impossible choices. I was lost and alone, and he was there. And for whatever reason, he wanted to be with me—maybe *because* I had no one else to cling to. Well, I don't need to cling to anyone anymore. I'm finally standing on my own two feet.

"I can't do this with you, Damian."

"Fine." He exhales in my ear. "Call me later."

"Listen very carefully." I speak slowly and clearly, so he fully comprehends this time. "We're done. Over."

"Are you seriously breaking up with me over the phone?"

The shock in his voice is almost comical, and I bite back a laugh.

"I should've done it a long time ago." Relief washes over me, chasing away the bitter taste of disappointment. "Have a great life, Damian."

"Come on, babe, I'm—"

I hit the end button, and the selfie Dash and I took under the giant guitar at Sun Studio smiles up at me from the screen. I drag the neck of his T-shirt to my nose and breathe in the lingering scent of fresh laundry detergent . . . and Dash. I have no idea what tomorrow will bring, but I'm ready for it, no matter what.

"Wow, you clean up nice." Dash's eyes light up as I slide in line behind him at the breakfast buffet. He focuses on my face, ignoring his Superman T-shirt and boxers hanging loosely from my slight frame.

I wish I could say the same for the rest of the breakfast crowd, openly eyeing me as I nervously tug the bottom of the shirt down my legs until it almost passes for a minidress.

I offer Dash a warm smile. "It's kind of amazing what a shower and a good night's sleep will do."

"You aren't kidding. I slept like the dead. That's the last time I stay up for two days straight." He piles his plate with scrambled eggs and bacon, then adds a biscuit and a scoop of fresh-cut fruit before taking his food to the table by the window. "You coming?"

I quickly fill my plate with a little of everything and join him, sliding my tote under the table by my feet. "I talked to my grandma last night."

"Yeah?" He unfolds a paper napkin and lays it across his lap. "So did I check out?"

My lips twitch. "I forgot to ask."

"Did you tell her about . . ." He lifts a brow and grins. "You know?"

I choke on a bite of dry toast, coughing until the whole room stares at me. "No. What she doesn't know won't get back to Jeanie. She'd never let me live that down."

Dash cocks his head to the side. "Jeanie?"

"My sister?"

"Oh, right." He shoves a piece of bacon between his lips, chewing and swallowing before finishing his thought. "You never said if she was older or younger."

"Older by two years."

"Ah." He nods like someone who's been tortured by an older sibling. "You'll definitely wanna take *that* story to the grave."

"Definitely." I slap a cold pat of butter on my toast and nearly tear the bread to shreds spreading it.

"So . . ." He takes a sip of coffee and waits for me to fill in the blanks.

"Oh!" I lick butter from my finger. "I told her I'm finishing the trip. I'll hang out here for a few days while they fix the car and then head for New York. So, I guess . . ." My mouth goes dry. The thought of saying goodbye sits like a brick in my belly. I know whatever we are has run its course, but I can't help feeling the loss.

Oblivious to the emotions brewing inside me, Dash chuckles. "A lot of shady characters in New York. You sure you're up for something like that without a bodyguard?"

"You mean a babysitter?" I roll my eyes and stuff a chunk of pineapple between my lips.

His smile curves up on one side, and he pins me with his stony gaze. "If the metaphor fits."

"I think I'll be fine. What about you?" The brick in my gut tumbles around like sneakers in a dryer, demolishing my appetite. "Where are you headed next?"

"Hmm. Haven't decided yet. Maybe east?" He shovels a forkful of powdered eggs into his mouth.

My hands tremble as I nibble on my shredded toast. "Who knows . . . maybe we'll run into each other on the road somewhere."

"Maybe." He nods, and his eyes glaze over for a quick moment. "Too bad you won't be in New York for the Fourth. Best fireworks in the country. My dad has a place there, so I've seen them firsthand."

I force a smile. "I hear Hicksville puts on a good show."

"No way." He laughs. "You can't even compare the two."

Resigned to my fate, I toss the crust onto my plate and slump into my chair. "Maybe someday."

"You know . . ." Dash takes another bite of his eggs, making me wait for the rest of his thought while he chews. "Since I'm heading east anyway . . . and New York *is* your next stop. And since your car won't be fixed until at least Tuesday, *if* they get the parts before then. Stuff gets lost in transit all the time."

Butterflies burst through my insides as I sit on the edge of my seat, waiting for him to get to the point. If he's thinking what I hope he's thinking, I'm ready to say yes. *Come on. Ask already!*

"You could maybe . . . tag along with me?" His eyes stay fixed on his plate, as if his offer is no big deal. "I've got room."

I snatch a strawberry from my plate and shove it between my lips to keep from squealing. "That's true. That car is ridiculously large for one person."

"So it's settled then." His lips curve into a dazzling grin as he lifts his gaze to mine. "Finish eating and we'll go get your stuff from Mack's. It's a long way to New York from here."

13

Moonage Daydream

Dash eyes me over his shoulder while stuffing at least one of everything from the hotel vending machine into his duffel bag. "Ready?"

I gape down at the assorted candy bars, bags of chips, and small packages of cream-filled cookies peeking out from inside, and snicker at his impressive snack haul. "Planning for the apocalypse?"

"Very funny. No hot Cheetos for you." He zips his bag, hauls it over his shoulder, and turns toward the closest exit.

Before I can formulate a witty reply, my phone rings. Without even looking, I know it's Damian . . . *again*. He's been blowing up my phone every hour on the hour since I ended things.

Dash stops in his tracks. "You need to get that?"

"Nope." I ignore the call, switch the phone to silent, and shove it deep into my pocket.

Damian can wait—until hell freezes over as far as I'm concerned. As much as I'd love to tell my ex exactly how relieved I am to be rid of him, that's a conversation I'd rather not have in front of Dash. He already has more than enough evidence of how messed up my life is.

Dash raises an eyebrow and locks his probing gaze on me, digging for answers I'm not prepared to give. "You sure?"

"Positive." Hiking my tote up my shoulder, I march to the exit and open the door. "You coming?"

Before hitting the highway, we swing by Mack's so I can reclaim my backpack and grab my pillow from the Betty. And for the first time in days, I change into a clean pair of denim shorts, and the faded pink FIGHT LIKE A GIRL cancer survivor T-shirt Mom wore until she'd basically accepted defeat. Then we hit the road.

On the long stretch of highway between Hicksville and Nashville, we pass a bright-yellow Volkswagen Beetle, and I punch Dash in the shoulder. "Punch buggy!"

"What the hell?" He gapes at me, shielding his arm from another attack. "What did I do?"

I burst out laughing at his horrified expression. "You've never played punch buggy?"

"No." He rubs his shoulder. "But it seems a bit . . . violent."

"Sorry." I swallow a giggle. "What road-trip games did you play when you were a kid?"

"My parents didn't really do the road trip thing. But if we had, I would've read a book." He eyes me as if he's afraid I might attack again. "Like a civilized person."

I roll my eyes. "Boring."

"Educational," he insists with another sideways glare.

"*Extra* boring." I laugh, but my heart aches for the little dark-haired boy I imagine sitting in the back of a fancy limo, a brand-new copy of *On the Road* in his lap, and a stern nanny by his side. "No license plate game? No I spy? No twenty questions?"

"No." His gaze darts my way. "But I'm up for a round of twenty questions if you're game."

"Only if you let me go first." I bounce in my seat, unable to hide my excitement.

He nods but keeps his eyes on the road.

I grin, thinking of his curious habit of scribbling secrets on napkins. "What are you always writing—"

"Pass." He tightens his grip on the wheel. "Pick something else."

Stunned by his lightning-quick refusal, I revisit the question he'd dodged at the diner. "Fine. What color crayon would you be?"

He snorts out a laugh. "What is it with you and crayons?"

I let out a frustrated sigh. "Supposedly, the color you choose directly correlates to the sort of person you are."

"Intriguing concept." He bobs his head a few times before turning the question back on me. "What color would *you* be?"

My withering look promises we'll be revisiting this subject later, but I let him off the hook . . . for now. "If you'd asked me a week ago, I probably would've chosen something sad . . . like gray."

"But today?" Dash turns his mesmerizing eyes on me, and I lose myself in their depths.

"I'm leaning toward sapphire . . . with a swirl of warm brown."

His brows draw together in a deep furrow. "What do those colors mean?"

"I-I don't know," I lie, as if I didn't just describe his eyes to a T. "So, uh, what's your favorite Bowie song?"

Dash presses a few buttons on the display, and "Golden Years" blasts through the speakers, effectively ending the conversation.

◆ ◆ ◆

June 29
I shoplifted today. Mom and I were trying on sunglasses in a Quiki-Mart about an hour outside Nashville, when she whispered, "Put those in your bag." At first, I thought she was kidding, then I saw her stuff a pair down her shirt. She distracted the guy behind the counter, flirting her butt off so I could pocket the pair in my hands. I've never been so scared in all my life. My hands shook so bad, I thought for sure the whole place knew what I was doing. But not a soul followed me as I walked out of there with

my butt cheeks clenched as tight as steel doors. My heart raced so fast, I thought I was having a heart attack. I still can't believe we didn't get caught. Best. Rush. Ever.

June 30
We climbed into the dumpster behind a bakery just after they closed, like a pair of dirty trash bandits, scavenging for bags filled with bread, little white boxes with assorted cookies and cupcakes, and probably a whole bunch of creepy crawlies. Thank God for the adrenaline rush, or I would've gained like fifteen pounds. I smell like spoiled custard, but it was totally worth it.

"Dumpster diving? Shoplifting?" I drop Mom's diary with a shuddering breath. I have no idea who this person is, but she's not the mom who danced around the kitchen singing old Bowie songs while flipping pancakes on Sunday mornings. I glare at the diary as if it has the power to destroy me. And maybe, in a million tiny ways I can't begin to understand, it does. For the first time since I discovered the damn thing existed, I wonder if Jeanie was right to keep it from me. Maybe I'm *not* ready. "I'm not sure I want to keep reading this thing."

"Why?" Dash's brows furrow as he glances at the journal in my lap. "What's wrong?"

How do I explain that I'm having a hard time reconciling Mom's memories with my own . . . that with every word I read, my perception of her changes, dredging up emotions I can't begin to understand. That I'm caught between this unquenchable desire to know everything about her past, and the fear of what I'll discover if I spend too much time looking. What if I somehow lose the mom I knew? How many of my memories am I willing to risk?

I lift my gaze to his. "What if I find something really . . . *bad*?"

"Zoey . . ." His eyes soften. "Whatever you find can't hurt you now. It's in—"

"Her past. I know, but . . ." My chest tightens as I struggle to find the words. "The rule-breaking girl who got drunk in Memphis and shoplifted a pair of sunglasses . . . I don't know her. The mom I knew was always so . . ."

"Boring?" he offers, using my own word against me.

"Serious," I say, choosing a more accurate description. "She was an assistant principal for god's sake. When she wasn't working, there was always some chore or school function that needed her attention."

"You never did anything fun?"

"We did," I assure him, as the memories come flooding back. "We went on vacations every summer. To the movies or bowling now and then. But her idea of getting wild was ordering pineapple on her pizza. She sure as hell never took us dumpster diving!"

"I get it." He nods. "Reading about her past is rocking your present."

"It really is." I release a jagged breath. "But if I stop reading now, I know I'll regret it for the rest of my life."

Dash offers a sympathetic smile. "You never mention your dad. Was he not around when you were growing up?"

"My parents got divorced when I was ten. It was just Mom, Jeanie, and me after that."

"Do you ever see him?"

My throat thickens, and I grab my pillow from the back seat. Hugging it to my chest like a shield, I stare out the window at the cows grazing in the distance. "He used to send cards—Christmases, birthdays, things like that. On the rare occasions he was in town, he'd take Jeanie and me to dinner. But other than the flowers he sent when Mom died, I haven't heard from him in two years. I guess he figured his responsibility ended with my high school graduation."

"What about your mom's funeral? Did he—"

"No." I shake my head, my eyes burning. "He sent a card saying he couldn't make it."

It wasn't even in his own handwriting.

"That's . . ." Dash frowns and faces the road, gripping the steering wheel until his knuckles whiten. "I'm sorry."

I blink a few times and force a smile. "What about your family? Are your parents still—"

"Together?" He laughs. "No. Dad's on wife number three. Mom never remarried. Once was more than enough for her. Plus, she'd lose that alimony if she did."

"Your dad must have a good job." I choke on an awkward laugh. "Sorry. That was kinda rude, but you said the car was a graduation gift—I assume from your dad."

He nods.

"A Model X isn't something you buy on a schoolteacher's salary."

He releases a slow breath. "He works in Washington."

"What about your mom?"

"She's a . . . *writer*." He doesn't seem sure of his word selection, but his eyes light up nevertheless. "That's what I'd like to do. My dad has *other* plans for me."

A chuckle escapes me. "Why don't you tell him no? You're an adult, he shouldn't really get a choice in the matter."

"It's complicated." He fiddles with the GPS. "Are you hungry? I'm starving."

And just like that, the conversation grinds to a halt as we search for the closest place to eat.

◆ ◆ ◆

"How can you hate 'China Girl'?" Dash pulls his eyes off the road to gape at me. "It's one of Bowie's greatest hits."

"You mean, besides the borderline racist undertones?"

He shakes his head and turns back to the deserted road. For close to fifty miles, it's been nothing but pastures and trees out every window.

"I don't think you can take anything he did at face value. I've read articles that said the song was a metaphor for exploitation, others claimed it was an allegory about drugs." He grows more animated as he lays out his argument. "I don't know what his true intentions were, but I *do* know Bowie spoke out against racism his whole career."

Ignoring his theories, I arch an eyebrow and glare at his profile. "That doesn't change the fact that I had to listen to it for more than four hours straight when it jammed in the 8-track."

Dash grins and breaks into a bad rendition of the chorus.

"Noooo . . ." I press my hands over my ears, trying not to laugh. "You can just shut *your* mouth. If I never hear that song again, it'll be too soon."

"Aw, come on, Zoey." He nudges my arm, giving me puppy dog eyes. "It's a classic."

A prickle of heat settles low in my stomach, and I look away, pretending his beautiful face didn't strike the match. "I heard even *he* didn't like playing it. There had to be a reason for that."

Dash snickers. "Maybe it got jammed in his 8-track."

My gaze snaps to the alert flashing across the car display.

Stay below 55 mph to reach your destination.

I straighten in my seat and point at the screen. "What does that mean?"

He blinks, as if trying to decide how to respond. "Battery's getting a little low. But we should be fine."

The red, glowing battery icon calls him a big fat liar.

"Five percent? You call that fine?" I take a deep breath and stare into the dense thicket lining the road on both sides. "How far are we from the next charging station?"

"Maybe twenty miles to the supercharger in Cookeville. But don't worry." He flashes a reassuring smile. "I've cut it closer than this."

As we crest the top of the hill, Dash's smile slips, and he curses under his breath.

The Tesla slows to a crawl as we approach a line of state police cruisers with lights flashing and an overturned tractor trailer blocking the road ahead. The trooper directing traffic from the middle of the road detours the line of vehicles off the highway.

Another alert pops up as we turn onto a rural road, following an old minivan and a newer pickup filled with trash bags.

I look up from the display and meet his gaze. "Are we going to make it?"

"We'll be okay," he mutters, as if trying to convince himself as much as me.

A mile or so down the road, the minivan turns onto a gravel drive, but Dash sticks with the pickup, following it up a winding hill for several more miles—and several more alerts.

The truck pulls into a church parking lot, then whips around and heads back the way we came. My stomach plummets. In the twenty minutes since we left the highway, we've passed three churches but not a single gas station, convenience store, or any other signs of civilization.

"Should we . . ." I gnaw on my bottom lip.

"It's too late to turn around." Dash points at a winding line on the navigation panel. "This road should circle back to the highway at some point."

My fingers drift to a loose string on my shorts. "If you say so."

We pass a small barn, where an old man loads a wire crate onto a rickety trailer hitched to a faded-green pickup. Several yards past that, with nothing but open road and rolling hills as far as the eye can see, Dash slows to a stop on the gravel shoulder.

I jerk my head around. Other than the old man with the green truck, the road is deserted. "What happened? Why are we stopping?"

Dash drops his head to the steering wheel with a dull thud and points at the battery icon.

The little red triangle winks, mocking me.

"It *died*?" My heart jumps into my throat. "But you said—"

"I know what I said." He bangs his forehead against the wheel. "I was wrong."

"You were *wrong*?" I gape at him. "Well, don't just sit there! *Do* something!"

"Do what?" He lifts his head and glares at me. "Give it CPR?"

I refuse to dignify his snarky comment with a response. Maybe he's content castigating himself all day, but I can't sit and do nothing.

I rifle through the clutter in my tote. "Jeanie's Triple A card is in here somewhere. A good jump should buy us a few more miles, right?"

"Triple A doesn't service Tesla batteries." He fixes his gaze on me. "But they could tow it to the supercharger." He grabs his phone from the console and flips it open, then stares at the tiny screen for the longest time.

"What?" I uncurl my fingers from my palms, itching to shake the answer out of him.

"No service," he croaks.

I check mine for a signal. Not only do I have no service, but my battery is almost dead. "Okay, so we go with plan B."

This is where he's supposed to come up with a brilliant, rich-college-graduate contingency plan. Where he reaches into his black bag of tricks and MacGyvers us out of our current situation, saving the day yet again. Right?

Wrong.

He throws his phone into the cup holder and drops his head to the wheel again, defeated. "I didn't think I'd *need* a plan B."

This is bad. Armadillo-in-the-radiator bad. But sitting here staring at the dead battery icon on my phone won't solve anything.

With a loud huff, I shove Mom's diary into my tote, unbuckle my seat belt, and throw open the door.

Dash jerks his head up, gaping at me. "Where are you going?"

"Unlike you, I'm actually going to *do* something." I climb out of the car, ignoring the stench of manure wafting through the air. "One of us has to."

"Zoey, wait!"

Tuning him out, I march toward the man in the green truck. Dash catches up to me halfway there, skidding to a stop in a cloud of dust.

"Oh, so *now* you want to rescue me." I cross my arms. "Hate to break it to you, buddy, but you're not actually Superman." I jab a finger into his chest. "And I don't need to be rescued."

He flinches. "I wasn't trying to rescue you, I . . ." He glances toward the old man and lowers his voice. "Were you really planning on leaving without me?"

Was I?

I frown, unwilling to consider the idea. "You're here now, so come on."

Dash and I walk the rest of the way together. The farmer has his back to us, fiddling with the chicken cages in his rickety trailer when we approach.

I clear my throat. "Excuse me, sir?"

The man lifts his gray head, his gaze alternating between Dash and me. "Y'all need something?"

"Actually, yes." I release a relieved breath. "Our—well *his*—car broke down, and we'd—"

Dash steps in front of me. "We really just need to call a tow truck."

I dial up my smile and elbow Dash out of my way. "But a ride to town would be great, if you're going that way."

14

Life on Mars?

"A ride to town would be great . . ." Dash grumbles, shoving a rusty chicken cage out of his way.

A giant white feather pokes out of his hair, and I resist the urge to pluck it.

"Oh, no . . . we don't mind sitting in the back with the chickens." He mimics my voice with annoying precision.

I scoot as far from him as I can get in the jam-packed truck bed but can't seem to dislodge his elbow from my ribs. "A ride is a ride."

The dirty white chickens in the cage beside him beat their wings against the bars, sending another batch of feathers into the air. A second one finds a home in his dark waves.

Dash pins me with a glare. "A ride is definitely *not* just a ride."

"You should be thanking me." I awkwardly cross my arms in the tight space, my left butt cheek going numb against the hard steel.

"Thanking you?" His mouth falls open. "For wedging me into the back of a truck filled with poultry and hay?"

I jut out my chin. "For rescuing you from your dead battery."

Dash laughs, and the menacing sound sends a ripple of heat through me.

"Sure," he says. "I'll thank you. If we actually make it to town instead of hanging from meat hooks in Leatherface's barn."

I suck in a breath and instantly regret it as the pungent aroma of fresh chicken poop coats the inside of my throat. Desperate for fresh air, I turn toward the scenery whipping by and get slapped across the face with my own tangled, windblown hair. Another day, another bad decision. I shift my weight again, wriggling sideways and sandwiching my bag between us like a cushion.

Dash loops a hand through the straps, preventing the contents from flying free. To his credit, he never questioned my decision to bring my tote with Mom's diary and ashes with us.

The truck jumps over a pothole, and one of the unsecured chicken cages hurtles toward me. Acting purely on instinct, I kick the side so hard it catapults the rusty thing skyward. The cage somersaults through the air before slamming into the truck bed, breaking the latch. The door flies open, and all three skittish chickens escape, wings flapping wildly in the air. Then the empty crate tumbles over the edge of the tailgate, where it gets wedged beneath the trailer's wheels. The rickety trailer lurches to the left before flipping upside down in the road, scattering the remaining chicken cages and releasing dozens of angry birds in a great big chicken jailbreak.

A cloud of dust and feathers trails the green pickup as it pulls away from the shoulder without us.

Dash stares at the taillights until they disappear into the horizon, then turns to me with his eyes narrowed into slits. He studies me until my skin prickles under his intense scrutiny.

Mouth too dry to form words, I shrug. What else is there to say? We're no worse off than we were before accepting a ride. No harm, no . . . *fowl?*

As if reading my thoughts, he exhales hard enough to dislodge a dirty feather from his hair. "You"—he jabs a finger toward me—"are a magnet for disaster."

"Me?" My mouth drops open. "What did *I* do?"

"You want a list?" Shaking his head, Dash stomps off in the opposite direction.

"Where are you going?" I chase after him, kicking up dust and feathers in my wake.

He picks up his pace. "Back to the car."

"We're stranded in the middle of nowhere." I release a bitter laugh. "Were you planning to fly there, *Superman*?"

Dash whips around, and the hurt in his eyes makes me wish I could take back every word. He opens and closes his mouth several times before speaking. "You think you're the first person to make that joke?"

I swallow the lump in my throat.

"You're not." He turns, putting a few more feet between us before turning back. "It's bad enough when my family—you know what? Forget it. It doesn't matter." With another loud exhale, he storms off again.

"It matters to me!" Guilt washes over me as I hurry after him. "Dash. Wait!"

He stops on the side of the road, as motionless as an ice sculpture. "What?"

"I . . ." I step toward him, an apology forming on my lips. Then I remember whose fault it is that we're stuck out here. "I forgive you for letting the battery die."

A dark chuckle crawls up his throat as he slowly turns toward me. "You *forgive* me?"

"I-I do." His menacing grin sends prickles of heat down my spine, and I step back.

Finger extended toward me, he stalks forward, his smile feral. *"You . . ."* He takes another step, head cocked to the side. "Forgive . . ." He pokes that same finger into his chest. *"Me?"*

God help me, I should not be this turned on right now, but I am. "Th-That's what I said." I lift my chin.

"This . . ." Dash rakes a hand through his hair, dislodging another chicken feather. It catches the breeze and floats away. "Is all *your* fault."

"M-My fault?" My muscles tighten, my insides coiling into a snarled knot. "*I'm* not the one who ignored the low battery warnings for God knows how long and got us stranded in the middle of nowhere!"

Dash nods stiffly, then turns on his heel and continues in the direction we left the car.

After following him for miles down the desolate country road, my resolve withers and blows away like those stinking chicken feathers. My feet ache from the sandbox forming in the soles of my Skechers. I'd kill for one of those Memphis sweet teas right about now. Every few minutes, thunder rumbles in the distance, and ominous dark clouds roll in. I can't shake the threat of impending doom.

A rainstorm would be the perfect end to a perfectly shitty day.

A banged-up blue hatchback rattles past us, blasting old-school hip-hop from its open windows. Just before it crests the next hill, it stops and reverses, backing onto the shoulder a few yards from us.

The driver pokes his blond head out the window and flashes a gap-toothed smile, reminding me of a grinning jack-o'-lantern. His lips move, but I can't hear him over the music. After repeating himself a second time, he ducks his head in and cuts the radio. My ears buzz in the sudden silence.

"Y'all need help?" With his close-cropped hair and wire-rimmed glasses, he looks like a redneck version of Reverend Tom.

Despite our long stretch of stony silence, Dash reaches for my hand, clinging to me as we cautiously approach the car.

"Funny you should ask," Dash says. "We, uh—"

"Whoa, dude . . ." The guy zeroes in on Dash's mismatched irises. "What happened to your eyes?"

Dash's grip tightens, and he pulls me behind him. "I was born with them."

"Spooky." The guy shudders. "So how'd y'all end up way out here?"

"Like I was saying," Dash continues with cool restraint. "We broke down a few miles from here."

Redneck Reverend Tom chuckles. "Ain't that a bitch? Guessin' you need a ride then?"

Dash turns to me, concern etched on his gorgeous face, and my racing heart stops cold before sputtering to life again.

"Your call," Dash says, brushing a lock of hair from my face.

Instead of acting on the overwhelming urge to kiss him, I slide my gaze to the crappy old Chevy, every bone in my body rejecting the notion of climbing into the rolling death trap. "I don't—"

A loud clap of thunder silences me seconds before the sky opens up, pelting us with fat raindrops.

Dash lets out a heavy breath. "We'd love a ride to town."

"Well, all right! Hop in. I'm Paul, but everyone calls me Itchy." As if demonstrating why, he drags his nails down his neck, leaving a trail of red stripes on his pale skin.

"I'm Dash, this is Zoey." Dash pulls the seat forward and helps me climb into the back before folding his long legs into the front with my tote.

"Y'all ain't from around here," Itchy muses.

Dash laughs. "Just passing through."

"Figured as much." Itchy bobs his head a few times, sliding his gaze toward Dash as he pulls onto the pavement. "Hope y'all don't mind, I need to make a quick stop."

Dash straightens his spine and goes rigid in the seat in front of me.

My pulse jumps as Leatherface's barn pops into my head, reminding me why hitchhiking landed in the top three on Jeanie's *What Not to Do* list.

Dash shoots me a nervous glance. "Sure. Why not?"

A few miles down the road, Itchy takes a sharp right onto a narrow side street. With my stomach in my throat, the little hatchback bumps and shimmies around the winding road until loose gravel replaces rough pavement and we pull into a sketchy trailer park.

Rows of ancient mobile homes line either side of the narrow drive. The little car creeps along, passing several crumbling walkways, at least two rusted-out cars on concrete blocks, and a sad, abandoned tricycle. The steady rain has turned potholes into swimming pools, and I keep waiting for one of them to swallow the hatchback whole.

At the end of the first block, Itchy parks along the curb in front of a shiny white Jeep Wrangler and leaves the engine running. He reaches behind his seat and grabs a red pizza delivery bag before hopping out.

"Be right back." He holds the vinyl pouch over his head like an umbrella and jogs up the driveway, but instead of going in through the front door, he disappears around the side.

Using a stray napkin from the floorboards, I wipe steam from the window and scope out the trailer. It doesn't look much different from the others on the street. The moldy white siding could use some attention, but someone took time to mow and pull weeds from the sparse flower beds.

"That bag didn't have a pizza in it, did it?" I ask.

Dash snorts as he pokes through the clutter in the center console. "No."

"Didn't think so. Maybe he's dropping off insulin to his sick grandmother, or . . ." My voice hitches up an octave. "Picking up Girl Scout cookies?"

He glares out the window. "If I were to hazard a guess, I'd say drugs. Either picking up or dropping off."

My pulse skyrockets. "I was afraid you'd say that. What are we going to do?"

He leans toward me, his warm breath washing over my lips. "Sit quietly, wait for Itchy to come back, and hope like hell he takes us to town."

I nod, swallowing the lump in my throat. What's the worst thing that could happen?

Other than the occasional dog barking and the angry wail of a baby in the distance, the neighborhood is deathly quiet. Then the deep, throaty growl of a motorcycle cuts through the silence. One motorcycle becomes two, and two becomes three. The roar grows louder and louder, making the windows in the little hatchback vibrate as a chrome army thunders toward us, engines snarling as they fan out in attack formation.

Dressed in collar-to-boot leather, with a massive beard almost as long as his flowing sandy-brown locks, and tattoos marking nearly every visible patch of skin, the clear leader of the pack climbs off his bike, his eyes alert as he approaches the trailer.

Oblivious to us sitting in the car, five similarly dressed men and one woman follow him through the front door. Almost instantly, angry shouting reverberates from inside the house.

"Zoey." The panic in Dash's voice pulls my attention from the trailer. "We need to get out of here."

"What? Why?"

"Have you seen *Breaking Bad*?" Dash pulls the passenger door handle, and it flies open. He jumps out and holds the seat forward so I can crawl out of the back.

My mind goes blank. "Is that the one with the Kardashians?"

"I'm gonna pretend you didn't—" Dash's whole body goes rigid as the shouting turns into a series of loud bangs. "Get out. Now!"

His terrified expression sends a jolt of panic rocketing through me. But instead of bolting from the car, I scramble over the gearshift into the driver's seat. Dash isn't the only one capable of being a superhero.

He leaps back into the passenger seat. "What are you doing?"

"Getting us out of here." *This is it, Zoey, your chance to show the world you're a total badass.*

My hands tremble and my pulse hammers in my ears as I grab the knob and put the car in drive. But instead of sliding in smoothly, the shifter fights me, and the gears rattle and grind. I yank my hand back and jerk my gaze to Dash.

"The clutch." Dash motions toward the floorboards. "You have to press the clutch."

I gape down at the three pedals between my feet. "Why are there—" As soon as the words pass my lips, dread washes over me. "I-I can't drive a stick shift!" I recoil from the wheel and tuck my hands against my chest. Why didn't I let Jeanie teach me when she offered?

"Yes, you can," Dash takes my right hand, places it on the gearshift, and holds it in place with his. "Use your left foot and push the first pedal to the floor." The moment the pedal touches the floor, he guides my hand, shifting the car into gear. "That's it. Now slowly ease off the clutch and press the gas at the same time."

The little car jerks forward, then just as quickly coughs and shudders before stalling.

"Damn it!"

"It's okay," he murmurs as if soothing a frightened puppy. "Try again."

With Dash quietly encouraging me, I follow his instructions again, this time jumping away from the curb and straight into a massive pothole.

"No!" I slam the steering wheel with both hands. "Not again."

With the front right tire buried deep in the hole, and at least one rear wheel spinning uselessly in the air, the little hatchback kicks up mud like confetti before stalling again.

"Let's go," Dash orders.

Vigorously nodding, I grab my tote and climb out. We barely clear the back bumper before Itchy comes flying out the front door with three members of the motorcycle gang on his heels.

"My car!" He clutches his head in both hands.

"You won't need it where you're going." The leader's thunderous voice freezes Itchy in place.

Rain soaks my hair and runs down my face as I flick my gaze between the biker and Itchy, too paralyzed with fear to flee.

Itchy raises his hands and turns. "Come on, John, cut a guy a break."

"You knew what would happen if you got caught peddlin' your shit in my town." The leader, John, pulls out a set of zip ties. "On your knees. Hands behind your back."

"Are you guys undercover cops?" The words fly past my lips before I can recall them. I slap both hands over my mouth.

The biker winks. "More like the neighborhood watch."

"Oh!"

A large hand clamps over Itchy's mouth, muffling his screams as two bikers drag him into the trailer.

Taking advantage of the distraction, Dash grabs my wrist, his eyes wild as he drags me behind the Chevy. "Do you have a death wish?"

"I can't help it! When I'm nervous, every thought in my head comes tumbling—" A siren wails in the distance, commanding my attention. "We need to get out of here."

"How?" Dash raises his eyebrows. "You broke the car."

I can't think of a single comeback. Maybe he's right. Maybe I am a magnet for disaster. But if my mom could dumpster dive and shoplift in broad daylight, I can sure as hell outrun a few out-of-shape bikers. I grab his hand and squeeze. "We run."

"Solid plan." Dash pulls me behind him. "Come on."

We sprint toward the snarled shrubs at the edge of the next yard, but John and the dark-haired woman catch up to us before we get past the wall of greenery.

"Where the hell do you think you're going?" the biker bellows.

"Please don't kill us," I whimper, licking rain from my lips and wishing I'd kissed Dash when I had the chance.

John looks down his long nose at me. "Do I look like a killer to you?" When I don't respond, he exhales a heavy breath. "We're just cleaning up the drugs in our town."

"That's good. Drugs are . . . they're . . . my grandma smokes a lot of pot." I shake off Dash's hands as he tries to pull me behind him again. *I've got this.* "That's why we're here. I was supposed to be spreading my mom's ashes with my grandma, but my sister fell off the roof, and I crashed into an armadillo, and then I met Dash, but his car died. Then we lost our ride. I swear I didn't mean to set the man's chickens free. And I definitely didn't know Itchy was a . . . a freaking drug dealer! Did you . . . is he . . . ? No. Don't tell me. I don't think I wanna know."

John bursts out laughing, putting an end to my word vomit. "Sounds like you've had a shitty day."

"You have no idea. This one—" Dash exhales a nervous laugh and glances at me. "Magnet for disaster."

My mouth drops open.

"What's this about your car dying?" John asks.

Dash blows out a breath. "My Tesla's battery died a few miles past the Baptist church."

John nods and then walks over to one of the motorcycles in the driveway and throws a leg over. "We'll give y'all a ride and send a tow truck."

I gape at Dash. "He's kidding, right?"

"I'm dead serious." John winks and pats the seat behind him. "Now, hop on."

"Shouldn't we have helmets?" I dart my gaze between the two bikers. I can only imagine what Jeanie would say right now.

John cocks an eyebrow, and Mom's voice pops into my head. *Just think, Zoey. This'll make for a great entry in your own diary.*

"Fine." I groan and throw a shaky leg over, then settle into the soft leather.

John cranks the bike to life, and the vibrations rattle my bones.

He turns to the woman. "You ready, Kitty?"

"Sure am." She blows him a kiss and climbs on her own bike, swiveling her head toward Dash. "You got a red *S* under that fancy shirt of yours?"

"No." Dash flinches and turns a bright red. "No letters under my shirt."

"He *does* have Superman under—" I start, but Dash's glare stops me cold.

John chuckles. "Not even gonna ask."

Kitty waves Dash over. "Come on. Don't keep me waiting, pretty boy."

With his face twisted into a sour frown, Dash climbs on behind her.

"Hold on tight!" John shouts. "And keep yer mouth shut or you'll be pickin' bugs from your teeth all night."

With my tote wedged between my front and John's back, I barely get my arms around him before his bike jumps forward over the loose pavement. We rocket down the highway, my hair flying behind me like a cape.

Less than five minutes later, we reach Dash's abandoned Tesla—right where we left it, like the bright-red cherry on our shit sundae.

15

China Girl

July 1

They say Virginia is for lovers. And I think I love Virginia. We stopped in Blacksburg today. Mom said she was tired of driving, but I think she secretly wanted to scope out the hot guys strolling around the Virginia Tech campus. Despite being right in the middle of summer break, it was still pretty packed with the college crowd. Everyone seemed to be gearing up for the 4th. We had a picnic on the lawn and met some nice people. At least one cute guy. Okay, several cute guys. As usual, Mom hogged them all. A few of the guys convinced us to stick around for a karaoke contest at Sammy's Pub. Not that she needed much convincing. All it took was the promise of free booze and lots of free-flowing attention, and Mom was sold. After drinking way too many shots, and flashing her boobs to the crowd, she dragged me onstage to sing. Bowie, of course. As wild as she acted, I totally expected to get kicked out, but nope. We won! The contest had to have been rigged. Sammy himself took our picture. He said our fifteen minutes of fame will be forever immortalized on the bar wall. Ha! Imagine that. Not like anyone I know will ever see it . . .

"We have to go to Sammy's Pub in Blacksburg, Virginia!" I snap Mom's diary shut and hug it, holding my breath until my head swims. I *must* find that undiscovered piece of her, left behind like breadcrumbs in a forest.

The corner of Dash's mouth tips into a smirk as he navigates us back to the highway, leaving the Cookeville Supercharger in the rearview mirror. "Change your mind about getting drunk?"

"No." I roll my eyes. "Mom's picture is on the wall."

Dash's smile slips, and I know what he's thinking. *What if they took it down?*

"Thirty years is a long time." His eyes soften. "Are you sure the bar is still in business?"

"No." My heart sinks. I never even considered that the *bar* might not be there.

A quick search for Sammy's Pub returns dozens of images of historic Blacksburg, and I scroll through the quaint brick buildings and tree-lined streets until I land on a fairly recent picture of the Sammy's marquee.

I skim the online description. "One of the oldest pubs in town . . . Hugely popular with the college crowd. And . . ." My pulse skips as I skim down until I find what I'm looking for. "The original wall of fame has grown to include all four walls!"

Relief sweeps through me, and I sink into the seat. Her picture *has* to be there.

"I'm afraid to ask how your mom ended up on the wall of fame," Dash says, his sexy smirk firmly in place.

I flash my teeth. "It may or may not have involved my granma's boobs."

He shudders, and a laugh bursts out of me.

"Sammy's has karaoke every Friday and Saturday night. Mom and G-Lo won a contest." I gaze out the window, trying to imagine Mom singing for a crowd. When I was a kid, she barely sang in the shower. "I wonder what they sang."

"'China Girl'?"

I groan. "*Anything* but that."

"Come on." He turns his dazzling smile on me. "It's a great song. I think you secretly love it."

Warmth flutters through my belly, and I tear my gaze from his face, focusing on the road outside to keep from climbing over the center console. Forget the damned song. The urge to kiss him is driving me insane.

I've never been the sort of girl who makes the first move, but if he doesn't make one soon, I may have to reevaluate that position.

The line of people in front of Sammy's stretches halfway down the block, and after almost an hour waiting with what appears to be half the Virginia Tech student body, our progress has slowed to a crawl. One by one, the streetlights come on, drawing every bug in Virginia. At this rate, the place will be closed by the time we reach the door.

"Stop fidgeting." Dash pries my fingers from a rip in my jeans.

I tear my gaze from the small group of people behind us, passing a silver flask back and forth.

"What if they don't let me in?" I whisper. Even if I had my stolen wallet and ID—both of which are probably sitting at the bottom of a dumpster somewhere in Cleveland—I'd still be three months too young to get in.

"Relax." His hand slips into mine. "Stay behind me."

The warmth of his palm seeps beneath my skin, and I nod, open to whatever it takes to get inside.

We finally reach the front of the line, and Dash lures the doorman aside, slipping something into his hand. They exchange a few words before the man grins and waves us through.

Hidden behind the quaint brick facade, Sammy's Pub is half sports museum and half pop-culture explosion, with a side of spring break at the beach. The place reeks of stale beer, furniture polish, and sweat. And nearly every square inch is packed wall-to-wall with people.

A swarm of twentysomethings, stacked three bodies deep, crowds the long mahogany bar running almost the full length of the front wall, and every high-top table perched on the worn wooden floorboards is standing room only. In the far corner, under the blue-and-red Sammy's marquee, a small crowd forms around the tiny stage, where a group of guys belts an off-key rendition of "Friends in Low Places."

Dash leans in and shouts over the music. "I'll look for a table."

With a quick nod, I set out to find Mom's picture.

Starting from just below my waist and reaching several feet above my head, a patchwork of assorted sports jerseys, trivia cheat sheets, and glossy black-and-white photos cover the weathered brick walls. The daunting task of searching the entire pub would take me days, maybe longer. If only I knew where to start.

I flag down a passing waitress. "Where can I find the original wall of fame?"

She points toward the back of the building. "There."

With a shiver of anticipation, I weave my way through the crowd, passing a row of arcade games, an empty table, and a stack of unused chairs on my way to the photo gallery wall.

I gaze up at the messy quilt of framed eight-by-tens. Each one is dated at the bottom, with a photo from 1996 sandwiched between one from 1989 and another from 2001. The odds of finding Mom in this mess are slim, but I have to try.

Working my way from one side of the wall to the other, I scan at least two decades' worth of pictures, each one so similar, my eyes cross. Hundreds of photos, hundreds of smiling faces, all posed under the same SAMMY's sign behind the stage. With no apparent pattern to their placement, the black-and-white images begin to blur, and my last shred of hope slips away.

Did we come here for nothing? Did her picture even make it to the wall all those years ago?

On the other side of the pub, another pair of singers stumbles their way through a classic party anthem, and it hits me. Mom and G-Lo were here, and whether I find their photo or not, their memories are part of this place. Just being here means I'm part of this place, too. With one last glance at the wall, I walk away.

I find Dash at a high-top table directly in front of the stage, jotting something down on a napkin. As soon as I sit beside him, he tucks the napkin into his pocket and slides a menu in front of me.

"If you want something, we should order now. Kitchen closes at eleven," he says.

"I'm not hungry." My stomach growls.

He lifts a brow. "Really?"

I shrug.

His lips turn down at the corners, and he sets the menu aside, his gaze focused on me. "You didn't find it."

I blow out a breath and shake my head.

"I'm sorry."

"Don't be." I force a smile. "I knew it was a long shot."

"Do you . . ." He glances at the stage as a young brunette steps up to the mic. "Do you want to leave?"

"I don't know." I focus on the singer. She doesn't look old enough to be here, and I wonder if she used a fake ID, or if someone slipped a few twenties to the bouncer to get her through the door. The mic trembles in her hand as she sings along to an old Britney Spears track. Her nervous excitement strikes a chord in me, and I imagine Mom standing on that same stage thirty years ago, stitching herself into the fabric of this place.

Butterflies flutter through my stomach, and I grab Dash's arm with both hands. "We have to sing."

"Oh, no!" He pries himself free with a nervous chuckle. "I'm not getting up there. You go right ahead, though."

"Please?" Alternating my gaze between his blue and brown irises, I coil my fingers around his wrist.

He swallows, his pulse racing beneath my fingertips.

"It'll be fun," I promise. "I'll even let you pick the song."

His lips curve into a diabolical grin. "Anything I want?"

"Sure." I release a shaky laugh. "As long as it's something I've actually heard of."

"Oh, you've definitely heard of the song I have in mind." He leaps from his chair and bounds to the DJ booth. "Just remember this was *your* idea."

For someone who hated the idea when I suggested it, Dash can barely contain his excitement when the DJ calls our names.

The song title flashes across the monitor, and I suck in a breath. "Dash, no!"

"You said I could pick." His grin turns sinful as he drags me to the stage and thrusts a mic in my hand.

"I know I did, but . . ." My stomach bottoms out. "Pick something else. *Anything* else."

I groan as the opening guitar riff of "China Girl" plays and the lyrics roll onto the screen.

Too late now.

Heat flares low in my belly as Dash rakes his smoldering gaze over me and sings the first line. His soft lips wrap around every syllable, his rumbling voice caressing me to the depths of my soul. Every off-key note slips through my crumbling defenses. What the hell is he doing to me? By the time he reaches the end of the first verse, I'm ready to kiss the hell out of him. And I'm certain one kiss won't be nearly enough.

"Come on, Zoey," he purrs. "Sing with me."

My stomach swoops, and the hungry gleam in his eyes turns my bones to jelly. Swallowing the lump in my throat, I join him on the second verse, giving it all I have. For one frozen moment in time, the whole room falls away, and it's just the two of us on that stage, singing our hearts out to one another.

And then I blink, and the moment is over, leaving me a trembling, blissed-out, needy mess as we return our mics to the DJ.

Dash throws a sweaty arm over my shoulders, leading me back to our table.

I open my mouth to tell him how much fun I had, but he presses a finger to my lips.

"Shhh." His pulse thrums against my skin for the longest moment before his gaze darts to my eyes. "Don't spoil the moment."

We stand there, in the middle of the crowded pub, for what seems like hours, and then he pulls his hand away with a lazy grin. "Told you it's a great song."

"It is." I catch my breath and glance around the room one last time. Singing a Bowie song—possibly even the same song Mom and G-Lo sang all those years ago—gives me the closure I need. "We can go now."

Dash dips his head, meeting my gaze. "You sure?"

"Why spoil the moment, right?"

Chuckling, he whips out a wad of bills and leaves it on the table. "Why, indeed."

As we reach the exit, the gritty guitar intro to "Rebel Rebel" blares through the speakers, and the hair on the back of my neck stands on end.

"Dash, wait." I grab his arm like a life preserver. "Before we go, I need to check one more time."

He slips his fingers through mine and squeezes. "I'll help you look."

We weave our way through the thinning crowd toward the back wall, where I start my search from the opposite side, working backward from where I searched before. One at a time, I run my gaze over every picture. Then, as if Ziggy Stardust himself has guided me to this very spot, the image of someone who resembles a young version of G-Lo catches my attention. Beside her is a young woman who looks almost exactly like . . . *me.*

Dash was right. I do look like Mom.

"There!" He points, finding the picture at the same moment I do. "Is that her? You could almost be twins."

Tears blur my vision as I gape up at my mom.

She looks so young, grinning at the camera with one arm around G-Lo's waist and a mic in her hand . . . so *happy*.

I dig out my phone and snap a few photos of the wall, zooming in on the picture of Mom and G-Lo for Jeanie. The angles are off, preventing me from getting a clear shot. If *Jeanie* were here, she'd climb onto a table, snatch that picture from the wall, and take it home. But Jeanie isn't here. I am.

Dash brushes a lock of hair from my face. "What's wrong?"

A spike of adrenaline kick-starts my heart, and I dart my gaze between Mom's picture and Dash's face. "Give me a boost?"

His answering grin sends a completely different sort of rush through my veins. Dragging an empty pub table against the wall, he glances over his shoulders before extending a hand to help me climb up. "You're turning into a regular Lois Lane."

"Don't make me laugh while I'm standing on a table." Rising onto my toes, I lengthen my limbs and reach as far as I can until my bones cry out in agony. Wrapping my fingers around the plastic frame, I pull it from the wall and pass it to Dash. "Take this."

He frees the photo from its frame and tucks it under his shirt, then offers his free hand to help me down. "Come on, Lois. Let's get out of here before someone catches us."

16

Young Americans

"Oh my God!" With a high-pitched squeal, I tip my face skyward, stretch my arms wide, and spin under the streetlight until my head swims. "I can't believe I did that!"

Dash grabs my hand and darts his gaze over his shoulder as he tows me toward the car. "We need to get out of here. Someone might've seen us take that photo."

"Noooo! I wanna celebrate." Riding my endorphin high, I lock my muscles and bring us both to a stop in the middle of the road. "I don't ever want this feeling to end!"

Dash tugs my hand, but I tug back, pulling hard enough to knock him off balance. He crashes into me, and I mold my palms to his chest.

His lips part, and he gazes down at me, dazed and out of breath. "What feeling?"

Up close, I can see the flecks of gold in his brown iris. I lick my lips, and his pupils dilate.

"This one." I brush a strand of hair from his forehead.

His next breath catches in his throat, and he steps closer, his nose brushing mine. "What does it feel like?"

"Dash . . ." My pulse skitters.

Coming to Blacksburg was supposed to be about my mom, but standing under the glow of the streetlight with Dash's eyes focused on my lips, all I want is for him to kiss me.

He dips his head, bringing his mouth close enough I can almost taste his lips. My mind blanks as every rational thought evaporates like morning dew in the midday sun. Instinct takes over, and I close my eyes and part my lips. My internal voice goes deathly silent while I wait for his mouth to collide with mine.

With less than half a millimeter separating us, he groans and steps back. "We need to go."

My eyes snap open, my emotions shuffling through confusion, grief, and anger in the time it takes to catch my breath. "Did . . . did I?"

"I'm sorry." He shakes his head as he walks off. "I can't."

With a frustrated whimper, I set off after him. "Dash, wait!"

"We need to get back on the road." He picks up his pace. "The Holiday Inn in Lexington has a supercharger. We can top off the battery while we sleep. I don't know about you, but I'm so exhausted I can't think straight."

"Did I do something wrong?" I catch up to him on the sidewalk.

"Of course not." Refusing to look at me, he frowns and wipes a bead of sweat from his forehead. "It's getting late, that's all. If we're gonna make it to New York in time for the fireworks tomorrow, we need to get going. *You* might be able to stay awake all night, but *I* need sleep every now and then."

"I could . . ." I release a breath, and the words tumble out. "I could drive. To Lexington. So you can sleep for a little while."

"I don't think so." Dash laughs darkly, his mask of cool disinterest firmly in place. "I've seen you drive."

"Hey!" I reach for him.

He darts away, and I stomp my foot on the cracked concrete like a toddler.

"Don't judge me based on what happened with that shitty Chevy! I'm usually a really good driver."

He pivots, flashing a cold grin as he walks backward down the sidewalk. "Tell that to the armadillo."

His barb stops me in my tracks, and I scramble for a witty comeback. "You . . . you can't blame me for the armadillo suicide rate in Tennessee!"

He shrugs and turns toward the Tesla, reaching the car in a few long strides, forcing me to jog to catch up. "I don't want to sound like a dick, but you know how much this car is worth. I trust the autopilot more than I trust you."

The brutal insult catches me off guard, and I flinch.

He unlocks the car and hands me Mom's photo. "Get in."

Stunned silent, I stare at him, unmoving and growing angrier by the second. What the hell just happened?

Dash leans out of the car, glaring at me from behind his stupid black-framed glasses. "Are you coming?"

A dozen snarky comebacks swim through my head, but none of them float to the surface. Every one of them makes me sound desperate and immature, so I swallow them down and climb in. And to think, I wanted to kiss this guy. Well, I won't make that mistake again. Screw him and his sinfully beautiful face.

I stew in my seat, wondering how the hell I'd misread his signals.

Dash lets out a loud sigh. "Don't be mad."

"Oh, I'm not mad," I snap, already plotting my revenge. "Why would I be mad? I'm just peachy. Didn't really want to drive anyway. Looking forward to catching up on my sleep." I grab my pillow from the back seat and punch it a few times.

"Yeah." He chuckles. "You don't sound mad at all."

"Because I'm not." I wedge the pillow between my head and my shoulder, then lean against the doorframe. "Now, would you please be quiet so I can fall asleep?"

"You got it." Dash switches on the radio and lowers the volume to a low buzz.

◆ ◆ ◆

"One day you'll meet the perfect boy, Zoey, and you'll fall in love." Mom dries my tears, brushes my hair back from my face, and presses a soft kiss to my forehead. "And you won't even remember the boy who broke your heart in second grade, or any of the reasons why you liked him in the first place. Because that new boy will be everything you didn't even know you wanted."

A door slams, startling me awake, and I blink against the orange glow of morning. With the sun barely clear of the horizon, the inside of the car is already as hot as a pizza oven—and, apparently, I'm the pizza. I lift my head from my sweaty pillow, sending pins and needles through my arm as blood rushes from my shoulder to my fingertips. My muscles scream as I unlock the tension gripping them in place. Even my jaw somehow glued itself shut as if I slept with a mouth full of honey . . . and woke up to the taste of old gym socks.

"Dash?" A quick peek at the empty driver's seat answers my question.

For a guy who didn't trust me behind the wheel of his car, he sure didn't mind locking me inside like an abandoned shih tzu. He could've at least cracked a window for me.

Outside, an older man connects his black Tesla to the supercharger. Across the parking lot, several people exit the Holiday Inn Express. I guess we arrived in Lexington while I slept. If I only knew where my infuriating travel partner disappeared to.

Afraid I'll set off his fancy car alarm if I open the door for air, I dig for my phone to text him instead. I get as far as the lock screen before discovering dozens of missed calls, most of them from Damian. Hell isn't nearly cold enough for me to call *him* back, so I scroll through the rest of the list. G-Lo's name pops up several times, along with several texts from both her and Jeanie, and at least one missed FaceTime request. With Dash who-knows-where doing who-knows-what, I decide to check in with my grandmother while I have the chance.

"Thank goodness you're alive." She doesn't sound nearly as concerned as she'd have me believe. "Jeanie was about to call the FBI."

"I could've used a little FBI intervention, or at least the local sheriff, in Cookeville yesterday. Between the pissed-off farmer, the drug dealer, and the motorcycle gang—" G-Lo cackles into my ear, so I hold the phone at a distance until her laughter dies down. "I'm glad you're amused. I almost died three times!"

"Don't pout. I knew you were fine. Jeanie traced your phone to Blacksburg last night."

"Jeanie what?" I gasp.

"She said she added your phone to her friend searcher app before you left. To be safe."

I'm too impressed to be angry.

"Modern technology." G-Lo snorts. "So, Blacksburg?"

I drop my gaze to my lap and pick at the loose thread on my jeans. "We stopped at Sammy's."

"Did you find it?"

I glance down at the photo peeking out of my tote. "I did."

The line goes quiet for so long I check the connection.

"We had such a good time that night," she whispers. "Your mom surprised me. I had no idea she could sing."

"I wish they'd taken a video instead of a picture."

"Me, too, honey. Me, too."

I bite back a grin, my pulse racing from the memory. "We stole it."

"The picture?"

"Dash helped me climb onto a table and . . ." Giddy excitement washes over me all over again. "I can't believe I did that."

"It sounds like you're having a wonderful adventure."

"I am. I even kinda-sorta learned to drive a stick shift, not that I'll be trying *that* again anytime soon. But . . ." I choke back a sob as the desperate desire to hear Mom's voice washes over me.

"Zoey, what's wrong?" G-Lo asks.

"I just . . ." The last thing I want is to ask my grandmother for advice about guys, but it's either her or Jeanie, and I'd sooner die than ask my sister. "I think I really screwed up last night."

"By stealing a picture? Oh, honey, I've done far worse—"

"No. Not that. I thought . . ." I touch my lips, the impression left by Dash's finger still seared in my memory, the taste of his hot breath still lingering. "I was so sure he was going to kiss me, but at the last second, he pulled away and got . . . mad? We both said some pretty harsh words, and we . . . we haven't spoken since." I let out a slow breath, resting my head against the glass. "I have no idea what I did wrong. Maybe it's for the best. We're from completely different worlds. But God, I really wanted him to kiss me."

"Is he . . . ?" She trails off.

"Gay? No. I already grilled him on the way to Memphis. Unless he's lying, he's straight. And he certainly *seemed* interested." My thoughts drift back to our almost kiss, and heat floods my cheeks. "Until he wasn't. And now . . ." I can't help wondering if peeing my pants repulsed him. Damian sure as hell would've been.

"What did he say when you told him you dumped the douche canoe?"

A bead of sweat slides down my temple, and I wipe it with the back of my hand. "I-I didn't."

Her breath hitches. "You didn't tell him?"

"No." I squeeze my eyes shut and slump into my seat. "I didn't want him to think . . . it doesn't matter now."

"Maybe *that's* why he didn't kiss you."

"You're right." I blow out a breath. I may not know much about Dash Hammond, but I'm pretty sure he's not the kind of guy who would steal another guy's girlfriend. "I'm so stupid."

"What are you waiting for?"

I scrub a hand down my sweaty face. "If I tell him now, he'll think it's because he didn't kiss me."

"Isn't it, though?" G-Lo laughs. "Give him a little credit. He may be relieved to find out you're unattached."

"But what if he's not?"

"Not what?"

"Relieved? Interested?" I glance at Dash's worn copy of *On the Road* and groan. "Why would a college graduate, who drives a damn Tesla and reads Kerouac for *fun*, be interested in a small-town girl with nothing but a high school diploma and zero life experience?"

"Why would he agree to drive you halfway across the country if he wasn't at least intrigued?"

"I don't know." My attention drifts as I search the distance for a familiar face. "Maybe you're right."

"You know, your mother had a steamy little romance the summer we took our trip."

My jaw drops. "She did?"

"Didn't you read her diary?"

"I haven't made it that far. I'm sort of reading along based on where she wrote each entry. So I can feel like I'm right there with her."

"Oh, honey." G-Lo clears her throat. "Why don't you skip ahead a little? Maybe it'll give you some fresh ideas. Follow her lead. Drag that boy into a tent for some—"

Dash peers through the driver's side window, and I jump.

"Gotta go! Call you when we get to New York." I end the call before she can finish her thought.

"Boyfriend?" Dash climbs in with a drink carrier and two white paper bags. His messy hair is even more disheveled than normal after spending the night in the car.

I shake my head. "My G-Lo."

He nods, his smoldering gaze drifting to my lips.

My mouth goes dry, and I swallow reflexively, squirming under his scrutiny. What a confusing creature he is. "W-What's in the bags?"

My question breaks the spell, my lips seemingly forgotten as Dash's eyes light up. He places the bags between us, last night's anger melting in the morning sun. "I got doughnuts. I wasn't sure which kind you like, so I got one of everything."

"Wow. Thank you." Once again, his thoughtfulness catches me off guard.

His head bobs, his cheeks flushing crimson. "And coffee. I figured we both needed a healthy dose of caffeine."

"Oh, thank God!"

Grinning, he hands me my cup.

I bring the coffee to my lips and release a groan as I inhale the fragrant steam.

"I added exactly three sugars and one and a half creamers," he says.

Pausing mid sip, I raise my eyes and lock my gaze on his. "How'd you know?"

Dash smirks. "I've spent the better part of three days with you. I think I know how you like your coffee by now."

An uncomfortable tightness grips my chest, and tears prick my eyes. "Damian would never . . ."

Confirming my earlier suspicions, he scowls and shifts his attention to the world outside his window. The man is too honorable to put the moves on someone he thinks is spoken for. I bet he'd never skip his girlfriend's mom's funeral, either. He's Damian's polar opposite. Just one more reason to like him.

Dash moves into my peripheral vision, and my quick intake of breath catches his attention.

"It's just coffee, Zoey." He fidgets with one of the white bags, his face turning even redder as he hands it to me.

"And doughnuts," I remind him.

My gaze drifts to his lips as I contemplate taking G-Lo's advice. Now would be the perfect time to tell him I broke up with Damian.

"Hey, Dash?"

He lowers his coffee and meets my gaze. "Yes?"

The confession rests on the tip of my tongue for several seconds, but instead of coming clean, I panic. As badly as I want to kiss him, I can't right now. I haven't brushed my teeth since yesterday. "Uh, thanks for breakfast."

"You're welcome." A deep furrow settles between his brows, as if he's trying to read my mind. "You okay?"

"Fine. Great. Starving." I reach into the bag and pull out the first doughnut my fingers touch—a cream-filled, chocolate-frosted delicacy—and sink my teeth in with a groan.

17

Drive-in Saturday

"I can *not* pee in there." I shudder, still clenching my toothbrush and toothpaste. "That place is practically a crime scene."

"Seriously?" Dash lifts a brow. "What's wrong with *this* one?"

I glare at the innocent-looking convenience store just beyond the front bumper as the horrifying, Jackson Pollock–esque images stitch themselves into the intricate quilt of my memories, where I'm certain they'll fester for all eternity. "Trust me, you don't wanna know."

Exhaling an exasperated breath, Dash backs out of the space and heads toward the highway. "You should've gone before we—"

"I didn't *need* to go in Lexington." *Oh, what a lying liar I am.* But it'll be a cold day in hell before I admit he's right. I cross my legs, squeezing my knees together. Did he seriously expect me to waltz into a hotel, without a reservation, and ask to use their bathroom?

"I know you're a camel—it's almost impressive how long you can hold it—but this is getting ridiculous. Promise me I'm not gonna have another princess and the pee situation on my hands. Because I'm running out of clean underwear."

I skewer him with a glare.

"Don't give me that look." One corner of his mouth tips up. "I'm only watching out for my leather seats."

I roll my eyes. "Find me a clean bathroom, please?"

"You've got it, princess." Dash hits the gas, heading east toward the next exit. He chews the inside of his cheek before speaking. "You know what you need?"

I still my bouncing legs and turn toward him. "No, but I suspect you're about to tell me."

"A GoGirl."

"A go-what?"

"It's a . . ." Flushing pink, Dash rakes a hand through his messy hair. "A funnel."

"What kind of *funnel*?"

"The kind you—"

"Stop!" I point at a store up ahead, everything but my nagging bladder forgotten. "Let's try this one!"

"The Quiki-Mart?"

"It looks clean. *Cleaner*, at least."

"If you say so." With a loud sigh, he pulls in and parks. "Third time's the charm, right?"

"A girl can hope." I hop out and bolt for the back of the store.

The restroom isn't the nicest place I've ever peed, but it's a huge step up from the last few places we stopped. After doing my business, I break out the toothbrush and toothpaste. Hopefully, fresh breath will be the good omen I need for the rest of the day.

◆ ◆ ◆

July 3
New York. The Big Apple. The city that doesn't sleep. I've never seen buildings so tall. The streets are still packed at eleven at night. In a shocking turn of events, Mom seems to know her way around the city. Our first night here, she dragged me to CBGB to see Sonic Youth, where she flashed her boobs . . . again, and we wrote our names

on the bathroom wall in permanent marker. Mom said adding our names to decades of graffiti would make us part of something bigger than both of us. We'd be immortalized for all eternity. I'm not sure I'm cool with being immortalized on a bathroom wall for all eternity, but if Mom's happy, I guess it's worth it. The next day, after getting lost in Chinatown for over an hour, my erratic mom dragged me to the building where my alleged father lives and almost got us arrested for stalking. After the doorman chased us away, we headed into Central Park and carved my name in a tree directly across the street. Took us forever because Mom wanted it to be perfect. We had to climb the tree first, so my name would "stand out above the rest." She said he might not realize it, but every time he looks out his window, he'll see me there. Once I got over the creepiness of the whole thing, I decided it was really sort of sweet. Could she be telling the truth after all? Wouldn't that be wild?

With her words still fresh in my mind, I pluck Mom's photo from the diary. I barely recognize her with her blond hair curled and teased like a *Cosmopolitan* cover model. She'd posed on the sidewalk in front of a grungy redbrick building. And her black T-shirt bore the same four bold-red letters as the ones printed across the white awning above her.

"What the hell is CBGB?" I mutter under my breath. Using the picture as a bookmark, I snap the diary shut and turn to Dash behind the wheel. "Is that some New York hashtag thing?"

"Are you serious?" He does a double take, and his eyebrows nearly reach his hairline. "Holy shit, you are. I can't believe you've never . . ." He huffs out a quiet laugh. "It's only the birthplace of punk rock!"

"Then we definitely need to go there . . . and Central Park."

"Central Park is no problem." He releases a breath. "Unfortunately, CBGB is closed."

"When do they open?" I tuck the diary into my tote.

His smile dissolves. "I mean, closed down. As in not there anymore."

"They tore it down?" The words rip from my throat. Not again. Not another piece of Mom's history, erased.

"The *building's* still there, but they converted it into a John Varvatos store." He rakes a hand through his hair. "We can go there if you want to get some pictures under the awning."

"Does it still say CBGB?"

Eyes darting to mine, he shakes his head.

"That's . . ." *Fan-freaking-tastic.* I fold my arms across my chest and stare into traffic.

"I'm sorry, Zoey."

I feel his gaze burrowing under my skin. "It's fine."

"You're a horrible liar." He coils his fingers around my wrist and pries my hand free. "Talk to me."

"I'm fine, really. We can skip it." I release a shaky breath and turn toward him, ignoring the pricking behind my eyes. "I've never even heard of John *Whoever*, so what's the point of going to his store?"

"Varvatos." He says the name again, enunciating every syllable. "Men's clothing designer. High-end stuff for a younger crowd."

"Like I said . . ." My throat constricts, and I swallow before it completely closes. "Why should I give a damn about his store?"

Dash's eyes soften, and he slips his fingers through mine, stroking the back of my hand with his thumb as if he can tell I'm barely holding on . . . that I'm a single breath from breaking. "What happened at CBGB? On your mom's trip—what made it memorable?"

The pricking behind my eyes becomes a steady burn, but the constant pressure of his thumb steadies me. "She wrote her name on the wall."

And now those walls are . . . ? Gone? Painted over? Little more than decades of blurry photos boxed up in someone's damp basement?

I stare out the window as if the clouds hold the answers. "But I'm not gonna find Mom's name written on the wall in some fancy New York boutique, so we may as well skip it."

He squeezes my hand. "Don't get your hopes up, but I think they left the walls intact."

"Seriously?" My soul tingles back to life, and I tear my gaze from the sky. "Because that would be *amazing*. We definitely need to check it out."

He offers a warm smile. "I'll take you wherever you wanna go."

"Jersey drivers are assholes." Dash tightens his grip on the wheel until his knuckles whiten.

For the past hour, he's barely taken his eyes from the road. A sea of glowing taillights snakes into the darkness as far as the eye can see, like miles of flickering red Christmas lights against the velvet backdrop of twilight.

"Guess we shouldn't have stopped in Washington," I mutter.

He glares at me out of the corner of his eye, his jaw ticking like a bomb, counting down the seconds before mass destruction.

"Point taken." I blow out a breath. So maybe it was my idea to stop, but I really wanted to drive past the White House. How was I supposed to know we'd have to park and walk the rest of the way?

The traffic slows to a standstill, boxing in the shiny red Tesla in a scene straight out of an apocalyptic disaster movie. So many lanes of traffic. So many cars.

"Do you think we'll make it to New York in time for fireworks?" I chew my bottom lip raw.

"It'll be close." He clears the current map from the display. "But I know a shortcut."

A shortcut the GPS apparently isn't aware of.

Taking advantage of a break in the traffic, Dash changes lanes, cutting off a black Lexus and earning a few rude gestures. He takes the next exit, winding around a series of ramps that remind me of a big bowl of spaghetti, then hops onto another section of highway, where we find ourselves in another bumper-to-bumper slowdown.

Every time I think we're in the clear, we hit another wall of traffic. Our quick shortcut turns into another hour of one exit after another, followed by several random side streets, roadblocks, and U-turns. The longer we spend in New Jersey traffic, the more agitated Dash becomes.

Darting his gaze to the clock, he exits the highway and cuts through a residential area before coming to an abrupt stop at a traffic light. We missed the green by a heartbeat.

Dash slams both hands against the steering wheel. "Damn it!"

"What's wrong?"

He rests his head on his knuckles. "We're on the wrong side of the Hudson River. On a holiday. We'll never make it through the tunnel in time."

The car behind us honks, and Dash lifts his head to glare into the rearview mirror before continuing forward.

I take a deep breath, hiding my disappointment behind a smile. "It's okay."

"No, it's not." His eyes soften as they dart to me. "I promised you fireworks. You're getting fireworks."

He takes the next turn, weaving around another series of side streets, toward downtown Jersey City. With every spot in the lot already taken, we park illegally on a strip of grass along the sidewalk.

"Ready?" He gets out and holds my door open.

I glance at the No Parking sign in front of the car. "Won't you get a ticket?"

He shrugs, his gaze meeting mine as if to say, *You're worth it.*

"Come on." He takes my hand, tugging me forward. "The view's better down there."

We pass several food carts, and my mouth waters at the tantalizing aroma of charred meat and spicy chili. Dash stops and buys a funnel cake, and then we cut through the crowd along the riverfront walkway to a vacant patch of grass facing the water. Dash sits, motioning me to join him, and we devour the funnel cake as if we haven't eaten in days.

Across the river, the glittering New York skyline captures my full attention. The water shimmers like glass, reflecting the lighted buildings and making the whole sky glow. "It's amazing."

"Especially at night," he agrees.

As if to punctuate his sentence, the sky sizzles with bursts of red and blue, and ribbons of glittering ash swirl toward earth, winking out before reaching the water.

"You were right." I glide a hand through the cool grass between us, inching toward him as if he has me hooked at the end of a line, reeling me in like a fish. "This is worth every minute of traffic and every nasty bathroom along the way."

Drawn by the same unseen force, Dash meets me in the middle, his fingertips barely grazing mine before he snatches his hand back.

Undeterred, I drag my eyes to his stunning profile . . . his perfect lips.

He shudders, as if he feels the heat of my gaze caressing his skin. "Being this close to you is absolute torture."

Heat engulfs my face, and I freeze, willing my muscles to move—*to flee*—before humiliation crushes me. "I'm sorry."

"Zoey, wait." Dash's hand closes over mine, holding me still. "That's not what I—" He releases a ragged breath. "It's taking every bit of self-control to keep from kissing you."

My heart flutters. "Self-control is highly overrated."

"Zoey . . ." He groans, and his trembling hand cups my face.

Prickles of warmth spread through my belly.

Another burst of color explodes across the sky with a series of pops and crackles, scenting the air with sulfur and smoke, but Dash locks his gaze on mine as he glides his thumb over my cheekbone . . . and the swell of my bottom lip.

His touch sets me on fire, and a needy sound breaks out of me.

He drops his hand, cursing under his breath. "I'm sorry. I can't."

"Why?" Blood races through my veins as I drag out the word.

He tears his gaze from me and scrubs a hand down his face. "You have a *boyfriend*."

The grip on my lungs loosens, and I release a breath. "Had," I whisper. "I *had* a boyfriend."

"Had?" Dash raises his eyebrows. "As in past tense?"

"I broke up with him after we got back from Memphis." G-Lo's words rattle around in my brain, urging me to make the first move, but my limbs won't cooperate. "Did I tell you he blew off my mom's funeral?"

"Dick move." His mouth curves into a sly smile as he gravitates toward me and cups my jaw in his warm palm.

The sky explodes with color again, but the spectacular pyrotechnics are no match for the sparks flying between us. The whole damn world could burn down around us, and I wouldn't notice.

He tilts up my face, and our gazes collide.

"What are you waiting for?" My breath stills, and my pulse quickens.

He drops his gaze to my lips and his eyes darken, sending my stomach into a free fall.

"Just kiss me already."

"I thought you'd never ask." He dips his head and presses his warm lips to mine.

Our mouths fit together like missing puzzle pieces, and my heart explodes at the first touch. Achingly slow and soft, each featherlight brush of his lips is like gasoline to a flame, sending a ripple of need racing through me and liquefying my insides.

I curl my fingers in the front of his shirt, drawing him closer and clinging to him like a raft in the middle of the ocean. He tastes of powdered sugar and sweet pastry, and I can't get enough of him.

The sound of his groan vibrates through me until I feel it everywhere at once.

Stars explode behind my lids as he angles my face for better access, parting my lips with his velvet tongue and kissing me as if the whole world really were coming down around us. As if nothing and nobody else matters but his hot mouth against mine.

Flushed and out of breath, Dash breaks the kiss and falls back against the soft grass, bringing me with him. "I've wanted to do that since Memphis."

18

Oh! You Pretty Things

With the last bang still reverberating through the air and the last plume of smoke still dissipating in the night sky, we say our goodbyes to New Jersey.

As we wander back to the car, Dash takes every opportunity to touch me—from stealing kisses under the moonlight to hooking his pinkie with mine and resting his chin on my shoulder while we gaze at the city lights. And every touch makes my heart soar and my pulse race.

Just before midnight, with the Tesla's battery dipping into the red, Dash pulls into the circular drive of a towering yellow-brick building. A small army dressed in crisp tan-and-black uniforms scurries between the line of expensive cars and shiny carts stacked with designer luggage.

"This is it." Dash unbuckles his seatbelt and climbs out of the car.

He walks around to my side and opens my door, then waits patiently for me to join him on the sidewalk.

Like Jack standing at the bottom of the beanstalk, I gaze up at the ornate facade jutting into the sky, and my insides curl into a ball. "You live in a hotel?"

Dash takes my tote and slings it over his shoulder as if he's done it a hundred times before. "I don't live here, my dad does. When he's in the city, anyway. And the upper floors are apartments."

"Will, uh, anyone be home?" Heat blooms across my cheeks. A sleepover in the front seat of his Tesla is one thing. A sleepover in his father's fancy New York apartment is something else entirely.

"Shouldn't be." He takes my hand and squeezes. "As far as I know, Dad's in Washington, which means his wife is with him . . . or in Paris, shopping."

"Paris?"

"She's . . ." He trails off as he turns to whisper a few words to the valet. "Let's not talk about her."

The uniformed man scurries to the back of the car, unloads our bags from the trunk, and places them on a shiny brass luggage rack. As he darts toward the building with our luggage, another man hops into Dash's seat and drives off with the Tesla.

I follow the taillights until they disappear into the night. "You sure we didn't just get carjacked?"

He laughs. "I'm sure. We'll get it back in the morning. Fully charged."

Suddenly self-conscious, I tug the bottom of my shirt, wishing I was wearing something a little less rumpled and sweaty.

"Come on." A slow grin spreads across his face as he tows me into the building.

The sweet fragrance of lemon and fresh flowers hits me the moment I step across the threshold. Giant arrangements of seasonal blooms and bowls of ripe lemons adorn a mahogany table—the first of several lining the walls and anchoring each matching pair of red velvet sofas. I keep waiting for someone to stop me and tell me I don't belong, but no one seems to notice the embarrassingly underdressed couple crossing the soaring lobby.

Dash leads me into a mirrored elevator and slips a key into the panel. He presses the button for the top floor and clings to my hand while we ascend. The doors open to the most spectacular view I've ever seen. Framed by floor-to-ceiling glass, and lit up like a shiny Christmas tree, the New York City skyline takes my breath away.

The view draws me in until my nose hovers a hairbreadth from the glass.

"Dash, you're rich." My heart sinks as I gape down at the Matchbox cars lining the street below.

We really don't live in the same world.

"Not me." His fingers circle my wrist, and he tows me away from the window. "My dad."

"Yeah, but your dad is, like, *uber* rich. That makes you rich adjacent." I gaze up at him.

His smile falters. "Please don't make this a thing between us. It really isn't a big deal."

"Not a big deal? Have you seen this place?" A sharp twinge stabs my heart, and I press my fingers to the spot. "And let's not forget that ridiculously expensive car of yours. Did you happen to see what I was driving? And that armadillo-murdering monstrosity isn't even mine. My piece-of-shit car wouldn't have made it to the Tennessee state line. I'd probably be stranded somewhere between Cleveland and Nashville with my entire electrical system shorted out."

Dash loops an arm around my shoulders and presses his lips to my temple.

"I don't even know who you are."

Would he have even given me a second glance if we'd met under different circumstances?

He wraps his other arm around me, tucking my head under his chin. "I'm the same guy you met in that shitty diner in Tennessee. The cars, the money, the fancy apartments . . . none of that is who I am."

I melt into him, burying my face in his chest. "My family isn't rich. And I'm not convinced most of them are even sane. My grandmother swears she gave birth to David Bowie's love child. And my mother clearly believed her if she made me promise to spread her ashes along that *specific* tour path."

Dash sucks in a sharp breath, and his arms tighten around me.

"And I'm just as crazy as the rest of them—thinking I could survive a cross-country road trip all by myself. God, what would we even talk about in the real world?"

"Trust me." He exhales slowly, pressing his lips to the top of my head. "I'd much rather talk with your family than mine. I do everything in my power to stay out of their orbit whenever humanly possible."

I nod, desperate to believe him.

"It's late," he says. "We should go to bed."

"Bed?" I stiffen in his arms like a schoolgirl.

Dash lets out a nervous laugh. "I'm certain there are more than enough beds to go around, if . . ."

Swallowing a groan, I lift my face to his. "If it's all the same to you, I-I'd rather sleep wherever you're sleeping."

He flashes a crooked grin. "As long as you promise not to take advantage of me."

"It won't be easy, but I'll try to control myself."

◆ ◆ ◆

"Who do you think she is?"

"Definitely Goldilocks. Look at her hair."

"Don't be ridiculous. Goldilocks doesn't wear Superman underwear."

"You don't know that. Maybe she does."

Hushed voices filter into my consciousness, dragging me from a magnificent dream where I'm floating through the air on a marshmallow cloud. *Am I still dreaming?*

The voices go silent, and I snuggle into the comfortable bedding again. I could float here forever.

"Should we poke her and see?"

I open one eye to discover Dash gone and two identical cherub faces leaning over me, the sun forming a halo behind them. Like tiny mirror images of each other, they wear matching floral tops, purple shorts, and the same dark ponytails punctuated with a lilac ribbon tied at the bottom of each one.

"She's awake," the little girl on the left whispers, her navy eyes stretching wide.

The other girl lets out a squeak, her mouth dropping open in a little pink bow. They smell like ripe berries, fresh from the vine.

With her blue eyes locked on me, the first girl elbows the second and whispers out of the corner of her mouth. "Should we get Tonya?"

A woman wearing a plain blue skirt and a crisp white blouse pops her head into the room. A severe bun pulls her auburn hair back from her face, making her look almost angry.

"What are you girls doing in your brother's—oh!" She flinches as her gaze lands on me. "I didn't—do I know you?"

"Uh . . ." I tug the zillion-thread-count white sheet to my chin. "D-Dash—"

"I should've known." She rolls her eyes, clearly judging me. "Come on, girls. It would appear as though your brother's home."

I want to tell her we didn't . . . it wasn't like that. Despite the overwhelming desire to rip his clothes off and have my way with him, we just slept. Nothing more.

But I don't dare say a word.

The girls squeal, jumping up and down beside the plush bed.

"She must be our present," one of the girls sings.

Do the disgustingly wealthy really give *people* as presents? If so, I should probably make a run for it while I still can.

"No." The woman grins. "She is *not* your present."

"She's mine." Dash wanders into the room, all rumpled and sexy in his gray flannel sleep pants and wrinkled white tee.

"Aww, Dash," both girls chime simultaneously. "But you always bring us presents!"

"Not this time, munchkins. I didn't even know you'd be here. Now, scram. Both of you."

Dash sweeps a hand through the air and clears everyone from the room before closing the door behind him with a quiet snick. With his glasses crooked across the bridge of his nose, he climbs into the bed and crawls toward me with a sleepy smile. "Sorry about that. I had to make a phone call. Did you sleep well?" He plants a sweet kiss on my lips before collapsing into the massive stack of downy pillows.

"I did." I giggle. "Almost too well. I forgot where I was."

For the first time since waking, I scope out my surroundings. Other than the massive windows framing Manhattan, the room is devoid of decoration. Nothing that would indicate Dash's presence. The stark white walls, crisp white bedding, and light-washed wood floors all blend together, but with a view that goes on for miles, it's still the nicest room I've ever stayed in.

Dash rests his head on my shoulder. "Sorry about the twins."

"Your sisters?"

"Yeah. I didn't realize Tonya and the girls would be here."

"Tonya? Your stepmom?"

He snorts. "The nanny."

"Oh."

"Could've been worse," he mumbles.

I wonder what he means by that, but let it go. "Should we leave?"

"We don't need to rush. We can take our time, have breakfast." Dash tugs me toward him and buries his face in my hair. "Shower."

I choke out a laugh. "Are you telling me I stink?"

"No." He chuckles. "I like how you smell. But we've been cooped up in the car for over twenty-four hours. I figured you might want to clean up."

"Yes, please. That would be great."

With another quick kiss, Dash hops out of bed. "I'll go scrape together something to eat while you grab a shower. The en suite is completely stocked, but if you need anything special—a clean pair of Superman boxers, maybe—let me know."

"I'm good." My cheeks burn. "I'm not actually a princess, you know."

His face lights up as he backs toward the door. "Sure you are."

◆ ◆ ◆

After taking the world's longest hot shower, I grab my bags and wander through the penthouse, dodging the tiny socialites and their uptight nanny as I search for Dash.

His angry voice carries through the cavernous space, and I follow the sound to a stark white kitchen.

Dash glares at his phone as he paces in front of the floor-to-ceiling window like a cornered animal, then presses it to his ear again. "You don't have to remind me. I know what I said!"

His icy tone freezes me in the doorway.

"No, I'm not—" He stops and rakes a hand through his hair. "Because I made a *promise*. You do remember what those are, don't you?"

Flinching at his tone, I melt into the shadows—unsettled, yet thoroughly transfixed by his anger.

"I told you I needed time to—" He huffs, growing more agitated with each passing second. "Well, I don't have to decide *today*!"

Afraid he'll catch me spying if I stay hidden, I step forward and clear my throat.

He spins toward me, his eyes widening as they meet mine. "Dad, I need to go. I'll call you later." He disconnects the call and shoves his phone deep in his pocket. "How long have you been standing there?"

"Not long," I say, hoping he doesn't see the lie in my eyes.

But he avoids my gaze and nods, as if constructing an invisible wall between us. "You, uh, ready to go?"

"Yeah. Sure." I force a smile. "Should I bring my stuff, or will we be—"

"Bring it." He stares out the window, his expression haunted. "I'd rather not have an excuse to come back."

"Dash . . ." Swallowing the questions clogging my throat, I take a step toward him. "Is something wrong?"

His head snaps up. "What? No. Everything's great." He blows out a breath and gives me a tight smile. "Great might be an exaggeration, but I'll be fine . . . as soon as we're out of here."

"Then let's go."

He reaches for my hand. "Ready when you are."

19

Rebel Rebel

"So this is CBGB?"

A floor-to-ceiling display of vintage record albums lines the front wall of the dark, moody space, greeting me as I walk in. Queen, Blondie, Lou Reed—and of course, David Bowie—among many others. Between the stacks of old records, concert posters, graffitied walls, and a mini stage decked out for a concert, I don't know where to look first. I definitely get the punk rock graveyard vibe. The whole place is a shrine to dead musicians. All that's missing is the stench of liquor and smoke.

My mom wrote her name somewhere in this room.

"No." Dash smirks and leads me through the store like a tour guide. "This is John Varvatos. They supposedly left most of the walls the way they were when the place was still CBGB but scrubbed away decades of filth and sticky floors."

The sandalwood notes of an expensive cologne waft through the air as I shift my tote to my other shoulder and gaze up at Dash. "This place is seriously cool."

He nods, admiring a vintage guitar behind glass.

"Even the clothes have attitude." I run my fingers over a rack of crisp shirts and pluck out a bluish-gray short-sleeved button-down from the bunch. "This one reminds me of you."

His cheeks flush. "I may have one similar to that."

"Hmm." Keeping Dash in sight, I tuck the shirt back where I found it and move to the next display. A table covered in rows of jeans draws me in, and I hold up a dark-washed pair. "And these?"

"Possibly." He chuckles, as if he's not wearing an almost identical pair.

My preoccupation with Dash's clothes temporarily satisfied, I shift my attention to the graffitied walls, tracing the different names with my finger, hoping to find even a hint of Mom. So much history. And yet, so much of it is buried behind racks of clothes or covered by framed photos, concert tickets, and other assorted memorabilia.

Tempted to pick at the old stickers to uncover what's hidden beneath, a wave of disappointment washes through me. "I could spend an entire day sifting through every inch of this place and still never find what I'm looking for."

Dash slips his fingers through mine and squeezes.

"It really is amazing, though." My heart clenches as I glance at the man folding shirts in the back. "But I seriously doubt they'd be cool with me tossing a handful of ashes into the air."

"Probably not." Dash smiles. "But we can get some pictures?"

Grinning, I hand him my phone. "So many pictures."

Dash plays photographer while I dance around the room like a kid in a toy store, posing in front of as many relics as I can without getting kicked out. I pick up a red guitar and pretend to play, then grab a stack of records and hold them up like Willy Wonka's golden ticket. I pretend to write my name on a heavy section of graffiti, making animated faces while Dash clicks away.

"Come with me." Dash drags me outside and snaps a few pictures of me under the black John Varvatos awning, in the same spot Mom posed when the awning was white with the CBGB logo.

Afterward, we take a few selfies of the two of us—my head on his shoulder, his lips on my cheek, and one of us kissing—before saying goodbye to the ghosts of CBGB and heading to Central Park.

◆ ◆ ◆

"She could've been a little more specific about which tree she wrote her name on." Even with the intoxicating aroma of fresh-cut grass and sunshine soaking into my pores, I stare into the vast park with an overwhelming sense of defeat.

For all I know, Mom's tree was turned into firewood decades ago, but I'm not about to let that stop me. "How will I ever find it?"

"Let's think about this logically." Dash scans the surrounding trees, then points to the high-rise looming behind us. "You said your grandma wanted your mom's name to be visible from those windows."

"Yes."

"Well, there's a finite number of trees directly facing that building, and anything big enough to climb thirty years ago would be even taller now, so we can rule out all the small trees." Dash's enthusiasm is contagious. He seems almost as invested in finding Mom's name as I am.

"So we should focus on big trees." I gaze into the lush green canopy overhead.

"As far as I can tell, we have three options." He ambles toward the smallest of the three and rests his hand against the trunk. "Let's start with this one. Just make it quick and don't draw too much attention to yourself. It's illegal to climb the trees in the park."

I laugh but his stiff expression doesn't crack. "You're not kidding?"

"No."

My stomach clenches as I set my tote against the base of the tree. I haven't been tree climbing since I was twelve, but if it means finding even a tiny bit of Mom, I'm all in. "That's a stupid rule."

"True." Dash nods, and his lips twitch. "But stupid or not, with your luck, we'll get arrested."

"Awesome." I place my hands against the trunk. "That's just *super*."

Dash rolls his eyes, but his smile tells me he wouldn't trade this moment for anything. "And I thought we were done with the superhero jokes."

"We're definitely not."

"I still can't believe Bowie was your grandfather," he whispers.

"Allegedly." I check over my shoulder before shoving a foot into the crotch of the tree. "And for the record, I don't buy it."

The fear of getting caught ignites a fire in my veins, and I shimmy up the trunk until I reach the lowest branch, then haul myself the rest of the way up. My arms burn as I move up the tree, running my fingers over rough bark and reading it like braille until I run out of branches that will hold my weight.

Bitterly disappointed I didn't find a single initial carved into the wood, I work my way back down the way I came.

Playing lookout and offering moral support, Dash leans against the trunk until I have both feet planted firmly on the ground. "Nothing?"

I shake my head and march to the next tree. After tossing another look behind us, I repeat the steps from the last one.

And again, nothing.

With a loud sigh, I drop from the lowest limb to the ground.

Dash hands me my tote and motions to the towering tree erupting from a mound of exposed bedrock. "Last one."

"Great." I hitch my tote onto my shoulder as the last shred of hope skips through my veins. "I was really hoping I'd find her name on one of the smaller trees."

"Yeah, me, too." Dash takes my hand, and we hike over the smooth rock outcropping.

Lifting my gaze skyward, I survey the massive oak towering overhead. Dappled sunlight streams through leaves the size of saucers. "I guess this is it."

Up close, the tree is even more enormous. The gnarled trunk must be close to three feet wide. As it rises into the sky, its limbs stretch out in every direction, daring me to climb it.

"How the hell am I supposed to get up there?"

"I'll give you a boost." Dash laces his fingers together and lowers his hands for me to use as a step. "Hop on."

After stealing a quick kiss, I rest my sweaty palms on his shoulders and plant my foot in his hands the way I did back in my cheer pyramid days.

"Hold on." His jaw flexes as he lifts me into the air.

My stomach flips completely upside down. As it turns out, climbing a tree is nothing like mounting a cheer pyramid.

"Can you lift me higher?" I grunt as I brace myself on the rough bark, keeping one hand flat on the trunk while stretching the other as far as I can reach. "I'm almost there."

Dash boosts me up the thick tree, and I grab the closest branch, muscles trembling as I hoist myself up. Once I get a foothold, I clamber to the next limb, resisting the urge to scream *I'm the princess of the world* at the top of my lungs.

From my dizzying perch, I can clearly read the Essex House sign. "You should see the view from up here. It's amazing!"

"That's great," Dash whisper-shouts from below. "But you need to look for your mom's name before someone sees you up there."

"On it!" My pulse hammers in my ears as I run my palms over the trunk, using the pads of my fingers to explore every knot. Every dip. Every imperfection.

A light gust of wind swirls around me, ruffling my hair and making the leaves flutter and dance. I wonder if the breeze is a sign from Mom to keep going . . . or maybe cut my losses. For an instant, I contemplate doing just that. Then my heart skips as my fingers settle into a slight indentation directly above my head. Using knots as footholds, I move upward to the next limb for a better look.

I've seen my mom's handwriting probably a thousand times before—twenty years of birthday cards, permission slips, and little notes left on the refrigerator—but seeing her swirling script, even sloppily etched into the gnarled side of a tree, takes my breath away.

Blinking back tears, I rest a trembling finger in the smooth indentation, slowly tracing each letter. Thirty years may have weathered the tree, but her name is almost exactly as it was when she carved it. The wound has long since healed over, but the scar tissue remains.

I can't help wondering how long Mom stood on this same twisted limb while she carved her name into the side. My eyes sting as I imagine her standing beside me. Resting my cheek against the scratchy bark, I wrap my arms as far around the trunk as I can while the tears I'd been holding back break free.

"Are you okay?" Dash calls up to me.

"Yes." I choke back a sob and then another. "No. Not really."

"Did you find it?"

"Mm-hmm."

"Did you get a picture?"

"Not yet." It takes me a full minute to pull myself together, but once I do, I snap a few pictures before tucking my phone in my pocket.

"Are you ready to come down?"

"I think so." The backs of my legs scrape the craggy tree as I lower myself to the next branch, inch by inch. I peek down at Dash, about a dozen feet below me, and my head spins. It would be so easy to do a basket drop into his arms if I could be sure he'd catch me.

When our neighbor's cat got stuck in a tree, I remember thinking it must've been the dumbest cat on the planet if it couldn't climb down the same tree it had just gone up. After today, I owe that cat an apology. Climbing down is way harder.

After what seems like forever, I reach the next branch, but there's no way I can slide the rest of the way. I won't have any skin left if I do.

"Jump. I'll catch you." Dash holds out his arms, but he doesn't have proper form. Or solid footing.

I snort. "I don't think so."

"Don't you trust me?"

"It's not about trust. It's about reality. It's a long way down, and I don't want to die." No matter how many times I'd dismounted a pyramid, it never failed to terrify me. The slightest miscalculation could mean death. I haven't done cheer in over two years, and Dash isn't trained to catch me. And this is no pyramid.

"You won't—" Below me, Dash freezes. Then, with a groan and a quick glance up at me, he slowly pulls his hands from the tree and turns toward the path . . . and the mounted New York City police officer.

"What are you doing?" the cop asks.

"Uh . . ." Dash chokes out a nervous laugh. "It's funny you should ask."

The horse snorts as if even *he* smells the bullshit in the air.

"I'm sure it's hilarious." The cop smirks and leans forward in the saddle. "Why don't you tell me anyway."

While Dash sputters, valiantly spinning an almost convincing fib on the fly, I suck in a deep breath and pull on my big superhero panties. When it comes down to it, I do trust Dash—probably more than I should after knowing him only a handful of days. But we've experienced a whole lot of living in those few days' time.

"Psst . . . Dash."

His head jerks up, a frantic question in his eyes.

I mouth the words "catch me" seconds before dropping from the lower limb in the cradle position, sending up a silent prayer for him to play basket.

Dash reaches out, snatching me from the air as if he really is Superman under those dark glasses.

"Nice catch, Clark." I grin.

"You're killing me here, Zo." He rests his forehead against mine, his pulse thundering beneath his skin.

"Okay, lemme see some IDs," the cop shouts. "I should cite the both of youse for unlawful tree climbing."

"Grab my tote," I whisper against his lips as I slide out of his arms.

Dash's eyes stretch so wide, I can see all the possible scenarios running through his mind. "Zoey—"

"On three." I calculate the distance between the cop and our tree, then from our tree to Fifty-Ninth Street. If my guess is right, and the cop doesn't cross the big rock on the horse, we should make it. If I'm wrong, someday I'll be able to tell my kids about the night I spent in a New York City jail. "One . . . two . . . *three*!"

Dash snatches my bag, and we make a break for it. Years of muscle memory from cheer come in handy as I dodge and weave through trees and over slick boulders. I lose my footing once, but somehow still beat Dash to the busy street.

"Do you think we lost him, or did he let us go?" My heart hammers in my throat, and I rest my palms on my knees while I catch my breath. "I can't believe I did that."

Eyes locked on mine, Dash stalks forward with purpose. He stops directly in front of me, takes my face in both hands, and fixes his lips to mine, kissing me until my head swims from lack of oxygen.

When he breaks free, he's panting every bit as hard as I am. "You. Are. Amazing!"

20

The Man Who Sold the World

After fulfilling my purpose in New York, sliding into the Tesla's warm leather seats at the end of the day feels like greeting an old friend. As much as I would love to explore the rest of the Big Apple, the open road calls to me, and I'm eager to see what Mom has in store for us next.

"You really don't mind leaving without seeing more sights?" Dash turns to me, stress lining his face. "Staying at my dad's place would save money, but—"

His muscles flex as I coil my fingers around his forearm.

"I promise, I don't mind. To be honest, your sisters freaked me out a little. It was like waking up in *The Shining*."

His laughter fills the car. "Margo, Dad's wife, insists on dressing the girls like that, and it's definitely creepy."

"So creepy."

"I guess we're heading to Boston." He taps the address into the GPS.

With his dad's building still looming behind us, a low hum vibrates through the quiet car.

"What is that?" I dig through my tote for the source, but it's not coming from inside my bag. It sounds like it's coming from the back seat, and I realize this isn't the first time I've heard it today. "Is that your phone?"

"Maybe." He glances at me as he fiddles with the satellite radio. "You've been ignoring calls all day, haven't you?"

"Have I?" He stares into the traffic, avoiding my gaze. "I hadn't noticed."

"You know what *I've* noticed?" I poke his denim-covered thigh. "*You* don't get calls. Like the whole time we were in Tennessee, all the way to New York, you didn't get a single call. Other than dialing Mack's for me back at the diner and talking to your dad this morning, I don't think I've seen you so much as open your phone since I've known you. Don't you have any friends? Should that worry me?"

"I have friends." He glares at me, as if mildly offended. "They just don't have this number. I didn't want anyone trying to influence my decision."

"If you say so." Narrowing my eyes, I attempt to uncover his secrets through telepathy. "For a guy who supposedly didn't give out his number, you've gotten a lot of calls in the span of an hour. Come on, Dash, what gives?"

His shoulders stiffen. "Probably a robo-dialer."

"A robo-dialer?" I glare at him and cross my arms.

"You know, a computer that dials a bunch of numbers and—"

"I know what it means. I just don't believe you." A twinge of something resembling jealousy flares in my gut. What if he won't tell me because it's the girl he mentioned before . . . the soulless creature?

Dash squirms in his seat, and his nervousness coils around my insides like snakes.

"It's whatever." I shrug. Two can play this game. "You don't owe me anything. We kissed a few times, big deal. I just didn't think we'd resorted to lying to each other already."

"I wasn't lying!" He blows out a breath. "Not exactly."

I arch an eyebrow and stare him down.

He lets out a low chuckle. "When you lay on a guilt trip, you lay it on thick." He rubs the back of his neck. "I told my dad I'd call him back, and I never did. Now he has his assistant calling me every fifteen minutes. She may as well be a robo-dialer."

The tightness in my chest loosens, but I'm not ready to let him off the hook. "What's so urgent?"

"He's . . ." Dash's jaw tightens. "Super intense. And he doesn't like to be ignored."

"Nobody likes to be ignored."

"Oh, it's worse than that." The iciness in his tone gives me chills. "He *really* doesn't like to be ignored."

"Why is he suddenly trying to get you on the phone?"

"Remember when we first met, I told you I was on a soul-searching trip?"

I nod.

"The minute I graduated—" He releases the wheel and rakes a hand through his hair. "Hell, probably since I spoke my first word, my dad has had a position ready for me at his firm."

"And let me guess, you don't want to work there."

He glances at me, then back to the road, his expression dour. "The summer between sophomore and junior years, I tried to change my major from economics to journalism. He hit the roof. He's never considered journalism a legitimate career. He'd much rather I follow *his* footsteps than forge my own path."

"You said he works in Washington. What does he do?"

"He's, uh . . ." Dash taps out a rhythm on the steering wheel and watches me from the corner of his brown eye. "One of the K Street bandits."

I stare at him, confused.

He blows out a deep sigh. "A political consultant. A lobbyist, if you will."

Everything I know about the inner workings of Washington comes from binge-watching political thrillers on Netflix, but I seriously doubt Dash's father is anything like *Miss Sloane*. "I've heard of them, but I don't really know what they do."

"A lot of things. From taking on the oil and gas companies for environmental protections to helping *roll back* those protections to keep the coal mines in business. Some lobbyists are actually out there fighting the good fight." Dash wipes a bead of sweat from his temple.

A series of red flags pop up in my head like gophers on a golf course, but instead of tiptoeing around the subject, I ask, "But not your dad?"

"Dad's a heavy hitter. Goes where the money is. Big pharma. Tobacco. Health insurance." He stares straight ahead, his knuckles paling as he tightens his grip on the wheel. "And he's not afraid to play dirty."

Despite the little voice in my head begging me to change the subject, curiosity gets the best of me. "I'm guessing you have a problem with that."

"Hell yeah, I do." Dash shoots me another glare. "He's been instrumental in getting potentially lifesaving procedures pulled from insurance coverage."

My brain scrambles to understand what he's saying. "Like my mom's cancer treatments?"

He nods once. "It's likely he, or someone like him, was responsible for her blowing through her savings. Possibly even prevented her from being treated at all."

"Oh." My stomach rolls, and I swallow back nausea. "That's . . . horrible. Why would anyone do that? Don't they realize those treatments *help* people?"

"It's all about the money. It's Dad's job to make sure the insurance companies get to keep it. And tobacco companies get to keep peddling their cancer-causing products. And whatever he does for the hundreds of other shitty industries he keeps in business."

"I see." Rage bubbles in my chest, but I'm not sure where to direct it. "I guess my mom spent her life's savings so your dad could buy you a Tesla?"

Dash throws me a panicked glance. "Zoey, I—"

"I'm not mad at you." Anger coils around my insides as I take in his John Varvatos shirt and his Gucci glasses. "Or maybe I am. For as morally outraged as you say you are, you sure don't seem to mind spending his money."

His jaw spasms. "I'm sure that's how it looks from the outside. Anything I say will probably sound like a shitty excuse, but I didn't know what he really did until I interned for him. Once I found out, I promised myself I would be better than he is. And I'm trying. I don't have everything figured out yet, but trust me when I say that's not the life I want."

"And yet, you let Daddy bankroll your summer trip?" I hiss, bitterness coloring my tone.

Dash flinches as if I slapped him, and the color drains from his face. "I earned every penny I've spent, busting my ass doing grunt work in Dad's office every day after class for the past two years. Running away may not seem like the mature thing to do, but staying under his thumb wasn't an option, either. I needed to figure things out without him—or anyone else—breathing down my neck. I only accepted the Tesla because I didn't want to get stranded driving some old beater."

His eyes dart to mine, and I snort out a laugh.

"So all the phone calls . . . I gather that means your dad is pressuring you to make your choice?"

He shakes his head, exhaling through his nose. "Remember what I said about strings? As far as he's concerned, choice is an illusion. No matter what decision I make, he'll expect me to come back ready to start work at the end of summer—to dive into his life with both feet."

"What *do* you want?"

"I'd like to travel and write about what makes people tick. You know? Tell the stories no one wants to tell."

"To be a writer? Like your mom?"

He nods.

Warmth blooms in my belly, and if we weren't sitting in the front seat of his car in rush hour traffic, I'd climb into his lap and kiss him. "You really are Superman, aren't you?"

"I'm far from super," he says softly. "But I'm definitely trying to be a better man."

"I wish I was as sure about my future as you."

"You don't know what you want to do?"

"I thought I did. I mean, I didn't plan out my whole life like Jeanie. She got her degree in engineering. I used to think she'd end up working in a pot dispensary somewhere, but she's starting this great job at a software company making six figures right out of the gate. But me? I always figured I'd end up becoming a teacher like Mom. Now . . ." My heart pounds as I get lost in his eyes. "I'm not so sure anymore."

For what must be the hundredth time, Dash's phone vibrates from the back seat.

"Maybe you should answer that. You can't keep dodging him forever. What if he reports you as missing?" The thought worries me more than I let on. From what Dash has told me, his father is capable of almost anything.

He laughs and my stomach flutters at the dark sound. "And risk the negative press when someone leaks the story? I highly doubt it."

"Well, I'm tired of hearing it buzz all day." Shoving his battered copy of *On the Road* aside, I grab his phone from the back seat. How hard is it to switch the stupid thing off?

"Zoey, no!" Dash tries to grab the open clamshell, accidentally answering the call.

"Hello?" A woman's voice plays through the car speakers, catching me completely off guard. My imagination runs wild, and the as-of-yet unseen "soulless creature" plagues my thoughts. "Dash?"

Panic flashes in his eyes as he reaches for the phone again, knocking it out of my hand in the process. He holds his breath as the device bounces off the leather, slides between my legs, and disappears under my seat.

He melts into his seat and closes his eyes. "Hi, Mom."

"Do you know why your father is calling me? I'm not exactly his favorite person. Hell, I don't even think I'm his favorite ex-wife."

He sighs. "I've been dodging his calls."

Her musical laugh trills down the line. "And you think avoiding him will solve anything? Surely you know better than that by now."

"He's pressuring me to come back, but . . ." He watches me from the corner of his eye as I fumble between my legs for the missing phone. "I can't. Not yet. I made a promise."

"Okay." All traces of humor disappear from her voice. "Who is she, Clark?"

With the phone finally in my grasp, I lock my gaze on Dash and mouth the word, "Clark?"

His horrified expression sends me into a fit of hysterics.

"Is that her?" she asks. "Is she with you now?"

He curses under his breath, snatching the phone from my hand and disconnecting it from the Bluetooth before pressing it to his ear. The heated glare he levels my way could melt steel. A furious Dash is a sexy Dash.

Sinfully sexy.

"Yes. She's right beside me." He flushes crimson to the tips of his ears, then whispers into the phone. "I really don't want to get into that right now. Can I call you later? Yes. I promise. Love you, too."

He doesn't say anything else for a long time, choosing, instead, to shoot searing glances at me as if he can't decide where to bury my body.

"So, uh . . ." I bite the inside of my cheek, fighting a grin. "Your mom calls you—"

"Do *not* go there." Fire dances in his eyes, but his gaze drops to my lips.

Heat flares in my belly, and I'm struck with the sudden desire to take him up on his unspoken invitation. "Dash, pull over."

He groans. "You can't have to go again. We just stopped—"

"Pull. Over." I arch a brow and drag my bottom lip through my teeth.

He cocks his head, and I can see the gears turning as his thoughts catch up to mine. His eyes widen, his lips parting a fraction before his tongue darts out to wet them. Without warning, he changes lanes and accelerates, taking the next exit a little too sharply.

After a few exhilarating turns, he pulls into an all-night diner, parks as far away from the door as possible, then quietly studies me in the glow of the streetlight before reaching over and unbuckling my seatbelt.

His gaze heats, the air crackling between us. "Come here."

"Thought you'd never ask." I crawl over the center console and straddle his lap.

"You are . . ." He slides his palms up my arms and over my shoulders. "So . . ." He sweeps back my hair. "Maddening." His eyes lock on my lips. "And yet . . ." He drags his gaze back to my eyes. "I still want to kiss you every damn minute of the day."

My insides swoop, warmth flooding my belly. "Then kiss me, Clark."

Before I get the words all the way out, he crashes his mouth against mine, gripping my hips and sliding my center over the bulge in his jeans, drawing a groan out of both of us. Our kiss grows frantic as I wrap both arms around his neck. His tongue delves in, mapping the inside of my mouth.

My phone wails from my bag, cutting through the sound of our heavy breathing. "Nooo . . . go away."

"It's probably your sister," Dash says between kisses. "Making sure I haven't buried you in the woods somewhere."

I suck on his bottom lip. "She'll figure it out eventually."

He nods, his mouth hot and insistent on mine.

The ringing starts all over again, and I let out a frustrated cry.

Dash pulls back, breathing heavy as he rests his forehead against mine. "Answer it. Tell her you're alive."

I reach for my phone and flinch at Damian's image on the screen.

Dash stiffens beneath me. "What does he want?"

"The same thing he's wanted since I ended things." I silence my phone and toss it into my seat. "He's having a hard time taking no for an answer."

"Are you sure?" He lifts his hands from my body and shifts as far away as possible with me still in his lap.

Unsettled by the sudden distance between us, I search the depths of his irises. "Sure about what, Dash?"

He draws in an uneven breath.

Is he jealous?

I lift my brows. "Am I sure I made the right decision dumping him?"

His throat works as he nods.

"I'm sure I should've ended it a long time ago. I thought . . ." I splay my fingers across his chest, over his heart. "I used to think he was the kind of guy I was supposed to be with."

His gaze meets mine. "And what kind of guy is that?"

"The complete opposite of you." I chuckle, bringing our bodies closer. "You're the guy who offers to give up his summer for a total stranger just because she needs a ride. The guy who would carry that same stranger through the streets of Memphis knowing her bladder could burst at any moment, then cut her out of her medieval torture underwear in a parking garage to rescue her from herself."

His loud laugh vibrates through me, and I shift closer, making sure he doesn't miss a single point I'm trying to make.

"And you're the guy who doesn't kiss girls with unresolved relationship issues. But since *I* don't kiss every guy I hitchhike across the country with, I guess that makes us perfect for each other."

Grinning, Dash glides his hands up my thighs and rests them on my hips. "As long as we're on the same page." He drags me closer, bringing his lips to mine again, stealing my breath with a searing kiss.

Definitely on the same page.

21

Jump They Say

"Where is that?" Dash peers over my shoulder at Mom's picture, taped to the page.

"I'm not sure, but it doesn't look like Boston Harbor."

His chin brushes my shoulder. Even after hours of being cooped up in the car, he still smells like fresh laundry and rosemary. "Why is she soaking wet and holding balloons and a charred muffin?"

I burst out laughing. "I have no idea why she's wet, but I'm pretty sure that's a lit match in a Little Debbie cupcake."

"That's weird."

The air in my lungs freezes as I zero in on the date scrawled on the photo. Just a few days from now.

"It was her nineteenth birthday." My throat squeezes shut. She won't be here to celebrate this year.

Dash reaches across the console, his warm fingers prying mine from the loose threads on my tattered shorts.

According to her diary, they hit all the cliché tourist attractions—the Harbor, the Freedom Trail, Faneuil Hall. Mom even dragged G-Lo to a museum and a Shakespeare festival. But before they headed to Detroit, they met up with some locals and went hiking, and . . .

"Holy shit! Listen to this!

"July 8

"For my birthday, Mom decided to get high with a few of the locals. This guy Shane and his girlfriend Kim talked me into taking a hit off their joint, 'since you only turn nineteen once.' Their logic was flawed, but what the hell, I did it. I figured, even with all the shit she smokes, Mom's still alive. Though I'll be shocked if she makes it to forty with enough brain cells left to count that high. Officially my first time doing drugs—not counting the time I accidentally took too much cough syrup and passed out in the backyard. I swore I'd never do that again after getting the worst sunburn of my life. And yet, there I was, high as a cat in a sycamore tree, walking through the woods, following a set of railroad tracks on some old patriot trail, like a scene straight out of a horror movie. We hiked for what felt like an eternity before coming to a huge lake and a rusty old trestle on concrete pillars. Not even the pair of No Trespassing signs stopped Shane, Kim, and their drunk-ass friends from walking across the narrow bridge. I inched my way behind them, careful not to trip over the train tracks or fall through the wide cracks where the boards didn't meet, until we reached the center of the bridge. Being up there felt a lot like playing the game Perfection, with the train whistle blowing in the distance taking the place of the ticking timer counting down. While Shane and Kim helped Mom scramble over the side and down a ladder to the top of the concrete pillar directly below us, the rest of us waited our turns, hoping like hell the time wouldn't run out and send our pieces scattering through the air. The old boards beneath my feet rattled as the train got closer, and I screamed so loud, my ears may never stop ringing. This cute guy, Ryan, helped me, and we barely made it over the side

before the train came flying overhead, blasting its whistle as it screeched along the tracks. The sound was deafening, and the bridge shook so hard I thought I'd fall headfirst into the lake. Even with Ryan holding my hand, I'd never been so scared in my entire life. Until the moment I jumped . . . Shane went first, then Kim, then Mom and this guy everyone called Scooter. I didn't catch all their names as they dropped like stones from the pillar into the dark water below. When it was my turn, I closed my eyes. With my heart clawing a hole in my chest, I pushed off the side. Then my chest went cold as I fell for what felt like forever . . ."

Dash's mouth drops open. "She jumped?"

"She freaking jumped." I wipe my slick palms on my shorts. My risk-averse mother had jumped. I would've never believed it, had I not read the words, written in her own hand.

"From a train trestle? With a train on the tracks?"

I nod, my pulse rocketing through my veins. "*That's* where I need to spread her ashes."

"How will we even find it?" Dash eyes the open diary as if searching for the answer, buried somewhere between the lines.

"I don't know, but we have to try." Thoughts racing, I skim the pages again, looking for clues. Anything that might point me in the right direction.

Swapping the diary for my phone, I search for *patriot trails* and *railroad tracks running through the woods outside Boston*. And come up blank.

"I think it's time to call my grandma."

◆ ◆ ◆

Despite Mom's prediction, G-Lo had plenty of brain cells left to tell me how to find the patriot trail and the train tracks. Bright and early the next morning, Dash and I set out to test her memory, skipping all the other Boston attractions listed in the diary to focus on the only one calling to me.

Of all the places I've scattered Mom's ashes, this is the spot that weighs heaviest on my mind. Jumping from the bridge had been an actual turning point, not just for Mom's trip, but for her life. She'd gone from visiting David Bowie concert stops to taking a literal leap of faith into adulthood.

"You okay?" Dash's brows furrow as he pushes thick brambles out of my way.

The deeper into the woods we trek, the harder it is to follow the overgrown trail, as if no one has come this way in a long time.

"A little anxious." I drag my tote higher on my shoulder. We have to be getting close by now. We've been walking for almost forty minutes.

His muscles bunch as he untangles a thick vine blocking the path. "Unless your grandma's directions were totally off, we should be almost there."

"I hope you're right."

Dash stops walking and tilts his head to the side. "Do you hear that?"

Blocking out the buzzing cicadas in the trees, I listen for whatever has Dash so excited. A low honk in the distance catches my attention, and my gaze snaps to his. "Geese?"

He grins. "We must be close to water."

"Come on." I grab his hand, towing him through the thick underbrush. Sharp vines claw at my bare legs as we sprint through the thicket, in search of the elusive train tracks.

We reach a break in the trees, and I slow to a brisk walk as I catch the first glimpse of the rusted trestle jutting into the horizon. Sunlight glints off the lake, stopping me in my tracks. The closer I get to the massive structure, the more space I see between the long, narrow bridge and the water below. My heart leaps into my throat. My imagination hasn't done it justice. Neither had Mom's description.

"She jumped from *that*?" The words rip from my throat as I cautiously make my way forward, swatting gnats from my sweaty face. My thoughts race to keep up with my pulse, the scent of musty earth and humid air so thick, I can taste it.

"Hey." Dash grabs my arm. "Be careful. Don't get too close to the edge."

Because we both know the fall could damn well kill me. That jumping off a freaking bridge is beyond reckless.

I tug my arm free as my conflicting emotions wage war. This whole trip was supposed to be about getting to know my mother all over again through her diary. But standing less than fifty feet from where she stood—where she *jumped*—has me questioning everything I thought I knew about her.

"Zoey?"

I angrily swipe a tear from my cheek. "My whole childhood was one big lesson on how reckless my grandmother was. Every time we rode off without our bike helmets, played too rough, or laughed too loud, we got the 'don't be like your G-Lo' speech. When Jeanie got caught smoking pot junior year, Mom flipped. She ranted for hours about Jeanie ruining her life the same way our grandmother had."

I knew Mom loved G-Lo, but I also sensed the unspoken tension between them.

"Jeanie idolized G-Lo and rebelled against Mom. And what happened to her? Nothing. She smoked pot and partied hard. But she still graduated college with decent grades and landed a six-figure job. *She* didn't waste four years with a stupid boyfriend who controlled her every move. But me?" Tears clog my throat, and I swallow, struggling to hold them back. "I was supposed to be the good, responsible daughter. Just like Mom."

But she wasn't responsible, was she? Not always. Not this one time, at least.

I swallow again, losing the battle with my emotions. How many new firsts did I waste on Damian because I was following the path I thought she wanted for me?

"Zoey . . ." Dash reaches for my hand.

Instead of accepting it, I take a step toward the bridge. I swipe at another tear, angry that she hid so much of herself from us—from *me*. Furious that I never got the chance to confront her about it. "This bridge represents the lie my mom perpetuated my whole life. Because at least *once*, she was as reckless as her mother. She got to experience that terrifying rush of adrenaline she so desperately fought to keep from us. And it's not fair that she's gone now, and I can't tell her how mad I am that she kept this from me."

Dash inches forward, his gaze locked on mine. "Maybe she never got the chance. Maybe that's why she sent you on the trip. So you could experience this with her in the only way she knew how."

"By spreading her ashes over a damn lake?" I stare down at the water, strangely jealous of what it represents.

"And going to all the places she went. Maybe this was her way of sharing that with you."

His theory—his wonderfully plausible theory—chips away at my anger. It would be just like Mom to send me on this epic quest to get to know her, to understand the parts of her she couldn't explain. If the trip—specifically this bridge—meant so much to her life, I can only wonder what it might mean for *mine*.

Shoving my anger aside, I pull Mom's urn from my tote, setting the bag on the ground beside the bridge.

Dash goes rigid beside me. "You're only spreading ashes, right?"

"Yes," I breathe—a cross between a sob and a laugh. "You didn't think I was gonna jump, did you? I'm enjoying this adventure a little too much to off myself."

He rolls his eyes at my weak attempt at humor.

Eyeing the rotting boards, I thrust the silver urn into Dash's hands. "Hold this. I don't want to carry the damn thing all the way out there."

His brows furrow. "What are you doing?"

"What do you *think* I'm doing?" I unscrew the lid and plunge my hand inside. Coarse sand spills through my fingers as I pull out a fistful of ashes. It doesn't escape me that only a few days ago, the mere thought had horrified me. Now I'm practically playing in it like a kid in a sandbox. I fill one pocket, then go back in for another handful and fill the other one.

"You want me to . . . ?" Dash nods toward the bridge.

"No." I force a smile. "I need a minute. Alone, if you don't mind."

Still clutching Mom's urn, he presses a quick kiss to my temple. "Be careful."

"I will," I promise as I take my first step onto the old boards.

Mom was right. The thick planks don't meet, giving me a peek at the shimmering water below through the gaps. It reminds me of something straight out of an amusement park, but there'd be absolutely nothing amusing about falling through.

Once I reach the center, I gaze out at the lake. It must be at least fifty feet to the surface. How did they survive that fall? With a shudder, I peer over the side and search for the ladder Mom wrote about. The rusty rungs don't look like they'd hold half my weight these days.

"Okay, Mom. I'm here."

I wipe my slick palms on my shorts, then fish into my left pocket and scoop as much of the sand as I can into my hand, memorizing the rough texture of the grains against my skin. Murmuring a silent, "I love you," I toss the ashes into the air, where they catch a light gust and drift across the lake.

The boards beneath my feet vibrate and I freeze, scanning the horizon in both directions.

"Everything okay?" Dash shouts.

"For a second I thought—" Laughing, I shake my head. "It's nothing. I'm imagining things. I'm almost done." I drag the second handful from my pocket and raise my fist in the air. A whistle blows in the distance, and I go rigid.

The train.

Air rushes from my lungs as Mom's ashes slip through my fingers, creating a dust cloud around me.

Dash shouts at me. "Zoey, get off the bridge!"

Paralyzed with fear, I stand in the center of the bridge, unsure of which direction to go. "Where is it?"

"Run!" Even from fifty feet away, terror shines in Dash's eyes.

"Which way?" The boards tremble, rattling hard enough to shake dust into the air. Nervous laughter rolls up my throat. Not dust. Mom. The whistle blows again, louder this time, and my thoughts scatter. The memories from her trip stitch themselves into the fabric of my mind until I replay her last moments on this very bridge in real time.

Ignoring Dash's frantic cries, I scramble over the side and cling to the rusted rungs of the ladder, my breath coming out in sharp bursts. Terror races through my veins as I release the bottom rung and land on top of the concrete pillar alongside decades of graffiti and fresh bird poop.

Not even Mom's memories prepare me for the train hitting the tracks above like a sledgehammer to my skull. My bones vibrate until I'm certain I'll break into a million tiny pieces and blow away like Mom's ashes.

I gape into the rippling water below, the concrete shuddering beneath my feet. And that's when it hits me . . . Mom stood right here.

A million questions swirl through my brain like fish in a bowl. What was she thinking at that exact moment? Was she scared? Was Dash right? Did she mean for me to find this place? My last thought replays inside my head, and suddenly I know.

This is why I'm here.

With Dash somewhere above me, screaming my name over and over, I squeeze my eyes shut and tuck my arms tightly to my sides. Then, inhaling one last deep breath, I point my toes and leap.

After falling through the warm air for what seems like hours, I slice through the icy water like a knife. The murky lake presses in on all sides, and regret hits me almost immediately. Jumping into a lake from a bridge is nothing like diving into the pool at the Y. Instead of resurfacing right away, I keep going down . . . down . . . down, until

I'm sure I'll hit the muddy bottom. But the lake must be a hundred feet deep, because I keep sinking. My lungs burn and my skull threatens to cave in. But still, I keep sinking. The farther down I go, the colder and darker the water is. I'm going to die down here without ever having sex with Dash.

Oh God . . . Dash.

My heart hammers in my ears, the bridge a blur above me as I reach for the surface. Stroke after stroke, I drag my arms through the dark water, my lungs screaming for air. As soon as my head breaks the surface, I suck in a breath, then another, bobbing in the water while I find my bearings. My pulse races like the world's worst caffeine and sugar high, and I know the eventual crash won't be pleasant.

"Jesus, Zoey, are you okay?" Dash's voice cracks as he shouts from the shallows, wading in up to his ankles, gripping his hair in both hands.

Arms trembling from the effort, I swim toward him. "It was touch and go for a minute, but I'm alive."

"When you jumped . . . my heart damn near stopped." He meets me knee deep in the lake and drags me from the water. "I thought I lost you."

I barely find my footing before his mouth closes over mine and he's kissing me senseless. This time when my lungs scream for mercy, I don't complain. I'd gladly drown in his kisses. At least I'd die happy.

22

Teenage Wildlife

With a deep sigh, I glance at the map on the Tesla's display. "How far to Detroit?"

"Detroit?" He frowns at the display as if seeing a completely different map than I do. "What about Chicago?"

I double-check Mom's diary, flipping through the pages and back again. "They went from Boston to Detroit . . . *then* Chicago."

"Chicago's supposed to be the next stop." He rolls his eyes at my blank stare. "The original tour? That *is* what we're supposed to be following, right?"

I cock an eyebrow. "I'm not even going to ask how you know that . . ."

Dash shifts his gaze to the road, his cheeks turning pink.

"Maybe they decided to be more efficient and hit Detroit first, since it's on the way."

"Detroit it is." Dash changes our route without complaint. "We'll have to find somewhere to stop for the night."

"Somewhere with a hot shower, please. I'm gross." I comb my fingers through my tangled hair and catch a whiff of my skin. "I still smell like the lake."

Dash leans over and buries his face in my hair. "I think you smell good. Like the woods."

"Like Sasquatch, you mean?"

"No." His lips twitch. "Like summer camp. You're making me crave bonfires and s'mores."

"I haven't been camping since cheer camp, the summer before senior year." I release a heavy sigh. It was the last time my life was semi normal. When I still believed Mom's cancer was beatable, and I could breathe without my chest cracking.

Dash's eyes twinkle. "Does cheer camp actually count as camping?"

"Not at all." I laugh, remembering the dorm-like space with twin-size beds and indoor plumbing.

"Didn't think so. It doesn't count unless you're sleeping in a tent under the stars."

"G-Lo said she and Mom went camping on their trip, but I haven't gotten that far yet. Maybe we could . . ." I let the thought trail off, remembering what G-Lo said about dragging Dash into a tent.

"Could what?"

"Figure out where they went and camp there?"

His eyes light up. "You'd do that?"

"We could totally rough it for one night, right?" So much for my hot shower.

"Hell yeah! Let's go camping!"

"You have a tent?" I gape at Dash's smug profile as he focuses on the road ahead.

"Not just any tent. A *Big Agnes*." The blazing midday sun has darkened his transition lenses to almost black, making it impossible to see the sparkle in his eyes when he glances my way, but I can tell from his tone, it's there. "And one of their arctic-rated sleeping bags."

I whip my head toward the back seat, but he obviously didn't stash it in there. "Where are you hiding all that?"

"It's all part of my secret serial killer kit," he quips.

I glare at him, and he laughs. If he looked any more pleased with himself, I'd slap him with his platinum card.

"I'm not hiding anything." He rolls his eyes. "I stored the camping gear in the back with my leather duffel, the tool bag, the flares, and the first aid kit. I didn't want to end up with no place to stay and no other options. Like I said the last time something like this came up, it's good to be prepared."

"Sorry, but I was a little *preoccupied* last time you had to open your Boy Scout preparedness kit." I cringe at the memory of the cold steel bolt cutters pressed against my skin.

Dash clears his throat, his cheeks flushing. "Eagle Scout, actually."

"Of course you were." I roll my eyes. "So where have you camped so far?"

"I, uh . . ." Dash scratches the back of his neck. "I haven't."

"Like ever? How'd you get your Boy Scout participation trophy if you've never camped?"

He snorts. "It's a badge, not a trophy, and yes, I've camped before—lots of times—just not during *this* trip."

"So you bought an expensive tent and an arctic-rated sleeping bag for show?"

"I wanted to make sure I was prepared for any eventuality."

"Right." With a quiet snicker, I nod. "Boy Scout."

He opens his mouth.

"Yeah, yeah, Eagle Scout, I know. What now, Mr. Eagle Scout? What else do we need in order to camp?"

"I suppose we should start with a specific location. Does your mom's diary have any information about where they stayed?"

I open Mom's diary and flip past Boston and the bridge jump until I find what I'm looking for.

> *Several hours after my leap from the bridge, my bones still ache. Hitting the water from over three stories high knocked the wind out of me. I couldn't breathe. Couldn't swim. I would've drowned if Ryan hadn't helped me to shore like my own personal Superman. Every time I look into his amber eyes, tingles run up and down my spine, making it hard to catch my breath. I've known him all of a day, but I already want to spend every moment with him.*

I press my hand to my chest, my heart thumping wildly beneath my palm. This must be the romance G-Lo mentioned. I don't know what I expected, but it certainly wasn't Mom gushing over a boy. She never acted that way with Dad. Not even when things were good.

> *Ryan's friends asked if we wanted to go camping with them, and I jumped at the chance. I expected Mom to be all for it, but surprisingly, it took her longer to warm up to the idea. For the first time I could remember, she pulled out the "Mom" card and asked a thousand questions first. Shane told her they were headed to . . .*

"Beartown State Forest." The words catch in my throat. "Apparently her bridge jumping friends were on their way there when they met up."

"See if you can find anything more specific."

While Dash inputs the location into the GPS, I get lost in Mom's swirly handwriting.

> *Mom refused to let me ride in Shane's van with Ryan, so I slid to the middle, and Ryan hopped into the front seat of the Cutlass to ride with us. We practically wore out Mom's Best of Bowie tape in the two and a half hours it took us to get to the campsite, and I loved every minute of it.*

> *Ryan even knew the words to almost all the songs. Mom said meeting him was "kismet." I don't know if I believe in all that, but I definitely feel lucky. And if everything works out tonight, Ryan will be getting pretty lucky, too.*

Dash pries my fingers from their vise grip on Mom's diary, startling me. "Are you okay?"

"Yeah, of course." I bite my lip and slide my gaze toward Dash. *My own personal Superman.* "Just trying to find clues." And wondering if my mom really got busy with a total stranger only hours after meeting him.

"Any luck?" he asks.

A nervous giggle bubbles out of me. I wouldn't mind "getting lucky" with Dash in a tent. "Not yet. But I'm hopeful."

Dash pulls into a grocery store about an hour away from the campgrounds and we stock up on food, bottled water, and the ingredients for s'mores. As soon as we hop back into the freshly charged car, I crack open Mom's diary and dive in again.

> *The gold in Ryan's hair shimmers in the firelight. After more than one warm beer, and another hit on one of Mom's joints, his eyes follow my every move. I want him more than I've ever wanted anyone. And as soon as Mom passes out, I'll have him, too.*

My hands tremble as I flip the page to skip ahead.

> *My head spun, as if I'd twirled around at least a dozen times. I wasn't drunk, or high—not from alcohol or drugs anyway—but I'd never felt so alive . . . so electrified. Not in all my life. Not even when jumping from*

the bridge. My skin was on fire, tingling like a fresh match strike. Ryan and I hadn't spoken an actual word in almost an hour, but we'd bared our souls through our eyes. One by one, everyone drifted off to their own private spaces—tents, back seats, and a few passed out in front of the dying fire. I wasn't the least bit tired as I draped the wool picnic blanket over Mom, snoring in her back seat. I took Ryan's hand and dragged him into his tiny tent, where we spent the rest of the night—

"Holy hell." I drop the diary to my lap before it bursts into flames and suck in a deep breath to calm my pounding heart.

Dash dabs my forehead with a wad of napkins, making me jump. "What the hell are you reading over there? You need me to crank up the AC? You're sweating."

"It's . . ." I groan. How do I tell him I'm basically reading diary porn? I'm equal parts disturbed and fascinated. The only reason I made it this far is because the person who wrote this diary is *nothing* like the mom I remember. And I can't help imagining Dash flirting with me across a campfire, and the two of us making out in a tent.

Dash glances at me from the corner of his eye. "Read me some."

I inhale and choke on saliva.

"Do I need to pull over and give you the Heimlich?"

It takes a few seconds of hacking and coughing before I can answer. "No! I need water."

Dash passes me an open water bottle. "Sip slowly. I haven't seen a place to stop in a while."

Smart-ass. I snatch the water from him and suck down half the bottle before taking a breath.

He grins and then nods at the diary in my lap. "Did you find what you were looking for?"

My face goes up in flames, and I put them out with another big gulp of water.

"You're acting weird." A groove forms between Dash's eyebrows. "Weirder than normal, that is."

"I'm not weird. You're weird."

"There she is." He laughs.

"Whatever." I roll my eyes, but I can't stop smiling. "Mom didn't leave any clues other than Beartown."

"We should be there soon."

Diary-worthy scenarios flicker through my thoughts as Dash fumbles with his fancy tent, his muscles bunching and tightening from the effort, and his skin glistening in the waning daylight.

My temperature spikes.

"You need some help?" I ask. God help me, I can't tear my eyes away. *Is this how Mom felt that night?*

"Nope. I've got this. You keep . . ." He lifts his head from the instruction booklet to catch me daydreaming. "What are you doing? I thought you were collecting firewood."

"Oh. Right." I shake the naughty vision from my brain. "On it!"

Keeping Dash within earshot, I set out in search of loose twigs and branches.

My quest takes me into the forest, where the heady scent of cedar and pine fills the air and scattered rows of soaring oaks draw me in, each one practically calling my name. The deeper I go, the farther the sun creeps below the tree line. And the farther I get from Dash, the less focused I am on cooking hot dogs and charring marshmallows. Even thoughts of kissing in front of a blazing fire take a back seat to visions of Mom walking this same path in another lifetime.

Scraping my fingertips over rough bark, I search each tree for my mother's name. No matter what I do, I can't shake the feeling that my reason for being here is bigger than simply spreading her ashes. *Come on, Mom . . . what are you trying to tell me?*

Dash curses, and I stop what I'm doing. While I'm out here feeling sorry for myself, he's wrestling with a tent, sacrificing his last summer of freedom so I can re-create moments from my mom's life.

I've never wanted to kiss anyone so badly in my life.

With a new plan forming in my head, I collect as many sticks and branches as I can carry and then hurry back.

"Tent's up. You need help with the—" Feet rooted in place, he cocks his head and studies me in the fading light. "Why are you looking at me like that?"

"I . . . uh . . ." Words stick in my throat as I wipe the stupid grin from my lips. With him standing right in front of me, all I can think of is how badly I want to drag him into his expensive tent.

Dash steps toward me and brushes a loose strand of hair from my eyes. "You're blushing."

"No, I'm not. I'm sweating. You're hot—I mean, *it's* hot out here." I clear my throat and turn back toward the forest before I blurt out something I don't want to say yet. "I was searching the trees. I guess I thought I'd find her name, but we're in a freaking forest. Even if it's out there, I'm never going to find it."

"I see what you mean." He stares into the woods for a moment before pulling a utility knife from his pocket.

I flinch. "What's that for?"

Dash presses a hand to his heart. "Your lack of faith wounds me." He marches to the nearest tree and begins carving a crooked heart.

Tears blur my vision as he adds our initials in the center. No one has ever written my name on a bathroom wall before, let alone a tree. This man—a man I barely know—cares enough to immortalize our names together in something that will outlive us both.

"There." He pockets his knife and takes my hand. "Now you're part of the forest, too."

23

Modern Love

"Oh my God." A moan of ecstasy rolls out of me as tingles work their way through every fiber of my being. "Where have you been all my life?"

Dash's eyes sparkle in the firelight as he gapes at me, so distracted he doesn't notice the ball of flame engulfing the marshmallow at the end of his outstretched stick. He clears his throat. "How have you never had s'mores before?"

With another toe-curling groan, I catch a glop of molten fluff and melted chocolate with my tongue as it oozes from between two graham crackers. "Clearly, I've been cheated and deprived my whole freaking life."

Dash shifts his weight on the log and his thigh brushes mine. "That's sad."

"Tragic, really." I stuff the last bite between my lips and lick the sticky residue from my fingers, one digit at a time.

He inhales sharply and chucks his burning stick into the fire, seconds before the flame reaches his hand. "You're killing me, you know that?"

A laugh rolls up my throat, because I know. I *totally* know.

With a devilish grin of his own, Dash dips his head and leans in. "You, uh, missed some . . ." His sweet breath washes over me as he rasps his tongue from my chin to the corner of my mouth, sucking my lower lip between both of his before releasing me.

A violent shudder cuts through me.

He chuckles, bringing his lips to my ear. "Now who's laughing?"

His dark whisper sends a prickle of heat rippling through my core.

"Not me." My voice cracks, my insides melting like a flaming marshmallow on a stick. "Definitely not laughing."

"Good." He brushes loose tendrils of hair from my neck and kisses along the curve of my jaw, fanning the out-of-control flames raging within me and sending molten heat spreading down . . . down . . . *down.* "Because this isn't funny."

"Not . . . funny . . . at all." I can barely breathe to get the words out.

Day-old stubble skims my cheek as he continues his sensual assault, his hot mouth moving to my exposed throat, kissing a blistering trail to my collarbone before nipping his way back to my ear.

Oh God.

Unable to think straight, I ball my hands at my sides, restlessly waiting for him to make his next move. He hooks a finger under my chin, tilting my head and dragging my gaze to his.

The crackle of the fire and the katydids singing in the trees fill the void as the silence between us stretches to the breaking point. Barely an inch separates us. All he has to do is lean forward to close the gap. All he has to do is kiss me.

He shifts again, resting his forehead against mine. The smoldering heat in his eyes challenges me to surrender. Begs me to give in. Little does he know how close I am to doing exactly that. Then he slips his fingers under my shirt, grazing my stomach as he inches his way toward the swell of my breasts. My nipples tighten with anticipation, and I let out a ragged breath.

Dash's lips curve into a wicked grin. He has me right where he wants me, and he knows it.

A moan escapes me. "Now who's trying to kill who?"

"*Killing* you is the last thing on my mind right now." He cups my face in his hands and closes the distance between us, capturing my eager mouth in a fiery kiss.

He tastes like toasted marshmallow and chocolate, and I don't care that I'm basically re-creating a page out of my mom's diary. Or that I've known him for only a handful of days. God help me, I've wanted him since the first moment he spoke to me in that greasy diner.

His thumb strokes my cheek as his warm tongue glides across mine, unleashing the wild beast inside me. Before I can stop myself, I tackle him to the ground, straddling his hips and pinning him to the forest floor.

Liquid heat floods my center as I settle over the hardness cradled between my thighs. Dash swells beneath me as he grips my hips and guides my movements.

"Oh God. Do that again," I whisper, digging my fingers into his shoulders and grinding my pelvis against his, chasing the tingles wherever they lead.

His head falls back, and a low groan works its way up his throat. *"Fuuuck!"*

My thoughts exactly.

"What are we doing?" he mutters, bringing his lips back to mine. "You don't really want our first time to happen on the cold hard ground, do you?"

I manage a breathy "no" but continue rocking my center against his growing erection. I know I should stop. He's right. I'd much rather our first time happened in a comfy bed, but the insistent throb between my thighs demands attention, and I'm too far gone for regrets. I snake a hand between us, palming him through his jeans.

A deep shudder runs through him, and he groans. "Zoey, no." His erection twitches as he wraps his fingers around my wrist and stills my hand. "Not here."

His words wash over me like a bucket of cold water, and I jerk back.

"Don't you dare," he whispers before claiming my lips in another toe-curling kiss.

Every sweep of his tongue sends ribbons of heat dancing down my spine and my stomach plummeting. He weaves his fingers into the tangled lengths of my hair and angles my head for a deeper, almost feral, kiss, making my head swim from lack of oxygen.

Out of breath, he rests his forehead against mine. "I want you so damn bad, I can barely think straight."

My lips part, my heart thundering in my ears. "Dash . . ."

"Just maybe not right *here*." He plucks a sharp rock from under his lower back and chucks it into the trees. "We should . . ." His gaze darts to the tent.

That's all the invitation I need. I jump from his lap and grab his hand. "Thought you'd never ask."

Halfway to the tent, Mom's voice whispers through my thoughts like a little angel perched on my shoulder, effectively kicking sand on the flames lashing my insides. *Are you being safe, Zoey?*

I slow my steps and let out a long sigh. Despite the fact that I've been on birth control since I was sixteen, she's right. There's no such thing as being *too* safe.

Dash tucks a lock of hair behind my ear, and I feel his touch everywhere. "Something wrong?"

"Um . . ." My cheeks heat as I fumble for the right words. "You were a Boy Scout, right?"

A smile tugs at the corners of his mouth. "Pretty sure none of my badges covered this."

"That's not what I—" A nervous laugh slips out. "What I mean is, you're always prepared. *Right?*"

As my meaning sinks in, his shoulders deflate. "Shit."

"Is that a no?" Horrified, I gape at him. "You don't have any . . . ?"

"No." His eyes widen, and he flushes to his hairline. "I mean yes! I do. In the first aid kit. In the car."

I exhale, equal parts relieved and confused. "I don't want to know why you have condoms in your first aid kit."

"Actually, they make excellent—"

I slap a palm over his mouth. "Don't tell me. Just go get one." Then I fist the front of his shirt and pull him in for a quick, but somewhat brutal, kiss. "Make that two! And hurry!"

Dash groans, adjusting himself as he backs away. "Be right back." He winks, then turns and jogs toward the break in the trees.

The second he disappears into the shadows, I exhale into my hand to check my breath and catch a whiff of my armpits. My breath still smells like chocolate, but the rest of me reeks of sweat and swamp water. And Lord help me, there isn't enough deodorant in the world to hide that.

With my heart rattling off the seconds, I crawl into the tent and snatch my tote, upending its contents onto the sleeping bag to search for the pack of wet wipes I tossed in there the other day.

Once I locate the only remaining wipe, I shove everything back into my bag and quickly get down to business. After stripping off my sweaty shirt and shorts, I unfold the wipe to its full size, pausing to glance at my flushed reflection in Mom's shiny urn.

"Sorry, Mom. I can't do this with you watching." I march the urn out of the tent and rest it on a log a few yards away.

As soon as Mom's ashes are safely out of the picture, I scrub the lone wipe across every sweaty inch of me before wadding up the tattered square and stashing it at the bottom of my tote. Then I give my dirty T-shirt a quick once-over before tossing it aside. If I'd known I would end up half naked, I would've worn something sexier than a plain white bralette and the bright-yellow Pikachu underwear I found at the bottom of my backpack. I don't even remember packing them. But at least they're clean. After going through everything else I'd packed—*and* Dash's Superman boxers—I was out of options.

My stomach flutters as I glance toward the shadows. What's taking him so long? He must be tearing his car apart, searching for a condom. If he doesn't find one, this will all be for nothing. But if he does . . .

A thrill runs through me, and my bladder clenches. No, no, no! This cannot be happening! I've already peed my pants once on this trip, I'll be damned if I let it happen again!

With a groan, I crawl out of the tent and stare at the tree line in the distance. There's no way I'm walking into the dark woods *alone*. And I'm sure as hell not going out in the open and have Dash catch me squatting against a tree. Talk about a mood killer. What I wouldn't give for indoor plumbing right about now.

Indoor plumbing?

The thought, combined with a flash of red in my peripheral vision, gives me a brilliant idea. I grab Dash's discarded plastic cup and crawl into the tent.

No sooner is my bladder empty than the sound of someone rustling around our campsite steals my attention.

"Don't laugh, but . . ." Balancing the full cup in one hand, I wriggle my undies up and over my hips with the other. "I had to pee . . ."

Swallowing a nervous giggle, I poke my head out of the tent.

In the half second it takes my eyes to adjust to the darkness, I realize it isn't Dash's sexy smirk waiting for me. Instead, a huge black bear lurks less than a yard from where I left my mom's ashes, grazing on chocolate bars and graham crackers. The animal raises its massive head, his fathomless eyes staring a hole through me.

A scream catches in my throat, the strangled sound becoming lost in the deafening buzz of the katydids in the trees.

Still gripping the red plastic cup in my trembling hand, I eye the urn just beyond the bear's reach, calculating my odds of beating him to it.

"Go on!" Heart racing, I attempt to shoo him away with my free hand. "Get out of here!"

The bear ignores me and ambles toward Mom's ashes.

Screwing up what little courage I can muster, I stab a finger in his direction. "Listen, Yogi! You lay one damn paw on that urn and, PETA be damned, I'll make a rug out of you!"

He chuffs, my empty threats doing nothing to deter him as he sniffs the shiny metal.

Mumbling obscenities under my breath, I scramble for anything I can use as a weapon. Where the hell are those bolt cutters when I need them?

The bear nudges Mom's urn with his snout, keeping his gaze locked on his own reflection as he rolls it forward, like a cat mesmerized by a laser pointer.

A spike of fear stabs my gut and, using the only weapon in my arsenal, I attack. Aiming for his head, I lob the red plastic cup like a Molotov cocktail, holding my breath until it hits the beast square in the muzzle with a splatter. The animal startles, flinching as if I'd pepper sprayed him.

"Take that, Yogi!" I shriek at the bear's retreating form.

Looks like Dash isn't the only resourceful one on this trip. I dart my gaze around the empty clearing. I finally get the chance to restore my tarnished dignity and show off a little ingenuity in the process, and there isn't a single soul around to witness my triumph. Figures.

24

Lady Grinning Soul

No sooner does the tail end of the bear disappear into the shadows than Dash comes running into the clearing, armed with a strip of condoms and another pack of wet wipes. "Holy hell, was that a . . . ?"

"Yes." With my hands shaking and my knees about to give out, I flash a proud grin. "But don't worry. I took care of it."

Pocketing the foil squares, Dash surveys the scattered chocolate wrappers and graham cracker packages at his feet. His gaze moves into the tree line again, and he palms his neck. "What—*how*?"

"I uh . . ." The sting of embarrassment rises in my cheeks as I nod toward the discarded cup. My nose wrinkles at the faint trace of fresh urine in the air. My self-defense tactics may have been somewhat unorthodox, but at least I got the job done. "I peed on him."

For half a second, I think maybe he didn't hear me. Then his face splits in a wide grin, and he barks out a loud laugh. "Looks like you finally found a use for your special talent."

"Very funny." Folding my arms over my chest, I tear my gaze from his, swapping embarrassment for a healthy dose of exasperation.

Either ignoring—or blissfully unaware of—my shifting mood, Dash collects a few stray marshmallows lying in the dirt and flicks them into the glowing embers. Then his gaze lands on the wet spot under the discarded cup. "I can't believe you fought a bear with nothing but a cup of pee."

I shrug and shoot an exaggerated glance at the yellow Pokémon character guarding my lady bits. "I must've left my Taser in my other underwear."

As if just noticing my current state of undress, Dash's smile slips. He swallows, his Adam's apple bobbing as his gaze drifts from my exposed shoulders to my bare legs.

A rough sound rolls up his throat, and my nerve endings flare to life. I'm afraid to even breathe as he traces the contours of my body with his eyes, as if memorizing every dip and valley, every line and curve between the tips of my toes and the top of my head.

A dull throb settles in my center as the thrill of anticipation evaporates every drop of my momentary irritation like water on a hot skillet. I release a jagged breath, drawing his attention back to my face.

Our gazes lock as we stand there in the clearing, the air between us crackling with unspoken promises. Moonlight sparkles in his mismatched eyes as he drinks me in. Then he licks his lips, and a slow grin curves his mouth. He hasn't even touched me yet, and I'm already putty in his hands.

Quickly closing the distance between us, he hooks an arm around my shoulder and pulls me into an embrace, shifting his weight and opening his stance until I settle between his parted legs.

"You did good," he murmurs, and his lips brush the shell of my ear.

My knees threaten to give out, and I melt into him, burying my face in his hard chest as tiny ripples of electricity dance down my spine. He smells of campfire, burned sugar, and the unique scent I've come to associate with Dash. If only it were possible to bottle that fragrance and keep it forever.

"Taking on a bear was pretty badass." His hot breath raises goose bumps over my cool skin.

I suck in a breath and let it out quickly, wishing we could rewind to before the bear showed up. "Badass or not, it wasn't what I had in mind for this evening."

"The evening doesn't have to be over. Not if you don't want it to be." His heart races beneath my cheek, but he doesn't move, doesn't breathe, as if contemplating the weight of his own words.

"But . . ." Torn between the dangers lurking in the dark and the desperate need building within me, I gaze up at him and drag my bottom lip through my teeth. "What about the bear?"

"You chased him away, right?" He glides his stubbled cheek along my jaw and traces a trembling hand up my spine, leaving a trail of heat in its wake.

Yogi could be anywhere, but Dash's fingers stroking over my bare skin chase away the fear until I can't focus on anything but him.

"What if . . ."

The thought dies on my lips, my concentration shattered as he nips my earlobe, clamping down just hard enough to send blood rushing from my brain to points south.

With a dark chuckle, he releases the lobe and soothes the sting with his tongue. "If what?"

My stomach bottoms out as his low purr unleashes another wave of liquid heat.

Abandoning my ear, Dash fixes his lips to the sensitive spot behind it, resting his fingers in the notches between my vertebrae while he ravages my neck. Every brush of his lips, every sweep of his tongue, pulls me under, drugging me, loosening my muscles and turning my bones to jelly.

My thoughts scatter like ashes in the wind as I cling to him, twisting my fingers in the back of his shirt, lost to the sensation of his lips, his teeth, and his tongue, caressing the column of my throat.

"If what?" he asks again, and his mouth curves into a smile against my neck, as if he knows *exactly* what he's doing to me.

My lips fall open to respond, but my mind goes blank. If he thinks he can coax any sort of rational thought from me while he slowly kisses his way to my collarbone, he's sorely mistaken. I can barely coax breath from my lungs.

Dash skates his large palms over my shoulders and down my sides, making my knees go weak and my core clench as his fingertips graze the swell of my breasts. Nonsensical ramblings about the bear tumble from my lips before I can snatch them back. Screw the bear. I'd willingly face down an army of predators for another minute of this delicious torture.

"Don't worry." He locks his gaze on mine and rests his wandering hands on the soft curve of my hips, lazily tracing the elastic waistband of my Pikachu panties with the pad of his thumb. "I'll protect you."

Lost in the hypnotic thrall of his eyes, I mutter, "Who's going to protect *you*?"

Dash brings his lips to my ear once again, his fingers flexing before sinking almost painfully into my hips. "I'm Superman, remember?"

His unexpected declaration snaps the remaining threads of my frayed willpower. My pulse quickens as I wrap my fingers around his neck and drag his face down to mine. Our mouths collide in a tangle of lips, tongues, and teeth. Again and again, his mouth slants over mine, his tongue delving inside. Tasting me.

Claiming me.

I don't care what color crayon he is. I want him. *Now.*

Without breaking the kiss, Dash walks me backward down the path, toward the Tesla. It wouldn't be my first time having sex in the cramped back seat of a car, though the expensive upholstery would be an upgrade from the last time—not to mention softer than a sleeping bag on the hard ground. But the lack of space would be too confining. And way too far from where we're desperately pawing each other under the stars.

Decision made, I dip a hand under his shirt, splaying my fingers across his taut abdomen, exploring every ridge and valley as I steer him toward the tent. He groans into my mouth, and the ache building between my legs becomes almost unbearable. The urge to drag him to the ground again overwhelms me, but I shove it back, squeezing my thighs together to answer the need.

Dash's large hands palm my ass, and he lifts me off the ground, guiding my legs around his waist and adjusting my position until his length rests in the cradle of my thighs. I shift my hips, and the hardness straining behind his zipper twitches, unfurling another wave of unquenchable need in me and drawing a low curse from Dash. With nothing but a thin strip of cotton separating my wet heat from the bulge in his jeans, I shift again, shamelessly riding him like a teenager on prom night.

As if he can hear every naughty thought skittering through my mind, Dash picks up his pace, slowing only long enough to scoop Mom's ashes from the underbrush. A different kind of warmth spreads through my chest as he gently leans the urn against the side of the tent, making sure my mom is safe before unwinding my legs from his hips and setting me down.

He gazes down at me, cupping my face in both hands as if he's afraid to let go. Afraid I might disappear if he blinks. "Zoey, if you're not sure, we don't—"

I press a finger to his lips. "Yes. We do. I've never been more certain of anything."

Dash wordlessly takes my hand, slipping his fingers through mine and towing me into the tent. He releases me long enough to zip the flap and switch on the battery-powered lantern before turning his attention back to me. He doesn't waste time, dragging his T-shirt over his head and tossing it aside, his taut muscles bunching and flexing with the effort.

Then he reaches for the strap at my shoulder, and my pulse quickens. *This is it.*

The faint glow of lantern light reflects in his irises as he slides the narrow elastic down my arm before repeating the action on the other side, exposing my breasts to the night air. He presses a kiss to the center of my chest, directly over my heart, then tugs the flimsy undergarment over my head and drops it at his feet.

A shiver runs through me as he rakes his gaze over every inch of my body. "God, you're so beautiful."

Heat flares in his eyes as he dips his head and brings his mouth to mine again. This time, the kisses are slow, every sweep of his tongue telling me how much he wants me without uttering a single word. His warm hand cups my throat and slides down between my breasts, guiding me down until he has me sprawled out on the sleeping bag and he's kneeling above me.

"Dash . . ."

I've had sex before, more times than I care to remember, yet his gentle touch makes me wish this was my first time. I've never felt this *revered*, this *adored.*

With his lips still on mine, he resumes his exploration, gliding his fingers over my breasts, pausing to circle each peak before blazing a path down my abdomen to my stomach. Anticipation sends shivers through me as he traces my belly button, teasing a moan from me before hooking his fingers in the elastic waistband of my cotton undies. He drags the thin fabric down my legs and over my feet, tossing them aside before skating a hand from my ankle up my inner thigh to the apex, where his skilled fingers discover the sensitive spot at the center.

Wave after delicious wave of pleasure spikes through me as his featherlight touches turn more deliberate. Every stroke of his fingertips over the swollen bundle of nerves between my legs intensifies the overwhelming need coiling around my insides.

My heart pounds a furious rhythm as I reach for the hardness straining behind his zipper.

"Not yet." He wraps his free hand around my wrist, stopping me. "Let me make you feel good first."

His declaration sends me spiraling. Damian would *never* put me first. I always had to take what I needed from him.

The moment I nod my consent, Dash increases the pressure on my exposed nerves, making my legs quiver as the coil of pleasure building within me tightens into a knot.

Pinpricks of light burst behind my eyes. “I think I’m going to . . .” My breath stills, my entire body going rigid. Then I break free, shattering into a million shimmering pieces in his hands.

“Your turn,” I whisper, reaching for his fly.

A low growl rolls up his throat as I slip the button through the hole and drag down his zipper. Without missing a beat, he kicks off his jeans, pulls the strip of condoms from his pocket, and tears one open with his teeth. Then he rolls it over his hard length and positions his body between my legs.

Like a greedy cat, I arch into him, my pulse racing as he slowly pushes into me. We fit together like missing puzzle pieces, and I match each thrust of his hips with my own, moving beneath him as if we’ve done this a hundred times before. As if my soul has known his forever.

Fire licks through my veins. The heat in my belly flares as I build toward something bigger than just another release. Something I’m not quite ready to put into words. Something that has the potential to be everything I never knew I wanted.

25

Panic in Detroit

"After all that, she just leaves?" I slam the diary shut with a loud sigh and shove it back into the tote tucked between my feet in the front seat of the Tesla. I don't know why I'm so disappointed. What happened on my mother's trip has nothing to do with me. But I can't help but feel cheated. "My mom was a player."

"What are you talking about?" A deep groove forms between Dash's eyebrows.

"Mom and Ryan. They had this epic romance going, then she dips out the next morning without a backward glance. No explanation. She goes on to the next stop as if it . . . as if *he* never happened."

Dash shifts in his seat, stealing glances at me while he drives. "Do you think maybe she knew it wasn't realistic to expect more with a guy she literally just met?"

The parallels between Mom's trip and ours hang between us like a thick fog.

"You'd think after having *sex* they would've at least exchanged phone numbers. I get this was before social media, but it's not like they lived on different continents. And even if they did, they could've been pen pals!"

A wide smile takes over Dash's features. "You wanna be pen pals?"

"Maybe?" I glance at his wrinkled shirt and rumpled hair, falling for him all over again. Our eyes lock, and I slip my fingers through his across the console. Saying goodbye to Dash once we've visited all of Mom's stops will be one of the hardest things I'll ever do.

"Maybe Ryan lacked a certain . . . *finesse*?" He locks his gaze on mine and brushes his thumb across my wrist.

Heat climbs up my throat, pinking my cheeks as I replay every glorious moment from the night before. There was no lack of finesse on Dash's part. In fact, he more than exceeded every expectation. Hours later, my bones are still jelly.

As I contemplate asking him to find somewhere secluded so we can pick up where we left off, a buzz from my bag drags me back to the present. With a wistful sigh, I dig out my phone and glance at the display before pressing it to my ear.

"Hey, Jeanie. How's the leg?"

She lets out a loud snort. "Hurts like hell. And it's screwing with my tan lines." Leave it to my sister to be more worried about her tan than broken bones. "You should be riddled with guilt for ruining my summer."

I roll my eyes, wishing she could see the gesture. "Did you really call to torment me again?"

"Actually, no." She laughs. "The Cleveland police just called to say someone turned in your wallet."

"No way." My eyes widen, and I turn to Dash. "They found my wallet."

"I know, right? I figured it was a lost cause. I mean, your money and your cards are long gone. They totally cleaned you out. But apparently your license and your library card were still inside. I can't believe you actually filled out the stupid ID card that came with the wallet. That's how they knew to call the house."

"That's what it's there for."

"If you say so."

"Are they mailing it home?"

"That's why I called. They said they could send it, or you could swing by the police station and pick it up. I checked your location on the app and saw you were a few hours away, so I figured I'd see if you wanted to grab it before they stick it in the mail."

Ignoring the fact that my sister is openly stalking me across the country, I turn my attention to Dash. "They said I can pick it up."

"Where?" He glances at our location on the display.

"Cleveland."

He smiles. "It's on the way."

With my temple resting on the passenger window, and my wallet—and license—back where they belong, I count the mile markers as we fly down the highway.

Dash pulls his gaze from the road and quirks a brow. "Food or sleep?"

"What?"

"That look. Are you fantasizing about food or sleep?" Less than a week together and he already gets me better than Damian did after several years. And if the grin is any indication, he knows it.

As if answering for me, my stomach rumbles. Other than splitting a few stale graham crackers and half a chocolate bar that escaped the pee-bomb, we haven't eaten since breakfast.

He chuckles. "Dinner it is."

He takes the next exit and pulls into a diner that reminds me a lot of BB's. All it needs is a giant guitar on the roof and it could be the same place.

Inside, the similarities end with the Formica counters and red vinyl stools. Instead of bright neon and rock and roll paraphernalia, the unadorned walls are covered in greasy stainless steel panels that are way overdue for a good cleaning.

The place is packed, so we grab the only two open seats at the counter.

"So what's the plan?" Dash side-eyes me over the dirty menu. "After the last few stops, I'm almost afraid to ask what your mom has in store for us next."

"Now that you mention it . . ." Smirking, I drag the diary out of my bag and flip to Mom's entry for the Motor City.

A yellowed photo of Mom standing in the rain in front of a run-down old house with hundreds of brightly colored polka dots painted all over the worn white siding brings a smile to my lips as I skip ahead and read a snippet of the entry to him.

> *Before we even hit the city limits, Mom told me she had a surprise waiting for me in Detroit. She wouldn't tell me what it was, but the familiar gleam in her eye has butterflies crashing around my insides like a bunch of drunks at a football game. I can only imagine the crazy plan she has percolating in her mad-scientist's brain.*

"Please don't tell me your mom rappelled from a skyscraper or boosted a car." Dash laughs, but the tremble in his voice gives his nerves away.

"Don't be a baby," I tease before picking up where I left off.

> *So much for my surprise. We got to Detroit smack in the middle of one of the coldest Julys on record. Cold and wet. It rained the entire time we were there. Most disappointing stop so far. At least we got to see the Fisher Theater and a few of the cool houses at the Heidelberg Project. Hopefully I don't end up with pneumonia.*

"Well, that's disappointing." I close Mom's diary and shove it into my bag. "No grand theft auto, and they didn't even jump from a single skyscraper."

Dash lets out a sigh of relief.

"Don't pack up your parachute quite yet." I pluck another laminated menu from behind the napkin holder and skim the selections. "There's always Chicago."

He snorts. "Don't even joke about spreading her ashes from the Sears Tower. I draw the line at BASE jumping."

Although beyond reckless and stupid, the thought *had* crossed my mind. "I make no promises."

"You jump off a building, you go alone." He drags his gaze back to the menu. "That's all I'm saying."

I grin. "Chicken."

After stuffing ourselves with burgers and fries, Dash grabs the check before the waitress has a chance to set it down.

"I can pay for my own food." I scowl at him. "I may not be rich, but I do have a little money, you know."

"I know." He brushes my hand as he slides his credit card onto the counter. "But I want to."

A minute later, the waitress comes back and eyes the shiny plastic card. With a sour expression, she points to the sign above the register. "Cash. Only."

Just after sundown, we stroll into the lobby of the Hotel Saint Regis, wearing the same clothes as yesterday—and reeking of campfire, sex, and the woods. The hair on the back of my neck prickles as dozens of eyes bore into my back, reminding me I don't belong in the fancy establishment. But by the time I'd finished spreading Mom's ashes at the park across from the Fisher Theater, it was too late to re-create her photo at the Heidelberg Project's Dotty Wotty House, so Dash suggested we find a nice hotel for the night, and I willingly agreed.

With my head held high, I tuck my tote under my arm and follow Dash to the registration desk, pretending I'm not tracking dirt all over their pristine tile floors. He tosses a wink over his shoulder, and the glimmer in his eyes tells me *sleeping* isn't all he has in mind. As long as I get a long, hot shower first, I'm all for that idea. Now that I've had a taste of him, all I want is more.

"Your card was declined." The dark-haired woman behind the desk slides Dash's card back across the polished stone counter.

"Declined?" Dash rocks back on his heels and rubs the back of his neck. "I've been traveling. Maybe the bank flagged my card."

The desk clerk raises a finely chiseled eyebrow. She glances at each of us in turn, making her chin-length jet-black hair sway from side to side. "Would you like to try another card?"

Dash nods, glancing at me as he pulls a shiny black card from his wallet.

She snatches the plastic from his fingers and shoves it into the card reader.

Several seconds pass before she flashes a pinched smile. "Declined."

"What?" Dash's voice echoes through the lobby. "Not possible. Run it again."

Lifting that thin eyebrow again in a silent challenge, she slides the card into the reader a second time and waits. "Declined."

"Fine." He huffs and pulls out his phone. "I'll just book a room and pay for it online."

"You'll still need a valid credit card to check in." The woman's cold smile sends a chill down my spine.

Dash's expression crumples as he turns to me. "I don't understand what's happening."

"Maybe you should call the bank," I whisper.

With a curt nod, Dash retrieves his card from the woman's bony fingers and storms through the lobby.

My dirty sneakers slap against the marble as I chase after him, barely catching the words *card* and *declined* before the double glass doors close between us. By the time I reach him, he's half a block away, pacing the sidewalk with his phone pressed to his ear and his fingers knotted in his tangled hair.

"How is that possible? Reopen them!" He comes to an abrupt halt and drops the hand from his hair. "What do you mean you can't? Who reported them stolen? I don't care what your system says, I didn't—" His eyes widen, and his breath stills. "I'll call back later."

He disconnects the call and turns his back to me as he dials another number.

"You crossed a line this time," he growls into the phone, his body trembling with suppressed rage. "You had *no* right! Those belong to me! I pay the bills, not you!" The vein in Dash's neck pulses as he works to keep his emotions contained. "I told you, I made a promise!"

Dash stops pacing, and a dark laugh rolls up his throat.

My stomach plummets.

"No, Dad. I never promised *you* anything. I said I would *consider* your offer, but I needed time. You agreed to give me the summer." His nostrils flare as he goes back to pacing. "The *whole* summer!"

The urge to go to him is so strong, and I grip my tote with both hands to keep from reaching out. Even arguing in hushed tones, his voice echoes through the night air as he lights into the person on the other end of the line.

"That's extortion! You wouldn't . . ." The color drains from Dash's face, and he comes to an abrupt halt again just a few feet away. "That was a gift! Hello? Dad? Damn it!"

For half a second, I expect him to hurl his phone into the dark abyss. Instead, he pockets it and grabs my hand, pulling me down the sidewalk.

"Slow down!" My pulse skyrockets as I struggle to keep up, tripping over my feet every few steps. "Talk to me."

"We need to hurry." Dash picks up his pace, dragging me into the parking garage.

"Why?" My voice echoes through the dark space. "Dash, you're scaring me. What's going on?"

"Stop!" Dash's panicked voice turns my blood cold. He drops my hand and runs toward a man standing at the back of a tow truck. "Please! You can't do this!"

"Sorry, man." The guy doesn't bother to make eye contact as he finishes securing the Tesla to the flatbed. He double-checks the cables and climbs into the cab. "I'm just doin' my job."

Dash stands frozen on the concrete as the truck growls to life and slowly pulls away. I want to scream at him to do something, but I'm as paralyzed as he is. Once the taillights disappear around the corner, I notice our bags sitting in the empty parking spot like abandoned orphans.

"How could your father do that?" I release a juddering breath. "Does he realize he's stranded us in downtown Detroit? At night?"

Dash turns to me, his face deathly pale in the eerie overhead light. With his hollow eyes shimmering, he reminds me of a lost child. "I don't think he cares. As far as he's concerned, he gave me fair warning, and I didn't fall in line."

"He told you he was going to have your car towed?" My voice comes out like vapor, dissipating into the shadows.

"Everything with him comes with strings. But I didn't think he'd actually do it. So much for my graduation gift." Leaning against the concrete wall, Dash deflates and slides all the way down until he's sitting in the empty parking stall. After a long moment of silence, he gazes up at me, his expression anguished. "I'll fix this, I promise."

"How, Dash?" A wave of panic threatens to drown me. "How will you fix it?"

He lowers his eyes. "I don't know yet."

"I'm sorry," I whisper as guilt chases the fear in my veins. This is all my fault. If Dash hadn't been helping me, this would never have happened.

"No." He squeezes my hand, flashing a sad smile. "You have no reason to be sorry. This is my fault. I'm the one he's angry with."

"But if you weren't here with me . . ." I swallow a sob.

I really am a magnet for disaster.

"Hey." He pulls me down beside him until we're hip to hip on the cool concrete. "There isn't anywhere I'd rather be."

I rest my head on his shoulder. "I heard you on the phone. This happened because of me. Because you promised—"

"Zoey, no." Dash wraps me in a tight hug. "None of this is your fault. If you'd said no to my offer, I would've found another way to tag along on your adventure."

"But what if your dad—"

"Does what? Has me evicted from my apartment? Even if that's possible, I can't do anything about it until I get back. And . . ." Dash scans the deserted parking garage. "At the moment, I'm more concerned about being swallowed by the bowels of Detroit if we don't find a safe place to shelter for the night."

I straighten my spine and tug my tote into my lap. "Hotels cost money, and we don't have a single working card between us. You heard Cruella. Even if we booked and paid online, we'd still need a card to check in."

"So we find a place that accepts cash." Dash digs in his pocket and pulls out a stack of wrinkled bills. "I have twenty-seven dollars. What about you?"

I do a quick calculation in my head. "Maybe twenty. And a few more in loose change."

"So, fifty?"

"About that. But there's no way we'll find a decent hotel for less than a hundred."

"Sure we will." Dash forces a smile. "You'll see."

"I doubt we could take an Uber across town for fifty, but if you say so." I rest my head on his shoulder. "I wish Hicksville wasn't so far away. The Betty should be ready by now." Thinking of G-Lo's car sparks a fresh idea, and I fish my phone from my pocket. "I'm gonna call my grandma. She offered to send me money the old-fashioned way. I think it's time to take her up on that."

Dash laughs. "Old-fashioned? Like mailing a check to the parking garage?"

"Western Union? MoneyGram?"

His blank stare speaks volumes.

"Come on." I gape at him. "You've seriously never heard of MoneyGram? Where I'm from, there's one in every Walmart and CVS—surely you've seen the big-ass sign in the window. And even small towns have Western Union kiosks at just about every grocery store. A big city like Detroit must have at least one location open late."

"I've never been much of a Walmart or grocery store kind of guy."

I roll my eyes. "Sounds like it's time to check your privilege, Dash. Must be nice having rich parents."

"Hold that thought." Dash's eyes light up, and he presses a quick kiss to my lips before jumping to his feet and pulling me to mine. "I need to make a quick phone call."

26

Fame

"Oh no. Forget it." A shudder runs through me as I gape down at the fuzzy image on Dash's phone display.

After making his mysterious call, Dash went to work searching for a cheap motel within walking distance of the parking garage.

"Can't we just take a bus around the city all night long? Or find a Walmart to wander through? We can grab a nap in a changing room. Either choice would be infinitely more sanitary than *that*."

"Come on." Dash chuffs. "I seem to recall one of us leaping from a rusty train trestle yesterday."

"So?" I steal another peek and shudder at the image on his screen. My skin crawls at the thought of staying anywhere that charges by the hour.

"I didn't hear you freaking out about bacteria or tetanus shots then. But now you're afraid of a little hotel room?" Dash stretches the image to its full, horrifying glory. "See, it's not that—"

"Look! Right there." I tap the lumpy blue bedspread in the center of the photo. "I can totally see the bedbugs from here."

"You can't—" Dash squints. "We can lay on top."

"Forget it. I'd need to disinfect my entire soul. And that's if we survived the night. I've seen this movie. I know how it ends."

As if proving my point, a bloodcurdling scream dissolves into loud cackles, and a rowdy group of drunken twentysomethings bursts out of the shadows.

A shudder cuts through me. "Walmart's looking better every minute."

"We'd spend all our money getting an Uber to the closest store."

My chest tightens as I consider bailing on the photo at Heidelberg. "Let's just go to Chicago tonight. It can't be more than four hours away, how much could a pair of bus tickets cost?"

"Zoey, no." Dash's eyes search mine. "You wouldn't get your picture."

"Really. It's fine." The lie catches in my throat, but I force a smile and swallow it down. "Mom would forgive me for skipping this one, given the circumstances."

"You've re-created her picture at every other stop."

"What does one picture matter in the grand scheme?" Fighting the urge to cry, I drop my gaze to the sticky garage floor.

"It matters to me." Dash hooks a finger under my chin, lifting my face until our eyes meet. "I wouldn't forgive myself if you missed a single moment because of me."

My stomach flips at the intensity of his gaze. "What about the all-night laundromat we passed on the way here? We could go there."

A smile tugs at his lips, and he pulls me to my feet. "I guess that's as good a place as any at this point. We can at least bleach the funk out of our clothes."

With my tote tucked under my arm, I squeeze Dash's hand and lead him out of the dark parking garage and down the block to the blissfully well-lit laundromat.

A far cry from the Saint Regis, but other than the burned-out light in the back corner, it's bright. And aside from an old woman with her nose buried in a book, the place is empty and relatively clean.

"See?" I nudge him with my shoulder. "Isn't this much better than some nasty hotel room?"

His dark eyebrows peek over the top of his black frames, sizing me up like a snack. "If you don't count the lack of a bed . . . or a shower . . . or—"

"I'm willing to make the sacrifice just this once." I spread out across a row of blue hard-plastic chairs attached to a single frame. "Besides, who needs a bed when we have these?"

◆ ◆ ◆

After digging up enough quarters to wash and dry a giant load, Dash and I use what's left of my loose change to split a nasty potted-meat sandwich from the vending machine and settle into a quiet corner to eat.

I do a sniff test before taking a tentative bite, chewing and swallowing before I change my mind. Who the hell decided putting meat in a blender would make for a good sandwich spread? "Jeanie would totally lose it if she saw me eating this."

Dash devours his half in just a few bites. "It's better than starving."

"If you say so." I snicker. "Wouldn't it be ironic if, after all the wild shit I've done on this trip, I die from a vending machine sandwich?"

Dash laughs and reaches for Mom's diary. "May I?"

I nod.

He flips through the pages, studying the photos in each section until he comes to the picture of Mom in front of the Dotty Wotty House. "Were you really considering skipping this photo?"

I shrug, unwilling to admit how close I'd been to bailing on Detroit.

"I can really see the resemblance here," he says.

Heat rushes to my cheeks. "I still think Jeanie looks more like her than I do."

"I didn't mean you." Dash lifts his head. "I see a resemblance between your mom and Bowie."

I rest my chin on his shoulder and squint down at the photo. With her head tilted to the side, and her wet hair plastered to her face, Mom doesn't look like herself, much less a famous rock star. "You can't even see her face."

"But look at that smile."

I shift my focus to Mom's mischievous grin. As far-fetched as the idea may be, I can *almost* see what Dash means. "Maybe a little. But that doesn't mean anything."

"She never told you the story?" Dash hands me the diary and pulls a knee to his chest. "About your grandma and the Ziggy tour?"

"Nope, never said a word. I mean, I always knew she liked Bowie. But I had no idea how much until the day he died." A thick lump forms in my throat, and I swallow it down.

"What do you mean?"

Memories rush back, and my eyes sting with unshed tears. Dash squeezes my hand as if he knows my heart is breaking all over again. He nods for me to continue.

I clear my throat. "I still can't get the look on her face out of my head. I'd never seen my mom cry so hard in my entire life. Not even three weeks later when she was diagnosed with cancer. I never got around to asking her why David Bowie's death hit her so hard. The topic never came up again, and she was so sick, it never seemed to be the right time." I lower my eyes to the pink-and-gray-speckled linoleum floor. "Then she died, and my grandma Lola rolled up in front of the church in her butt-ugly Cutlass—over an hour late for Mom's funeral—and the pieces started falling into place like a giant puzzle."

"That's . . ." Dash lets out a long breath. "Wow."

"I don't believe a single word of it. My best guess is that my grandma came up with the story back in the day to cover her shame. It was the pre-Roe seventies, and she was young, pregnant, and probably didn't even know who the guy was. I'm guessing she told the lie so many times she started to believe it herself."

"It's a stretch, but not entirely impossible." Dash opens the diary again and flips to the picture of my mom in front of the junk house.

I chuckle under my breath. "I love my grandmother, but she's the original wild child. And definitely not firing on all cylinders."

"But your mom believed it?"

"She must have." I snatch the diary from his hands, close it, and slide it into my tote, hoping to close the subject along with it. "Why else would she send me on this crazy mission?"

"Come on." Excitement oozes from Dash's pores. "You can't tell me some small part of you doesn't think it's possible."

"Sure." I heave out a breath. "I still believe in Santa and the Easter Bunny, too."

"Listen." Dash rakes a hand through his hair. "Bowie did a lot of interviews where he talked about all the indiscriminate sex he had back in the day. So it's not impossible."

"Maybe not." I stand and stretch, putting some distance between us. "But it *is* highly improbable. I really don't care either way. This trip isn't about who was or wasn't my mom's sperm donor, it's about honoring the promise I made her."

"You've got to admit, it would make for a great story."

"Right. Because I'd love the whole world to think my mom and my grandma were crazy . . . or liars." A nervous laugh rolls up my throat. "No thanks."

Dash jumps up and follows me across the room as I check on the clothes. "But you must be curious, at the very least."

"Maybe, in the beginning. But now, I'm just glad I get to connect with Mom this one last time." I reach into the dryer and drag out the still-damp clothes, stuffing them into a wire laundry cart. They need at least ten more minutes, but quarters aren't the only things I'm out of. "In my head, I know she's gone. But in my heart, I swear she's been right beside me this whole time." I glance around the dingy laundromat and snicker. "Maybe not *here*."

Dash fishes his things from the cart, folding them before placing them in his bag. "You know you could probably make a fortune selling your story."

"To who?" I snort.

"I don't know. *People*?"

"What people? The bottom-dwellers of *Tattle Tale* magazine? No thanks, I'm not interested." I shove my clothes into my backpack with more force than necessary. The idea of exposing my family secrets to a bunch of strangers turns my stomach. "All I want is to get back on the road and finish what I started."

"About that . . ." Dash leans against the block wall and fidgets with his glasses.

I study him out of the corner of my eye.

"I, uh . . . came up with a plan to get money."

"I told you." Abandoning my laundry, I drape my arms over his shoulders. "I'm gonna call G-Lo and Jeanie, and have them send—"

He presses a finger to my lips. "This one's on me. It's my fault we're in this situation."

"I'm a big girl, Dash." I let out a breath. "I don't need—"

He pulls me into a tight embrace. "I got us into this mess, please let me get us out?"

I reluctantly nod, and his smile lights up the room.

"Okay, then." He presses his lips to my temple. "By the time we finish getting your picture at Heidelberg, I should have enough to get us to Chicago. From there, we can head to Hicksville to pick up your grandma's car."

Curious, I tilt my head to look at him sideways. "How'd you pull that off?"

"Oh, you know." He shrugs. "Sold my soul to the devil."

Warm arms wrap around me, and Dash's voice rumbles beneath my ear. I sit up and wipe drool from my chin. The flowery aroma of fabric softener and laundry detergent fills the air. "What time is it?"

"Just after seven." He tucks a few napkins and a pen into his back pocket, then brushes his lips across my bare shoulder.

Dappled sunlight streams through the dirty windows, highlighting an army of dust motes floating in the air. Across the room, a pair of old women steal glances at us as they unload their baskets into open washers. "I can't believe we slept here."

"*We* didn't. *You* did." As if he can't stop touching me, Dash presses another kiss to the top of my head. "I was busy standing guard."

"Oh. Thank you." Memories from the night before race around my head like rats in a maze. I drifted off to the sound of Dash's voice as he shared his hopes and dreams for the future. "I didn't mean to fall asleep on you."

"I really didn't mind." He gives my hand a squeeze and nods toward the open restroom in the corner. "But you should probably clean up so we can head out. It's a long walk to Heidelberg from here."

Nodding, I climb to my feet and grab my tote.

When Dash said it would be a long walk, he wasn't kidding. Over an hour after leaving the laundromat, loaded down with our bags like a pair of refugees, we finally reach the whimsical art displays on Heidelberg Street.

The entire block is one large evolving, open-air gallery, attracting tourists from all over. The actual houses look as though someone passed out paintbrushes, glitter, and glue sticks to the neighborhood kids and said, "Go wild!"

Ignoring the growing swarm of people, I focus on the main house. It looks like it's evolved since Mom was here. The paint looks fresher, the dots bigger and brighter.

"Do you think . . . ?" I turn toward Dash, but he's lost in his own thoughts, eyes riveted on the crowd.

The color drains from his face.

"Dash?"

My voice snaps him out of it. He locks his gaze on me and cups my face in both hands. "Do you trust me?"

"Of course. Why?" Confusion turns to concern as Dash slips his fingers through mine and pulls me forward. "What's wrong?"

His grip tightens as he steers me away from the throng. "I'll tell you as soon as—"

"There she is!" A woman's excited shriek cracks the air. "Zoey!"

It never fails to surprise me when I hear my name in the wild. Curiosity gets the best of me, and I search the crowd for the other Zoey.

"Zoey, over here!" another voice—a man this time—shouts.

Startled, I whip my head toward the sound and lock eyes with a tall, silver-haired man. With a prickle of anxiety zipping down my spine, I turn to Dash. "He can't be talking to me, can he?"

Gripping my hand, Dash freezes, his mismatched eyes as wide as stop signs. He moves to step between me and the strangers, but there are too many of them.

A petite brunette rushes toward me, a recording device in her outstretched hand. "When did you first find out? How did that make you feel?"

"Find out about what?" Beside me, Dash pales, and my heart skips a beat. "I think you have the wrong person."

"How much did your mother tell you about her father?" The woman takes another step forward until she's within the bubble of my safe zone.

Before I can process what's happening, a stampede of people armed with cameras, microphones, and selfie sticks descend upon us. Questions come at me from all sides, the voices blending into one, like a swarm of locusts buzzing around me.

"Did your mother talk about Bowie?"

"Did Bowie know?"

"Is that why he didn't leave you anything in his will?"

"Where's the proof?"

"Did you get a DNA test?"

"Do you really believe your mother was Bowie's love child?"

"Why spread her ashes along the tour?"

"Did your mother really die of cancer?"

My heart stills, my next breath frozen in my lungs. They know. About Mom. About Bowie. About *everything*.

Dread seeps into my bones as I whip around to face Dash. "How did they know we'd be *here*?"

Dash scrubs a hand over his face. "I—"

"Dash Hammond?" A stocky man in an orange-and-pink Hawaiian shirt shoves his cell phone camera in Dash's face. "Aren't you supposed to be working on the Hill with your dad?"

"Over here, Dash." Cameras click and flashes go off as the mob moves in on Dash.

"Does Daniel know you're slumming it with a gold digger?"

I tear my gaze from the stranger and gape at Dash again. "What did he just call me?"

"Where's your mother, Dash?" Hawaiian Shirt Guy pushes his way to the front of the pack. "Did Lauren send you?"

"Your mother?" My head spins from the constant barrage of questions, the contents of my stomach churning. "Why would she—"

"She doesn't know?" Hawaiian Shirt Guy barks out a laugh.

My mouth goes dry as I gaze up at Dash, probing his eyes for answers. "You said your mother was a writer."

"Oh, she's a writer, all right." One of the circling sharks, a petite woman with a spiky pink pixie cut, smirks at Dash. "His mother is only *the* Lauren Michaels. Editor of *Tattle Tale* magazine."

Dash points a trembling finger at Pink Hair. "This has nothing to do with my mother."

"Did you scoop her, Dash? I'll bet Lauren's beaming with pride!" Hawaiian Shirt Guy raises his hand for a high five, but Dash glares at him.

My chest tightens, and I gape at Dash as if seeing him for the first time. A light gust ruffles my hair, my last shred of hope desiccating and blowing away with it. "Is *that* who you called last night?"

Dash rakes a hand through his hair, his eyes wild. "I know what you're thinking, but you're wrong."

For the first time since we met, I don't believe him.

"If I'm wrong, explain how all these people knew where to find us." The remains of my breakfast threaten to make a reappearance as his words from last night rush back to me. *You could probably make a fortune selling your story.* "Is *this* how you're getting the money?"

"No!" Dash's eyes widen behind his dark frames. "I wouldn't! You know me better than that!" His anguished gaze locks on mine, and he reaches for me.

Yesterday, I would have latched on to his hand and never let go. Yesterday, I didn't know any better.

Heart thundering in my ears, I step back out of his reach. "Do I? Really?"

I'd trusted him. More than that, I'd shared intimate details with him that I'd never shared with anyone. I willingly gave myself to him, body and soul. And he—

Sold my soul to the devil. His words replay in my mind.

Every fiber of my being yearns to believe him, but the truth won't be ignored. "Maybe you're more like your dad than I realized. What is it they say about the apple not falling far from the tree?"

His jaw tightens. "I'm *nothing* like my dad."

"So, maybe, you're like your mom, doing whatever it takes to get the story. Your entire family is a bunch of vultures. Why should I believe you're any different?" A horrible thought bubbles up from somewhere deep. "The napkins. You've been scribbling secrets down since I met you. Have you been writing about me this whole time?"

Dash flinches as if I slapped him. "What? No!"

"What about your cards? And the Tesla? Were we ever really stranded?" I do a quick scan along the curb, hoping his betrayal doesn't run that deep. Not that it matters anymore. "Never mind."

Ignoring the relentless interrogation, I push past the circling sharks, determined to get as far from the feeding frenzy as possible.

"Zoey, wait!"

Dash matches my stride as I flee, easily catching up to me at the intersection. Outrunning him is impossible. He's too fast. No matter which way I turn, he blocks my path, dipping his head to look me directly in the eyes.

"Let me explain. Please?" His eyes beg me to listen.

"What?" Cornered, I throw up my hands. "What could you possibly say to me that would change anything?"

Gaze locked on mine, he takes another step toward me. "You're right. I've been keeping a secret from you, but it's not what you think. It's a career. A way for me to cut all those damn strings keeping me bound to a life I don't want. I couldn't risk anyone finding out. Not until I figured out what to do about my dad."

I'd trusted him with everything, and he'd given me nothing in return. Vibrating with anger and on the verge of tears, I tear my gaze from his and stare at my filthy sneakers. Oh, the places they've seen. "I've heard all I need to hear."

Between Dash's looming presence and my erratic pulse thrumming in my ears, I don't notice the sweaty, out-of-breath reporter approaching us until he shoves his phone in our faces.

"One question, Zoey!"

"Get that goddamned camera out of her face!" Dash knocks the guy's phone from his hand, and it lands on the pavement with a crack.

The reporter scoops his broken device from the road, muttering a few choice obscenities as he drags his disgusting gaze from Dash to me. "Did Hammond sleep with you before or after he got the whole story?"

My lungs seize, expelling my last breath in a loud hiss. Icy dread washes over me as my stomach does a death spiral.

"Zoey, no," Dash croaks, as if he's finally choked on all his lies.

The reporter nods, and his mouth hooks to one side in a knowing grin. "Like mother, like son. He learned from the best."

Bile crawls up my throat, and I swallow before I retch all over the sidewalk. Was I just a means to an end for him? A wave of panic washes over me, and I scan my surroundings for a way out. I'll walk all the way to Hicksville if it comes to that. "I can't be here anymore."

Dash invades my personal space, his gaze riveted to mine as he cups my face in his hands, forcing me to make eye contact. "I know how bad this must look to you right now, but don't listen to him. You know me. What happened between us was real. *We're* real."

"What color crayon, Dash?" My heart clenches as the fears I'd buried deep resurface. Were my instincts about him wrong? Could he have been red this whole time?

The firm grip on my face relaxes, and he backs up, his eyes drifting shut. "Zoey, please believe me. I didn't—"

"I don't know what I believe anymore." I turn my back on him and head toward a small group of people waiting in front of the bus stop at the next light.

"Zoey! Please . . . stop." Dash reaches for my arm, but I yank it away before he can get a good grip.

"Don't. Touch. Me!" My skin tingles, the aching need to be close to him battling with the truth, staring me right in the face. "They knew about my mom's cancer. And the diary. And *us*. How else would they know those things unless *you* told them?"

Dash's mouth goes slack, his breaths coming out in shallow pants. "My mom. But I didn't know she'd send reporters."

"Oh, okay." I roll my eyes and push forward. "As long as you didn't know."

"I didn't mean—"

"Like I said before, I've heard everything I need to hear. You're no better than Damian. I should've stayed in Hicksville and waited for them to fix G-Lo's car." When we reach the intersection, the growl of the approaching bus catches my attention, and I break into a run, not sure if I'm trying to outrun the paparazzi . . . or Dash.

"Where are you going?"

"Anywhere but here." My throat closes, my vision blurring with unshed tears as I inhale one jagged breath after another. It takes every ounce of self-control not to cry. As soon as the bus doors open, I jump in. The hurt in Dash's eyes breaks my heart, but I've learned my lesson. "Don't follow me."

The doors close behind me, leaving Dash alone on the sidewalk.

27

Sound and Vision

With Dash's betrayal lodged in the center of my chest like a thorny spine, embedded so deep it would take a team of surgeons to dig it out, I plop into a cracked vinyl seat and sit on my hands to stop the trembling. Shifting my eyes from the road outside the window, I drag in one shallow breath after another. Numbness radiates through my bones, quickly morphing into sharp pain and spreading like a virus until every nook and cranny screams for mercy.

Damn you, Dash Hammond. Damn you and your smirky grin and stupid shiny Tesla.

Part of me wants to set fire to his memory, to burn it out of my system until it doesn't hurt anymore. But a weak, pathetic piece of me refuses to let go. I kissed this man with my eyes closed and my heart wide open. I gave him a part of myself I can never get back, and he betrayed me as though I meant nothing to him.

Utterly devastated and alone, I drag out my phone and scroll through my favorites, pausing with my thumb hovering over Mom's number. For the longest half second ever, I stare at her contact info. Then the fog clears, and fresh tears spill over my lashes. *She's gone.*

The weight of her loss settles into my chest as I wrap my arms around my tote, hugging Mom's urn and diary as if the inanimate objects might hug me back. I wish I could rewind the clock to before she died. Wish I'd listened to Jeanie and waited for her leg to heal. There are so many things I wish I'd done differently.

Resting my head against the cool glass, I watch the world outside the window pass by as, bit by bit, the wall of ice around my heart begins to melt, freeing the emotions I've held in check for the past two years.

For the first time since Mom died, I dissolve into bone-racking sobs.

Almost an hour later, after riding three full circuits of the city bus's route, reality sets in. I can't stay on this bus forever. I need to find a way to get out of Detroit and back to Hicksville. And the Betty.

A quick online search tells me the nearest Greyhound station is just a short walk from the next stop. Using PayPal, and most of what I had left in my checking account, I book two tickets. First, a seat on the next bus to Chicago to spread Mom's ashes, followed by a ticket from there to Hicksville on the last bus tonight. I refuse to let Dash Hammond derail my mission any more than he already has.

With my eyes and nose leaking like a rusty faucet and my heart shattered into a million pieces, I exit onto Michigan Avenue and walk the rest of the way to the bus station.

After picking up my tickets, I hurry on board the first bus before it leaves the station. Ignoring the blank stares of the other passengers, I lug my tote and backpack behind me until I reach an empty window seat near the back. After tucking my backpack behind my feet, I loop my arms around my tote, cradling it like a baby. With Mom's diary open to her Chicago entry, I settle in for the long ride.

July 12

My mother is like a cat with nine lives, only instead of lives, it's get-out-of-jail-free cards. After sneaking into a sightseeing tour of Lake Michigan, Mom talked our way into Wrigley Field for a Cubs game, and then we swam in Buckingham Fountain . . . all without ending up in striped jumpsuits. Sometimes, I swear she's playing an epic game of tag, and the loser gets an all-expenses-paid trip to the county lockup. One of these days, she's going to run out of cards, and I just hope I'm not caught in the dragnet when she does . . .

◆ ◆ ◆

More than five hours, and several stops, later, the bus finally pulls into Union Station. Easily the size of several football fields and filled to the brim with travelers rushing off in every direction, the palatial building looks like something ripped right out of the pages of Fitzgerald or Hemingway. Decades of history ooze from the walls and the marble floors, and I nearly get swept into the crowd before even making it outside.

I need to conserve what little cash I have, so with less than an hour before I lose what's left of the light, I head west. According to the guy at the information desk, Grant Park and Buckingham Fountain are only about a twenty-minute walk.

Burnt-orange and purple shafts of evening sun slice through the gaps in the buildings as I make my way through downtown Chicago. I don't have time to take in the scenery, and I refuse to think about walking back in the dark.

By the time I reach the massive three-tier fountain, it's lit up like a damn space station. Classical music accompanies the light show as plumes of water erupt from the center spout.

Eager to get my picture and get the hell out of town, I push my way through the tourists and run straight into an ornate green metal fence surrounding the perimeter. I could easily step over the low barrier, but I can't help noticing that out of the hundreds of people here, not a single soul stands on the other side.

. . . the loser gets an all-expenses-paid trip to the county lockup.

I take one last look at the picture of Mom in Buckingham Fountain before tucking it between the pages of her diary and shoving them both deep into my tote.

"I'm about to regret this, aren't I?" I toss the question into the wind.

"If you're thinking about getting into that fountain, then yeah. Big-time regret."

I whip my head around and stare at the stocky guy in the shiny new Cubs jersey. "What are you talking about?"

His wide grin exposes a gap between his front teeth wide enough to park a number-two pencil. The sweat forming on his dark skin reflects like diamonds in the light. "There's a security system around the fountain."

"Oh." Eyeing the fence with fresh eyes, I step back. Great. "Is it electrified?"

The Cubs fan shrugs. "I heard a couple got arrested a few months ago after swimming in the fountain. No one mentioned them getting electrocuted."

"Hmm." My plan to get a selfie from inside the pool just got a bit more challenging. "Not impossible then."

The guy gapes down at me, his thick eyebrows jutting into his forehead. "I guess that depends on your goal. Is a night in jail on your scavenger hunt list?"

If he only knew.

"Not exactly." A loud laugh explodes out of my throat, and I bite down on my bottom lip to keep from blabbering my life story. "I only need a picture."

"Oh, if that's all." He rolls his eyes.

I huff. "My mom climbed into that fountain thirty years ago to have her picture taken."

He shrugs. "So?"

"So she died a few weeks ago, and—" I snap my mouth shut. "Never mind, I'll figure it out on my own. Thanks for the info."

"I'll take it."

The guy's sympathetic smile triggers my tear ducts again, and I sniff back the waterworks. "Take what?"

Cubs guy looks away and blinks a few times before turning back to me. He exhales a long breath. "Your damn picture."

"Really? You'd do that?"

"Yeah, really. But I don't know what triggers the system. Could be the fence. Could be the actual fountain. You need to get in and get out. Make it fast. You've got ten minutes, tops, before the cops get here."

"Got it! Thank you!" I bring up the camera app and hand the guy my phone. "You just—"

He rolls his eyes again. "I know how to work an iPhone."

Less than four yards of freshly cut grass separates the fence from the pink marble fountain rim. A little voice inside my head—Dash's voice—reminds me to be careful. I can only imagine the look on his face if he knew what I was about to do. I wish he *were* here to see how I don't need him to cover my back anymore. I've got this. I may not qualify as a full-blown rebel quite yet, but I'm also not the same timid damsel I was a week ago when I set out to spread my mother's ashes.

"I'll be right back." I set my backpack against the fence and leap over with my tote still slung over my shoulder. I might risk my phone and my clean underwear with a total stranger, but I'm not about to let Mom out of my sight. My heartbeat counts down the half seconds as I race across the grassy border. It takes me four long strides to get the edge of the fountain, and after setting my tote safely on the grass, less than a second to glide over the slippery side into the cool water.

My accomplice signals he's ready, and I quickly pose with one of the green seahorses behind me. His thumbs-up tells me he got the photo, and I don't waste any time dragging my soaked butt out of the pool and back across the grass.

My partner in crime hauls me over the fence and presses my phone into my wet hand.

Resisting the urge to hug him, I throw my phone into my tote and shove my arms through my backpack straps. Giddy excitement oozes out of my pores until I can taste the adrenaline. "Thank you!"

"Go!" He nudges me toward Columbus Drive with a gruff nod. "Get the hell out of here while you still can."

With a quick wave, I bolt into the crowd, hoping to blend in, and make my way back toward the crosswalk in the distance. My hair flies behind me as my feet pound the pavers, water squishing out of my sneakers with every step.

I choke out a loud laugh. Dash would never believe I made it in and out of the fountain without peeing my pants.

As I reach the busy street, I realize I forgot to spread Mom's ashes. I stop dead in my tracks and fumble with the urn. As soon as I get the lid off, I grab a fist of ashes and throw them into the air, ignoring the horrified looks from the crowd as I bolt across the road. The bus to Hicksville won't wait if I don't make it to the station on time.

The eventual crash from my adrenaline rush hits me somewhere between the last stop in Illinois and the first stop in Missouri. The fear of being robbed can't compete with the need to sleep. With my eyes drooping, and my mind wandering to places I really wish it wouldn't go, I start to drift off when a little boy with shaggy dark hair pops his head over the back of the seat in front of me. His big blue eyes stretch wide behind a pair of black plastic frames with no lenses. He watches me for a few seconds before opening his mouth. "Are you riding the bus all by yourself?"

"I am."

He nods and flashes his tiny teeth in a devilish smile. "My daddy said you prolly ran away from home."

I snicker at the low groan coming from the aisle seat in front of me. "No, I didn't run away."

"Gabriel!" The boy's name comes out in a sharp whisper, and Gabriel drops into his seat again. A haggard man leans into the aisle and turns to me with an apologetic smile. "I'm sorry, he's a little bored. It's been a long ride, and someone fed him way too much sugar." He rolls his eyes at the word *someone*, obviously implicating himself.

"Don't worry about it." I swallow another laugh. "He's not bothering me."

"See? I told you she was nice." Gabriel pops his head above the seat again, holding on to the back with both hands. "If you didn't run away, how come you're all by yourself?"

"Because no one wanted to come with me." The fib burns on the way out, and I point to his fake glasses. "Are you supposed to be Harry Potter?"

Gabriel groans and rolls his eyes in a perfect imitation of his father. "I'm Superman!" He lowers his voice to a whisper. "In disguise."

"Oh." A sharp twinge in my chest brings tears to my eyes. "I used to like Clark Kent a lot."

His dark head cocks to one side, and a small furrow forms between his little eyebrows. "You don't like him anymore?"

I swallow my conflicting emotions and shrug. "I haven't decided yet."

"Come on, Gabe." The man tugs the boy from his perch, leaving me alone with my feelings. "Let's get some sleep before the sun comes up."

After a two-hour layover in Memphis, I finally board the bus for Hicksville—tired, hungry, and reeking of sweaty feet and stale chips. The air-conditioning went out during the first fifteen minutes, and even at quarter to ten in the morning, the outside temperature must be hovering somewhere between deep in the heart of Texas and the bowels of hell. To make matters worse, the bus is as packed as a box of broken crayons, and other than a quick sponge bath in the laundromat, I haven't washed since Boston. Only the stench seeping out of the nearby toilet can outrank my foul odor.

I've spent the better part of an hour fighting sleep and avoiding the creepy guy across the aisle. His camo board shorts and bow-tie-with-suspenders novelty T-shirt make him look like he escaped from one of Jeanie's serial killer lineups.

Just when I'm about to lose the battle and drift off, my phone vibrates in my pocket. I'd basically given up on reaching G-Lo or Jeanie. They'd been either intentionally avoiding me or hungover. Maybe both. So when a picture of G-Lo, leaning against the Betty, smiles up at me from the display, I accept the call and press the phone to my ear. "Where have you been?"

"Who?" The surprise in G-Lo's voice almost makes me laugh.

"You!" I whisper shout. "I've been trying to reach you for hours."

G-Lo cackles down the line. "You didn't really expect me to answer the phone before nine, did you?"

"Did it ever occur to you I might've needed help?"

G-Lo clicks her tongue. "Not until you mentioned it. But you don't sound like you're calling from jail. Wait! You're not calling from jail, are you?"

"No!" My shriek draws unwanted attention from the creep across the aisle, so I turn toward the window and lower my voice. "But that's not the point. Do you think your car is ready for me to pick it up?"

"Why would you need my car? You already have a ride."

I press my fingers into my temple. "Had. Past tense."

"What happened?" G-Lo snickers. "What did you hit this time?"

"A whole family of vultures."

The line goes so quiet, I think I must have lost the call.

G-Lo clears her throat. "I guess that means you've met Dash's parents."

"You could say—wait. What do you know about them?"

"Oh no. Ask Dash. It isn't my story to tell."

"I can't exactly do that right now." I huff.

Part of me wants to tell her everything, but to do that, I'd have to relive it. I'm not ready to admit how stupid I was for putting my trust in him. How much I'd started to care about him. How I'd slept with him.

"Why? Did something happen? Is he okay?"

"*He's* perfectly fine." I grind out the words, irrationally angry at her misplaced concern.

"Honey, you sound upset. What's going on?"

I let out a long breath. Rehashing the past twenty-four hours is the absolute last thing I want to do. "I just need to get to Hicksville and pick up your car if it's ready."

"I spoke with the mechanic just the other day. She's better than ever and ready to go, but—"

"Good." I don't give her a chance to ask anything else. Now that the floodgates are open, I can barely hold back the tears as it is. "I should be there in an hour or so. I don't suppose you could wire me some money? I still don't have my cards, and I'm kinda tapped out."

"Of course! How much do you need?"

"As much as you can send? I can't use Apple Pay until I get a new debit card, and not everywhere takes Venmo. I promise I'll pay you back as soon as I get home."

"Don't worry about the money, sweetheart. I have plenty."

"Thank you." I swallow the growing lump in my throat.

"Zoey—"

"I have to go. I'll check in again later." I disconnect the call before the last thread holding me together completely unravels.

28

Soul Love

I never thought I'd be this happy to hear Bowie blasting from the crappy old speakers again. Somehow the mechanic managed to pry an entire armadillo out of the grill without dislodging the tape stuck in the 8-track. But since the stupid thing finally skipped to the next track, I'm willing to let that slide.

I couldn't care less that "Criminal World" has played on a loop for going on four hours straight. Or that the odds of getting the backs of my legs unstuck from the vinyl seats without losing a layer of skin are pretty slim. In fact, I solemnly swear I'll never complain about the broken gas gauge, the Whac-A-Mole windshield wipers, or the overwhelming stench of old tacos and unfiltered Camels again. At this moment, the Betty is my very best friend in the whole wide world, because absolutely nothing about the ancient Cutlass reminds me of Dash.

Best of all, the grumble of the Betty's geriatric engine drowns out the voices in my head for the better part of the drive to St. Louis.

After an unexpected detour and a few wrong turns, I finally catch a glimpse of the sleek, futuristic Gateway Arch towering over the city—on the *other* side of the Mississippi.

Uttering a string of obscenities that would make my sister proud, I backtrack to the highway in search of the closest bridge. As I cross the river into Missouri, sunlight glints off the curved steel monument, reflecting in the water below and taking my breath away.

I follow the signs to the Gateway Arch National Park and find an empty spot in the lot adjacent to the Old Cathedral, just a short walk to the monument and the riverbank beyond. According to Siri, the original concert venue is long gone, but surely Mom visited St. Louis's most famous landmark when she was here.

Determined to put the whole Dash debacle behind me, I step out of the car and straight into another scorching-hot summer day. Sweat trickles down my back as I take in my surroundings and get my bearings straight. The weight of Mom's ashes in my bag provides a much-needed reminder of why I set out on this journey to begin with.

What now, Mom? Where do I go first?

As I reach for her diary for guidance, I catch a glimpse of the historic church in front of me. A glint of gold draws my gaze up the polished stone facade—from the four heavy columns marking the entrance to the clock on the stone bell tower and then all the way to the shiny gold ball and cross at the very top of the towering steeple.

Other than going to Sunday school as a child, I've never been a regular churchgoer, but something about the centuries-old basilica calls to me. Maybe if I hadn't stopped going to church . . . if I'd prayed harder when Mom was sick . . . I shake off the thought before I tumble down a rabbit hole I'm not prepared to explore.

Would it be wrong of me to go inside . . . to say a prayer for her now, even though I'm not Catholic? After her funeral, I was in such a hurry to flee Reverend Tom's attempts to console me, I didn't pause long enough to consider the emotional ramifications. I glance down at my wrinkled shirt and tattered shorts. I look exactly like someone who slept on a Greyhound bus last night. But no one knows me here. Maybe I can slip in and out without being noticed.

The moment I enter through the heavy double doors, a sense of peace washes over me. Every detail, from the delicate moldings on the curved ceiling above and the sunlight streaming through the vivid stained glass windows, to the tall, graceful columns and stone floors, radiates serenity.

Without drawing attention to myself, I slide into a polished wooden pew near the back and offer up a silent prayer for my mom's soul—and another for my own. Then I pull out her diary and flip to the entry for St. Louis.

Instead of a worn Polaroid of Mom, posed in front of some landmark or another, a folded paper flutters from between the pages and lands squarely in my lap. The edges are yellowed and crisp, and I carefully unfold it, hoping it doesn't fall apart in my hands.

After scanning the fifty-something-year-old newspaper clipping announcing David Bowie's October 1972 concert in St. Louis, I carefully fold it again and set aside the memento to read Mom's account from that day.

> *July 14*
> *We made it to Kiel Auditorium about two months too late—technically six months if we'd hoped to see the 1930s Art Deco building in all its glory. And more than five decades since Ziggy Stardust played his final set on center stage. Mom cried as we pulled up to the vacant lot. There wasn't a single brick, stone, or fluted column marking the spot. We sat alongside the curb for a solid fifteen minutes while she mourned a loss I couldn't begin to understand. Then she dried her tears and drove away without a word. We wandered around the city for almost an hour, as if she expected to find the old building hiding around the next corner . . . down the next block. When she didn't find whatever it was she was looking for, we left the city without a backward glance. And we never spoke of St. Louis again.*

Why did they leave? She could've at least gotten a picture under the arch. And why would she want her ashes spread in St. Louis if she never even got out of the car?

The question still haunts me nearly half an hour later as I exit the basilica and wander toward the banks of the Mississippi and the Gateway Arch, skipping every opportunity for a selfie in solidarity.

Gazing up at the monument, framed by the clear blue sky, I trace the steel curve with my eyes until I reach the very top, hundreds of feet above my head, then follow the slope back down the other side. There's only one person who might know why they left town so quickly—why Mom never got her picture here.

With Mom's words flickering through my thoughts, I turn back toward the Betty, pulling out my phone and keying in my grandmother's number as I walk. I scrape my teeth across my bottom lip while I wait for her to answer. One ring turns into two, then three. Just when I think the call will roll to voicemail, she picks up.

"Well hello, sweetheart!" G-Lo's smile carries down the line. "Did you have any problems picking up the car?"

"No." I unlock the door and sit sideways in the driver's seat, facing the river. "I got it just fine."

"Good. Good. Did you, uh . . ." She hesitates for an instant. "Work things out with—"

"No." I stop her line of questioning before it has a chance to take hold. The irony of me digging into her past while avoiding questions about my own isn't lost on me. "That's not why I called. I actually have a question I'd like to ask you. About your trip with Mom."

"Sure. Go ahead. Ask me anything."

"I'm in St. Louis, and—"

G-Lo sighs. "I had a feeling this subject would come up eventually."

"You just left." I hook my finger around a loose thread on the Betty's upholstery but stop myself before tugging it free. "No pictures. No sightseeing. Nothing."

"We did." She lets out another heavy breath. "I simply couldn't bear to stay."

I glance toward a riverboat, lazily floating down the Mississippi. "What happened here that upset you so much?"

"St. Louis held so many fond memories for me. I was excited to show your mom the place . . ." Her voice cracks, and she takes a steadying breath. "But when we got there, they'd torn it down. Finding an empty lot where the building should've been . . . it broke my heart."

Anxiety gets the better of me, and I wind the long thread around my finger again and tug, snapping it off at the seam. "But why?"

The question hangs like a dark cloud between us, and for a moment I think she'll ignore it completely and move on to another topic, the way I did when she asked about Dash.

But she doesn't.

"Back in '72, nobody in St. Louis knew who the hell David Bowie was. The concert promoter barely sold enough tickets to fill the front row that night."

"So they canceled the show?" I don't remember St. Louis being scratched off the list of tour stops, but maybe I missed something.

"Cancel?" She scoffs. "Honey, that was the best damn show on the whole tour!"

Her outburst makes me laugh. "What made it so great?"

"There couldn't have been more than a few hundred people in the crowd, so he had us gather around the stage, right there in the orchestra pit. He bantered back and forth with us all night as if we were old friends." She lowers her voice to a whisper. "I was close enough to reach out and *touch* him."

The word comes out with such reverence, my pulse jumps. "Did you? Touch him?"

She laughs like a schoolgirl. "We made eye contact as he sang 'Soul Love'—it was the first time he'd performed it live. Hand to God, I swear he was singing it directly to me."

The line crackles between us for a long moment, and I wonder if the call dropped. Then she clears her throat.

"Your mother was conceived that night."

I suck in a sharp breath and sputter as saliva goes down the wrong pipe.

"You okay?" G-Lo chuckles. "I wasn't planning on sharing the dirty details, if that's what you were expecting."

"No! Definitely not. You just surprised me is all." Her confession brings up more questions than answers, but I sure as hell don't want to know any more of the intimate details when I already feel as though I'm eavesdropping on her memories. I steer the subject back to the present. "So if you didn't actually stop in St. Louis, where do I spread Mom's ashes?"

"We didn't stay in the city, but we did stop about an hour away for another little *adventure*. Keep reading. You'll love it!"

29

Space Oddity

First thing the next morning, I glance at a photo of Mom standing in what looks like the Upside Down, surrounded by inverted mountains and shafts of otherworldly light, and a hard shudder runs through me.

"You'll love it!" G-Lo said, but I'm beginning to think we have very different definitions of the word *love*.

> *July 15*
> *After bailing on St. Louis, Mom suggested we sign up for a guided caving expedition on our way to Kansas City. My stomach rolled into a ball, clenched itself tight, and it didn't let go the whole time we hiked the path to the first cave. The shallow opening carved into the rock face barely seemed big enough for a woodchuck, let alone a human. I was sure I'd get stuck, and the next person dumb enough to crawl in would find my favorite pair of Vans at the end of my rotting bones. As I crept along the damp earth on my knees and elbows like a slug, I couldn't stop wondering what was crawling around me in the dark. Every wispy web had me imagining the spider who built it. Every time I thought we were almost there, the*

walls closed in a little bit more, making my heart flutter like the flapping of tiny wings. And then it wasn't my heart at all . . . it was hundreds of leathery black wings clinging to the earthen ceiling above me. When we finally reached the end of the narrow passage and spilled into the open cavern, I could've sworn I'd dropped into the pages of Treasure Island. *The musty air smelled like old coins and fresh grave sites, and the light dancing off the crystals reminded me of the disco ball at prom. Best. Trip. Ever.*

I stow Mom's diary and climb behind the wheel of the Betty with my heart lodged in my throat and an Egg McMuffin sitting like a stone in my stomach. I'd always heard Missouri was the "Show Me" state but I had no idea about the labyrinth of caves.

A wave of Pavlov's claustrophobia sweeps through me at the mere thought of crawling into a dark cave alone. Or with a handful of strangers—doesn't really matter either way.

Where the hell is Dash when shit starts to get real?

Fresh anger spikes my blood pressure to the redline. He's probably cashing all his new checks and preparing to follow in Daddy's footsteps. Traitor.

Shoving Dash out of my thoughts, I take the next exit and follow the road signs to Satan's Butthole or whatever the hell the place is called. After circling around for over a mile, I park next to a brown Jeep wrapped with a cheesy "Bat Man Caving Adventure" ad and wait for the next guided tour to start. If Mom had only been as vague with the caves as she'd been with the campsite, I might've skipped it altogether, but no. This time, she had to be specific. And thanks to Google, it's as if she drew me a freaking map.

Once again, I fill my pockets with Mom's ashes and then shove her urn and diary back into my tote and store them in the trunk with my backpack. I already know there won't be enough room to drag anything but my phone with me.

One look at our guide, and I regret my decision. "Bat Man" obviously thinks he's clever wearing a black shirt with a giant yellow bat signal emblazoned across his chest, but I've had my fill of phony superheroes on this trip. The overgrown twelve-year-old corrals me and a half dozen middle-aged spelunkers, takes our money and stashes it in his khaki cargo pants, then passes out the safety equipment and leads us to the cave. Just like Mom described, the opening isn't much bigger than a medium-size dog door.

Whispering a silent prayer for my favorite jeans, I drop to my knees and follow the Shrek look-alike in front of me into the hole. With any luck, if his hulking frame gets stuck, I can make my escape before anyone even notices. No one would blame me for bailing if there's a great big dude wedged in the tunnel ahead of me.

Unfortunately, Shrek is pretty quick for his size and puts quite a bit of distance between us, leaving me alone in the dark. I guess his pallid complexion should've been the first clue that he spends a lot of time in caves. Pushing down panic, I crawl forward, chasing the glow from his headlamp while dampness soaks into my knees. Every inhaled breath tastes like our basement after a heavy rain. Memories of playing hide-and-seek in the dark with Jeanie keep me from completely losing my mind. If I concentrate, I can almost see the boxes of Christmas decorations and half-empty paint cans.

In front of me, Shrek pauses and rips one before quickly crawling forward with a snicker, effectively Dutch-ovening me.

My gag reflex kicks in and I dry heave in the tight space. "Thanks for the warning, asshole," I mutter to myself.

"Everyone still with me?" Bat Man's voice bounces off the walls from somewhere ahead of us, making it impossible to tell how far away he is.

I add my "here" to the chorus and keep moving. We must be close to the open cavern by now. The shadows looming in the small space make the low ceiling look like a mouth full of jagged teeth. *Come on, Shrek! Use your jet propulsion and crawl faster before the cave eats us both!*

As we reach the end of the tunnel, the opening widens enough for me to go from a low crab-crawl to my hands and knees. Finally, I climb to my feet as the cavern opens into a massive cathedral of draping rocks. The walls remind me of melting candles. Overhead, the glittering daggers hang like yellowed fangs, dripping water from them like slick saliva, conjuring images of a hungry T. rex.

Bat Man corrals us into a loose circle and rambles on about stalactites and the types of crystals forming them, but I have a mission to complete, so I wander off in search of the place Mom stood in her picture.

When I find a spot closely matching the photo, I hold out my phone to catch a selfie, but my arm isn't long enough to get the stalactites behind me in the shot.

"You need some help?" Bat Man holds his hand out with a smile. "It'll look a lot more impressive from farther back."

"That would be great, thank you." I hand him my phone and strike a pose, imagining what Dash would say if he were here. Something appropriately nerdy about Superman totally taking Batman in a fight, I have no doubt.

You're not thinking about Dash, remember?

"Yeah. Who needs a stupid superhero-obsessed man anyway?" I mumble. "I don't need to be rescued! I'm perfectly capable of managing on my own."

"Uh . . ." Bat Man holds out my phone to me, his smile faltering. "I'm sure you are. I didn't mean to imply—"

"No! I didn't mean you." I take my phone, fumbling and almost dropping it in the dirt. "There's this guy, and he, uh . . . he didn't actually *say* I couldn't do it. In fact, he was always super supportive. Until he wasn't. Then he totally betrayed my trust, and it's not like I can forgive him for that, right?" I can almost see Dash rolling his eyes. "It's so weird." I let out a breath. "After everything he did, I still miss having him around. Even though I don't *need* him to be here, I really sort of wish he was."

◆ ◆ ◆

After snapping a photo and spreading Mom's ashes at the historic Memorial Hall in Kansas City, I close the book on the Midwest leg of the tour and hop back on the highway, letting GPS plot the course to California. I know I won't make it in one night, but I have every intention of driving until I can't keep my eyes open.

Two tanks of gas and at least a dozen unanswered calls later, my phone vibrates from the passenger seat again. I glance at the screen, my snarky inner voice refusing to let me get my hopes up. It's not him. It's never him. I ignore several more calls from Jeanie, a few from Damian, but not a single one from Dash. No calls. No texts. Nothing. Not that I want him to call me. I don't. But he hasn't even tried to apologize for single-handedly ruining my life. And I'd really like to know why.

The urge to call him is overwhelming. Fear of *accidentally* dialing his number has me answering Jeanie's latest call instead. I quickly fill her in on my recent exploits and G-Lo's explosive revelation.

"Do you think maybe . . ." She lets her thought trail off, but I know exactly what she's thinking.

I've been asking myself the same damn thing.

Was David Bowie actually Mom's father?

I gaze into the horizon as I collect my thoughts. "If you'd asked me two weeks ago, I would've said not a chance, but today? You didn't hear G-Lo talking about that night. I don't know anymore. Her story was pretty convincing."

"She's old." Jeanie snorts. "And after more than fifty years of smoking pot, she probably can't remember everyone she slept with."

"I wish I could say the same," I mutter under my breath.

Jeanie lets out a knowing sigh. "Oh, Zoey . . ."

"I shouldn't have come, Jeanie." My voice cracks. "I should've waited for you."

"Tell me you didn't actually fall for the serial killer."

When I don't answer, a bark of nervous laughter echoes through the car.

"You did, didn't you?"

"Shut up." I choke back a hollow laugh of my own. "He wasn't a serial killer. Just a serial *liar*."

Jeanie's laughter dries up, and she uses her "Mom" voice on me. "What happened?"

Despite my better judgment, I tell her everything.

After an unexpected show of sympathy for my wounded pride, Jeanie cuts to the chase.

"I haven't seen a single picture of you online, Zo. And not a single rumor about Mom or G-Lo on the internet or in any of the grocery store tabloids. Trust me, with you gallivanting all over the country, I've searched your name multiple times a day to make sure you weren't lying in a morgue in the middle of bum-frigging Egypt. I would've known if there was even a whisper of a story about you out there."

I let out a heavy sigh. "Doesn't mean the *pictures* aren't floating around out there . . . just waiting for the worst possible moment to show up on my social media feed."

"Did you ever stop to think maybe he was telling the truth?"

"What happened to 'he could totally be a serial killer, ditch him before you end up as a statistic'?" I do my best Jeanie impression.

"I know." She groans. "I did say that. But hear me out. If he was going to kill you, he would've done it in the middle of the forest and blamed it on the bear."

"No. He slept with me instead so he could sell me out to the tabloids."

The silence stretches between us, and I keep waiting for a snarky response that never comes.

"How can you be sure he was the one who sent the reporters?" My sister poses the question as if challenging me to a freaking duel.

Since when did Jeanie climb on the Dash Hammond bandwagon? And why am I so damned desperate to join her there?

I heave out a breath, but it does nothing to release the tension holding my muscles hostage. "The fact that anyone knew we'd be there at all means *someone* told them."

"But he denied it, right?"

"So?"

"So maybe he was actually telling the truth!" she insists.

For several long seconds, I stare at her name on my phone display, almost convincing myself I answered a wrong number. No such luck. My sister has simply lost her ever-loving mind.

"Jeanie, we were swarmed by reporters shouting my name and asking things no random stranger could've possibly known." I drag my lower lip through my teeth, still tasting him there nearly two days later. "Would you have given him the benefit of the doubt?"

"I don't know." She lets out a long sigh. "But the more I think about it, the less sense it makes. He already had your trust. You'd already told him everything. So why risk losing the exclusive by blabbing to anyone else?"

Swirls of doubt float through my vision like black smoke, clouding my thoughts. "He didn't want me to know he was selling me out?"

"And how well did that work out for him?" I can almost hear her arched eyebrow. "You really just hopped on a bus and left him there?"

"Yeah."

"That's some stone-cold shit, little sis."

I groan and shift in my seat. "Why are you suddenly trying to convince me Dash is a good guy?"

"Because not one of those pictures showed up online or anywhere else. And if a guy's gonna go to that much trouble to sell you out, he's not doing it for nothing."

A nagging wisp of doubt spirals around me, gripping my throat until my voice comes out in a faint whisper. "It's only been a few days."

"Be real, Zo. It takes less than thirty seconds to post a picture on social media."

"Maybe." A flash of something resembling hope punches me in the gut, and it takes me a whole second to catch my breath. "Or maybe they're waiting to drop a bomb."

"Zoey, listen—"

"You're wasting your breath." I refuse to get sucked into Jeanie's unsubstantiated theories and allow the hairline cracks in my heart to split wide open.

Jeanie growls. "You can be so stupid sometimes."

"I'm not stupid!" Her words sting, but I refuse to let her hurt my feelings. She just doesn't get it.

"You really jumped off a train trestle?"

"I really did." My lips curve into a smile. "Are you bummed you didn't come? We could've jumped together."

"Screw that!" She laughs. "I've had my fill of falling from heights for the rest of my damn life."

"You don't know what you're missing."

"Oh, I do." Her tone softens. "But it's okay. This was your turn to be first."

"Thank you," I murmur. "For letting me go."

"Don't mention it, sis. So where to next?"

"My next *official* destination is Santa Monica. I'll probably stop somewhere to sleep, but other than that, I'm driving straight through."

"That's one hell of a long haul. You can't tell me Mom and G-Lo didn't stop anywhere between Kansas and California."

"They did the typical touristy stuff: Dodge City, Santa Fe, Flagstaff, Barstow. Nowhere worth revisiting as far as I'm concerned. It's not like I'm planning to spread her ashes in any of those places."

"Did you say Flagstaff?" Jeanie's voice vibrates with excitement.

"Yeah, why?"

"I was flipping through G-Lo's *Groupie* magazine, and apparently there's some big Bowie tribute concert in Flagstaff Saturday night."

"That's like"—I check the date on my phone—"tomorrow night, Jeanie."

"I know. You should totally go."

"Even if I could somehow make it on time, I don't have—" Before I get the word *tickets* out of my mouth, I remember G-Lo's press pass buried somewhere under fast-food wrappers in the back seat. In the span of a few seconds, a really bad idea begins to take shape. "I think I have a plan."

30

Hallo Spaceboy

Seventeen hours, four tanks of gas, three stops to pee, and one less-than-restful stay in what may as well have been the Bates-freaking-Motel later, I roll into downtown Flagstaff with the same damn song still blasting from the Betty's speakers. With the sun hanging low, and craggy mountain peaks jutting into the sky behind the old redbrick buildings, the quaint city reminds me of a cross between an Old West mining town and a ski resort—just one heavy snow away from being a Hallmark Christmas movie. But I don't have time to enjoy the scenery. Not after spending half the drive replaying my conversation with Jeanie over and over until I'm even more confused than I was before. I spent the other half of the drive trying to convince myself sneaking into a concert isn't a disaster in the making.

A combination of nervous energy and sick curiosity drives me to pick up the newest issue of *Tattle Tale* from the local newsstand. After tearing through the pages from cover to cover, searching for any mention of me, Mom, or even Dash, I come to the same conclusion as Jeanie. Someone buried the story. And not in the fine print between "Elvis Sighted in Oregon" and "Rock Star's Housekeeper Spills Dirty Secrets."

If a guy's gonna go to that much trouble to sell you out, he's not doing it for nothing.

Was Dash telling the truth after all?

I hit the speed dial on my phone, tapping my toe on the brake until G-Lo picks up.

"None of the pictures were published. And not just the pictures. I can't find a single mention of me or Mom or any of us. Not anywhere. Jeanie thinks that means Dash found a way to bury the story, but does that mean he had nothing to do with the reporters showing up?" The words come tumbling out in a rush.

G-Lo laughs. "Well, hello to you, too!"

"I'm sorry." I glance at my frantic expression in the rearview mirror and cringe. "I'm just so confused. What am I supposed to do now?"

G-Lo clicks her tongue. "For starters, I'd stop worrying about some nonexistent exposé and start figuring out how you're going to get past the concert gate."

"I know." I groan and sink into my seat. "You're right. Got any suggestions?"

After G-Lo fills me in on the finer points of sneaking into a rock concert, I pull into the only empty parking spot within five blocks of the venue and get down to business. Less than an hour before showtime, I plot my next move like Bonnie about to pull off a heist without Clyde.

What the hell am I doing?

After rescuing the press pass from beneath a bag of stale fries, I crawl between the front seats and do a little dumpster dive in the back seat. With a shudder, I dig through the assorted food wrappers, empty cigarette packs, and petrified chicken nuggets. I should've packed rubber gloves. Once I reach the elbow-deep stash of concert tees, I dive in as if I've discovered the Victoria's Secret sale bin. Not even the countless hours spent in the Betty could prepare me for the treasure trove that's been hiding in plain sight the whole damn time.

The stash is worthy of the best CBGB has to offer. The Kinks. The Stones. The Police. The Dead Kennedys. My fingers dance over the crackled lettering on an ancient *Dark Side of the Moon* T-shirt.

How am I supposed to pick just one?

After sifting through every shirt in the stack, I settle on a vintage Bowie T-shirt with a washed-out red lightning bolt emblazoned across the front. Ignoring the herd of concertgoers passing the window, I change out of my sweaty Harry Potter tee and strip off my dirty shorts, swapping them for a pair of G-Lo's artfully ripped jeans. The shirt's a little big, but the jeans fit like a glove.

With every bit of makeup I'd packed, plus a few things I found in the car, I get to work, with a little help from a YouTube beauty influencer. Layers of black eyeliner, mascara, and red lipstick transform me into someone I barely recognize—someone sophisticated and confident. Once I'm satisfied there's nothing left to do, I shove a twenty into my bra, tuck my phone into my front pocket, and lock everything else I own in the trunk of the car.

Everywhere I look, cosplayers representing Ziggy Stardust, The Thin White Duke, Aladdin Sane, and even the Goblin King from *Labyrinth* fill the streets as if I've stepped into a carnival in full swing. Joining the eclectic crowd making their way toward the historic theater, I catch my reflection in a plate glass window. Dressed in my own version of Bowie, with my features hidden behind a mask of makeup and my blond hair twisted into a low knot, I could totally pass for a rock journalist, even if I look nothing like the photo on the pass hanging around my neck.

Nervous excitement courses through me as I struggle to keep up with the pack. Of all the risks I've taken on my trip, this one seems the most personal. Everything else I've done has been for Mom. This one is for me. I'm on my own here with no road map or trail to follow. No urn. No ashes. Just me and the adventure of a lifetime.

Following G-Lo's instructions to the letter, I linger near the entrance until I spy a few guys with passes like mine. Then, pressing my phone to my ear as if talking to someone important, I follow them to the glassed entrance and jump in line behind them. With my stomach lodged in my throat, it's a wonder I can breathe. My heart pounds so hard, G-Lo's stupid press pass practically vibrates against my chest. When the guys flash their passes, I smile and flash mine, then walk through as if I belong there. I follow them all the way backstage, where they introduce themselves to the band and a flame-haired Bowie impersonator. Electricity crackles in the air as people scurry around with their last-minute details.

This time, before I press the phone to my ear, I actually dial.

"Well?" G-Lo's voice bounces down the line.

Pure excitement oozes from my pores. I haven't felt this sort of a thrill since I jumped from the trestle. It's all I can do to keep my voice to a whisper. "I did it! I'm backstage."

"Aww, honey, that's great. I know the feeling well. Enjoy every second of it."

"Trust me, I will!" Not for the first time on this trip, I realize how true that statement is. I love the rush I get from flying by the seat of my pants, diving into one adventure after another. I started this trip to say goodbye to my mom and ended up discovering my true self. I don't know if I can ever go back to being who I was before Mom got sick. I'm not sure I want to.

"Go," G-Lo shouts as the first guitar licks of "Ziggy Stardust" roar through the speakers. "Have fun!"

"I will. I'll call you later."

The tribute concert is laid out in several acts, each era of Bowie's life represented by a different lead singer. After seeing the Ziggy version onstage, I finally understand why G-Lo got so caught up in the young Bowie. The current version—a platinum blond in a baby-blue suit—gyrates onstage while belting out "Modern Love." When he's finished, the familiar opening chords of "China Girl" send a ripple up my spine. Feelings I can't begin to reconcile wash over me, and the words "our song" fall from my lips before I can stop them.

Memories of Dash singing karaoke pop into my head, and I laugh. For half a second, I swear I hear his horrible, off-key warbling coming from the audience.

You're totally losing it, Zoey.

From my vantage point, I scan the wall-to-wall people crowding the stage. More than half are at least two or three times my age. G-Lo would've fit right in. A flash of light reflects off a pair of black-framed glasses, and my heart jerks to a full stop. The lights dim so fast, I can't make out the face behind those glasses, but the dark hair, the tall frame . . .

I shake the absurd thought from my head. Why would Dash be in Flagstaff? And even if he is, would I want to see him? Jeanie's words come back to haunt me. Dash swore he would fix everything. Then someone buried the story. I was so angry with him and said so many cruel things. What if he was telling the truth? What if he meant it when he said what we had was real? It was certainly real for me. Shouldn't I at least give him a chance to explain?

It takes me all of two seconds to realize how much I want Jeanie to be right, and how much I wish Dash were in Flagstaff. I need to know what really happened back in Detroit, and I need him to tell me face-to-face.

With a step forward, I hold my breath and squint into the dark. The Clark Kent look-alike disappears into the shadows, but I can still make out his silhouette clapping along with the beat.

The strobing lights pan over the crowd again, and I catch a fleeting glimpse of the guy. My pulse thunders in my ears. I'd know that smile anywhere. Despite my best efforts, I've thought about nothing but his smile since the minute I boarded that bus for Memphis.

"Dash!" I scream his name from the wings, making several people, including the bass player, glance my way. Cursing under my breath, I slink back to the shadows, quickly making my way to the nearest exit.

Pushing past the music journalists and photographers, I weave around speakers, dodging wires and assorted other equipment, searching for a way into the audience.

The lone security guard standing between me and the long hallway raises an eyebrow at my frantic escape attempt. "Where's the fire?"

"How can I get into the audience?"

"Without a ticket? You can't."

"I have a press pass!"

"And that gets you right where you are."

"But you don't understand." I squeeze my palms together, pleading with my eyes. "I'm pretty sure I saw someone I know, and I wasn't very nice to him the last time I saw him, and I need to let him apologize, but if I don't get out there right now, I might not get another chance!"

"Oh, well, if that's all." The guard nods and motions me to follow him down the hall toward a metal door. "You can go right through here, and down the stairs."

"Thank you!" I shove the heavy door open, then fly down the stairs and through another door at the bottom. But instead of landing on the stage floor, I end up in the rear parking lot. Before I can grab the door, it locks behind me.

Damn it! So much for *that* adventure.

Almost an hour later, after sitting on a bench across from the theater watching the last of the concertgoers trickle out of the building, I begin to think I hallucinated the whole thing. Not a single person looks remotely like Dash.

Why do I keep seeing him everywhere? First, it was the little boy dressed like Clark Kent on the bus, and then I insulted the caving guy because I was imagining Dash. And now this. It's as if I have Dash Hammond stuck in my brain, replaying like a broken Bowie 8-track.

With one last look at the theater entrance, I drag myself off the bench and make my way back to the car. No more interruptions. I need to get to California and finish what I started.

31

Changes

With Mom's diary in my lap and her urn at my side, I sink my feet into the cool sand. The early-morning fog hovers over Santa Monica Bay like an invisible sponge, coating everything in a layer of dampness and raising goose bumps on my bare arms. The marine layer will supposedly burn off by midday, but after driving through the freezing desert all night, the slightly warmer ocean breeze is a welcome change.

"I guess this is it, Mom." I scoop her urn from the sand and hug the cold metal to my chest. "Last stop on our tour."

Just as I'd done at least a dozen times since leaving home, I open Mom's diary and flip to the next entry. The photo of her riding a carved wooden carousel horse slips from the page into the sand. I rescue the picture and gaze into her soft expression. She looks older, as if she'd uncovered the secrets of the universe since her last entry. I wonder if I look different, too. With her image still burned into my retinas, I switch my focus to her swirly script.

July 22
As soon as we finished doing all the standard touristy stuff, like visiting the Chinese Theatre and Hollywood Walk of Fame, Mom and I headed to the beach. We

spent the afternoon on Santa Monica Pier, stuffing ourselves with funnel cakes and cotton candy, and riding the merry-go-round. After getting booted off for taking lewd pictures on the horses, we wandered to the arcade. I totally kicked her ass at Skee-Ball, walking away with bragging rights, a strip of tickets as long as my arm, and a stuffed penguin. We walked down to the sand, past the cute boys in board shorts and the kids building castles, to watch the sunset over the Pacific. I knew we still had the whole trip home ahead of us, but with the tide rolling in and the sun going down, it felt like the last day of summer vacation. And I guess in a way it was. First thing tomorrow morning, we head home. Mom didn't say anything, but I knew she felt it, too. I almost wish we could stay in paradise forever, bare toes in warm sand, no responsibilities, no worries about the future. I'm pretty sure if I say the word, Mom would make it happen. I tuned out everything but the sound of the tide crashing against the shore, pushing thoughts of tomorrow to the back of my mind, and listened for the sizzle when the sun finally sank into the ocean.

I rest my chin on her urn, my breath hitching as I fight back tears. A light gust ruffles my hair, and I close my eyes, imagining Mom running her fingers through the long strands the way she did when I was little. Part of me wants to believe she's standing over me while I see this through.

A few tears make it past my defenses and slide down my cheek. "I think I finally understand why you wanted me to come. I know I wasn't thrilled with the idea at first, but I'm really glad you made me promise."

As if Mom's trying to tell me something, the wind flutters through the pages of her diary, uncovering something I hadn't noticed before: The last two pages are stuck together.

What the hell? Careful not to rip the paper, I peel the pages apart, revealing a new entry. Mom's handwriting is less swirly—almost serious. And instead of the faded-blue ink of the earlier entries, this one was written with a black gel pen.

> *I've often wondered where life would've taken me if my mother hadn't dragged me all the way across the country that summer to chase after the ghost of Ziggy Stardust. Even before Mom dropped her little bombshell in my lap, I loved Bowie's music. I don't know if that was Mom's influence or simply something that was meant to be. Maybe he really was otherworldly, because from that first stretch of road, I was forever changed. I didn't even realize until we were already heading home that not one minute of our journey had been about David Bowie . . . or my real father, for that matter, whoever he may be.*

Wait! What? Confusion morphs into disappointment. I shake off the conflicting emotions, suddenly realizing how much I'd invested in the fairy tale. G-Lo's story. Mom's diary. The pictures. None of it had anything to do with Bowie?

"Why send me on this trip if you didn't even believe her story?" A gust of wind ruffles the pages again, as if Mom's spirit is urging me to keep reading. I heave out a breath and pick up where I left off.

> *Bowie may not have been my father—and as caught up as I was in the idea, I don't think I ever really believed he was—but he was definitely the catalyst that brought Mom and me together again. His music provided the soundtrack of my life. And he was the glue that cemented my relationship with my mother. No matter where on the globe she may be, I feel closer to her when one of his songs plays. I'll always treasure the summer*

we spent together—pretending I was someone we both knew I wasn't—because that was the summer I discovered who I really was. I still don't know if I was actually conceived on the Ziggy Stardust tour—knowing Mom, I guess it's possible—but somewhere along the way, the dream of meeting my father was replaced with the reality of getting to know the woman who brought me into the world. Mom was, and always will be, an adventurous free spirit with a heart as big as an ocean. But as much as I love her, we're as different as two people can be, and I had to follow my own path. I chose the life I wanted—a life that couldn't be further from my mother's world if I tried—and I have no regrets. Because for one special summer, we were heading in the same direction, and I'll carry those memories with me for as long as I live.

I close Mom's diary and stare out at the ocean, rhythmic waves breathing in and out, lapping at the shore with every exhale. In the distance, a lone surfer rides the swells toward the beach.

Now I really do get it. This trip was never about a concert tour or an obsession with a rock god. Mom wanted her ashes spread across the path she'd taken with G-Lo—the one time in her life she and her mom traveled the same road. A road that forever after diverged.

I laugh, and the ocean swallows the sound. It hits me that we both came to the same realization—we both needed to forge our own paths. I always thought I wanted the safe path, because that was the one Mom chose. But unlike her, I *did* inherit G-Lo's free spirit. I want—no, I *need*—adventure in my life. The two years I spent caring for Mom changed me. This trip changed me. So maybe college isn't in my future. At least not now. I'd like to experience everything life has to offer while I can. Travel . . . take pictures . . . keep a diary of my own. But before I can do that, I have to finish what I started.

Another gust tosses my hair over my shoulder. It's time.

"Mom, no matter what happens next, I want you to know I'm really glad I made the trip." I drag myself to my feet and unscrew the lid from the urn.

This is the moment I've dreaded since leaving home. I've always known I'd have to say our last goodbye at some point, but until now, I wasn't ready. My stomach tightens into a painful knot as I tip the urn toward the ocean, letting the cool breeze reach into the vessel and swirl Mom's ashes into the air. With a flick of my wrist, I shake the rest of the contents out until they scatter to the wind like snowflakes.

Instead of sadness, a sense of pride and accomplishment washes through me. I close my eyes and picture her the way she was before cancer ravaged her body, stealing the life from her eyes and the breath from her lungs. *I did it, Mom.*

"I'm so proud of you, Zoey." Mom cupped my cheeks in her cool hands and pressed a kiss to the top of my head.

I was nine—no, ten. It was only a few months before Dad moved out. Mom had to come to school because I'd gotten into a fight with a boy. He'd pulled up my skirt, and I punched him in the mouth, leaving him with a fat lip and a chipped incisor. I was so afraid she would be mad at me. But she wasn't.

"Proud of me? But I hit Mason."

"You defended yourself."

"He did sort of deserve it." I snickered. "But I thought hitting was bad."

"Hitting for no reason *is* bad, but there will be times in your life when you have no choice but to take matters into your own hands. I won't always be around to protect you."

"Like your mom isn't around to protect *you*?"

"That's true." Sadness washed over her features. "Your grandma hasn't always been around for me. But in her own way, she taught me everything I needed to know to be able to take care of myself. And now I know you'll be able to take care of *yourself*."

"Yup!" I wrapped my arms around her middle and squeezed. "I'm going to be just like you when I grow up."

"If that's what you really want. But Zoey"—Mom squatted so we were eye to eye—"you'll have the whole world at your feet. You can be anyone you choose to be."

"Even Grandma Lola?"

Her laugh quickly turned into a groan. "I'm hoping when the time comes, you'll choose to be yourself."

With my mom's ashes still floating through the air, I pack up her diary and the empty urn, tucking them both into my bag with my shoes. Tomorrow, I can decide what to do with the rest of my life. But today, I'm ready for my next adventure.

The guy I'd seen riding the waves steps out of the surf carrying his canary-yellow board. With his wetsuit peeled down to his waist, his long sun-bleached hair matted and twisted from salt and sand, and his skin glowing with a deep nut-brown tan, he looks like an extra in the movie *Point Break*.

"Hey!" I call out to him as I walk to the water's edge. "Will you teach me how to do that?"

He stops and rests the end of his board in the sand, eyeing my wrinkled Bowie shirt and G-Lo's jeans—rolled up almost to my knees. "You wanna surf? In *that*?"

"I know I don't have a board or anything, but can you show me a few things?"

"No way." He shakes his head, sending icy water droplets flying. "Water's too cold without a wetsuit, bruh."

A little voice tells me I should probably take his advice, but I'm too eager to start my next adventure. "I'm from Pennsylvania, I can handle the cold."

"Okay." He smiles, exposing his perfect white teeth as he picks up his board and jerks his head toward the shore. "Let's do this."

"Sweet!" A twinge of fear grips my insides, but the newly minted adventurer in me refuses to let it stop me.

Following "Point Break," I run headlong into the surf, soaking my jeans to mid-thigh and nearly falling on my ass. "Holy crap, that's cold!"

"Come on, Pennsylvania. It's just right." He throws his head back in a hearty laugh.

"I think I'll come back later." I stumble back to the beach, squeezing brine from the drenched denim. "Maybe I'll see you around."

"I'll be here." He waves before turning and paddling out to sea.

Lugging my bag over my shoulder, I hike through the wet sand toward the pier access.

Instead of rinsing my feet in the beach shower, I brush them off as best as I can and shove them into my sneakers before climbing the wooden steps. Maybe there's a surf shop up there . . . not that I could afford to buy anything.

I grab a funnel cake and a Diet Coke on my way to the Looff Hippodrome, the building housing the hundred-year-old carousel. I don't find anyone selling surfboards, but I do pass the sign marking the end of historic Route 66. I can't help wondering if Dash made it back to his own *On the Road* trip.

How's he supposed to finish his trip without a car, Zoey?

"I dunno, maybe he flew." I answer my own question with a snort. It can't be a coincidence that Ziggy Stardust was an alien and so is Superman.

I board the merry-go-round and scramble to find the same standing horse Mom rode thirty years ago before someone else gets it. As soon as I mount my trusty steed, I catch the attention of a woman riding with her little girl.

"Will you take my picture?" I ask.

"Sure." She smiles and holds out her hand for my phone just as the organ music starts to play. After snapping a few pictures, she hands it back and lifts her daughter onto the jumping horse beside me. "Your battery is about to die."

“That figures.” I check my messages, deleting another unsolicited text from Damian without reading it and pocket my phone, hoping I won’t need it before I get back to my charger.

“What’s your name?” the little girl asks.

She reminds me of me at that age—no more than about four or five—with wispy blond hair and curious blue-green eyes.

“Zoey.”

Her eyes widen and her little mouth pops open. “That’s my name, too!”

My stomach does a free fall. “Really?”

She nods, and a weird sense of déjà vu sweeps over me.

“Hold on tight, Zoey.” Her mom shoots her a stern warning. “No standing in the saddle this time.”

“She stood on the horse?”

“She did. Almost did a header onto the floor, too.” The woman laughs. “She’s a thrill seeker, this one.”

“I think all Zoeys might be.” A single thought pops into my head. This can’t be another coincidence.

32

The Supermen

After taking a few turns on the merry-go-round, I say goodbye to my daredevil namesake and head down the pier to Pacific Park for some thrill seeking of my own.

On my way, I duck into the Playland Arcade where Mom and G-Lo had their epic Skee-Ball battle. The place is practically a museum, packed with a combination of modern video games and vintage arcade machines—some I've never even heard of before—plus an air hockey and foosball mecca.

Following the blue-and-white-checkered floor, I make my way to the back of the building where a row of Skee-Ball machines from different eras call to me. As I bend down to put a coin in one of the newer machines, a man clears his throat, catching my attention.

The old man watches me from the end of the row like Benjamin Button in a faded-blue Superman T-shirt and bright-red board shorts big enough to swallow him whole. What am I, a Superman magnet? *Okay, universe. I hear you.*

He eyes the quarters in my fingers and gives a subtle shake of his head, ruffling his silver hair. "I wouldn't do that."

"No?" I glance at the ancient chassis in front of him. Based on the impressive strip of tickets pooling at his feet, he's been playing a while.

"Nope. See these?" He nods to his machine and the one beside it. "They've been bringing joy to generations since long before you were born. I suspect it'll continue long after I'm gone."

"You think the old ones work better?" I can't help but smile at his logic.

"I prefer to think of them as classics." He chuffs. "And yes. They most definitely do. There's nothing like years of wax buildup to make these babies glide up the alley." He holds up the polished wooden ball in his hand, and the sparkle in his eye makes me giggle.

"That's a good enough reason for me." I abandon the modern machine for the classic and shove my coins into the slot. A row of balls rumbles down the chute.

On my first try, the ball sails up the lane and over the hump, bouncing right into the fifty-point bull's-eye ring. I let out a squeal. "Did you see that?"

"See what I mean? You can't let old age fool ya."

I immediately think of G-Lo. "You're so right."

My second roll doesn't go as well. The ball drops into the lowest ring for ten points. "So much for thinking I could go pro."

"Keep at it. You'll get the hang of it." The man rolls his next ball and scores forty points. "This isn't my first rodeo. I've been doing this for a long time."

"Not me." I laugh. "I'm only here because my mom played here with my grandma when she was about my age, so when I saw the sign, I had to come check it out."

"Play a lot of Skee-Ball, do they?"

"They did when they were here."

He throws another ball up the alley, hitting the bull's-eye again. "They don't play anymore?"

"My, uh . . ." I draw in a deep breath. "My mom died recently."

"I'm sorry to hear that." His pale-gray eyes bore into mine. "Was she sick?"

"Cancer."

He nods and lowers his head, his shoulders slumping under an invisible weight. "Cancer took my wife last fall."

Tears well in my eyes. "I'm so sorry."

"No, don't be." A sad smile curves his lips. "I'm a lucky man to have had her as long as I did. We were married for the best damn sixty years of my life. Through a whole lot more good than bad. She loved the pier. Every Sunday we came to play Skee-Ball and watch the sunset."

"Was she as good as you?"

A loud bark of laughter cracks the air. "Even when she was sick, she was hard to beat. I called her Wonder Woman." He pats the big red *S* on his chest. "And she called me Superman."

My eyes glaze over, and a lump forms in my throat.

"Listen to me, rambling on. You don't want to hear about my life." He shakes his head and turns back to his lane, rolling another fifty-point bull's-eye. The light above his machine spins, flashing red, putting the sparkle back in his eyes. "I don't suppose you'd be interested in a friendly wager?"

"You let me win," I admonish him with a smile.

He waves his hand in protest, but he won't look me in the eye. "You won fair and square. Just not my day, I guess."

I laugh and tear off a few of the tickets I won, tucking them into my pocket before handing him the rest. "Here."

"What's this for?"

"For teaching me how to be a Skee-Ball shark."

He hesitates a second before taking the tickets. "You don't want to claim your prize?"

"Nah." I pat my pocket. "I have these as a memento. You get something cool to remember me by."

"I'll do that." He flashes a mouth full of dentures and opens his arms. "Your momma would be proud of you."

Swallowing a sob, I hug my new friend goodbye and head toward Pacific Park.

The moment I step under the steel octopus marking the entrance, I'm caught in a wave of sensory overload. My stomach rumbles at the savory aroma of greasy burgers and fries, fresh-baked pizzas and spicy tacos, and the decadent scent of funnel cakes and coffee. But the bells and the flashing lights of the midway make me eager to try my luck.

For the bargain price of three dollars, I can either join the group of kids armed with water guns, hoping to win a one-eyed Minion, or join the teens wielding cushioned mallets and viciously bashing plastic moles over the head for a chance at a stuffed elephant. Or I could skip both and use those three bucks on another funnel cake. Flashing blue lights go off almost simultaneously on both games, signaling the winners, and I move on to what I really came for . . . the rides.

Above me, under a clear blue sky, the roller coaster rattles over the track to a symphony of shrieks and squeals. Behind it, the massive Ferris wheel looms large against a backdrop of the Pacific as I queue up for tickets.

Blocking the sun with my hand, I stare up at the umbrella-covered red and yellow gondolas swooping past. The Pacific Wheel must be over a hundred feet tall. One hundred thirty according to the sign.

The slow spin of the wheel mesmerizes me, and I must be losing my mind because I swear I see Dash in a red gondola. I pull my eyes away and shake my head, refusing to fall for the same hallucination again.

After paying for an all-day pass, I head for the Scrambler.

By the time I line up at the Ferris wheel, I've ridden every other ride at least once and eaten my weight in popcorn and cotton candy. I'd love to stay longer, but I haven't slept more than four hours in the past twenty-four, and my battery is reaching critical mass. Thanks to sleep deprivation, my Dash sightings have exceeded a healthy level. Does everyone in Southern California own a Superman shirt?

I seriously need a nap.

Sleep is highly overrated, imaginary Dash whispers in my head.

Since the real Dash is probably still stuck somewhere in the Midwest, I glower at my feet. "Overrated or not, I'm finding a place to hole up for the night as soon as I get off this ride."

Since park rules forbid single riders, the attendant pairs me with the Golden Girls. From their coordinating pastel capri pants, large floral-print T-shirts, and floppy straw hats and bags, all the way to their matching white hair, orthopedic sandals, and giant sunglasses, the four remind me of a way cooler version of Reverend Tom's church lady group. I can almost smell the tuna casserole and lime Jell-O.

Once the last of the ladies climbs in, I follow them into the circular booth and settle in.

"No lap restraints?" The lady with purple lilacs on her shirt gapes at the attendant.

"Nope." The stone-faced guy slams the tiny doors across the opening, closing us into the giant red teacup.

"Is that even safe?" The lady with the red rose shirt grabs ahold of the center pole as our gondola jerks forward.

As we begin to climb, the guy shouts, "Don't lean over the side."

We stop halfway to the top while the attendant fills another gondola, and Pink Peony grabs Purple Lilac's hand, practically climbing into her lap. "Oh, my word!"

Red Rose sighs. "Look at that view!"

"Stunning," Daisy agrees with a nod.

The wheel rotates on its steel skeleton, taking us well over a hundred feet into the sky. All I can think is: *I wish Dash were here.*

Instead of gazing into the horizon like everyone else, I scan the pier below. I'm not sure what I'm looking for, but I'm certain I won't find it in the ocean.

Purple Lilac cranes her neck and peers over the side. "Did you lose something, dear?"

"Not exactly." If she only knew how much I've lost lately. "Wishful thinking."

"Nothing wrong with making wishes," Daisy says with a smile.

"I guess." From the top of the Ferris wheel, everyone looks the same. Anyone down there could be Dash.

The wheel rounds the top, and as we descend, faces come into focus again. My breath hitches as a familiar crop of artfully disheveled dark hair catches my eye. I shake my head and ignore it. Same hallucination, different city.

The guy turns toward the beach, giving me a clear view of him. All the blood rushes to my head, my heart hammering in my ears as if I'm trapped underwater. But it isn't his hair, or his tall lanky frame, or even his black-frame glasses kicking my pulse into high gear.

It's the royal-blue Superman shirt. *I slept in that shirt!*

I launch myself forward, coming off the seat and scrambling to my knees. The gondola wobbles, and all four of the Golden Girls gasp as I lean over the side and scream his name. "Dash!"

He whips around as if he heard me, but the Ferris wheel climbs into the sky again, and I lose him in the crowd. I reach for my phone to call him, then remember the dead battery.

"Damn it." I slump back into the seat.

Rose presses a hand to her chest and catches her breath. "I was sure you were about to jump."

"Oh, like that man in North Carolina? Such a tragedy, bless his soul." Lilac lowers her head as if saying a quick prayer.

"Dear," Daisy whispers. "May I ask what was so important you'd risk your life to get a peek?"

"It's a long story." The wheel circles back around, and I peer over the edge again. If he's there, I can't see him at this height.

Daisy leans forward. "Then tell it quick."

"It all started when I met this guy in a diner outside Memphis—"

"And you saw him just now?"

I nod.

"Is he good looking?" Peony's eyes twinkle.

"Yes." I sigh, seeing his smile in my head. "He really is."

"What are we waiting for?" Daisy grasps the edge of the gondola in her gnarled hands. "Let's find him!"

The others follow suit, and four pairs of arthritic hands clasp tightly to the side of the gondola as they peer over the edge. This time, no one says a word when the gondola lists to one side under our combined weight.

"What does he look like?" Daisy asks without pulling her eyes from the pier below.

"He looks like Clark Kent just before he turns into Superman."

"Should be easy enough to spot." Rose releases an unladylike snort, and I'm not sure if she's being serious or snarky.

"Oh! Is that him?" Lilac points at a guy in a Spider-Man shirt.

I laugh. "Wrong superhero."

"There!"

I follow Daisy's pointed finger to a dark-haired guy in a blue shirt standing near the pirate ship.

"Yes!" An overflow of endorphins has me bouncing in place. "Dash!" I scream his name again, but a gust of wind swallows the sound.

Panic sets in as I realize I may not get off this ride before he disappears into the crowd.

The wheel jerks to a stop again in midair as the attendant swaps riders below us.

"I need to get off." I search for a nonexistent escape route.

"You aren't going to jump, are you?" Rose's eyes stretch wide until the whites are exposed all the way around.

"No." I laugh, but the idea has merit. "Not from the top, anyway, but maybe once we get close to the ground."

"I have a better idea." Daisy leaps into action. Shoving the other ladies aside, she scoots all the way over to the small doors keeping us from falling to our deaths. She waits until we're almost at the bottom, then rattles the cage and shouts to the man at the controls. "Help! I think my friend is having a heart attack!"

Rose quickly slumps into the seat and clutches her chest, as if they've practiced this maneuver before.

With a sly grin, I join the charade. "Hurry! She's turning blue!"

The dark-skinned attendant freezes, his mouth hanging open. Then, after giving his head a quick shake, he brings the wheel to a standstill before guiding us to the bottom. A small crowd rushes the gondola.

"Go!" Daisy whispers. "Find your Superman."

When the attendant opens the doors, I slip out unnoticed. As soon as I'm free of the wheel, I hop the fence and break into a run, slamming into people as I fight my way back to the midway. Like a roadblock in the middle of town, a couple holding hands blocks my path. A quick glimpse of a blue shirt near the Scrambler sends a jolt of electricity straight to my heart. *Please don't let this be another hallucination!* For half a second, I consider hurdling their linked hands, but thankfully, they move to the side, letting me pass. With my eyes locked on the back of the blue shirt, I crash into a Steelers jersey. The familiar scent of Old Spice Fiji deodorant curdles the cotton candy in my stomach.

Oh no, no, no . . .

My brain shuts down for a full second, my next breath caught in my throat.

What the hell is *he* doing here?

"Whoa." Damian grabs ahold of my shoulders to steady me before pulling me in for a tight hug. "Thank God I found you." His confident swagger makes it clear he expects me to be happy to see him.

A host of emotions flickers through me, but *happy* isn't one of them. What the hell did I ever see in him? Everything I thought I liked about him—his hulking muscles, his bossy personality, the overpowering stench of piña colada—suddenly turns my stomach. It takes every ounce of my self-control to keep from slugging the cocky grin from his lips.

Across the park, Dash turns toward me and our eyes meet. His face lights up, and every fiber in my being screams to go to him.

"I've missed you, Zo." Damian's grating voice breaks the spell, and reality crashes down like a suicidal armadillo.

I know the second Dash realizes I have another man wrapped around me. The corners of his mouth take a sharp downturn, and he pivots toward the exit and stalks away before I can get his name past my lips.

This can't be happening.

"I need to go." I break free of Damian's embrace and take off running.

"Zo!" Damian shouts. "Wait!"

Ignoring his pleas, I shove my way through the growing crowd, racing toward the place I last saw Dash. Damn him and his freakishly long legs.

Relinquishing every drop of self-respect, I cup my hands around my mouth and scream his name until my ears ring. But between the chattering voices, the tinkling carnival music, the bells, the whistles, the sirens, the ocean, and my own heart hammering in my ears, I can't hear the sound of my own voice.

Once upon a time, I thought I wanted easy, but absolutely *nothing* about falling for Dash Hammond has been *easy*. He's a risk to everything I always thought I wanted. A risk I'm more than willing to take. Because in just a few short days, he's reignited the spark I'd buried beneath layers of grief and helped me find myself again.

"Where the hell are you going?" Damian grabs my arm and roughly spins me toward him. "I used the last of my frequent flyer miles to get here. I think you owe me more than five minutes of your damn time."

"I don't owe you *anything*." Fighting back angry tears, I wrench my arm free of his painful grasp. "Why are you here, Damian?"

"What do you mean, why am I here?" His brow wrinkles, his lips forming a tight smile. "Where else would I be?"

With the imprint of his hand raising a bruise on my skin, I cross my arms, creating a barrier between us. "I can think of at least a dozen places more likely than the Santa Monica Pier."

He dips his head to catch my eyes, and his cocky smile boils my blood. "But *you* aren't *in* any of those places."

"I never asked you to come." I hold his gaze, willing him to take the hint. Absolutely nothing he says will change my feelings. We're over. I think we've been over almost since we began. "How did you even find me?"

"Your phone."

A spark of fury ignites in my belly. "You tracked my phone?"

The son of a bitch grins, clearly proud of himself.

I blow out a breath and clench my trembling hands. "Listen, Damian. Whatever this was has run its course. We're not the same people we were in high school. *I'm* not the same person. Too much has happened since then. We don't want the same things. We just don't *fit* anymore."

"I think we fit pretty great." He waggles his eyebrows.

Narrowing my eyes to tiny slits, I glare at him. "You're a dick, you know that? I should've dumped you when you no-showed Mom's funeral."

"I'm sorry I missed your mom's funeral." He shrugs. "But I told you I wasn't letting you break up with me."

"And what? I'm supposed to fall in line and do what you say? Like I don't have my own opinions or control over my own life?"

He shrugs again. "That's what I like best about you. You'd rather let someone else call the shots. You *like* when I take the lead."

He tries to put an arm around me again, but I recoil from him.

"Come on, Zo, what're you gonna do without me? Your mom is gone. Your fake-ass friends forgot all about you the minute they settled into their dorms and started pledging sororities. Everyone else left you behind, but I'm still here. I'm all you have left."

My last nerve snaps with a loud crack, and I curl my fingers into my palm, squeezing until my nails cut into my flesh. Before I can stop myself, I throw my fist forward. It connects with his nose, making a horrific crunch.

Damian crumples to his knees, cupping his face in both hands. "Jesus Christ, Zoey. What the hell was that?"

"That was me breaking up with you. For good this time." Relief—and a little pain—pulses through me as I turn my back on him and march toward the exit, cradling my bloody knuckles.

33

Lady Stardust

With Damian finally out of my life, I search for Dash's trail, but it's gone ice cold. After searching the pier from one end to the other and coming up empty, I give up. He's gone. Just like my hopes. Too tired to imagine what G-Lo would do, I wander to an empty bench. The second I sit, the dam breaks and tears of frustration spill down my cheeks. I drop my head into my hands and let them fall.

Suck it up, Zoey. This trip was never about a guy.

"I know, but . . ." *I really like this one.*

Bone-weary exhaustion finally catches up to me, and I slump against the back of the bench to stare out at the ocean. If I'm being honest with myself, I don't just like Dash, I *more than* like him. It's way too soon to say the *L* word, but it wouldn't take much for me to get there. And for at least a little while, I thought maybe he felt something for me, too.

He saw me at my worst and didn't run away.

A bitter laugh catches in my throat, turning into a sob on the way out.

"He didn't run away until he saw me with Damian." I choke out the words, certain I'll never see him again. And it's all my fault for pushing him away to begin with. For not letting him explain when he begged me for a chance.

The old bench creaks as someone sits at the opposite end.

Straightening my spine, I focus my gaze on the ocean, using my shoulder to dry my tears. The last thing I want is a total stranger asking a slew of invasive personal questions I'm not prepared to answer.

The person beside me clears their throat. "Did you know Bowie recorded a live album in Santa Monica?"

My breath catches, and I jerk my head toward the sound, gaping at the familiar profile.

At least a hundred relevant questions float through my brain, but I can't get a single one to come to the surface. "I had no idea."

Picking at a funnel cake without eating it, Dash nods but doesn't look at me. "*Live in Santa Monica '72*. But plot twist . . ." He leans in and lowers his voice. "*Bowie* didn't actually record it. It was a bootleg recording that wasn't released until more than twenty years later. And then rereleased in 2008." He shrugs and leans back against the bench again. "True story. A fun bit of local trivia I picked up."

Shock . . . confusion . . . elation . . . the conflicting emotions swirl inside my head like goldfish. I have no idea how he found me. The only thing I'm sure of is that he didn't use his stupid phone to track me. "I thought I'd never see you again."

Dash turns to me, wonder reflecting in his mismatched eyes. "Are you kidding?" He bumps me with his shoulder. "You and me? We're like pee and carrots."

A semihysterical laugh bursts from my throat as a combination of exhaustion and relief turns my stomach inside out. The same question I'd asked Damian pushes its way past my lips. "Seriously, Dash. What are you doing here?"

"Come on, Zo, where else would you go to spread your mom's ashes?"

"But . . ." I fumble for words that never come.

Dash picks up my hand and inspects my split knuckles. "Nice right cross, by the way. Does it hurt?"

"A little." *Not nearly as much as thinking I'd lost you again.* I gently extract my throbbing hand from his and rest it in my lap.

"I wanted to rush in and defend your honor, but I figured the badass who fought off a bear with a cup of pee could take care of herself." He shrugs, his gaze focused on the ocean. "Guess I was right."

"Yeah, I think he finally got the hint." Fighting the urge to lean into him, I glance at the rippling waves and then back to his face. "How'd you know I'd be on the pier today? *Now?*"

"Oh." He flushes to the tips of his ears, and his gaze drops to the mangled funnel cake in his lap. "Your G-Lo sort of told me."

The second her name crosses his lips, it hits me. "The pictures. I texted her from your phone."

He nods but still doesn't make eye contact.

"She *sort of* told you how to find me?"

Dash flashes a sheepish grin. "She basically drew me a map. But I gotta tell ya, you're a hard woman to track down. I was so sure you'd be at the tribute concert in Flagstaff, but—"

"You were there?" My mouth drops open as shock turns to vindication, and I do an internal fist pump. "I *knew* I saw you in the audience. I was backstage, but I got kicked out trying to get down to the floor. I waited for like an hour, and you never came out so I figured I'd hallucinated you."

Dash relaxes against the back of the bench and scrubs a hand over his face, laughing.

"What's so funny?"

"While you were outside waiting, I searched inside until the roadies started packing up."

"That figures." With a wry laugh, I reach over and pull off a piece of his funnel cake, shoving it between my lips. I chew slowly, trying to decide how to bring up the proverbial elephant in the room. We can't move on until I know . . . "Dash, what happened? Back in Detroit. You swore you didn't have anything to do with the reporters, but after making your mysterious phone call, you came back and said you'd sold your soul—"

"I did. But not like you think." He turns toward me, pinning me with his stare. "I called my dad."

"After he took everything from you? Why?"

Dash rakes a hand through his hair. "Because I didn't know what else to do. I told him I'd come back, but I'd need two weeks and he'd have to give back the damn car."

"So, if you didn't tell them, how'd the reporters know where we'd be?"

Dash leans forward and rests his elbows on his knees. "I swear to God, I didn't sell you out. But in the end, I guess it's still my fault."

"What happened?" My fingers itch to take his hand, but I resist the urge.

"I was so pissed when Dad had the car towed and reported my cards stolen, I called Mom. She said she'd send a car to pick me up, but if I wanted her help, she wanted your story in return."

"That's . . ." What kind of mother does that?

"I told her to forget it, but I guess I'd already given her everything she needed. She took what I said in confidence and sold us out. I'm so sorry, Zoey."

"And you really had no idea?" I hold my breath, waiting for him to confirm what my heart already knows.

His gaze collides with mine. "Not a clue. Not until we got there, and I saw the media swarming. I thought if I could just get you out of there and explain . . ." He blows out a breath. "But by then it was too late. Everything had snowballed."

I search his eyes for any hint of a lie. When I don't find one, I lean into him and rest my head on his shoulder. "I'm sorry I doubted you."

He takes my hand and slips his fingers through mine. "Under those circumstances, I probably wouldn't have believed me, either."

"I still don't understand what happened to the pictures. They never showed up online or in *Tattle Tale*. It's like it never happened."

"That was Dad, too." Dash heaves out a breath, and a shudder rolls through him. "But he wasn't going to tackle a problem that big without certain *assurances*."

I lift my head and meet his gaze. "What did he do?"

"He got an injunction." Dash shrugs, but his stony expression tells me there's more to the story.

I'm almost afraid to ask. "At what cost?"

"I had to agree to come work for him. Give up my dreams for his."

Fiery rage floods my veins, and I jump to my feet. "But you . . . you *despise* what he does. You hate everything your father stands for!"

"I do." His curt nod says far more than his words.

"So why would you agree to something like that?"

Dash wraps his fingers around my wrist and tugs me back down beside him. "Because it was the only way to stop those pictures from getting out. To stop your story from going public."

"Dash . . ."

"No, Zoey. Don't." He squeezes my hand and rests his forehead against mine, bringing his lips closer than they've been in days. "Do you know why I wanted to go with you on your trip?"

I swallow hard and shake my head.

"It wasn't because you're tenacious and beautiful." He cups my cheek in his palm. "Or because I couldn't stand the thought of you walking out that door and never seeing you again."

I raise an eyebrow.

He smiles. "It's true. But you were also driving across the country for a chance to be closer to your mom, and I was doing the same thing to get as far away from my parents as I possibly could. You remember asking me what I've been writing on napkins?"

I nod.

"I submitted my first freelance article the summer before senior year. I never expected anyone would pick it up, let alone *pay* me for it. But I've been getting paid to write ever since."

"How—"

"I use a pen name. You're the first person I've told."

"Why keep it a secret?"

"My dad won't hesitate to sabotage anything that isn't what he wants me to do, and this is the first thing in my life that's been all mine. No strings attached. He's never once asked me what I wanted to do with my life, because he doesn't care. And my mom? She used to be a real journalist. Used to write about things that matter. Not anymore. And when it came right down to it, she sold out her own son for a story."

"That isn't your fault."

"Maybe not directly, but I'm the one who put you in that position to begin with. Zoey, I want to do something with my life I can be proud of. And up till now, I haven't. I should've never told my mom—"

"You couldn't have known she'd use it against you." Thoughts of his mother betraying him are all that keep me from kissing him.

"I should have." A dark chuckle rolls out of him like distant thunder. "That's who she is."

The realization that we're on borrowed time hits me square in the chest. "If you promised your dad you'd go back, why are you here and not there?"

"You didn't really think I'd pass up a trip to the beach, did you?" He winks.

"Dash . . ." I groan, my stomach twisting with dread. "We both know your dad isn't gonna wait forever, so please get it over with and tell me when you have to go back."

"See, that's the thing." His crooked grin turns into a full-blown smile. "I don't."

"I . . . I don't understand."

"Because you aren't the only badass in your family." Dash laughs. "I can't believe you didn't tell me you're related to *the* Lola Stone. Her piece on the underground punk scene is literally the reason I started listening."

"That's great, but what does G-Lo have to do with a promise you made your dad?"

"Do you remember telling me she was running a background check on me?"

A light goes off in my head, and G-Lo's cryptic comment about Dash's parents comes back to me. "Yeah."

"As it turns out, she knows my mom from way back in their early journalist days. And apparently, your grandma has some juicy dirt on my parents. She wouldn't tell me what, but whatever it is, Dad doesn't want it out there."

My jaw drops. "G-Lo blackmailed your dad?"

"Yup. Like I said, your grandma's badass."

"She really is." I laugh. "She must have something really good if she got your dad to let you out of that promise."

"Without a doubt." He shudders. "Remind me to never end up on her bad side."

"You and me both." I gaze out at the blue Pacific, remembering all the moments that brought me here. "You know, I've learned a lot about G-Lo on this trip. And a lot about my mom. But mostly, I've learned a lot about myself."

He pulls our joined hands into his lap. "Oh yeah? What have you learned?"

"I used to think Mom and I were just alike. Before she got sick, I was fully prepared to go to college, get married, find a nice stable job and a minivan."

"Really?" Dash cringes. "A minivan?"

I smack his shoulder and giggle. "Shut up and let me finish. I might look like my mom, and maybe I am like her in some ways, but there's way more of my grandma in me than I ever realized."

Dash strokes his thumb across my knuckles. "Are you saying I need to stay on your good side, too?"

"I'm saying, I jumped off a freaking train trestle! Me! And I outran a New York City cop, and snuck backstage at a concert, and waded through Buckingham Fountain."

Dash's eyebrows jump up at the last one. "Seriously?"

As I nod, I'm struck with a sudden WWGLD moment. What *would* G-Lo do? She certainly wouldn't wait for a guy to make the first move. I inch closer to him on the bench. "I've done a lot of thrill seeking on this trip. I even risked my life a time or two. But the biggest thrill I've had since leaving home was meeting you."

"Zoey, I—"

Without giving him a chance to finish his thought, or me a chance to chicken out, I grab both sides of his face and kiss him. The moment our lips touch, electricity crackles between us, and I know. *This* is where I'm meant to be. As soon as the shock wears off, Dash pulls my hands from his face, slides them around his neck, and we melt into each other.

God, I've missed this.

A chorus of loud *whoops* interrupt our moment, and we both turn toward the source.

"You go, girl!" Daisy screams from the park entrance.

"Friends of yours?" Dash rests his forehead on my shoulder as he catches his breath.

"Just some girls I know." I wave at Daisy and the other Golden Girls as they wander down the pier toward *their* next adventure. Then I turn my focus back to Dash and his swollen lips. "So you know, I'd like to do a lot more of this as soon as I get some sleep."

Dash's slow smile sets my skin on fire. "Sleep is highly overrated."

With my back pressed to Dash's chest and his arms wrapped tightly around my middle, we sit on the beach waiting for the sun to sink into the ocean.

He rests his chin on the top of my head. "A deep cerulean blue."

"The sky? The water? My eyes?"

"And sunny yellow." His lips brush my ear, sending shivers through me. "With swirls of emerald green."

I crane my neck, trying to catch a glimpse of his face over my shoulder. "What are you talking about?"

"The answer to your crayon question." Dash leans around and peers into my eyes. "Blue like the sky on a clear summer day, because it represents peace and tranquility in my life. Yellow because it's happy and fun, like sunny days and baby ducks."

"Baby ducks, huh?"

He chuckles.

"And green?"

"Green signifies life, and growth, and vitality. And hope for the future."

"I like that."

He rests his cheek against mine, letting out a satisfied hum. "So you really waded into Buckingham Fountain to get a picture?"

"Sure did."

"You do realize there's a security system around the perimeter?"

"It's not like I robbed a bank."

He hugs me tighter. "So badass."

"I know." I beam. "I'm so much more like G-Lo than I ever imagined. And you know what? I'm totally fine with that. My grandma is a national treasure. But if I start dyeing my hair red and smoking Camels, you have my permission to kill me and bury me in the desert."

"Deal." Dash rests his chin on top of my head again and blows out a breath. "So I was thinking."

"Dirty thoughts?"

He snorts a laugh. "Maybe later."

"Too bad."

"Pay attention." He nips my ear. "Santa Monica wasn't the last stop on the Ziggy Stardust tour."

"It wasn't?"

"Nope. That was only the halfway point. From here they went to San Francisco, Seattle, Portland, *Phoenix* . . ." He kisses a path down my neck as he rattles off the rest of the cities. "And once they were done in North America, they went back to the UK, ultimately finishing the tour in London in '73."

I spin around in his arms. "Are you saying what I think you're saying?"

"If you think I'm saying we should see this thing all the way through, then yeah. I think we should finish what we started."

"I don't have anything else planned for the rest of my life."

Dash pushes my hair away from my face and kisses me. "You do now."

Acknowledgments

Where do I begin?

Long before I wrote the first sentence in *Chasing Stardust,* David Bowie's music had already left its mark on me. As a longtime fan, I often tuck little Bowie references into the pages of my books—typically a song mentioned during a pivotal scene or a character wearing a colorful Ziggy Stardust T-shirt. And my go-to writing playlist almost always includes at least one of his songs. "Young Americans" has been a personal favorite of mine for as far back as I can remember and never fails to conjure the perfect emotions when I'm struggling to write those difficult scenes. But when Bowie died in 2016, my casual devotion became rabid obsession. I dove in headfirst, digging up and devouring old concert footage and every interview I could unearth, going all the way back to his early career. After spending countless days immersed in the world of Ziggy Stardust, Aladdin Sane, and The Thin White Duke, the whisper of an idea began taking shape. But 2016 was a rough year for many reasons, and it took me two full years before I was ready to put pen to paper . . . to give life to that little story that had taken root. I officially started writing *Chasing Stardust* in 2018, and not even a personal battle with cancer could stop my momentum. Then, not long after I finished the book, a global pandemic shut down the world.

But out of the ashes comes hope . . . and hope never dies if you have a spark to keep it alive.

Chasing Stardust has been a labor of love—a literary love letter to David Bowie. A story not as much *about* him but rather *inspired* by him and set to the soundtrack of his music. And I'm so thrilled to finally share this story with the world.

First and foremost, I need to thank my wonderful agent, Cathie Hedrick-Armstrong, and my fantastic editor Nancy Holmes. To Cathie, for believing in me and this novel when I'd almost given up hope. And to Nancy, for loving *Chasing Stardust* almost as much as I do. From the deepest depths of my soul, thank you both!

To the rest of the team at Lake Union Publishing—you're all so amazing, I don't even have words. To Jarrod Taylor for creating a cover worthy of rock gods and legends . . . I can't even imagine a more perfect cover for this book! To the extraordinary editing team—Faith Black Ross, Sarah Engel, Sarah Vostok, and Ashley Little—thank you a million times over for polishing my book into the gem it is today! And to Emma Reh and everyone who worked tirelessly behind the scenes to make *Chasing Stardust* a reality. Thanking you will never be enough, but I'll start there anyway.

And thank you to my crew of critique partners and beta readers, who pored over this manuscript almost as many times as I did. Specifically Karissa Laurel, my all-time ride-or-die writer bestie; Casey Dembowski, who doesn't always get my humor but never fails to offer excellent advice; Rashida T. Williams and Deborah L. King, two fantastic authors in their own right who always hold my feet to the fire and make sure I don't phone in those tough scenes; and my cousin Louise Flynn, who reads literally everything I write and isn't afraid to tell me when something isn't working. To them and the many others who offered insight and guidance on getting this book just right . . . I literally wouldn't have made it this far without you!

Special thanks to my family for their continued love and support. Some may not read my books because they find the idea cringey, but they still shout my praises from the rooftops. I love you guys! And an extra special thank-you to my poor husband for (sort of) understanding when I listen to the same song on a loop while I work through a scene, playing it for hours on end, almost as if an 8-track got stuck in the player.

And to all the readers who have been with me from the beginning—from that little blog that could—thank you from the bottom of my heart. You're the force that drives me to keep going. I hope you love this book as much as I do!

About the Author

Erica Lucke Dean writes stories that explore the complexities of relationships, with engaging and relatable female characters who navigate the ups and downs of life and love. For over a decade, her novels have captivated readers of romantic comedies and paranormal romances alike, thanks to her ability to blend humor and authentic emotions. Erica was born in the Twin Tiers of upstate New York and lived on both coasts before ultimately settling in the scenic north Georgia mountains, where she and her family live with two ginormous English mastiffs and a diabolical Frenchie hell-bent on world domination. For more information, visit www.ericaluckedean.com.